THE
CHANGELING

THE
CHANGELING

HELEN FALCONER

CORGI BOOKS

THE CHANGELING
A CORGI BOOK 978 0 552 57342 9

Published in Great Britain by Corgi Books,
an imprint of Random House Children's Publishers UK
A Penguin Random House Company

 Penguin
Random House
UK

This edition published 2015

1 3 5 7 9 10 8 6 4 2

Copyright © Helen Falconer, 2015
Cover imagery © Trevillion Images
Cover design and montage by Lisa Horton

The right of Helen Falconer to be identified as the author of this work has
been asserted in accordance with the Copyright, Designs and Patents Act 1988.

All rights reserved. No part of this publication may be reproduced, stored in a
retrieval system, or transmitted in any form or by any means, electronic, mechanical,
photocopying, recording or otherwise, without the prior permission of the publishers.

Penguin Random House is committed to a sustainable future for our business, our readers
and our planet. This book is made from Forest Stewardship Council® certified paper.

MIX
Paper from
responsible sources
FSC® C018179

Typeset in 13/18 pt Adobe Caslon by Falcon Oast Graphic Art Ltd.

Corgi Books are published by Random House Children's Publishers UK,
61-63 Uxbridge Road, London W5 5SA

www.randomhousechildrens.co.uk
www.totallyrandombooks.co.uk
www.randomhouse.co.uk

Addresses for companies within The Random House Group Limited
can be found at: www.randomhouse.co.uk/offices.htm

THE RANDOM HOUSE GROUP Limited Reg. No. 954009

A CIP catalogue record for this book is available from the British Library.

Printed and bound in Great Britain by CPI Group (UK) Ltd, Croydon CR0 4YY.

A story dedicated to Alana Quinn
9th March 2001 –
6th July 2005

BOOK ONE

PROLOGUE

THOUSANDS OF YEARS AGO, IN THE WEST OF IRELAND . . .

He was a handsome boy of seventeen when he chanced on her, washing her red-gold hair in the soft water of a pool surrounded by hawthorns. She looked up at him and smiled as she wrung the water from her hair – and that was the end of everything for him. He forgot his mother, his father, his brothers and sisters, his duties as a young warrior of the Fianna. And when the girl slipped feet first into the pool, he threw aside his cloak and sword and followed her.

At first the water only came to his knees, but very soon it was up to his waist and then to his shoulders. It was as cold as ice. The hawthorn blossoms floating on the surface gave off a sweet, dizzying scent. The girl smiled back at him, her red-gold hair floating out around her on the surface of the water. He held out his hand but she took another step further into the pool and the freezing water closed over her head. And, a moment later, over his.

Wahu: Greeting used in the west of Ireland,
possibly derived from the Irish *Ádh-thu*
(luck be with you).

CHAPTER ONE

Aoife was texting while picking her bike out of the flowerbed, when the phone slipped from her grip, skittered across the dry-stone garden wall and disappeared. She climbed after it into the field behind the house and poked around in the nettles with a stick, finding first the main part of the phone, and then the casing off the back. It was while she was trying to get at the battery without being stung that she found the tiny heart locket half buried in the earth.

She fixed her phone, then rubbed the heart clean. The dirt was hard to shift, as if the locket had been lost for a long time. Scraping with her thumbnail, she found that the gold underneath was engraved: *Eva*. Interesting. Aoife was 'Eva' on her birth certificate, although everyone, including her parents, called her by the softer version of the name. She flicked the heart open and found two portraits – one of her parents looking ridiculously young and the other of a pink-faced baby. Even more interesting. Her parents had lost all their photos in the move from Dublin, so this was the first time she had ever seen a picture of herself under the age of four – there had been no Facebook then, keeping its eternal record.

She tried the locket on. She had a slender neck, but the fine gold chain was meant for a little girl and she could only just fasten the clasp. As it clicked into place, an image sprang into her mind – two little girls with glittering wings, wandering hand in hand through the long grass of this field. Herself and Carla, years ago, playing at 'follow the fairy road'. She turned to see if the 'road' was still there, and it was – a narrow stripe of paler green that ran straight from where she was standing, up the steep slope, then over the high bank at the top of the field. A badger run, perhaps, or the sign of a stream hidden underground? As little girls, they had never made it over that thorny bank. Now Aoife was filled with a desire she had long forgotten: to see if the road continued on through the next field, and if so, where did it—

Her phone beeped. Then beeped again and again – incoming texts, stacked up while she was hunting for the battery. All from Carla:

orange too tight
Im so fat ☹
where are u
u there?
help ☹
WHERE ARE U

Aoife texted:

not fat ☺ wear the orange, dropped fone, ON
WAY 20 mins

Carla texted:

HURRYUP!!!!!!!!!!!!!!!!!!!!!!!!!!!!!

Aoife scrambled back over the wall into her
garden, ran the bike down the side of the small
house and out of the front gate, threw her leg over
the crossbar and set the stopwatch on her Nokia. Her
record to Carla's: nine minutes, thirteen seconds. She
hit START and shot down the narrow flowery lane.
The potholes had got deeper in the last two weeks
of solid rain, and she was forced to swerve or risk

her wheels. Two kilometres on, she came up behind Declan Sweeney's tractor and had to wait for him to turn left onto the Clonbarra road before herself heading right for Kilduff. She picked up speed, past the garage, the empty estate, left at the shop. A steep sweaty climb in the sun, standing on the pedals, up past the GAA pitch where a game of Gaelic football was in noisy progress, past the builder's huge three-storey house, the secondary school, then downhill all the way to the Heffernans', skittering to a halt outside the yellow dormer. She dropped her bike on the step, checked her time – nine minutes, fourteen seconds – '*Aargh!*' – took the stairs three at a time into Carla's room and collapsed, panting, full-length on the bed. '*What* are you on about? That dress is pure gorgeous on you.'

Carla was contorting herself in front of her wardrobe mirror, judging herself from every angle in the close-fitting orange dress. 'It's not. I'm a pig. Nothing fits me any more. I wish I was beautiful like you.'

'Don't talk crap. You're gorgeous, everyone says it.'

'Ha ha. Sinead admired my curves?'

'Carl, she's just jealous of your boobs. And that dress is perfect for showing them off.'

For a moment Carla brightened – 'You really think?' – then she checked the mirror again and her freckled face fell. 'No. My arse is way too—' A faint beep, and she stopped to scrabble through a pile of clothes like a dog after a rat, emerging triumphant with her phone. Then panicked. 'Jessica says what are we wearing to the cinema? What will I tell her?'

'Snapchat her what you've got on, 'cos that's what you're going in.'

Aoife's phone also vibrated. It was Killian, asking was she going on Sinead's birthday trip – like he'd 'forgotten' the whole class was invited.

'Aren't you going to answer that?'

'Vodafone top-up reminder.'

She never lied to Carla, but Killian Doherty, with his ridiculously pretty looks, was Carla's crush. Not only Carla's, unfortunately. Half the girls in their year – and the years above and below – had already gone out with him, yet every time he dumped the latest one (by text) Carla prayed (literally, in church, to God) that it would be her turn next. Which was why Aoife had also lied – or at least, not told – about the builder's son trying to chat her up at last month's Easter disco. (She had ignored him then, the same way she'd pretty much ignored his texts ever since, but still he failed to get the hint. Did he imagine she was *shy* around him like the other girls still waiting their turn? Good joke. Maybe he was one of those boys who was only interested in what he couldn't get.) 'Come on, Carla, let me do your face, I'll make you irresistible.'

'Some chance of that.'

'Will you stop. Sit over in front of the mirror and do your foundation while I stick on some decent music.' Aoife knocked off One Direction, scrolled through Carla's iPod for Lana Del Rey, and stuck it back in the dock. *Born to Die*. One day she hoped to write a song like that. She'd written hundreds already, but none she felt were any good; maybe a few that were passable. She chose a white eye-liner. 'Tilt your head back. Keep your eyes open.'

Carla said, straining not to blink: 'I'm loving the necklace. Is it new?'

'No . . .' Aoife drew the point of the pencil along the inner edge of Carla's eye. 'I found it in Declan Sweeney's field, the one behind our house. I must have lost it years ago. I don't even remember owning it.'

'Then how do you know it's yours?'

'It has my name on it – I'll show you in a sec. *Don't blink!* Mam and Dad's picture is in it and me as a baby.' She glanced towards the window, towards the distant mountains, hazy in the summer heat. 'Do you remember the fairy road?'

'Do I or what! All that sheep shite and thistles!'

'Ah, it was fun!'

'I'll never forget that time you got nearly to the top of the bank and I had to run back for your mam, I was so sure you'd get into the next field and be trampled by a bull, and she went pure mental—'

'*Anyway.* Do you remember me wearing this locket ever?'

Carla sighed, and tilted her head back again. 'No. Is it in any of the early photos?'

A hundred Blu-tacked memories of their childhood selves gazed down on them from all four walls. As Aoife worked on Carla's face, she kept pausing to look around but she couldn't see the necklace anywhere, though she did spot the fairy wings. As a little girl, she had been a lot smaller than Carla and appeared to have been in a constant state of surprise – her blue-green eyes wide open, her short red hair a tangled mess. Later, the wings had become school uniforms, and by the time they had donned huge amounts of make-up and started pouting at their own camera phones, Aoife was the taller of the two by several centimetres. She fired the blusher and mascara back into the drawer.

'Now – you're lovely. Just let me get changed, I won't be a sec.' She stripped off her trackies and T-shirt, and took her favourite dress out of Carla's wardrobe – a pale green A-line. She pulled it over her head, slipped on her navy Converse, fixed her hair – now very long and a deep red-gold – into a ponytail, grabbed one of Carla's many shoulder bags for her phone and purse, then checked herself in the mirror. 'Aaargh! Way too short! What else have you got?'

'No point – all my dresses will be like that on you now. Like on me they're too tight. At least you've got taller. I've just grown *out*.'

'You have not. I'll change back into my trackies.'

'You will not! Your legs are amazing: let everyone see them. Sinead will be sick – serve her right.'

'Nice of her to bring us all to the cinema, though.'

'Whatever. *Don't take off that dress.*'

Downstairs in the kitchen, Carla's mother,

Dianne, was putting ten euros into a birthday card for Sinead. 'I hope ten's enough – I don't have a twenty.'

Zoe, Carla's four-year-old sister, plump with light brown hair and freckles (the image of Carla in the early photos), looked round from the television. 'Can I come?'

Carla ignored her. 'Ten's plenty, Mam: no one puts twenty in the cards any more, no one has the money.'

Dianne Heffernan sighed. 'I suppose. It seems so little.'

Aoife said, 'No, Carla's right, everyone gives a tenner now . . . Oh, for—'

Carla said, "S up?'

'Left my card at home.' All she had in her purse was one euro twenty.

Dianne offered, 'You want to add your name to Carla's?'

'No, you're grand. I'll give it her in school on Monday.'

Zoe said again, louder: 'Can I come?'

Aoife smiled at her. 'I'll bring you back something.'

'Chocolate chip ice cream?'

'No, it'll only melt. I'll get you a bar.'

Even though Carla's house was only half a kilometre from the town, the journey back to Kilduff took over ten minutes. Carla's bike was rusted, and stuck in a low gear. The green dress kept riding up, and Aoife kept having to pause to tug it down, worried her pants were on show to passing drivers – it was true what Carla said: nothing fitted them any more. The day was getting hotter, and flies bombed them every time they stopped. Finally they crested the hill and cruised down past the school, a long white one-storey building with high glittering windows, then the field of cows. As they passed the builder's wrought-iron double gates, Killian Doherty swung out on a clean, mean, electric-blue racing bike and overtook them in a spurt of gravel; a great pumping of legs and narrow arms. He shouted over his shoulder as he raced ahead of them: 'Love your dress!'

Carla wobbled. 'Did he mean me or you?'

'You – he was looking at you.'

'Oh God . . . Are my boobs falling out?'

'Course not – don't mind him, he's an eejit.'

'Don't *mind* him? You think he was being sarcastic?'

'*No!*'

'Maybe you were right, maybe it is OK to have big boobs.'

'Trust me, I'm right.' Aoife pedalled on at Carla's side, except where the potholes were too deep to allow it.

There was a bevy of lads piling out of the GAA clubhouse, still pink from running non-stop for seventy minutes, though their short haircuts were spiky from cold showers. A couple of them were in Aoife's school. She slowed as she overtook them. 'Hey, Ciaran, how'd it go?'

'Crushed them in the last minute – they were one point ahead, eleven–twelve to them, but then we scored a goal.'

'Who got the goal?'

'That lad from your year. Shay Foley. He's pure fast. Burned them off. Zinger of a goal. He'll be scouted for Mayo when he's sixteen, I'd say.' He nodded ahead, to where a tall, black-haired, sun-browned boy walked on alone, long-legged in faded jeans, his Gaelic football kit slung over one shoulder.

'Really? I didn't know he was that good.' The sight of Shay Foley walking by himself vaguely annoyed her. Anyone else would have been in the thick of it, celebrating, but he was such a typical lad from back the bog: silent as the mountains he lived among; utterly unconcerned with social goings on. He'd turned up at Kilduff Secondary only last September, after his school in the Gaeltacht got shut down. In three terms, Aoife had never heard him say one word except in answer to a direct question from a teacher.

As they cycled past him, Carla called out: 'Well done! Coming to the cinema?'

Shay glanced at her, and kept on walking.

'I'll get him to talk to me one day,' said Carla.

'Good luck with that. Why bother? He's pure anti-social.'

'Gorgeous looking, though. You know both his parents are dead?'

'Seriously?' Now Aoife felt bad for having bitched about him. She glanced over her shoulder; he had turned into the path behind the shop, taking the short cut to the square. 'You never told me that.'

'Sorry – only found out last week. It was my granddad's birthday and we were putting flowers on his grave, and my nan pointed out the Foley grave behind. Both in the same year, when Shay was five.'

'Oh God . . . Car crash?'

'Don't think so. Nan said the mam died in an accident all right, but his dad died later of something fatal.'

'Bad. Does he live with his grandparents or something?'

'No – still on the parents' farm. He has a much older brother. Come into the shop – I'm busting for a Coke, you can share it.'

'Sure, I need to get that bar for Zoe.'

There was a queue for the till and the twenty-seater from the community centre had its engine running when they came out. Sinead was sitting near the front with Lois; she rolled her pale green eyes when Aoife apologized for forgetting the card. 'Sure, if you're that skint, don't worry about it . . .'

'I'm not. I have it at home, I'll give it you Monday.'

'Like I said, don't worry about it. Find a seat. There aren't any left together. Pity you didn't get here sooner.'

Lois grinned fakely at Aoife, all apple-red cheeks and frizzy black hair. Aoife grinned hugely back again. After the school talent show, Lois had accused Aoife of being an attention-seeking anorexic who wrote crap songs. Lois was a lot more direct in her insults than Sinead.

Annoyingly, Sinead was telling the truth – there were only two seats left: one across the aisle beside Killian, and the other near the back beside . . . For a moment Aoife was so surprised she just stood staring blankly up the coach. Then someone tugged at her dress and the blond, silver-eyed builder's son was smiling up at her, patting the seat beside him.

She kicked him lightly in the leg. 'Come on, gorgeous, move your arse up there next to Shay Foley. Me and Carla want to sit together.'

He scowled, making a big show of rubbing his shin. 'I wasn't asking *you*, Ginger. I was saving this seat for the girl in the sexy orange dress.' He tossed his floppy hair, and turned his boy-band smile on Carla.

'Oh . . .' And Carla spectacularly disintegrated before Aoife's eyes, grinning like a psycho, soft brown hair standing out like an electric charge had been shot through it.

Aoife couldn't resist kicking Killian again – not so lightly.

'*Oi, bog off!*'

'Sorry, Carla, bad luck — looks like he's super-glued to the seat. You'll have to put up with him.'

'Sit down, everyone!' Sinead's father was backing in alarming fits and starts across the potholed square. 'Oh, for . . . Where's first gear on this crate?' He stalled and restarted, with a hideous scraping of the gears and a stink of burning clutch. 'Everyone, sit down!'

Shay Foley was plugged into his phone, earphones in, eyes closed. He was occupying the aisle seat, and showed no sign of moving over. His knees almost touched the seat in front, and Aoife had to clamber over them, tugging down the short pale green dress. The bus kangarooed forwards, and she nearly fell on top of him. In a quick reaction, without even opening his eyes, he grasped her arm and steadied her.

She murmured, vaguely mortified, 'Thanks.'

He didn't answer but remained with his head tilted back, listening to his music. A thread of song drifted from his earphones. *Little Lion Man* . . . Mumford and Sons — cool London folk. She glanced back down towards the front. Carla had turned to see was she all right — anxious but still looking like the cat that's got the cream. Aoife smiled back; a reassuring wave of her hand. Then sat down and pressed her forehead to the glass.

The bus lurched off down the Clonbarra road, past the garage, then the turning to Aoife's own boreen. Fields of yellow irises juddered by. She tried to retreat to that place in her head where she created her songs, but couldn't stop thinking about her first day in junior infants. A little boy with white-blond curls had been chasing a plump girl with a worm, and Aoife had taken it off him and stuffed it down his shorts, sending Killian in pant-wetting hysterics to the teacher. That's when her and Carla's friendship had started, and it had just gone on and on, no reason to change it. She swallowed and the tight gold chain pressed against her throat – she pushed a finger under it, running it back and forth, looking towards the hazy mountains. A faint pale line wriggled across their slopes – a distant dusty track. She thought of the fairy road, and herself and Carla in their wings, when the games they had played were so simple.

A light touch on her arm.

She moved her elbow away.

Another touch – this time, definitely deliberate. Slowly Aoife turned her head. Shay was looking straight at her. 'Don't worry about your friend,' he said, in the soft rain-washed accent of the mountains. 'Killian's only a gobshite but she's well able for him, more than you think.'

Aoife stared. He smiled suddenly. The deep curve in his upper lip flattened out when he smiled.

'You see, I do talk,' he said. 'If there's something needs saying.'

It was Aoife who couldn't speak. She just kept on staring at Shay. How had she never looked at him before? Properly looked at him, that is? Apparently unperturbed by her scrutiny, he continued to gaze back at her, still with that same smile. His jaw was slanted, and his cheekbones strong and slightly flushed under his sun-browned skin. His eyes were dark green mottled with chestnut – the colour of woodland growth; his eyelashes were as black as his thick close-cropped hair. He had a single silver earring, worn near the top of his ear. He was wearing the Mayo jersey, and a well-worn leather belt slotted through his faded jeans.

The bus lurched wildly, and Aoife managed to

drag her eyes away from him. Sinead's father had taken a sudden right turn, swinging the bus up a steep, narrow road towards the mountains.

'*Dad, where are you going?*'

'Settle down, Sinead. There's a short cut up here to the back road – we'll get there faster this way.' The bus climbed steeply between dry-stone walls, brambles squealing painfully along the paintwork.

Shay said under his breath, 'We won't be getting anywhere this way.'

Aoife turned to him again, frowning. 'Are you sure?'

'This here is an old bog road – it'll take us straight west into the mountains.'

'Crap. Go up front and tell him, before he goes any further.'

He shrugged. 'Sure, there's no talking to the likes of Tom Ferguson when he gets a notion in his head. Whatever wild thing led him astray, he'll have to come to his senses by himself.' He stuck his earphones back in and closed his eyes.

Aoife stared out of the window, annoyed and not knowing what to do. How could Shay Foley so casually predict disaster and then just wash his hands of the whole problem? She was right about him, he was anti-social. He had no reason to think Thomas Ferguson wouldn't listen – it was just a lame excuse not to get involved.

Sinead was on her feet, strawberry-blonde pony-tail trembling with indignation. 'Dad, are you sure about this?'

Thomas Ferguson's bald head flushed pink. 'Sinead, sit down. I know *exactly* what I'm doing and where I'm going.'

Aoife glanced quickly at Shay. But his eyes remained shut, long thick lashes resting on his cheeks. His silver earring glittered slightly in the sun. His mouth was deeply curved, at rest. His lashes flickered. She pulled her gaze away.

The bus kept on relentlessly climbing. Before them, the dusty road unwound through endless heather. The mountains rolled away into the west. No other cars, no farms, just this sweeping lilac-orange land.

A united groan went up as all the phones went out of range.

'Dad. Are you—?'

'*Sinead, relax!*'

This must be the pale track she had seen from the road, crossing the mountains. Even if Thomas Ferguson wasn't so set on going in the wrong direction, there was no place to turn – it was far too narrow, and the soft margins of the bog on either side wouldn't take the weight of the bus. In the distance, a small green hill rose from the bog, capped with a white circle of hawthorn.

A little girl was running down the hill, in the direction of the bus.

Aoife blinked, looked again, saw nothing for a while. Then did – the same small figure, now struggling across the soft terrain of the bog between the hill and the road, standing, falling, crawling. Impossible at this distance to be sure it was a girl . . . or a child at all. It could be a lamb. It must be a lamb. Or some other animal. How could a little girl – or boy – be out here in the middle of nowhere, all on their own? There was no house anywhere, not even a car parked by the road.

It was a lamb.

It was a child, she was sure of it.

The bus passed a low outcrop of grey rock, and the tiny stumbling figure was blanked from view. When

Aoife could see back past the rock again, there was only empty bog.

She sat very still for a moment, thinking about it. Then stood up and climbed out over Shay's long legs. He pulled out his earphones, eyebrows raised. She said, 'Sorry – saw something . . .' and strode quickly down the aisle. 'Could you stop the bus for just a moment?'

'Why? Are you going to be sick?'

'No, I saw a little girl out there on the bog, all by herself.'

'Out here?' Sinead's dad started to slow down. 'Where?'

'Back there by the hill.'

Killian's voice said, 'Hey, Aoife saw a leprechaun.'

'*Dad! We're going to be late!*'

Thomas Ferguson stopped looking over his shoulder and speeded up again. 'No, you must have seen a lamb.'

'Please, just for a minute, while I check—'

'Aoife, if you're not going to be sick, sit down.'

Shay was on his feet. He called across the seats in his soft westerly accent, without even seeming to raise his voice, 'You might want to stop the bus,

Thomas. If there's a little girl lost out here on the bog, we wouldn't want to be the ones to have driven off on her.'

The bus slowed again, tentatively.

Lois shouted, 'Aoife's only trying to ruin the day for everyone because Killian's going out with Carla and Aoife fancies him!'

Speeding up—

Aoife screamed, *'I'm going to be sick!'*

Thomas Ferguson slammed on the brakes.

CHAPTER TWO

As soon as she'd jumped off the bus, she sprinted back up the road.

'Aoife, get back here!'

She increased her speed. All around, acres of bog stretched to the horizon, broken only by the small green hill, crisscrossed with sheep paths and crowned with white hawthorn. Nothing moving.

She had seen a child.

She had.

The bus did a clumsy three-point turn on a stretch of grass and came rumbling up the road behind her.

Aoife cut left across the bog, round the back of the rocky outcrop. It was painfully slow going across the soft ground, her feet sinking in at every step, but after a few minutes of struggle she hit on a trail of mossy stones laid side by side in a regular pattern, as if they had once formed an ancient pathway. A thought came to her: *Down.* Yet the stone track brought her straight to the foot of the hill, and the only way forward was up. Maybe from the top she could get a better view. She mounted the steep slope, turning at the top to scan the landscape. Slopes of rusty and purple heather, dotted with fluttering white scraps of bog cotton, stretched away to the mountains and a distant glint of sea. A few sheep with their lambs. Nowhere to hide in this wild empty land.

The bus drew up at the side of the road and two figures got off: one in a bright orange dress and the other in the green and red of a Mayo jersey.

Aoife hurried on across the summit towards the circle of hawthorns. Maybe the little girl had taken fright and run back the way she had come, and had hidden herself among these trees.

The densely woven hawthorns were wound together as tight as a roll of barbed wire. There seemed no easy way into the thicket. She tried to pull the branches aside, but the thorns hurt her hands; she peered in between them, and saw only whiteness. This close to her face, the scent of the hawthorn blossom was overpowering, so strong it made her feel strange and floaty. A hand touched her arm, and she spun.

'Jesus, Carla, you nearly gave me a heart attack!'

'Sorry.' Carla was breathless and pink with the effort of struggling across the soft ground and up the steep slope. 'I'm so sorry about that stupid crap Lois said about Killian.'

'Not your fault. Here, help me find a way in—'

'Stop pulling at those thorns, you'll hurt yourself! Sinead's dad sent me to tell you to come back.'

'Help me—'

'I *have* been helping. I was looking all around me all the way across the bog and up the hill. Shay Foley's looking as well, on the other side of the road.'

'Really?' She would never think badly of him again, ever, even if he never said another word to her or anyone in all his life.

'Aoife, stop doing that . . . *Stop it, you're bleeding!*'

'It's all right, I've found a gap – come on.' She pushed her way through into the circle. Inside, the canopy of flowers above and the carpet of blossom made a pale, sunlit dome filled with sweetness. At the centre of the clearing lay a round pool, so flat and black it was like an oil spill on snow.

Carla came complaining bitterly in her wake. 'Ouch, yuck. Aoife, let's go, there's nobody here and I'm scratched to pieces, and this dress is ruined and my dress that *you're* wearing is ruined . . .'

Aoife walked across the soft carpet and looked into the pool. Blackness. Nothingness. She crouched down on the bank, and felt around in the water. It was freezing and deep, deeper than her arm could reach. She lay down on her front. Carla said in a panicky voice, standing over her, 'Oh my God, have you seen something?'

'No, but what if she's in here? I can't reach the bottom.'

'What? You can't see anything in there but you think she's *drowned*? Aoife, this is crazy. Even if you did see her, she can't have had time to—'

Aoife sat up, kicked off her shoes and slid into the pool. The coldness of it nearly stopped her heart.

'Aoife, what the hell? Get out of there!'

The water was up to her chest. She took a deep breath and crouched, letting the iciness close over her head, feeling blindly around the soft bottom of the pool, her knees sinking into the mud, fearing yet longing to put her hands on a small cold body buried in the mud. Sinking down, down . . . Her lungs were straining, and her head was ringing. *Down. Down.*

She was numbingly cold; her veins had filled with the waters of the pool. *Down, down . . . Under the ground . . .* Hands seized her, dragging her to her feet; her head surfaced, lungs expanded; she choked down air.

Carla was sobbing, shoving her along in front of her onto the bank. 'Get out of the water, you stupid fool . . . *Get out!*'

Aoife's head was spinning, light and dizzy; vision black; her tongue felt thick. 'Let go of me—'

'*Get out!*'

'But the child—'

Carla screamed at the top of her voice: '*There is no child!*'

The release was immediate, as if Carla's despairing scream were a full-strength hammer blow that had shifted a heavy blockage in her head, allowing the darkness to drain, letting in the light.

Carla was right.

There was no child.

Thomas Ferguson took one look at the two of them – soaking, muddy and shivering – and announced that he was driving them back to Kilduff before taking everyone else to the seven o'clock showing instead.

Killian refused to let Carla sit beside him because he didn't want to get wet; he went to sit beside Shay. Shay moved over into the window seat to make room for the builder's son, plugged his earphones in and closed his eyes. He would probably never speak to Aoife again, not after he had broken his long silence to stand up for her only to be made a fool of.

Carla sat beside Aoife, staring gloomily out of the window, eyes full of tears.

In the seat across the aisle, Sinead was being loudly comforted by Lois. 'Don't let her spoil your day.'

'There won't be time to get a pizza after!'

'There will, and if not we'll go next week, just you and me.'

Behind, Killian was on great form, leaning across the aisle to crack pointed jokes about leprechauns with his cousin, Darragh Clarke. 'Two leprechauns walked into a bar. Ouch! It was an iron bar.'

As they neared Kilduff, Aoife touched Carla's hand. 'I'm so sorry.'

Carla said stiffly, without turning her head, 'It's all right.'

The bus drew up outside the church.

Aoife paused beside Sinead. 'I'm really, really sorry . . .' Sinead ignored her. 'OK, well, I hope the film is OK.' Silence, and a prolonged sigh from Lois. She followed Carla off the bus.

As she was picking up her bike, she heard a man's harsh voice shouting: 'Shay! Get over here!' across the square. She turned, and Shay Foley had dismounted from the bus – he caught her eye, hesitated, then walked rapidly away towards a beaten-up, three-door red Ford that had just pulled out of the pub car park. The driver who had summoned him was a big, black-haired man in his mid-twenties – his brother, presumably. Shay got in, and the Ford drove away. So he really had decided not to talk to her any more.

Carla was standing beside her gazing forlornly after the departing bus. She said, without looking directly at Aoife, 'That was pretty mean of Sinead's dad to make us come home.'

'You can't really blame him, though – look at the state of us. We're not just wet, we're filthy wet. I'm really sorry.'

Carla shrugged. 'It's OK.'

'Will I come home with you and explain to your mam?'

'You're all right, I'll just say what we said to Sinead's dad – that you fell in a bog hole by accident and I helped you out.'

'I don't mind telling her the whole thing—'

'*No.*' Carla paused, and sighed. 'I'm not being funny, but you know, it was a bit weird and she might not understand.'

'OK.'

'Are you feeling all right now?'

'I guess. Here's that bar for Zoe.' She pulled it from her bag and held it out.

Carla took it but then just stood there holding her bike, clearly working herself up to something else. 'Look—'

'Carla, don't worry, I know I didn't see a child. Or a leprechaun. I swear on my life I haven't gone mental on you—'

'No, no, I don't mean about that, I mean about Killian. Do you really fancy him? I don't mind – just tell me.'

Aoife said, taken aback, 'No, really, I don't.'

'Because actually he said to me on the bus that he thinks you do.'

'*What ... ?*' But she stopped herself in time.

34

Telling the truth would just be the poisonous icing on Carla's already very bad day. 'No, he's grand and everything, but seriously, no.'

Carla shrugged, not looking any the happier. 'Anyway, I don't know why I'm even asking, 'cos it doesn't matter now. He couldn't stop laughing at me when I got back to the bus all covered in mud and my hair in a big frizz.'

'Oh, Carla.' Aoife wanted to say something like *If he really likes you, something like that won't matter to him*, but that was the sort of thing only mothers said, and it was never true. 'I wish . . . Look, I'm sure he'll text you.'

Carla said stiffly, 'He won't. Don't worry about it.'

Aoife hugged her – awkwardly, because they were both holding their bikes.

As she rode out of the square, her phone beeped. Carla.

i love u more than any boy

Warmth flooded Aoife's heart.

me too

She set the stopwatch and rode home as fast as she could, as if through sheer physical effort she could leave her own bad day behind. Past the unfinished estate on the edge of the village, where her dad, a carpenter, had been working before the recession. Past Kilduff garage and then slightly downhill, the breeze drying the last of the dampness from her short green dress. There was a tractor ahead of her, and she overtook it. After the tractor was a car, and she had a sudden urge to overtake that too – and did. The elderly man at the wheel gave her a startled glance as she powered by. This was strange – and a bit frightening. How fast was she going? The old man must have been driving very slowly . . . The turning to her house was coming up, and she only just made it, skittering left in a wide spray of gravel into the boreen. This was terrifying – the pedals were spinning so fast her feet could barely keep up. If she didn't slow down, she'd destroy her wheels on the potholes . . .

And yet she did not brake, because suddenly all fear had drained away, and she was filled instead with a mad, unnatural pleasure. There was no need to slow down for the potholes – she was flying over them. The hedges were a green and flowery blur, the cows in the field mere streaks of black and white . . . The small stone house appeared in its nest of trees, and seconds later she was dumping her bike on the lawn, panting, exhilarated, her hair a mess. She checked her phone to see how long it had taken her. Two and a half kilometres in two minutes, two seconds. That morning it had taken her over nine minutes to cycle the three kilometres from her place to Carla's.

For a brief moment Aoife was giddy with triumph. Two minutes! Then reality intervened. It wasn't possible; she must have set the timer wrong. Still breathing hard, she dragged her fingers through her tangled hair. Hawthorn blossoms showered out. Her dress was still covered with mud from climbing into that icy pool. *Down . . . Down . . .* She had set the timer wrong. She took a deep breath, and walked into the house.

Her mother was in her usual place at the kitchen table, working on local farmers' accounts, her dark blonde hair dragged back into a scruffy plait. The sink behind her was stacked with plates. She glanced up as Aoife passed. 'I thought you were going to the cinema, sweetie?' And stayed staring, pushing back her chair and standing up. 'What on earth . . . ? Hey, wait, don't go – what happened to you?'

Aoife came back to the doorway. 'We went for a walk and I fell in a bog hole.' At some point she would tell her mother the whole story, but right now she needed to get her head in order. And she wanted a shower. 'Is there any hot water?'

Maeve, shocked but half laughing, was coming towards her with her arms held out. 'You poor thing. Are you all right?'

'Grand.'

'Oh. Oh my God.' Now Maeve had both hands pressed to her mouth, eyes staring – she seemed to be becoming more shocked as the seconds passed, not less.

'Mam, calm down, it's just a bit of mud. Is there any hot—?'

'Where did you find that?'

Aoife said, confused now, 'Find what?'

'That. *That.*'

'Oh, you mean this.' She touched the heart locket. 'I dropped my phone in Declan Sweeney's field and I found this when I was looking for it. Weird, isn't it, how it turned up after all this time? I must have lost it when me and Carla used to play in there – do you remember we had this game called—'

'Let me see it?'

Aoife unclipped the chain. 'Are you all right, Mam? You look kind of . . . It's nice, isn't it, having something from when I was a baby? After all the photos were lost.'

Maeve didn't answer; just took and studied the locket very closely, reading the name. Opened it. Kissed the picture of the baby. Closed it. Tears were leaking down her face.

After a while Aoife said, not knowing how else to break this strange emotional impasse, 'It's too tight on me now.'

Maeve looked up at her vaguely; the tears were still trickling, and she kept wiping them away with the back of her hand.

Aoife said, 'It needs a longer chain. Do you have an old one lying around somewhere, if you don't want to buy one?'

There was a long pause, in which her mother seemed to have a hard time understanding what she'd just said.

'Mam, a chain? You know, so I can wear it.'

'You want to *wear* this?'

'Well . . . Yes. I'd like to. Isn't that OK?'

'Sweetie, it's kind of a precious memory.'

'I know it's the only photo of me we have, but I'll take care of it, I promise. I really like it, it's so pretty.'

But Maeve kept the locket in her hand, turning away from Aoife like she was afraid of being robbed. 'I'll just put it away somewhere safe for now.'

'Mam—'

'Have a shower, Aoife, before I use all the hot water doing the washing-up.'

In the spotty bathroom mirror, she looked even worse than she'd realized. She had streaks of mud on her high cheekbones, like an ancient hero going into battle. The green dress was ripped under both arms. Her hands were badly scratched; on her right, new red scratches crisscrossed the long silvery scar she'd got from falling off her first bike and grabbing hold of a line of barbed wire – she didn't remember that happening, but her parents had told her about it. She pulled off the dress, dumped it by the washing machine, and stood in the sputtering shower, shampooing. More cream blossoms poured out of her red-gold hair and swirled in a pale whirlpool down the drain.

She went upstairs to her bedroom wrapped in the towel and rummaged for a T-shirt and jeans. While in the shower, she had received nine texts from Carla:

killian message me from ifone!!!!!!!
on Facebook!!!!!!!
hey text me
killian message me again!!!!!!!!
killian thinks film terrible ☺ ☺ ☺ ☺ ☺
txt!!!!!!!!!!!!!!!!!!!!!
hey text me
txt
☹ dinner

Aoife left it till later to text back. Dianne Heffernan always put her daughter's phone on top of the dresser when the family was eating, and the beep of an incoming text would only be a torment to Carla. She brushed the space bar of her ancient PC, waking her Facebook page. In between texting

Carla, Killian had managed to post a clip of a leprechaun jigging at the foot of a rainbow, pulling gold out of his pockets. Darragh had liked it a few minutes ago. The birthday film was a romantic comedy. The lads must be getting bored.

Darragh posted:

I saw a goblin today

Aoife typed:

Where? In the mirror?

and got an instant 'like' off Killian.

She thought about deleting the leprechaun post, but there was no point getting defensive. She'd made a mistake about the child. She'd just have to live it down.

She sat cross-legged on her bed with her back against the wall, pulling her guitar into her arms. Eminem, Nirvana and Lady Gaga gazed down from tattered posters. So much history on these walls – photos of herself and Carla, same as in Carla's bedroom. Old drawings of Manga characters, done in national school. Other singers' song lyrics, her favourites, written out by hand. One or two of her own, but she hadn't put her name to them.

She started picking out a tune that had been running through her mind for days. She hadn't had any words before, but now she sang under her breath:

'Drifting like a ghost in the water –
Could have been anybody's daughter . . .'

And shivered. Was that the answer to what happened today, rising from her subconscious – had the child been a ghost? Maybe a little girl had drowned in that pool a long time ago.

Stop. There was no child.

Aoife heard her father come through the front door downstairs, struggling under a heavy load, dropping it in the hall. More old books, no doubt. He had been at a car boot sale in Clonbarra, and he wouldn't have been able to resist buying boxes of cheap second-hand hardbacks. James O'Connor was obsessed by the old stories – ancient Irish tales that nobody else under the age of eighty gave any thought to now. He was a carpenter, but the collapse of the building trade in the recession had left him plenty of time on his hands to read. He had so many books now that he had run out of shelf space in the back room. Tattered volumes were piled everywhere in the house, including up both sides of the already narrow staircase.

'James?' Maeve called her husband into the kitchen. He went in; she murmured something, and he shut the door.

After a few minutes he cried out – a deep painful cry, as if horribly wounded.

Aoife leaped down the stairs, into the kitchen. 'Dad, are you all right?'

Her parents were standing in the middle of the room with their arms around each other. Her father's shoulders were bent and head was lowered, resting against his wife's cheek.

'Dad, what happened? What's the matter?'

Looking past him at Aoife with a weak smile, Maeve said, 'Nothing's the matter, darling. Did you finish your shower?'

'Yes, ages ago.'

'Then go and dry your hair.' Her mother's hand

was folded into a soft fist, resting against the small of her husband's back.

'It *is* dry.'

'Finish drying it properly, sweetie.' A glint of gold was visible between her mother's fingers.

'Mam, is this to do with me finding my necklace and it having my baby picture in it?'

Her father trembled. Maeve tightened her grip on the heart locket, hiding it from view. 'Nothing's to do with anything, sweetie. Go dry your hair.'

That night, Aoife was woken by small icy fingers squeezing her wrist. Still half asleep, she moaned: 'Who's that?'

'Come with me.' The freezing fingers tightened. 'You have to come with me.'

Aoife opened her eyes. The ghost child was kneeling over her, staring down at her. Aoife screamed, but no noise came. She tried to free herself, but couldn't move.

'Come with me,' said the little girl.

With a desperate effort, Aoife heaved herself sideways, frantically trying to shake herself free. The child came scrambling with her across the bed, beseeching: 'Come with me! Come with me!'

She got her hand to the bedside light; the moment it flashed on, the child sprang from the bed, raced across the floor and scrambled out of the window into the starless night. Aoife lay in a tangle of sheets, sweating, shivering, her heart hammering.

A terrifying dream.

The window had come loose from its catch and was creaking in the night breeze. As soon as she had her courage back, she got out of bed. Rain was blowing in, wetting the curtains. When she reached out into the dark to pull the window shut, cold fingers caught at hers.

She pushed them away with a cry. Wet leaves swept around in the rainy wind. The ash tree outside her window sighed and the rain rattled heavily on the slates above her. No moon, nor stars. The black garden stretched to the black wall. Beyond were invisible fields. The sudden downpour had released the sweet scent of hawthorn from all around, and the smell of it made her feel dizzy, like she'd been spinning in circles and suddenly stopped.

CHAPTER THREE

Aoife studied her father out of the corner of her eye, from under her lashes. He didn't often come with her and her mother to Sunday Mass, but today he had seemed to feel the need for God. He was even listening to the sermon, his dark brown eyes fixed on the priest.

When she'd found her father's picture in the locket, it was the first time she'd ever seen him with black hair – as far back as she could remember, his hair had been a thick silvery grey. Nor had she ever seen him cry – until yesterday, in the kitchen, with her mother's arms around him. By this morning, he seemed to have recovered from whatever dark upsetting memory the locket had brought back to him. As the priest droned on, he caught Aoife's eye and smiled. She smiled back.

Father Leahy blew his nose, and turned a page. 'There is no other,' he carried on in his flat, snuffly voice. 'There is no God but Me.'

A subversive lyric drifted into Aoife's head:

Your God says he's the holy one,
But you know he's not the only one . . .

Yes, she liked that. She needed to remember that and put it in a song.

I think he's just the lonely one . . .

The words were still running through her head when she went up to take communion, and as Father Leahy placed the wafer on her tongue, she found herself raising her eyes to his gaze. *Maybe he's the phoney one . . .* The priest's eyes widened; he snatched his fingers away as if he thought she was about to bite, and quickly sketched the sign of a cross.

Instead of returning to her pew for the rest of the Mass, Aoife carried on past it up the aisle and straight out of the church into the fresh air. She felt shaken – had Father Leahy really flinched from her, as if she had bared her teeth at him like a dog?

You know he's not the only one . . . The persistent lyric was beginning to annoy her; it had set itself to a chirpy tune.

To block it out, she turned on her phone, and texted Carla:

U dead yet?

Carla had woken up that morning with a cold, presumably from getting soaked in the hawthorn pool the day before. But she must have gone back to sleep, because she failed to text Aoife back.

Restless and still troubled by the priest's reaction, Aoife wandered the gravelled paths between the graves. The sun was warm on her head, and there was a scent of mown grass. An old man in a black jacket was tidying away dead flowers – John McCarthy, whose nephew owned the small supermarket. The old man was a heavy drinker and steadily losing his mind; he had taken to telling everyone that his nephew's wife was a witch, although that didn't stop him going there for his Sunday dinner. Aoife read the gravestones as she walked. Familiar Kilduff names: Heffernans and Burkes, Fergusons and Dohertys. A rake of O'Connors – her father's family, the remains of which were spread thin around the world in Canada, Australia, Hong Kong. She realized suddenly that she was reading the stones because she was looking for the grave of a little girl, one who might have drowned out on the bog. She stopped looking. Then carried on.

Instead of a little girl, she found:

HERE LIES MOIRA FOLEY,

BELOVED WIFE OF EAMONN FOLEY,

BELOVED MOTHER OF JOHN JOE AND SEAMUS FOLEY.

Shay's mother, laid to rest eleven years before, around the time Aoife's family had moved home to Kilduff. Under his name, another inscription:

HERE LIES EAMONN FOLEY,

BELOVED FATHER OF JOHN JOE AND SEAMUS FOLEY.

Poor Shay, losing his mother and then his father in the same year.

'That's not Moira Foley in there.'

Aoife nearly jumped out of her skin.

John McCarthy was reading the gravestone over

her shoulder, arms folded and elbows sharp in his old black jacket. 'People say she was after jumping off that cliff, but they're wrong.'

She got her breath back under control. 'She killed herself? But that's so sad!' No wonder Shay was so quiet at school, never talking to anyone, keeping his own company.

'Do you not listen? I said, that's what they *say*. But she never did. If she had, the sea would have given her body up in the end.'

Surprised, she looked back at the gravestone. 'But it says she's buried here.'

'Fool's talk. 'Tis a log of driftwood. They fairies do love to play tricks on human fools with logs of wood.'

'Oh, I see.' People were trickling out of the church. 'I think my parents are coming now . . .'

John McCarthy caught the sleeve of her hoodie in thin urgent fingers. 'A fairy, that's what she was. A lenanshee. A fairy lover. Eamonn knew it about her, God rest his tormented soul. He told everyone who would listen, even as he was painting and painting her portrait over and over again. "My wife's a lenanshee," he would say. "I'm not long for this world, and as for her, she was never of it."'

His hand seemed so thin and brittle, Aoife didn't like to shake it off. 'I didn't know Shay's father was an artist . . . ?'

'But he wasn't. A farmer was what God meant him to be – it was she who made an artist out of him, and it killed him. Your lenanshee is one dangerous fairy. She steals your heart and burns you up. Beware of the *leannán sídhe*, Aoife O'Connor. Stay away from the lover from the otherworld.' He tightened his fragile grip on her arm. 'Do you know what it is to have a *grá*?'

Aoife said faintly, 'To want something really badly?'

'Badly. Yes. Very badly. A *grá* is no ordinary, comfortable, fireside sort of a love. It is a mad love, a wild love, a hunger, a longing, a terrible insatiable desire that cannot be turned aside. If a lenanshee ever takes a *grá* for you, Aoife O'Connor, your life will be as short as a candle in the wind. My own nephew is married to a lenanshee, and look at the state of him – he can't work in the shop, he'll barely eat or drink, he's an old man at thirty, and all he does is write poetry. *Poetry.*' John McCarthy made a noise of disgust, whistling through his yellow teeth. 'What good is poetry to a man? It feeds no one. It burns you up. You know what a lenanshee even is?'

'Don't they cry outside people's houses when someone is about to die?'

'You don't know much, do ye?' His eyes were bulging blue marbles in his lined brown face. 'That one's not a *leannán sídhe*, them's a *bean sídhe*. A ban-shee. A woman of the fairy hills. She steals human babies to sell to the devil, and leaves fairy babies in their place. You can always tell a fairy baby. Bright red hair and evil in its heart. No souls, see, which is why they're no good to the devil. My grandchildren – every one of them is from the otherworld.'

'There's my mam and dad now – I have to go.' Relieved to have an excuse to get away, Aoife ran to join them. Sinead's mother was talking to Maeve; Sinead shot Aoife a most un-Christian glare. Aoife changed direction sharply, and went to her father's green Citroën.

When her parents got into the front of the car, Maeve said rather stiffly over her shoulder, 'Mary says you made everyone late for the film by saying you saw a little figure running across the bog, but no one else saw anything and it turned out to be nothing.'

Aoife winced. 'I was going to tell you about that. Sorry.'

'Mm. It would have been handy to know in advance. I felt a bit ambushed.'

'Sorry again.'

James kept glancing at Aoife in the rear-view mirror as he pulled out of the square. 'So what was it you saw, do you think?'

Aoife sighed and leaned her head against the window. 'Nothing. A lamb, maybe. Can we stop talking about it? People kept making stupid jokes about leprechauns. It was awful embarrassing.'

Early afternoon, Carla began bombarding her with texts about being so bored she could die. Apparently Killian had texted Carla twice ☺ but her mam wouldn't let her have visitors ☹.

Aoife texted back:

Be there in 20 mins

Halfway up the long narrow lane, she realized that it was happening again. She was going ridiculously fast – dangerously fast; if she met a car coming in the opposite direction, something horrible was going to happen, she was going to end up smeared across someone's windscreen . . . Yet while her mind was having these alarming thoughts, her physical body was being flooded by utter joy – *Don't worry about death, this is how it feels to alive!* Bending over the handlebars, torn between fear and ecstasy, she flew recklessly on. She made the skidding ninety-degree turn towards Kilduff without even looking to see if anything was coming the other way. The white lines down the centre of the road strobed past . . . The garage, the unfinished estate . . . A terrible squealing filled the air, ringing in her ears – the sound of metal screeching along the tarmac. She came to her senses, coasted the bike to a halt and got off to have a look. Disaster. Both tyres destroyed.

Panting, Aoife carried the bike across to the estate side of the road and laid it on its side on the grass verge, crouching down to get a better look. The thick rubber had worn right through and the inner tubes were shredded. What on earth had happened? She'd bought new tyres from the garage shop only a year ago, and they'd cost her thirty euros. Had she really ridden fast enough to wear them out? She checked the timer on her phone. Just over a minute since she'd left the house. No. One minute, to bicycle nearly two and a half kilometres? No. Impossible. *Insane.* She was imagining things, just like she'd imagined the child in the bog. Early Alzheimer's? Paranoid delusions? The last of the energy drained out of her, and she suddenly felt a bit ill. She sat down on the grass. Then lay down, flat on her back.

Seconds later, her phone vibrated, and she worked it out of her trackies pocket and held it up, shielding her eyes from the sun.

U left? mam says not even you ☹ thinks I have foot and mouth ☺

Aoife texted with her thumb:

No prob all good only just left

Then let her hand drop, and lay there with her eyes closed.

A car was coming slowly up the road from Kilduff, loud as a fleet of motorbikes – the silencer gone. She kept her eyes closed. The car thundered past her, then stopped. Then reversed and stopped again, right next to where she was lying. Unable to ignore the racket any longer, she opened her eyes. A red beaten-up three-door Ford with no registration plates. She recognized it from the day before – Shay's brother's car. Puzzled, she sat up. The black-headed driver leaned across from behind the wheel, winding down the window on her side. '*Wahu.*'

It was Shay himself.

Aoife was so startled, she forgot to be surprised that he was actually talking to her and blurted out: 'You're driving? You're only fifteen!'

He looked faintly offended. 'Nearly sixteen. You want a lift?'

'No, you're all right . . .' She scrambled to her feet, and picked up the bike. 'I have this with me.' She hesitated. 'Look, I'm really sorry about everything, and thanks for sticking up for me yesterday, and I'm really sorry – I'm an idiot, OK? I'll see you in school tomorrow.' Then walked off towards her lane, pushing her bike, relieved to have got it said.

He drove slowly along beside her. 'We could put it in the back, on top of the chickens.'

She glanced into the car. There was a big cage on the back seat with about ten annoyed-looking chickens in it. 'I don't think it would fit.'

'Maybe you're right. I was just on my way into Clonbarra to sell this crew for a few quid. You want to come? We can fold the cage flat after and get the bike then.'

Aoife could feel a smile forming inside her, right in the centre of her chest. 'No, you're grand.' She kept on walking, past the garage. She could see Dave Ferguson, Sinead's uncle, in the yard behind the shop, tinkering with an old cream-coloured car.

Shay kept on driving along beside her. She stopped. He stopped too, engine idling. She walked on again. He followed. She stopped. He stopped. 'I can drive, you know. I run her around the farm all the time.'

Aoife leaned the bike against the hedge and got in. It took three slams to properly close the badly-hung door. The foot well was full of straw, sweet wrappers, Coke cans and an old sketchbook.

Shay said, 'Just kick that stuff out of the way.' He revved the engine, pulled away from the verge, jammed a tape into the ancient radio-cassette. After much hissing, Christie Moore burst out of the tape deck – *Ride On*. Old folk, cool in its time.

Aoife shouted over the music: 'Won't you get in trouble driving into Clonbarra? I mean, you're not insured, are you?'

Shay turned the music down to a background crackle. 'Ara ya, they let me into the scheme young, 'cos I'm a class driver.'

'Really?'

'No.'

She laughed. 'But the guards . . .'

'Sure, what will they do, ban me?' Shay drove on at what seemed to be the car's maximum speed of forty kilometres an hour. His hands were curled loosely over the wheel, his long fingers tapping lightly in time to the music. He had rolled up his white sleeves and the skin of his arms was a dark golden brown. His tight-cropped black hair and collarless shirt revealed the strong curve of his neck which ran from his shoulder to his sloping jaw. The single silver earring glinted high in his ear. Without moving his head, his hazel gaze flicked towards her, a very slight smile in it.

Aoife quickly turned her head away. A song lyric had popped into her mind:

I dream of this:
Under the hawthorns he raises me with a kiss.

Worried she was going to blush, she leaned down to pick up the sketchpad lying in the foot well among the straw and opened it on her lap. On the first page, in black pencil, an old sheepdog slept in the sun, flies circling its nose ... 'Hey, this is really good!'

With an alarmed glance, Shay said, 'Don't look at those.'

She turned another page. 'Oh—'

He jerked the pad out of her hand and tossed it over his shoulder into the back, setting the chickens off squawking and crashing about in the cage. 'You don't want to be looking at my old rubbish.'

Grinning as well as now actually blushing, Aoife put her hand up to hide her face, staring out of the passenger window across the fields. She'd only got a glimpse, but she could have sworn the next picture – done in watercolours – was of a red-haired girl in a short green dress running up a hill towards a hawthorn circle.

They had reached the point where the Clonbarra road pushed up closest to the mountains. Wild rhododendrons piled across the dry-stone walls. Somewhere near here was the old bog road, which Thomas Ferguson had for some mad reason decided to take and so had got them lost, and so had led to all the trouble.

Lost . . . A coolness suddenly trickled through Aoife's blood, fizzy and tingling. She could see her now, in her mind's eye, as clear as anything – a little girl stumbling across the bog. Scared. Alone. Lost.

Not a lamb.

She took down her hand, and stared up at the passing mountains. In the distance, a pale ribbon wound across their purple slopes. The road across the bog. Any moment, they would pass the turning. She had to make Shay stop. She had to make him take the old boreen, the same as Thomas Ferguson had done . . .

Suddenly Shay was wrestling with the steering wheel. 'Holy Mary, what's the matter with her? Holy— How the—? Whoa! Stop!' The car spun hard right, straight across the road towards the turning, just failed to make it and smashed hard into the corner of the wall.

The old Ford's bonnet was drawn back in a lopsided snarl, the bumper twisted like a circus ringmaster's moustache. A headlight dangled from its socket like a hideously gouged eye. In the cage on the back seat, the chickens were going demented.

Shay stood in the road, clutching his black hair. 'Ah Christ, what am I going to do – it's a write-off. Mary and Joseph, John Joe is going to beat the bejaysus out of me.'

Aoife turned to him, horrified. 'What do you mean, *beat* you?'

He looked startled and uncomfortable, as if he hadn't realized he'd spoken his thoughts out loud. 'Nothing, it's grand – I just mean he'll go mental at me. This is his car and he doesn't even know I took it.'

'But it wasn't your fault—'

'That's right – I didn't hit the wall, the wall hit me.' He peered into the engine, which he could do without having to lift up the bonnet. It was still running, even louder than before. 'She's still going, anyways.'

'It can't have been your fault, it's not like you were speeding—'

'Aoife, calm the form, John Joe will be fine – I can handle him.'

She couldn't help feeling responsible – she had been thinking so hard about making him turn right, and then he did. 'Look, seriously, something must have broken.'

'I was thinking it might be the drive shaft . . .' Shay was checking under the chassis now. 'Nope. Can't see anything wrong. Maybe I can fix her up.' He jumped into the driver's seat and reversed in a wheel-spinning semicircle, setting off a fresh explosion of anxiety from the chickens in the back. Then he pulled up beside Aoife. 'Not a bother on her! I'll hammer her back into shape, and she'll be as good as new. Hop in.'

She didn't move. The narrow dusty road wound up away between green fields brilliant with gorse.

'Are you coming? I don't blame you for being a small bit careful but I swear I'll drive like a nun . . .'

Oh God. Before she could change her mind she

blurted out in a rush, 'All right, I know I'm mad, but I can't help thinking, *What if I really* did *see a little girl and she's still out there somewhere, wandering around on the bog – she could die, she could drown—*'

'Aoife.'

'She was lost and I didn't help her—'

'*Aoife*. Stop.' Shay was gazing at her steadily; he didn't seem exasperated with her for being a total idiot – just genuinely concerned. 'You don't need to get all up in a heap about this. If there was a child gone missing, then we'd have heard about it. I listened to the news yesterday, every hour on the hour, and there was nothing.'

She felt a rush of gratitude towards him – at least he had taken her seriously enough to check. 'But what if she was abandoned by someone who didn't report it to the police? Her own parents, even?'

'Ah, Aoife—'

'I'm sorry. I have to go look. You go on. I'll walk.'

CHAPTER FOUR

She stood on the rocky outcrop near where she'd seen the child, staring around. The landscape was still empty, dotted with white tufts of bog cotton, steaming in the May sunshine. Creamy clumps of sheep. A shining stroke of distant sea. No houses. No one visible for miles. No little girl.

Shay waited patiently beside her, arms folded, shirt sleeves pushed up above his elbows. A short way off was the hill capped with the tightly wound circle of hawthorn trees. Aoife could smell the blossom – the breeze must be blowing directly towards them.

There was no reason to return to the hawthorn circle. She knew exactly what was there.

Nothing.

She shoved her hands into the pockets of her hoodie.

If she could take one look, just *one*, in the pool, it would surely satisfy this insistent worry, once and for all. Like double-checking a door was locked, or a light turned off. She said, 'Look, I'm crazy and I know it, but I think I'll just take another look up there by the trees.'

'Don't go falling in any bog holes again.'

She said with a flash of irritation, 'I feel stupid enough about this already – no need to rub it in—'

'Ah, I was only joking you. Come on. Look at me.' Shay's voice was teasing. 'Come on, Aoife. Look at me.'

She looked, frowning. As soon as she met his green gaze, a wide grin spread across his face. 'Race you!' And without any further warning, he sprang down from the outcrop.

Aoife scrambled down after him and out across the bog. He had almost twenty metres on her, leaping long-legged from patch to patch of the firmest ground, arms stretched out at his sides to retain his balance, everything about him taunting her. But she was gaining on him. His trainers were leaving deep prints in the soft ground while, unlike yesterday, her own feet barely bent the heather. She was gaining, gaining . . . She was fast, she was feather-light . . .

Yet now Shay had reached the stony track, and was himself able to display the unnatural speed he showed on the GAA pitch. He had reached the foot of the hill before Aoife caught up with him, but just as he started up the slope, she managed to grab the back of his shirt, and that slowed him down enough for her to slip past him and take the lead.

'Cheat!' He made a grab for her, but she dodged and scrambled on up the green sheep-trodden mound. Nearing the summit, she felt safe enough to turn and do a little victory dance, but he surprised her by being right behind her, and she turned and fled again with a shriek – but not before he'd seized her by her hood. Aoife flailed her arms and stumbled and slipped, and twisted to free herself, and suddenly she was on the ground with Shay on top of her, and his face was so close to hers that she could see herself reflected in his dark green eyes. His expression became suddenly very serious, thoughtful, his mouth drawing closer to hers . . .

He rolled away, laughing. 'Jesus and Mary, but you can run. I never knew anyone could run faster than me. Let me get my breath here for a minute.' He lay on his back, panting lightly, staring at the sky.

Feeling confused and slightly disappointed by his sudden change in mood, Aoife lay with her arms by her sides and concentrated on breathing. Her heart stilled. The sun was beautiful on her face. Around them, the bog hummed softly under its gauzy net of flies and bees.

'Hey, Aoife, look at this . . .'

She rolled onto her side, to face him.

Shay was leaning on his elbow, with his other hand palm up – a green caterpillar was crawling across it. As soon as he was sure she was watching, he closed his fingers over it, holding her gaze with a smile, the gold-brown depths of his green eyes lighting up.

She said, 'What?'

'Wait . . .'

'For what?'

'Now.' He opened his hand. A blue bog butterfly fluttered upwards.

Aoife was delighted. 'How did you do that?'

'Something my mother taught me . . .' Shay's eyes darkened for a moment, and then he was smiling again. 'A magic trick. Good, isn't it?'

'Show me how you did it! Did you have the butterfly up your sleeve? Where's the caterpillar? Give it here to me!'

She held out her hand, but he was laughing at her.

'Gone! Turned to a butterfly!' Then, glancing at her palm: 'What happened to your hand?'

For a moment Aoife thought he meant the scratches from the hawthorn circle, but they seemed to have healed already. 'Oh, that . . . A scar from when I was a little kid – I fell off my first bike and grabbed a barbed-wire fence.'

'Let me look . . .' Shay was reaching out to take her hand, but then seemed to change his mind about touching her and turned onto his front, pulling up blades of grass.

Aoife sprang to her feet and ran the rest of the way up to the circle.

She couldn't find her way in through the trees. She could see the way she and Carla had gone in and out – their footprints were still clear in the soft ground, running right into the wall of thorns. But where the gap had been, the flowering branches were locked together, as if they had grown again overnight. She pressed her palms against the thorns. Instead of giving way, as they had yesterday, they remained as tightly woven as the rest of the circle. *Locked*.

Shay came up behind her. 'Careful now, they'll stab you.'

'It's weird – I got through here yesterday, right at this spot, but it's like the branches have grown back.'

He tried to part them himself, then swore and stood back, sucking a large thorn from the base of his thumb before wiping the red blood on his faded jeans. 'Are you *sure* this is where you got in before?'

'Yes – see, look at the ground – you can see the treads of our shoes, going in under the hawthorn— What's that?'

'What?'

'*That!*'

Not far from their footprints, a small dead animal was lying covered by wind-blown blossom. No, not a dead animal – but not a living one, either. Aoife fell to her knees on the grass, gently brushing aside the flowers. A rabbit, with long grey ears and a fluffy white tail, and round black eyes. A child's toy. She sobbed in horror: 'She *was* here!'

Shay crouched beside her, his hand on her shoulder. 'Ssh, don't be worried. This doesn't mean anything. Any child could have dropped it.'

'*How?*'

'Any family could have stopped by to look at the fairy fort.'

Aoife swallowed and wiped her face with her sleeve. 'All right. I know. When I'm thinking straight like you, I *do* know she wasn't real. But the minute I stop thinking about it, I go back to feeling like she was. I just keep going round and round, and every time I have it sorted in my mind, everything gets mixed up again.'

There was a long pause. She turned her head to look at him. He had dropped his hand from her shoulder, but was still squatting on his heels beside her, gazing straight at her. There was an odd expression in his green-brown eyes, like he wanted to say something to her, but wasn't sure quite how to put it, or how she would take it.

She said defensively, 'What? I know I'm an idiot.'

Shay said, 'I saw a sheóg myself once, when I was a kid.'

'*A sheóg?*' For a moment Aoife was seriously angry with him. It was bad enough Killian taunting her about leprechauns, or Darragh going on about goblins. 'Oh, of course, stupid me – why didn't I think of that – a fairy child, of course, that explains everything.'

But instead of laughing at her burst of temper,

or getting annoyed himself in return, he just settled himself down on the green hill beside her, his arms clasped around his faded jeans, and stared out over the endless orange-lilac sweep of bog, saying nothing at all.

Aoife sat grumpily beside him until her irritation subsided. After few minutes she even started to feel bad about having snapped at him. He'd only been saying something to comfort her – that any fool can make mistakes about what they see. She lowered her head and examined the rabbit, and stroked its well-chewed ears. It had been well-loved once, before it had been forgotten. The toy looked back at her with small dark eyes, the black plastic scuffed with rough patches like the pale cataracts of old age. She sighed and shoved the rabbit into the pocket of her hoodie. Some child had loved it once. It seemed wrong to leave it outside, lonely and cold in the rain.

Shay said, 'I was out helping my father with the lambs, and a little girl came walking towards me along the cliff top, out of the early mist. She was even younger than me, not even old enough for school, and she was wearing a little red shawl, the way they used to on the islands. When she saw me, she seemed to get a big fright and turned and ran off again. I would have chased after her, but for my dad stopped me.' His voice softened when he spoke of Eamonn Foley. 'He said I should never, ever follow a sheóg. He said they liked to lure human children out across the bog to drown, to keep them company as ghosts.'

Aoife suggested softly, 'Maybe he was telling you a story to stop you running off on him.'

'No, he really believed it. A young woman disappeared out of the next valley soon after, and everyone said she'd run off with a travelling man, but my father said the sheóg had fetched her away.' Shay raised his dark green eyes and looked straight at her.

She looked straight back at him, saying nothing. She was remembering mad John McCarthy in the graveyard, and how he'd said Eamonn Foley was convinced his wife was a lenanshee.

The softness went out of Shay's face, like he knew full well what she was thinking. He turned his face away. 'Sure, my father believed in a lot of things.'

Instantly Aoife felt terrible. Shay Foley never spoke to anyone about anything, and now here he was opening up to her about his father, and she had just stared blankly at him like he was talking nonsense.

She said quickly, putting her hand on his arm, 'Your father was an artist, wasn't he?'

He glanced at her in surprise, and his expression softened again. 'Where did you hear that? I didn't think anyone remembered that.'

'They do, of course. Is that where you get your own talent from?'

'My . . . ? Oh . . .' He became suddenly self-conscious, more his old withdrawn self. 'No, that's nothing. I'm no good, not compared to him.'

'You are – the drawing of the dog was brilliant.'

He shook his head, flushing slightly across his cheekbones. 'Seriously, he was a real artist. Other people thought so too, people who knew, but he never would sell to them. After he died some Galway fellow auctioned his paintings for us, and they went for a good amount. I didn't want to part with them but my brother needed the money to get the farm going again.'

It came to the tip of her tongue to say *I'm sorry for your troubles* like everyone said at funerals. But it seemed stupid and pointless, so long after the fact. Instead, she said, 'What sort of thing did he paint?'

Shay hesitated. 'Portraits.'

She nearly asked of who, but John McCarthy's voice piped up just in time: *Painting and painting her portrait over and over again.* Eamonn Foley painted his wife, nobody else. 'Did you not keep any of his paintings?'

'Just one. A small one. I have it in my room.' His eyes were bright. On impulse, Aoife took his hand; he didn't pull it away. His palm was hard – a typical farm boy's hand. He ran his thumb absently over the back of hers. A surprisingly intimate gesture for the boy who usually kept his distance from everyone.

In the silence between them, two lines passed through Aoife's head:

*Her body lies beneath the sea
But in my room she watches me.*

She shivered, and Shay looked worried and disengaged his hand as if it might be the touch of him that bothered her. 'Are you all right?'

'Fine – just the breeze is a bit cold. I guess you need to get on to Clonbarra.'

He checked his phone. 'Bit late for the mart now.'

'Is it? Oh God, I'm sorry . . .'

'No bother – live chickens don't go off.'

So there was still no room for the bike in Shay's car, and Aoife ended up having to push it home after all. That evening, she lay on her bed and had a long conversation with Carla about the amazingness of Killian, who had actually texted Carla to ask how she was.

'Wasn't that lovely of him?'

'Yeah, really nice.'

'I said I was fine and I'd see him in school tomorrow.'

'That's great, well done.'

Carla said suddenly, 'Aoife, are you all right? Has something happened?'

Aoife flopped over onto her back, stared up at Lady Gaga. 'Mm. A couple of things.'

'Well, like what?'

'I ruined my tyres.'

'Ugh, bad luck – those potholes in your lane are getting ridiculous.'

That's what it was! Two days in a row she had ridden right over the growing potholes instead of going round them. No wondered she'd ruined her wheels – nothing strange was happening to her. She said more cheerfully, 'And I saw Shay Foley. You won't believe this, but he was driving.'

'Are you serious? He's only fifteen!'

'Nearly sixteen.'

'So? He's not allowed till he's seventeen. I suppose that comes of having no parents.'

'Yeah, it's so sad for him.'

'No, I mean it's kind of cool not being told what to do all the time. That must be why he's so independent. I get forced to not even have visitors because I have a stupid cold, and he gets to drive around the countryside in a car. Where was he when you saw him?'

'On the Clonbarra road.'

'The main road! Are you sure it was him?'

'He stopped to talk to me.'

'No way! What's he like when he actually opens his mouth?'

'Nice.'

'Serious or funny?'

'Serious. Funny. Both.'

'And gorgeous! Did he ask you out?'

'No! He was just being friendly. We drove around for a bit.'

'Oh my God! He wants to ask you out!'

'Give over, Carla. We had a conversation, that's all.'

'So? I've never even had a conversation with Killian.'

'Ah, come on. You must have talked to him about something on the bus.'

'Not really. To be honest, I think that's where everyone else has gone wrong with him – he's not really one for conversation. It kind of tires him out.'

Shay Foley's first words to Aoife: *Don't worry about your friend. She's well able for him, more than you think.* Thinking about it, Aoife found it amazing that the quiet, reserved farmer's son, who had never spoken to her best friend – who never socialized with anyone – still somehow knew that Carla Heffernan was well able for Killian Doherty. While Aoife, who had known Carla almost her whole life, had in this case got her best friend completely wrong.

CHAPTER FIVE

Just as Aoife was pulling on her grey school coat, Carla called her on her mobile and carried on the conversation as if they'd never left off. 'This is mank – Mam's keeping me home in bed.'

'She is?' Aoife heaved her concrete-heavy school bag onto her shoulders, swapping the phone from one hand to the other. 'What's wrong with that?'

'I'm so bored and Zoe's annoying me—'

'Still, you're better off in bed if you're ill.'

'What are you, my other mammy?'

The front door was standing open and it was pouring, netting the world in silver-grey, flattening the grass. Maeve was waiting in her old Volvo at the gate. Aoife tried to judge whether if she lingered in the hallway for another few seconds the rain would ease off for the time it would take her to reach the car. 'I'm just off to school now.'

'Rub it in, why don't you. Tell everyone "hi" from me.'

Maeve beeped impatiently.

'Two secs – I'm not hanging up...' Aoife sheltered the mobile under her jacket while she dashed through the rain and threw herself into the Volvo. She got straight back on the phone. 'Here again.'

Carla said, 'By everyone, I mean Killian.'

'I realize that.'

'Do you think he's more pretty-boy or more sexy-boy?'

'My mam's driving.'

'I think both. Will you tell him "hi" from me?'

'Sure.'

'And don't let him go off with anyone else till I get out of here.'

'I won't.'

'By anyone, I mean Sinead. She was expecting to go out with him next – it's why she dumped Darragh.'

'Carla, I swear on my life I won't let her lay a finger on him.'

The first lesson was double history. At the lockers Aoife ran into Lois, also late, who checked her up and down with narrowed eyes. 'God, Aoife, you're even thinner than you were two days ago. Do you ever eat at all?'

'Yes . . . no . . . what?' Aoife was rummaging through the rubbish in the bottom of her school bag. 'Crap, I've forgotten my locker key.'

Lois raised her voice. 'I dare say it's just that you feel so guilty about messing up poor Sinead's birthday and poor Carla being ill. I suppose guilt would make you lose your appetite. You poor thing.'

Yet when Aoife rested her hand on the metal locker, the catch clicked and opened. For a moment she was worried someone had been messing with her stuff, but everything seemed in order – or at least everything was in the exact same total disorder as she had left it. Where were her history books? Right there, as if by magic, neatly on top of the pile.

Lois slammed her own locker shut. 'I can't believe you didn't even give Sinead a present.'

'Ah Jesus . . .' It was annoyingly true: the envelope with the ten euros was still on the windowsill in her bedroom, and she'd gone and forgotten it again. She grabbed her books. 'You're right, I'll sort it.'

Pleased with herself at finally getting a proper

guilty reaction, Lois said, 'But don't imagine that's going to make up for anything.'

The history class had already started. Mr Vaughan, a thin man with a fierce red comb-over, was writing on the whiteboard. The history room had long fixed desks; the rows near the front were fairly full, growing emptier towards the back. Lois marched up to the front and slid in next to Sinead. Aoife hesitated by the door: no Carla to sit with. Several heads turned towards her, clearly interested to see how she would deal with her first day back in school after making such a show of herself on Saturday. Shay was sitting by himself in the back row, slightly turned away from her towards the window, doodling left-handed on the cover of his copy book, his right hand shielding his face from her view. Lois nudged Sinead and shrieked in a high squeaky voice, 'Quick, there's a leprechaun hiding behind that rock! Oh no, it's a sheep.'

'Quiet!' snapped Mr Vaughan, without turning round from the board.

As the laughter died, Shay said loudly without looking up, 'Quick, there's a rock. Oh no, it's Lois's head.'

'*Quiet!*'

Grinning, Aoife slipped into the empty row in front of him, scooting along to sit by the window. Yet when she turned to smile her thanks, Shay had twisted the other way so that he was now facing the door instead of the window, resting his face in his left hand instead of his right. Confused, she turned back to her desk and opened her textbook.

At the front of the room, Lois was still trying to get Sinead's attention with repeated jabs of her elbow. But her friend was having a whispered conversation with the boy on her other side, smiling up at him from under her lashes. *Crap!* Carla was right. Sinead was already trying to move in on Killian. Now it was too late for Aoife to go and sit near them herself, and there wasn't a lot of point in glaring at them from behind. She raised her forefinger and squinted along it, at a point between Killian's shoulders. In her head, she said, *Bang*.

Killian jerked, gasped, and spun in his seat. 'What d'you do that for, ya fool?'

Darragh, sitting at the desk behind him, made a big show of innocence. 'Wha'? What are you on about? I done nothing!'

'Don't give me that – you jabbed me in the back with your biro . . .'

Aoife, grinning, felt oddly powerful – she'd been wanting to annoy Killian, and then it had happened, as if by remote control. Clearly Darragh was feeling the same way as herself – no doubt because Sinead had dumped him only just before the weekend.

'*Settle down!*' Mr Vaughan turned to face the room. 'Page forty-two, Vikings. Pillage in the village, et cetera. Sinead, before we get to the fun bit, perhaps you can remind us about the arrival of Christianity from last week?'

Sinead wasn't paying attention to him either, any more than to Lois; she was practically leaning against Killian.

'Sinead, the arrival of—?'

With an indignant cry, Sinead shot up in her seat, clapping her hand to the back of her neck. The history teacher took a startled hop backwards. Sinead turned vengefully on Darragh. 'Quit poking me, or I'll rip you!'

Killian's cousin threw his hands up in the air. 'Leave me alone, the two of ye. I'm doing absolutely nothing to either of ye.'

'Sure you're not—'

'*Sinead. The arrival of Christianity.*'

Aoife hastily locked her hands together on her desk. This time she'd been looking straight at Darragh, sighting along her forefinger over his shoulder at Sinead – and she knew Darragh hadn't done anything. It was almost as if it had been *her* that had poked Sinead . . . She glanced back at Shay, to share her puzzlement. But still she couldn't get him to meet her eyes. His hand was a barrier between them; the frayed cuff of his jumper was pulled up all the way over his knuckles instead of being pushed back to the elbow as it normally was. She could see the tilt of his jaw and the curve of his mouth no more.

Disappointed, she turned back to her book, riffling through it for page forty-two. Despite what she'd said to Carla about Shay only meaning to be friendly, she had kind of wondered – that time on the hill, when he had caught her and pulled her down and his mouth so close to hers – she had kind of hoped . . .

I dream of this:
Under the hawthorns he raises me with a kiss.

Maybe he had only wanted someone to talk to for a while, about his childhood. Maybe she'd just been around at the right time, when he'd needed company. Maybe he now regretted opening even that small window into his soul.

Several feet above her head, a bee was hitting off the high window, trying again and again to take the obvious way out. Aoife knew how it felt. It would be so good to fly out of this concrete box of a classroom and run for miles and miles, all by herself, up into the damp and lonely bog.

Mr Vaughan said, 'All right, Darragh, perhaps you can tell us why the Vikings came to the west of Ireland.'

'God only knows, sir.'

'*Darragh!*' Mr Vaughan scowled down the room-wide shout of amusement. 'Serious answer.'

'I *am* being serious. Why would anyone come here? I mean, there's no gold or decent women, just rain and sheep.'

Sinead said, 'Don't pretend you don't prefer sheep.'

'*Page forty-two!*'

The buzzing above Aoife's head was becoming demented, rising even above the laughter. The bee had one wing caught in a strand of web, and was spinning and tugging on it like a balloon in the wind. A spider with a red back abseiled down the strand and sank its teeth into the bee's fur. As soon as its victim stopped vibrating, the spider wove a grey shroud around it, then hung it, paralysed but alive, from the topmost corner of the window, three metres above the ground. Never to fly again.

As soon as the bell went for first break, Shay stood up abruptly and left. All Aoife saw of him was the back of him disappearing out of the door. She gathered her books together slowly, letting everyone else leave before her. He had gone back to his old silent self, and she had her pride – she didn't want him to imagine she was following him.

A heavy squall of rain rattled the high window. Far above, the shrouded bee dangled, a grey bead on a string; the spider sat waiting. A very tall but flimsy set of shelves stood against the wall. Could she? No, she'd pull the bookcase down. *I'm feather-light . . .* Aoife glanced around to make sure she was alone in the room, then ran up the bookcase, leaned across to pluck the bee's body from the web, and sprang from the top shelf to the floor, landing with her knees bent and her heart pounding with shock and exhilaration. When did she get to be able to do such things? She'd never been unfit, but this was like being an Olympic gymnast.

She'd think about it later. Right now, she had to rescue the living creature from its shroud. There was a loose end of thread hanging from the pointed end. She pinched it between her fingertips and pulled. The sticky thread started to unwind. She pulled some more. The bee spun round and round on her palm like a cotton reel being unwound.

'Aoife?'

She glanced up sharply, closing her hand over the bee. Sinead had come back in and was sidling towards her between the desks. 'Aoife, there's no need to hide away from the rest of us just because of what happened on my birthday.'

'Thanks, I'm not hiding, I was just doing something.'

'Because it's OK. Lois says you're feeling really guilty about ruining the trip for everyone, but I just want you to know I forgive you. I mean, you must feel bad enough about Carla ending up with the flu . . .'

A peculiar tingling sensation rushed into Aoife's fingers, like lemon juice had been squirted into her veins. She said, 'If you're feeling sorry for Carla, maybe you should quit trying to steal her boyfriend.'

Sinead's mouth formed every shape under the sun before she spluttered out, '*Oh!* You jealous cow! It's you that fancies Killian!'

Aoife laughed; she hadn't meant to be quite so direct, but while she was at it she might as well continue. The fizzing in her blood was surprisingly pleasant, like the time she'd been given champagne at a neighbour's wedding. 'I wouldn't go out with Killian if he was the last person on earth. I've no idea why Carla even likes him. But while she does, I'm going to make sure he doesn't upset her – and you're going to keep your thieving paws off him.'

Sinead's cat-shaped face flushed crimson, her eyes flashed. She spat, 'You've got no right to say who goes out with who – you can't tell me what to do, and what Killian does is none of your business, and I'll go out with whoever I like, when I like, and you can't tell me any different.'

'Be careful,' said Aoife. Her blood felt icy now.

'Don't you point your finger at me, Aoife

O'Connor! Carla doesn't have any reason to think Killian is her boyfriend or anything just because he sat next to her on the bus. He was only messing and it's not like she's pretty, she's not even in his league— Aargh!' Sinead jumped backwards with a scream, crashing into the desk behind her.

Aoife cried out, alarmed, dropping her hand. 'Are you all right?'

Sinead retreated towards the door. 'Keep away from me, you maniac!'

'But what happened?'

'You punched me, you bitch!'

'I didn't—'

'Get away from me!' And Sinead turned and rushed from the room.

Aoife stared after her, bewildered. She hadn't gone anywhere near Sinead, let alone punched her – although she would have done, given half a chance. How dare Sinead say Carla wasn't pretty . . . In a fresh rush of rage, Aoife clenched her fists. And a terrible pain stabbed through her left palm.

Her heart sinking, she uncurled her fingers – the bee lay dead. Sadness overwhelmed her – she'd crushed the poor little creature she'd been trying to save. All it had wanted to do was get out into the fields, and fly, and drink nectar from flowers, and make honey, and be happy. And now it was dead, and it would never see the sun again, or drift on the warm breeze.

There was a bin by Mr Vaughan's desk, but she couldn't bring herself to throw the tiny body away like rubbish. Instead, she opened the window and climbed out.

Outside, the rain had eased to a soft dampness, and the sky was brightening. Aoife breathed in deep. The breeze coming down from the bog was flowery with heather. So much better to be outside than be stuck in a glass-and-concrete box. She was standing on the path that ran round the school building, but there was a long stretch of grass between the path and the boundary fence. She knocked a divot out of the soft soil with her heel, dropped in the bee and footed the earth back over its corpse.

Her hand throbbed; the bee's sting was still buried in her skin. She eased it out with her fingernails, and a little blood welled from the puncture wound. No, not blood . . . She peered at the centre of her palm. The round drop of fluid was a shimmering silver, rainbow-tinged. Poison from the sting? She licked it off her hand. It tasted sweet.

Before climbing back in through the window, she squatted down and prodded the roots of a displaced daisy and a few shoots of grass into the earth of the bee's grave. And as soon as she had done so, she knew with sudden joyful certainty that through this process the bee would be transformed. The roots of the daisy and the grass would sink into the bee's flesh and draw up its energy as through a straw, and as a flower it would feel the sun and wind again, and bees would drink from it, and make other bees.

Life would spring from death. There was no end.

CHAPTER SIX

She was starving. The school canteen was open for first break, but she had no money on her. Still, she checked her pockets just in case and found she did have a few coins after all, and they added up to quite a lot – almost four euros. Odd, because her uniform always got washed over the weekend, and her mother would have emptied the pockets. And even stranger, she didn't remember having had the money in the first place. It wasn't like there was a lot of it to spread around – since the recession, James O'Connor had been out of work and the family relied on what her mother earned from doing the accounts for local farmers.

The canteen was a long open-plan area with plate-glass windows that looked out into the gravelled courtyard in the centre of the school building. Everyone from her class was sitting at the same table.

No, not everyone.

Shay sat perched sideways on the wide low

windowsill, with his feet up, staring out into the rain-swept courtyard, drinking a cup of tea. He was wearing his school coat now, with the collar pulled up.

Aoife lingered at the counter. She was so hungry she felt she needed a *serious* quantity of calories. Maybe it was all the mad cycling and running she'd been doing yesterday. She hesitated between a strawberry and a chocolate yoghurt, then bought both, then a bag of salt-and-vinegar crisps, then an apple, and then, just in case that still wasn't enough, an extra-large Mars bar. The white-capped woman behind the counter said, 'How nice of you to treat all your friends.'

'What? Oh, right, sure.'

She sat down beside Jessica, whose brown eyes widened. 'Hungry?'

'Starving.'

'I don't *how* Lois gets the idea you're anorexic.'

Lois, hearing her name, glanced over. She did a double-take at Aoife's loaded tray and whispered in Sinead's ear, loud enough for the whole table to hear: '*Bulimic.*'

But Sinead just said, 'Stop shouting in my ear,'

and shot Aoife a sour look. It was as if she were slightly scared of her – maybe she really did imagine Aoife had punched her in the history room.

Aoife ate her way steadily through the food in front of her, all the time feeling vaguely troubled by what had happened. Sinead was sitting a long way away from Killian, and that was a good result of the fight. But at the same time, even if she hadn't attacked Sinead, she did owe her for messing up her outing – and she still hadn't given her a birthday present. She should have hung onto the four euros, and added it to the card. She checked to see if there were any more coins, and to her astonishment there was an actual note, folded small and pushed right down into the corner of the same pocket. A brown note. Ten euros.

She went round the table to Sinead, who said tightly, 'What do you want now?'

'Nothing. Just, here's your present – sorry it's late.'

Sinead glanced down at the folded note, then went slightly pink. 'Oh. That's . . . Thank you . . .'

'Sorry it's not more.'

'No, really, thank you, that's really generous.'

Aoife suddenly realized that the brown note she

was handing Sinead was not a ten-euro note but a fifty. The shock was so sudden, it took all her will-power not to snatch it back again. She said as brightly as she could manage, 'No problem, and sorry about Saturday.'

'That's all right . . .' Sinead pocketed the fifty, exchanging a round-eyed look with Lois.

Aoife was so shaken she hardly knew what to do next. How had there been a fifty-euro note just lying around in her school trousers? Had it been there for a long time, and been washed and forgotten about? Yet when had she ever been rich enough to forget about fifty euros? Why hadn't she checked what sort of a brown note it was before handing all that wealth to Sinead? She could have bought those tyres for her bike.

'Hey, Aoife, any more of those to give away?' Killian had been watching the exchange from the far end of the long table; he was one of those types who could smell money. Aoife remembered Carla had made her promise to give him a message. She moved on down the table. He stood up as she got to him, smiling, making eye contact. 'You gonna give me money as well?'

'No. Just, Carla asked me to say she says "hi".' She looked away as she was speaking. Shay was finishing his tea, getting ready to leave the canteen.

Killian said, 'What about you?'

She looked back at him, surprised. 'Me?'

'Do you say "hi" to me?'

Aoife sighed. Why couldn't Carla have crushed on someone a bit less irritating? 'Don't be such an eejit.'

'Ah, come on, you know you like me. That's why you didn't tell Carla about kissing me at the disco.'

Her blood cooled. She looked steadily at Killian; her fingers tingled, and she flexed them slightly, experimentally.

Killian winced, and touched his stomach. 'Hey . . .'

'What?'

'You poked me . . .'

She felt a faint, startled flicker of triumph. 'I didn't *touch* you. And I wouldn't, if you were the last boy on earth.' Again, her eyes strayed towards the windowsill; Shay was gone, his cup abandoned.

Annoyed, Killian said, 'What d'you keep looking over there for? I know Bogger Boy chatted you up on the bus, but he's not so pretty now, is he?'

'*What do you mean?*'

He brightened again at her reaction, though still prodding at his stomach tenderly with both hands. 'What? You didn't notice the state his brother left him in?'

'His brother?' It was as if a hand had reached in and squeezed her heart.

'Yep, Bogger Boy stole his brother's car yesterday and crashed it, and my dad says John Joe Foley was in the pub last night getting drunk and guilty about beating Shay up for it— *Aargh!*' Killian doubled up, clutching his stomach.

Shay was already halfway down the corridor towards the gym.

'Wait!' She was damned if she was going to let him keep disappearing on her, just because he was too proud to let her know he'd been beaten up. 'Shay, *wait.*' Aoife sprinted down the empty hallway and grabbed his sleeve, and finally he stopped walking and stood with his back to the wall, his arms loose by his sides. There was a violent crimson bruise over his cheekbone, and a black cut on his mouth. 'Oh, Shay . . .'

He half smiled, although it was more of a lop-sided grimace, presumably so as not to split open the newly healed cut on his lip. 'Not as bad as it looks. Crashed again and hit my face off the wheel.'

'You did not – your brother did this to you.' She was having a hard time keeping her voice steady, between fury at John Joe's violence and fear for Shay with no parent to stand up for him at home, and above all the despair of not knowing how to make things right.

'No, I crashed the—'

'Don't lie to me.'

'I'm not, I—'

'*Shay*. People know. John Joe was telling everyone down the pub.'

He looked taken aback and annoyed. 'Was he indeed, the gobshite? I hope he told people I gave as good as I got.' He showed his knuckles to her with a look of pride; they were bruised and cut. So that's why he'd had his sleeves pulled up over his hands, as well as hiding his face.

Aoife, who had been feeling so light, felt suddenly weighed down. 'I'm so sorry about this.'

'Not your fault. It was me crashed the car, and

99

now he's got no wheels apart from the tractor and I owe him, that's all.'

She said fiercely, 'You don't owe him, he's a brute.'

Shay's face closed down; he looked off to the side. 'He's not, he's just mad strong and he forgets his own strength. And I do owe him. He's minded me since I was five years old. The social had foster parents lined up for me. He was only seventeen but he fought for the right to raise me, and he got me back after a year and I was right happy to get home.'

'OK, I'm sorry, I didn't know that.' Though it didn't really change her mind about John Joe.

He said, 'I can work off what I owe him by doing stuff around the farm. I'm good at lambing. I never lose a lamb, never.'

Aoife felt even worse now about giving the fifty euros to Sinead. If only she'd known that she'd had it and that Shay needed it. She longed to stroke the dark cut on his mouth, to heal it somehow. She shoved her hands hard and deep into the pockets of her school trousers, to keep herself from touching him. 'I want to help.'

'Aoife, it's not your problem. I'll sort it.'

In her pocket, her left hand closed on a slim

packet. She fingered it – absently, and then with growing puzzlement. She pulled it out. An envelope full of hundred-euro notes.

For a long moment she just stared, incredulous. This finding money was getting . . . ridiculous. She flicked slowly through the thin sheaf of notes. Three, four . . . Her heart gave a frightened thump . . . Six, seven, eight . . . *Twelve hundred euros?* What . . . ? Where . . . ? She looked up at Shay; he seemed dazed yet transfixed by the sum of money she was holding. On a wild impulse, before she could think about it, she thrust it at him. 'Here. There's plenty enough there to buy a decent second-hand car.'

He came to with a start, pushing it back at her like it might burn him. 'No! Jesus! Where did you get that?'

'I don't know. Take it!'

'You don't *know*?'

'I mean it's . . .' She scrabbled in her head for inspiration. 'It's an early birthday present! From an aunt! *Take it.*'

Shay's green-brown eyes grew hot, cheekbones flushed. 'I will not – are you cracked? I don't need your money.' He said 'money' in a fierce voice, like he really meant 'charity'.

'Look—'

'Aoife, *leave it*!' And he was gone, striding away round the corner towards the gym.

He should have been in the next class, business, but he wasn't. He must have been so annoyed with her that he'd walked out of the school.

Aoife sat scribbling flowers in her copy and thinking very seriously about the money. As much as she'd wanted Shay to take it, it was probably just as well he hadn't. It couldn't have come out of nowhere. It must be the money Declan Sweeney owed Maeve for doing his accounts, and somehow she had picked it up, thinking it was a note for school. She did most things on auto-pilot in the morning. Her mother would be going demented, turning the house upside down – hysterically berating herself for always putting things in a safe place and never being able to find them again.

When the bell rang between classes, she went to the school secretary, a maternal pinkish woman.

'Rose, I feel really peculiar – could you phone my mam and ask can she come and sign me out?'

Reaching for the phone, Rose said, 'You should eat more, Aoife. You're too thin. You teenage girls are always on a diet, and then you wonder why you get tired and have headaches. Have a proper breakfast tomorrow.'

Aoife, thinking of everything she had eaten at first break, said earnestly, 'I will, I promise.'

Maeve arrived with her dark blonde hair tied up on top of her head and wearing the shabby old green cardigan that she'd owned ever since Aoife could remember. She seemed very relaxed; clearly she hadn't yet noticed that she'd mislaid a fortune. As they walked from the school to the car, she asked Aoife, 'So, do you need to go to Doctor Lynn?'

'No, I'm grand.'

Maeve shot her a look. 'Grand apart from the splitting headache that's making it impossible for you to concentrate in school?'

'Yeah, apart from that.' Aoife touched the envelope in her pocket. 'Did Declan Sweeney pay you yet, by the way?'

'Tomorrow.'

'Oh. Are you sure?'

Maeve stopped walking for a moment, her hand on Aoife's arm. Her expression had changed to one of concern. 'Is this headache brought on by worrying about money? I know I'm always moaning about how poor we are, but we're not going to starve.'

'OK. Good.'

After they'd driven through Kilduff, Aoife said, 'Did you or Dad lose any money at all recently?'

'None to lose, sweetie. Why?'

'Declan didn't pay you anything in advance?'

Maeve sighed as she turned left into their lane. 'I'm starting to feel like I'm missing something here, sweetheart. What's really bothering you?'

'Nothing. I found some money.'

'Well, that's a good complaint. How much?'

Aoife opened her mouth to say twelve hundred. But then didn't. If it really *wasn't* her parents' money, she needed to think about the whole thing a bit longer. At the same time, it seemed mean not to share her new-found wealth. So instead, she said cautiously, 'A hundred euros?'

'*A hundred?*' Maeve, who was in the middle of

changing gears, stalled the car. Instead of restarting it, she sat staring at Aoife in astonishment. 'Where did you find it?'

'In my trousers.'

'An old pair?'

'Mm . . .' Her school uniform was pretty old, although she suspected her mother was asking if she'd found the money in a pair of trousers that she hadn't worn for ages.

Maeve, shaking her head in amazement, started the engine again. 'Well, lucky you. It must have been left over from your confirmation or something like that. I wish I could find a forgotten hundred-euro note lying around.'

Aoife took one of the several hundred-euro notes out of the envelope in her pocket, and laid it on the dashboard. 'You have it.'

Maeve smiled, pleased by this act of solicitude – very tempted, then resolute. 'No, God no – you found it. Buy yourself that fancy pair of trainers you've been wanting.'

'Really. Take it.'

Maeve weakened again, picking it up. 'Aoife, that's so sweet of you. Maybe just . . . I could borrow it until Declan pays me tomorrow? He's giving me three hundred.'

'Sure, whenever.' She turned to gaze out of the window. So it could never have been the farmer's money anyway.

Pulling up in front of their house, Maeve said, 'If I'd known you were going to lend me a hundred euros, I'd have bought some lamb chops for dinner! But I really have to work.'

Aoife offered quickly, 'I'll go to the shop for you if you like.'

Maeve gave her another look. 'Headache better already?'

'The fresh air will do me good.'

Her mother laughed, maybe softened up by the hundred euros, pulling out her ancient yellow leather purse. 'Oh, go on then. You sure you don't mind walking that far?'

'It's not that far. I need to clear my head. What will I get?'

'You choose – your money. Lamb chops?'

'And cheesecake?'

'Perfect.' Maeve opened the purse. Frowned. Hunted through the different compartments. 'What the . . . ? I must have put it . . .' She dug around in the pockets of her old green cardigan. 'God, this is so annoying. I know I put it somewhere safe, I know I did.'

'Oh, Mam—'

'Don't say anything! Just help me find it!'

Aoife picked up the purse from the dashboard. 'Will I . . . ?'

'Feel free.' Maeve was rifling with increasing anxiety through the driver's door pocket, pulling out old letters, tissues, sweet wrappers.

Aoife checked through the untidy purse. In the zipped section were a lot of coins, but none worth more than twenty cents; in the wallet section were shop receipts, stamps, three raffle tickets, a library card, and the crushed skeleton of an oak leaf. 'Try the floor. Maybe you dropped it.'

Maeve got out of the car and checked frantically around in the foot well, then under the seat. Nothing but old newspapers. 'Oh God, this is a total nightmare . . . I can't believe I've lost it. I feel so stupid – I'm such an idiot. I'll still pay you back tomorrow . . .' There were tears in her voice.

Aoife said hastily, 'Maybe it's in the back?'

'*Why would it be there?*'

'I don't know – you had the window open, maybe it blew there?'

While her mother searched the back seat, now almost sobbing, Aoife quickly took another hundred euros out of her pocket and 'found' it in the glove compartment.

Maeve stood wiping her eyes with the corner of her cardigan. 'Well done, Aoife. Thank God . . . I remember putting it there now, that's my safe place in the car . . .'

'Will I go to the shop now?'

'Yes! Quick before I lose it again!'

CHAPTER SEVEN

The rain was still holding off, and a watery sun was breaking through. Strolling up the flowering lane, flies annoying her head, Aoife flicked through the remaining eleven hundred-euro notes.

She couldn't even begin to understand it.

Maybe everything else that had happened to her in the last couple of days could be explained away. Imagining she could bicycle so much faster than normal could be down to the timer on her phone not working. Secretly believing that she was responsible for Shay Foley crashing his brother's car, just because she'd wanted him to turn right? OK, that had to be delusional. Like the way she believed, deep down – no, far from deep down – that she'd shoved Sinead into the desk and poked Killian in the stomach without touching either of them. (An entertaining idea, but surely way too good to be true.)

But the twelve hundred euros was not an illusion. They existed. Her mother had seen two of these notes – had held one of them in her hand. Shay had seen the money too, when she offered it to him to buy his brother a car.

Because that was what it was for . . .

A new determination filled her. She wasn't going to tell her mother about this. She would have liked to give Maeve more than a hundred euros, but she couldn't risk her mother deciding that when it came to this amount of cash, finders wasn't keepers. Yes, now she thought about it, she was pretty certain Maeve would hand the money over to the guards.

Reaching the garage, Aoife turned into the yard. Shay's brother had beaten him, and nobody else seemed to care. She wanted to help him. She *needed* to help him. This money was the answer to her prayer. Didn't people pray for all sorts of things? Health, love, good exam results? Why not money for a car? Maybe it was crazy to believe that it was literally a gift from heaven, but for now she was going to go with it.

Dave Ferguson's garage consisted of two petrol pumps, a tin-roofed shed where he did his repairs, and a small shop selling bits and pieces to do with cars, motorbikes and push bikes. The owner was in the yard, prostrate under a green post office van. Aoife crouched down to speak to him. 'I need some new tyres for my bike.' It seemed an easier place to start than just coming straight out with wanting to buy a car.

'Five minutes . . .' He hit something fiercely with a wrench.

While waiting, she wandered around the yard. There was a rusty Toyota for sale at seven hundred and fifty, a small Honda for six hundred, and a very old but very beautiful cream-coloured BMW convertible, with no price on it – the vintage car she had seen Dave Ferguson tinkering with yesterday afternoon. She peered inside. It had red leather seats.

'Like her?' Dave Ferguson had finished with the post office van and was now standing at her shoulder wiping his oily hands on a rag. He was bald, red-faced, and wore small wire-framed glasses – just like his brother Thomas, Sinead's father.

Aoife said, 'The seats are nice.'

'They are nice, surely, and there's nothing more essential to a car than to have nice seats. Who needs an engine?'

'How much is it?'

'You're after buying a car off me, are you? How old are you now?'

'Fifteen. But could you sell it to me, just to have?'

'Good joke. Now, what size of a bike tyre did you say you were after?'

'What if I paid a thousand in cash, right now?'

Dave Ferguson laughed, shoving the blackened rag into the pocket of his overalls. 'Done. Yours for a thousand euros.'

Aoife experienced a strong stab of satisfaction. 'So it's a deal?'

'Surely it's a deal. Now about those—'

She pulled out the sheaf of notes.

There was a long, long pause, during which Dave Ferguson stopped chuckling, went even redder than normal and lit a cigarette. Aoife waited, holding out the money. Deep down, she was certain that the garage owner would have to stick to the deal they had just made.

After several lung-filling drags, and a coughing fit, he flicked the half-smoked cigarette into a nearby puddle. 'Nope. Not possible. Your parents will murder me if I let you spend all your savings on a car. Especially this one.'

In one way, Aoife was relieved. So she couldn't just *make* something happen, just by wishing it. Yet still she kept on patiently holding out the envelope towards him, hoping he would change his mind in the normal way. 'A deal is a deal.'

'Not with someone your age it's not . . .' Yet even as Dave Ferguson was saying 'no', his left hand was moving towards her. He glanced down at it with a frown. 'Look, I can't take your money . . .'

'A deal is a deal,' repeated Aoife, dropping the thousand into his outstretched palm. He groaned and turned redder still as his fingers gripped it.

In the shop in Kilduff, she broke into the remaining hundred-euro note to buy nine pink lamb cutlets and a strawberry cheesecake, then, because she was starving, a packet of chocolate Hobnobs. She set off home with the shopping bag in one hand and two new bike tyres over her shoulder, eating her way thoughtfully through the biscuits.

Buying the car for a thousand euros had been amazing, and had felt like the right thing to do at the time – but now she wasn't so sure. The garage owner had clearly felt terrible about selling her the BMW, even though she'd assured him that she wouldn't be driving it herself. When she'd tried to pay him for the tyres as well, he had insisted on giving them to her for free. Had she tricked Dave Ferguson, somehow? She had paid with real cash – yet it still felt wrong, as well as utterly bewildering. For another thing, it was ridiculous to pretend that the money was a gift from heaven. God was mysterious and never behaved in such a direct, uncomplicated fashion – not according to Father Leahy, anyway. In fact, if she was to believe the priest, God usually answered prayers by doing the exact opposite of what He was specifically asked to do.

Maybe he's the phoney one . . .

Yet it was also ridiculous to pretend to herself that there was a rational explanation for her finding the money in her pocket. There was no getting away from the fact that she had wanted the money, and it had instantly appeared.

Sticking the last biscuit into her mouth, she slipped her hand into her trouser pocket. Empty. Shifting the shopping bag to her other hand, she tried the other pocket. Nothing. She made a big effort to imagine a million euros, in one huge colourful note. And tried again. Nothing. She wasn't sure if she was more relieved or disappointed. Disappointed, to be honest.

In the evening, Aoife cooked the chops for dinner herself, and it was the best meal she could ever remember eating – maybe because she was yet again so incredibly hungry, even after eating the whole packet of Hobnobs. But her parents also declared themselves amazed by her cooking. They seemed to have fully recovered from the strange shock that the locket had given them, and talked cheerfully and aimlessly to each other about the upcoming elections and where they would go for a holiday in the sun, if only they had the money (Aoife quietly checked her pockets again – still nothing).

Afterwards, Maeve stayed in the kitchen to work at the table, humming tunelessly as she battered away at the keyboard of her laptop. 'Got to get this finished and printed out for Declan, or we won't be eating like that again for a while.'

Aoife went into the back room to watch television. Her father was already sitting in the armchair by the empty fireplace, television off, reading one of his 'new' second-hand books.

She knelt at the hearth. 'Do you want me to light a fire for you?'

He looked up from his page. 'Do you think we need one? It's a warm evening.'

'I know, but it's nice for the smell of the turf burning. I'll just make a small one.' She took two pieces of turf and a firelighter from the wicker basket. While she set the fire, she glanced at the broken spine of the old leather book. 'What's that you're reading?'

'The *Lebor Gabála Érenn*. A good translation from the Irish.'

'What's it about?' Aoife had never given her father's hobby much thought, or wondered why he was so fascinated by the old stories – it was simply the way he was and always had been in her memory of him, just as she couldn't picture him without silvery-grey hair. Now she wondered if there might be something he had come across in his books that could explain what had been happening to her. She had flicked through the odd volume, taken from the piles of second-hand books on the stairs, and she knew ancient Ireland was full of strange goings on: St Patrick battling snakes and giants, and beautiful St Dympna plucking out her eyes and causing a holy well to spring up from where she threw them down.

'You haven't heard of the *Lebor Gabála Érenn*?' Her father half closed the book, showing her the cover. 'It's the ancient history of the Irish fairies, the Tuatha Dé Danann.'

'Oh. Right. Fairies.'

He laughed. 'I take it you don't believe in such things.'

'There is a limit to what I can get my head around. I am fifteen.'

'Well, grown-up girl, your great-grandmother was a firm believer, and she was eighty-eight when she died.'

This time, it was Aoife who laughed. 'OK.'

Her father said suddenly, with a very sad, straight look at her, no humour in it at all, 'She didn't like my parents buying this house, you know. They only got it cheap because it was built on a fairy road.'

That was news. 'Seriously? When me and Carla were young, we were always playing at—'

'I know it. Your mam kept having to drag you back home before you disappeared over the hill.'

She was still amazed by his revelation. 'I never

realized the road was like a real thing. I thought we'd made it up. I must have heard you talking about it. Why didn't your nan want your parents to buy this house?'

'Because the road would bring the fairies to our door, and she was a Mayo woman, and afraid of them. She thought they were dangerous, evil creatures.'

Aoife looked away, stirring the fire with the poker. She felt unsettled now, and strange. So the fairy road had been more than a game. 'From what I've heard over the past few days, it sounds to me like your nan was right.'

'Have people been teasing you about leprechauns again?'

She looked up, surprised by how upset her father sounded about it. He was leaning forward in his chair, staring intensely at her. 'Dad, chillax! I can cope with a bit of slagging. Anyway, I didn't mean that, I meant I heard a couple of stories about real fairies.'

'Real fairies?' He still sounded suspicious.

'Well, you know what I mean – real as in not little men wearing green coats and pointy hats.'

He settled back in his seat. 'And what did these great experts on Irish folklore tell you?'

Aoife threw another piece of turf on the fire, and sparks of orange drifted up. 'That sheógs lure human children out across the bog to drown, and lenanshees suck the life out of anyone they fall in love with, and banshees steal human babies and sell them to the devil.'

'*No!*' Now her father seemed even more upset, his dark eyes large and shocked. 'Don't listen to that sort of rubbish, it's all—'

'Dad.'

'. . . superstitious nonsense—'

'*Dad.* Like I said, I'm fifteen.'

He stopped; pulled a self-deprecating face. 'Sorry. I know you're too sensible to believe in the old country stories. Your great-grandmother had my head wrecked when I was a boy. I had to do a lot of reading to find out the truth about the Tuatha Dé Danann.' He nodded at the shelves of books, the tattered volumes piled in every corner.

She arched her eyebrows mockingly at her father. 'There's a *true* story about the fairies?'

He mimicked her expression, peering at her over

his glasses. '*There are more things in heaven and earth, Horatio*—'

'Yeah, yeah – so what's this "true" story, then?' Aoife settled herself cross-legged on the hearth rug. 'Impress me, Professor O'Connor, with the results of your extensive research.'

'Well, then, I will.' He reopened the volume on his lap. 'This is one of the best accounts of the Tuatha Dé Danann. It was written about a thousand years ago.' He pushed his glasses back up his nose. 'Here's the story of their arrival in Ireland.' He cleared his throat and read aloud:

'They landed with horror, with lofty deed,
in their cloud of mighty combat of spectres,
upon a mountain of Conmaicne of Connacht . . .
Without ships, a ruthless course
the truth was not known beneath the sky of stars,
whether they were of heaven or of earth.'

'Sounds like they came from outer space.'

'No, they were from the earth.' He smiled at her with sudden warmth, the way he had when she was little and he was about to tell her how much he loved her. 'They were magical, Aoife – beautiful to look at. Tall, slender. And immensely powerful. A true fairy race.'

'Cool beans. So, where did they go?'

'Into another world.'

'There's another world?'

'Many other worlds. Under the ocean to the west are the blessed isles. Under Munster lies the land of the dead. But under Mayo and the rest of Connaught lies Tír na nÓg, the land of the young, and that's where the fairies went.'

'And what's it like down there?'

Aoife's father was no longer gazing at her but somewhere over her shoulder, towards the window that faced out onto the garden. 'It's a beautiful world where no one grows old or dies. Where life is eternal, and death has been defeated.'

'Something like heaven?'

'Something like that, please God.' He looked down at the book again, but he wasn't reading it; his eyes were nearly closed, like he was dreaming.

'Dad?'

'Yes?'

She was going to say: *Do you* really *believe in*

fairies? But it seemed a bit too much like asking him if he was mad, so instead she said, 'That's a lovely story.'

There was a strong scent of rotting hawthorn. She sat up and turned on her lamp. The sickly stench was coming from the toy rabbit, which had been under her pillow since she'd brought it home from the bog. Hawthorn blossoms seemed to have got into its leaky body, replacing some of the stuffing.

What had she been thinking of, bringing the dirty thing home with her? God knows what wildlife it was crawling with. Getting up, Aoife rummaged through her drawers for an old T-shirt, mummified the rabbit and pushed it to the back of her jewellery and make-up drawer.

Later, the scent of hawthorn grew even stronger. She got up again, to shut the window. She didn't need to turn on the lamp this time, because there was a silver glow in the room – yet as she reached out to close the window, she saw that it was a black, moonless night.

For a moment she couldn't bring herself to turn back into the room. She had a sudden terrifying thought that if she did, she would see a pair of glowing fairy eyes gazing at her from the dark. Not one of her father's fantasy angels, but a creature of the night, of the old country stories . . . She turned quickly, and there was nothing. Yet there was still a silvery light in the room. The PC screen was dark, as was her phone.

Aoife went back to the bed, and when she moved aside the duvet, she realized that the light was coming from her own hands. She looked closer. The veins were shining through her skin, as if her red blood had been drained out of them and replaced with liquid, shining silver.

She must be dreaming.

In her dream, she got back into her dream-bed and closed her eyes.

CHAPTER EIGHT

'*Come to me.*'

Aoife lay rigid in the dark. A child's voice had woken her. She raised her head very slightly from the pillow, listening. No creak of movement in the room. Maybe the leaves of the ash tree whispering against the half-open window . . . She must have been dreaming again.

'*Come here to me.*'

Her heart raced, and her skin prickled with cold sweat. She reached to switch on her lamp and sat up. No child in the room. Everything normal: the tangled mess of clothes on the carpet; the ancient PC still asleep; her guitar leaning in the corner; Kurt Cobain and Lady Gaga still gazing down.

She got out of bed and went to the window, opening it to listen. A thin yellow rectangle of light stretched out from behind her, pointing its way along the fairy road; her shadow was long and narrow on the grass, overlaid by the flickering movement of the ash tree. Something rustled in the hedge and a young fox strolled out across the lawn, appearing and disappearing as it moved in and out of the light. The dark breeze from the mountains plucked at Aoife's T-shirt and ran across her skin like cold fingertips.

'Find me.'

Heart hammering, she slammed the window shut. Without knowing why, without even thinking first, she wrenched open her jewellery drawer. The rabbit lay bundled in the back. She took it out and unwrapped it from the T-shirt. The stench of rotting hawthorn was sickening.

'Come to me.'

Aoife dropped the rabbit on the floor. She thought now that the faint voice was coming from somewhere inside the house. *Think straight.* Had the television or radio been left on downstairs? She moved cautiously across the messy room, trying not to step on anything that would make a noise by breaking, like a DVD or a biro; she turned the handle of the door very slowly; she stepped out onto the landing. Dead silence from below. Across the way, her parents' door stood ajar. Maybe one of them had been talking in their sleep? She flicked on the landing light and peered through the crack.

The two of them lay humped back to back under the duvet, silent. Aoife felt a sudden weird and terrible certainty that if she stepped into their bedroom she would find the ghostly little girl from the bog – the sheóg – perched on the sugán stool by their bed, watching over her parents as they slept. She braced herself, and thrust wide the door. Nothing. Her father snored briefly, then settled.

The bedroom was small and low-ceilinged, and packed tight with old oaken furniture left from her grandparents' time: the big double bed with a patchwork quilt thrown over the duvet; a double-fronted wardrobe with a curly carved top, like a fringe; the oak press with two small drawers and three long ones; an old-fashioned dressing table with a hole for a china bowl, long broken; the sugán stool.

'*Come to me!*' Very faint; frighteningly near.

Acting on the same helpless impulse that had driven her to unearth the rabbit, Aoife went straight to the chest of drawers and crouched down. The long bottom drawer was slightly deeper than the others. It was locked, as it always was, because this was where Maeve stored her clients' accounts. (Or so she had told Aoife, when Aoife had asked about it in the past.

Except, of course, now Aoife actually thought about it, that was a lie – the few files were always in the kitchen, and stored in nothing more secretive than plastic shopping bags. So why had her mother . . . ?) She touched the lock, and heard the brass mechanism click.

It was as if there were someone in there willing her to find them; someone who had just turned a key on the inside. It took her several long seconds to get up the courage to slide out the drawer. A terrifying image had come into her mind of what she might find: a little girl lying on her back, eyes closed, hands folded on her chest— Stop. Madness. She yanked out the drawer.

No child.

No accounts, either.

Just a 'Baby's First Year' photograph album bearing Aoife's name and date of birth, and stacks of green envelopes stuffed with old photos. Video cassettes from another era, and the ancient video camera with which they had been filmed. And the locket, stored in a small plastic bag of the type banks use for coins. So this was where her mother had been keeping the necklace.

Her mother grunted something incoherent in her sleep. Aoife held her breath, keeping very still. Too weird to be found creeping around her parents' bedroom, looking in places she was clearly not supposed to look. She pushed the drawer back in, slowly and carefully, so that it didn't scrape.

Then pulled it open again. This was crazy. Years ago, when she had asked Maeve were there any pictures of their time in Dublin, her mother had told her that all the family photographs had been lost in the move to Kilduff. Yet here was her own baby album, and envelopes of photographs dating from years ago.

Maeve turned over in the bed, and a pillow fell to the floor.

Sliding the drawer all the way out of the press, Aoife carried it into her own room and dumped it on the bed. She was shivering now and pulled on a hoodie over her Nirvana T-shirt, and then a pair of trackies, before kneeling on the rug to sort through the photographs. The plastic bag containing the locket was the first thing she took out; she made to set it aside, but then shook the necklace out onto her palm and thrust it into the pocket of her hoodie. Why not? It was hers. She jumped up and went back to the window, pushing it open again. The moon was rising over the mountains, casting a wide silvery line across the fields, across the garden, right to the foot of the ash tree outside her window. She had a sudden urge to climb down the tree . . . To run away, far away, through the cool, silvery night . . .

It felt like an effort to return to the photographs. The 'Baby's First Year' album had a padded white cover printed with curly gold lettering – *Eva Sarah O'Connor* – her own full name, in its original form, as it was written on her birth cert. The date of her birth was written underneath the name. Why had Maeve told her these pictures were lost? What could possibly be secret about Aoife's own baby pictures? Stapled to the first page was a black-and-white scan, dated six months before Aoife was born. The white comma-shape must be a barely-begun Aoife in her mother's womb. Extraordinary to see herself unborn. The next pages featured the baby from the locket, squash-faced and bald, looking like every other baby ever born. Here was her mother, gazing at the drooling identikit blob like it was uniquely beautiful. Here was her father, looking like he'd won the all-Ireland Gaelic football final. The rest of the album documented Aoife sitting, crawling, standing, and ended up with her smeared in cake at her first birthday party. In the party photos, her parents were pictured together for the first time; someone else must have been holding the camera. There were other grinning adults in attendance, none of whom she recognized, all eating cake and drinking wine in a small city garden surrounded by a high stone wall.

Had Maeve *forgotten* about these pictures? Had she maybe lost the key to the press and misremembered what was in there? No, because she'd hidden the locket in the drawer.

Aoife inspected the video camera, but it needed batteries.

She took one of the green envelopes and eased out another photograph. She was about two years old in this one, and her shoulder-length hair was still blonde, not red-gold, her eyes a very pale blue, not the greenish blue they had become. In the next photograph, she looked another year older and her soft blonde curls were very short. She was wearing a lacy fairy dress with small stiff wings; she was sitting on a new swing in the same small garden, and her father was standing behind her, smiling down at her, the way he had always smiled at her when she was little, when he was about to tell her that he loved her.

Then there was a posed studio shot. Aoife's parents were side by side on the photographer's sofa with their arms around her. Aoife's dress was blue velvet, her shoes white, and she was wearing a matching blue velvet beret, completely covering her hair.

In the next photo she was wearing the same beret, but apart from that was dressed in a Sleeping Beauty nightie, sitting cross-legged on a rug in a room of stripped-pine furniture. In her arms was a well-worn toy rabbit.

Aoife threw an astonished glance at the grey rabbit flopped on its side in the middle of her floor. Identical. How was it possible that her childhood toy had got lost out on the bog? No, it must be just one of the same make—

'Aoife?' Her mother was standing with her hand on the bedroom door. 'Are you . . . ?' Her gaze fell on the photographs, and her question trickled away to nothing. Aoife remained kneeling speechless by the bed, holding a picture of herself cutting a cake with four candles, surrounded by the same grinning adults who had been at her first birthday party. Her mother came further into the room, stooped to pick up the rabbit and pressed it lovingly to her cheek. She said in a low, trembling voice, 'Hector.'

Aoife found her voice. '*Hector?*'

'Where did you find him, Aoife?'

'How did I even *lose* him? I don't understand!'

'Is everything all right?' Her father was standing in the doorway, tousle-haired in his paisley pyjamas, yawning, awkwardly putting on his glasses. Once they were on, he took a moment to absorb the scene: the bed covered in Aoife's childhood pictures, his wife hugging the toy. His eyes settled on the rabbit, and he went deathly pale. 'Hector.' His voice was choked. He came forward and took the rabbit from his wife. And kissed it tenderly. Just as Maeve had kissed the baby photo in the locket – although at the time, Aoife had assumed that this was because it was the only picture of herself as a baby in existence.

Not true.

Despair welled in her heart. She'd always thought her parents were ordinary, normal people, like everyone else's parents. Yet they'd clearly been keeping some terrible secret from her – something about her childhood, before they'd moved here from Dublin, away from their house, their friends, their jobs, their everything. And never gone back. She jumped angrily to her feet, flinging the birthday photo down among the rest. 'What was the big emotional deal about my finding the baby locket, when you had all these pictures of me already?'

'Aoife, sweetie—'

Fists clenched, cheeks burning, she cried, 'Don't *sweetie* me! I don't want to be comforted! I want to know why you locked away all the photos of me as a baby and told me you'd *lost* them!'

Her mother had her face in her hands, shaking her head from side to side. 'I'm so sorry—'

'Did I do something terrible when I was a kid?'

Maeve dropped her hands, horrified. 'Of course not!'

'Then why do we never go to Dublin? You had loads of friends – they're in the photos of all my parties. Why aren't you in touch with any of them any more? It's like you ran away from something. *What happened?*'

'Aoife—' Her mother was coming towards her, trying to pull her into a hug.

'I told you, I don't want comforting! I just want you to tell me the truth!'

But Maeve wrapped her arms around her anyway. Keeping her own arms rigid by her sides, Aoife twisted to stare fiercely at her father. He was sitting slumped among the photographs, still cradling the rabbit to his chest. 'Dad. You tell me. What happened?'

He said in a breaking, haunted voice, 'This isn't fair on her, Maeve. I think we have to tell her.'

'But what about the promise—'

Aoife, feeling sick, broke out of her mother's embrace. 'What promise? Tell me! I have a right to know! *Tell me!*'

'Darling, we love you—'

'*Dad! Tell me!*'

Her father sighed and wiped his face, and laid the toy rabbit on the bed, stroking its head as if he were hushing it to sleep. Then stood up and put his own arms around his wife. 'We were always going to have to tell her sometime, my love. And I think she knows already, in her heart.'

'*Knows what?*'

'Oh, James, I can't do it . . .'

He sighed and kissed his wife's dark blonde hair. 'Then let me tell her.'

CHAPTER NINE

It was peaceful in the west of Ireland, and it was spring, and so it seemed like the right place for the O'Connors to bring their daughter. Eva loved all baby things – fledglings, calves, lambs. Maybe a country holiday away from Dublin could make her happy, and create one last sweet memory of her for themselves.

James O'Connor's family home had stood empty for the last two years, since his parents had gone to visit his sister Aileen in Australia and had found the sun so good for their bones.

Maeve pushed the leather couch over to the window of the back room so that Eva, who was very sick, could see Declan Sweeney's lambs bouncing around the field like white balloons. The only trouble with having lambs nearby was that foxes were on the prowl. That first night, a vixen cried in the garden for hours. Maeve and James couldn't sleep for the racket, although their daughter lay in a deep drugged sleep with Hector tucked under her chin.

The next morning in the shop, James overheard old John McCarthy – whose nephew was the owner – talking to the farmer who rented the field across the lane. They were discussing how the banshee had spent last night wailing outside the O'Connor house, just as it had 'when poor young Michael passed on' – Michael being James's unmarried uncle, who had died in his seventies of a heart attack.

'So I hear Jimmy and Nancy's lad has a wee girl who is sick?'

'Cancer, they say.'

'God send them a miracle, then. The banshee means no good.'

The woman behind the counter sold James the paper with an expression that declared she had heard nothing and didn't have an opinion on the subject either way.

That evening, three visitors came to the house.

The first was Declan Sweeney, the young farmer who owned the sheep. He had a tiny newborn lamb with him, wrapped up in a blanket. They couldn't let him into the house in case of infection, but Maeve brought the lamb to the doorway of the back room for her daughter to see.

The second was Father Leahy, who was the one person they did let into the house – banking on the power of prayer to outweigh the risk.

The third visitor came to the house after dark. It was a tall woman, very beautiful, wrapped in a red hooded cloak; in the shadow of the hood, her eyes were so black they were like the space between the stars. She had a small child by the hand, a skinny little weather-browned thing in a simple purple dress and bare feet. She said to Maeve, 'Well, now, I've come for the little girl.'

Maeve said, 'I'm sorry, she's asleep and she can't have visitors anyway, because she's ill.'

The woman said, 'I might come in.'

Maeve said, 'No – you see, the doctor says that she's not allowed visitors, in case of infection.'

The woman said, 'Do you not want her to get better?'

And Maeve said, with a catch in her throat, 'You're very good to offer a cure, but the doctors said definitely no visitors.' And she closed the door, then went to the window and watched as the woman walked away down the garden path; the moon caught her in a flickering spotlight as it moved in and out between fast-moving clouds. The tiny girl broke away from her mother and leaped right over the hedge into the narrow boreen, even though the brambles were as high as her head. Instead of being amazed, Maeve found herself thinking angrily: *Why is that child so alive, when mine is dying? Unfair, unfair.* She stormed into the back room, where Eva was still asleep on the couch.

James said, 'Who was that?'

Maeve snapped bitterly, 'Some traveller woman, selling cures. She must have heard there was a sick child in the house.'

'Unbelievable.'

'She asked me did I want her to get better. As if I might not. Oh, it's cruel, what some people will say.' They both looked over at their daughter, whose short hair framed her sleeping face. Gripped by a crippling self-doubt, Maeve said, 'But what if that woman really knows of a miracle cure . . .'

James said, 'She *doesn't*. You know that. No more than all the other hundreds of quacks out there. We've gone down that road enough. I refuse to force one more vile-tasting potion down my daughter's throat.'

Outside, the vixen started up again very close to the house, wailing like a broken-hearted woman. By midnight, James had been driven so demented by the noise that he decided to see if could he frighten the fox away. He got a torch and unlocked the kitchen door. When he opened it, the woman was standing facing him on the step. *'Jesus Christ . . .'* He grabbed hold of the doorframe; he thought for a moment he was going to drop dead of a heart attack, like his own uncle.

'I might come in,' said the woman in the red cloak. She still had her skinny child by the hand.

'It's nearly midnight! Go away!'

'I am here for your little girl,' said the woman.

'No!' And he shut the door – *slammed* it – although he felt bad about leaving the child outside, because the night was cold and a needle-sharp rain had begun to fall. He hurried back to Maeve. 'That woman you were talking to earlier? She was on the back step when I opened the door.'

'No!'

'Yes, and she still had the child with her.'

'Oh God – at this time of night, in this weather . . . Should we let them in?'

James hesitated. Somewhere deep inside himself, he knew that this was no traveller woman. 'No . . . She's gone now and hopefully that's the end of it.' The vixen was off again, wailing. The next moment there was a furious banging at the front door.

Maeve cried, 'Look, maybe she's just after money. I'll give her twenty euros to leave us in peace.'

'*Don't let her in!*'

But Maeve was already at the front door. The beautiful woman seemed pleased to see her and gave the child a small push forward into the light of the porch. She said: 'I might come in.'

Maeve thrust out the twenty-euro note, at arm's length. 'Look, this is for you. Now, please, leave us alone.'

'I've come for your daughter, Mrs O'Connor.'

'I've told you already, we don't want your help! Please, take the money . . .'

'Don't you want her to live? Where I come from she will never grow old.'

'*Leave us alone!*' She tried to close the door, but the woman slipped her red shoe in the way.

Maeve shrieked: 'James, call the guards! Now!'

But the woman looked straight past Maeve at James, who had followed her into the hall, and said, 'Mr O'Connor. Look there in the boreen.'

He peered over his wife's shoulder, trying anxiously to see into the darkness beyond the garden. Nothing there but the black shapes of trees, rustling and dripping. 'I can't see anything . . .' Then his heart missed a beat. Through the light patter of rain he could hear the heavy sigh of a horse and the rattle and creak of leather and wood, like the sound of the old farm cart on which he had once hitched a ride as a boy to school. And as he stared, the moon came out like a bruise against the clouds, and rising over the top of the blackberry hedge was the roof of a black carriage, of the type travellers use as a hearse for funerals.

Maeve shrank back into the hallway. 'James?'

His throat felt dry as sandpaper. He said hoarsely to the woman, 'Who is that?'

Again, the woman urged the child forward into the yellow light of the porch. 'You know well who it is, and who I am, or you are not a Mayo man at all. Give me your daughter and she will be cured. And you will mind this child as your own in her place.'

Maeve slammed the door and punched 999.

The Clonbarra guard turned up two hours later with the elasticated waist of his pyjamas visible over the belt of his trousers. He refused a cup of tea, and asked to see the little girl that the traveller woman had threatened to steal. He wasn't too impressed when they explained that he wasn't allowed to go near their daughter in case he might be infectious with something. He took one quick look around the garden, shone his torch on the fresh marks of a traveller's caravan wheels in the muddy lane, and violently yawned his way back to the squad car.

Eva remained in her deep drugged sleep on the couch in the back room, with Hector under her chin. She couldn't be left in case she woke and needed extra pain relief. James took first watch while Maeve went up to bed for a few hours. He sat for a while, hunched in the armchair, brooding on what he'd seen. Then he closed the old wooden shutters on the window, and secured them with their iron latch. Then he took down a chocolate-box-style painting of a thatched cottage from over the couch and, using a piece of fencing wire, hung up the iron fire tongs in its place.

Maeve was from Dublin, which is why James had moved there when they married – that and all the carpentry work, with the new houses being built and old ones renovated. Yet while you can take the man out of Mayo, you can't take Mayo out of the man. James knew that fairies hated iron. His grandmother had insisted on these same tongs being hung over his own cradle when he was a baby, to stop the fairies stealing him and leaving a changeling, a child of their own, in his place. She hadn't liked his parents buying this house, because it was built on a fairy road – a road, invisible to the human eye, that ran straight across the fields towards the bog. But James's parents were hard up and took the risk; they bought the old place cheap. And now a fairy woman was at his door wanting him to raise her child, and to bring his own daughter to the Land of the Young, that paradise beneath the earth where she would be cured and live for ever.

Or rather, in the real world, the world his wife believed in, a mad woman had been pestering him to buy some useless folk remedy, using the sight of her own child to soften him up, while her traveller husband waited for her in the lane, idly flicking the reins of their horse-drawn caravan.

At five in the morning, exhausted, James checked that the black coach in the lane had not returned, then shook his wife awake to take over from him.

At eight in the morning he woke to Maeve screaming his name.

Hurling himself down the stairs, he knew for certain she'd woken and found their daughter dead. But he was wrong. Their daughter wasn't dead. She was just gone. And sitting cross-legged in her place on the couch was the little red-haired child from the night before.

Maeve was running around clutching her hair, screaming at the top of her voice: 'She's been stolen! Stolen!' The iron tongs were back on the hearth. (He would discover later that his wife had removed them from the hook last night, afraid they would fall.)

James grabbed hold of the tiny girl by her shoulders. '*Where is she?*' But the urchin just burst into tears. 'God help us, she must be here somewhere . . .' He rushed through every room, searched every cupboard, then burst out into the garden – checking the turf shed; the coop where once there were chickens; the dark stinking space under the coop. In the boreen, tractor tyres had crushed all signs of other wheels; he searched the banks and ditches, under brambles and nettles and elderflower bushes. He ran back to the house.

Maeve was screaming down the phone to the guard: 'No, she hasn't just wandered off, she's *sick*, too sick to move! No, she's not hiding! *Why won't you listen to me! Our daughter has been stolen!*'

James shouted to her: 'I'm going to ask the kid again – she has to know something . . .' and threw open the door to the back room. For a moment he thought the child was gone, but then he saw her squatting by the bookcase, on all fours with her knees bent up like a little frog and breathing in the same panting, rippling fashion. She seemed to have hurt herself – she was bleeding from a long cut on the palm of her hand – strange, sparkling, luminous blood. He moved very slowly towards her, his arms held out, not wanting to scare her as he had before. The child shrank back. He whispered, 'I'm not going to hurt you . . .' Then burst out loudly, 'Oh, good God!'

Because as he reached to pick up the little girl, she had sprung out of his way and run up the bookcase like a squirrel, and was now crouched on top of it, staring down at him with blue-green eyes.

Maeve came in. 'The guard is coming. Where's the—? *How did she get up there?*'

'I don't— *Jesus Christ!*' Because the child had flown through the air – *literally* flown – hurling herself with a bang at the nearest set of shutters, where she clung, screeching, not touching the iron catch but trying to force her small fingers into the gap. James rushed to stop her escaping. 'Maeve, help me! We have to mind her!' He caught hold of the tiny girl but she scratched his face and burst from his arms, leaping and flying around the room, smashing his mother's porcelain figurines, even breaking the light bulb dangling from the ceiling.

'*What's happening?*' shrieked Maeve. '*What is it?*'

'She's a changeling! We've to mind her, and that way Eva will be cured and live for ever!' Because he knew it was true. He'd known it deep in his Mayo heart as soon as he saw the carriage in the lane. It was what his grandmother had warned his parents of, and why she had hung the fire tongs over his cradle. The fairies had taken his beautiful little girl for themselves, and in return had left him this fierce changeling child.

It was a long hard battle to catch the changeling and calm her down, but slowly the fight went out of her. At last she sat on the couch with her little face buried in her knees and her red hair hanging down, and her arms wrapped around her thin brown legs, and just wept and wept. Maeve also wept, as James begged her over and over to say nothing to the guards – because they couldn't afford to lose this fairy child: she had to be minded if Eva was to be cured and live for ever with the fairies in the Land of the Young.

When the Clonbarra guard turned up an hour later, with boiled egg on his stubble, they showed him the changeling (now sleeping) and said she was their own daughter, who'd been hiding in the wardrobe. He was heavily unsurprised. 'Sure wasn't that the way with the O'Sullivan child: his mother had him drowned for sure, and him in the barn all along, with the new puppies. Don't cry, Mrs O'Connor – she's found now, and what else did I have to be doing on a Sunday morning?' And away he went.

*

It was five in the morning, and dawn was rising. The bedroom was full of clean clear early light.

Aoife stared at her father in bewilderment. He sat on the bed among the photos, his head in his hands. The story he had told . . . Did he really imagine it was true? Had his fascination with old folk tales come to this – that he believed in the fairies, like his grandmother had done? Like mad John McCarthy? Maeve had her arm around him and her cheek pressed to his shoulder, eyes closed, as if she were lost in the mythical world of his strange tale.

Aoife slid off the windowsill where she'd been sitting, quietly crossed the room and touched her mother on the shoulder. 'Mam?'

Maeve opened her eyes and caught Aoife's hand, pressing it. 'Always remember we love you. You're our beautiful, clever, amazing daughter and we both love you very much.'

'I don't understand what Dad is saying . . .'

'Darling. He's saying the fairies stole our daughter.'

'I know, I heard him! But, Mam, I'm your daughter, aren't I? I'm Aoife – I'm me!' She caught up her baby album from the bed. 'Look, see – me, Eva!'

Maeve took the album from Aoife's hands and hugged it to her chest, saying nothing.

Aoife cried, trembling, 'I'm Eva Sarah O'Connor! That's the name on my birth certificate!'

'We love you, darling.'

'Dad? Look at me! I'm Eva!'

Her father raised his head and gazed straight at her, his eyes full of tears. He said, 'I'm so sorry. You are the fairy child.'

CHAPTER TEN

She rushed for the window; the curtains blew open wide and the casement swung back in a blast of wind. She sprang onto the windowsill. The sun was rising over the mountains, and there was a pale green streak up Declan Sweeney's field.

'Aoife, stop, you'll fall!'

She leaped and clung to the outer branches of the ash tree. The slender twigs gave way beneath her, the leaves tearing off in her hands, and she was tumbling headlong through the air . . .

'Aoife!'

In mid-fall, she leaped again, and for a moment it was as if she had purchase on the wind, and somehow she was gliding across the garden and over the wall, and had landed in Declan Sweeney's field. The rage drained out of her and she was filled with a joy and energy so bright, it was as if she had been flooded by the rising light of dawn. If her parents weren't mad – this made sense of everything . . .

'Aoife! Come back!'

She fled on up the stony field in her bare feet, following the fairy road as she had as a child, but this time she wasn't going to stop . . . She could run so fast, she could leap any obstacle . . . The bank was as high as her head. She sprang over it easily and hit the next field still running. A crowd of young bullocks came thundering towards her out of the dawn mist, silver spools of saliva swinging from their great mouths; Aoife darted straight as an arrow through the middle of the herd, scattering them in noisy panic, and vaulted over a metal five-barred gate, one hand on the top, without breaking stride.

It was true, it was true! She was not made of dull human flesh and bone, but sun and wind! Exhilaration lifted her, like wings. A stream flowed across the next field; she raced across its misty surface, the water fizzing up between her toes. *I can walk on water. I am the fairy child.* Three more fields of long grass and kingcups, leaping the high hedges in between, and then it was the Clonbarra road that crossed her path – and there, panting, Aoife was forced to stop. The joy ebbed slightly from her veins.

On the far side of the road was a small white modern bungalow, its porch supported by plastic Greek-style columns, fir trees densely planted around the border of its garden. This was Lois Munnelly's house and, like Aoife's own, it had clearly been built on the fairy road, and it was blocking her way. She could hardly knock on the door at this time of the morning and demand to walk straight through and out the back. Yet if she changed direction around it, she felt she might lose her way . . . Extraordinary thought – could she go *over* it? Up the drainpipe and over the roof? Could she? Why not? Imagine Lois waking up to see Aoife gliding down from the roof, past her bedroom window, the way she had glided down from the ash tree . . .

Lois would probably decide it was just more attention-seeking.

Oh, this whole thing was crazy.

Aoife had to talk to someone down to earth, or her head would explode. Carla. Carla would know how to explain this. She checked her phone. Just gone six thirty. She tried calling anyway, but the other end rang out. Sometimes Dianne Heffernan took her daughter's phone away at bedtime, to make sure she went to sleep. Aoife would have to throw stones at the bedroom window. She turned away from the fairy road and took the ordinary human road towards Kilduff, towards her friend.

Passing the turning to her own house, she glimpsed the roof of her father's car making its way up the winding boreen between the hedges. She scrambled over a gate and crouched down behind brambles. She wasn't ready to face her parents yet, not while she was still trying to figure things out. A few seconds later, the car turned out of the lane towards Kilduff. Aoife stayed low, peering through the brambles, until they were gone. Her parents had clearly guessed exactly where she would be headed – towards Carla's.

A hundred metres further on, the garage was already open for early business. Dave Ferguson was walking around inside his little shop, phone to his ear, gesticulating furiously with his spare hand. Bent low so as not to be seen, Aoife hurried past the shop and shed, into the yard behind.

The cream BMW's FOR SALE sign had been removed. She opened the driver's door and slipped in behind the wheel. She would hide here for a while, just till her parents had given up driving around looking for her, and until Carla woke up and saw the missed call, and phoned her back. The soft red leather seat embraced her; she leaned back in it and tiredness swept over her. She'd had no sleep at all. She closed her eyes.

And opened them. The clock in the walnut dashboard said just after seven. She'd been asleep for only twenty minutes, but felt wide awake and refreshed. The key was in the ignition. She touched it lightly, and the car started. Alarmed, she tried to turn it off again, but couldn't. What if Dave Ferguson heard the engine running and came storming out of his office? Yet she wasn't doing anything wrong – it was her own car and she wasn't driving it anywhere, she was just sitting in it, here in the yard.

The BMW slid forward across the tarmac.

Panicking, she slammed her foot on what she thought was the brake, but it clearly wasn't, because the car turned and glided luxuriously up the slope by the side of the workshop. Sweating with fright, Aoife grabbed the steering wheel and stamped on the other pedal. The BMW carried straight on past the pumps and out onto the Clonbarra road, in the direction of Kilduff. Now she was afraid to touch anything, in case the car went even faster. As she entered the square, a Gardaí car passed her coming the other way. She shook the steering wheel frantically. '*Stop, you stupid lump of—!*'

The car pulled in by the church and parked. Aoife got out as fast as she could, and stood there, half laughing, half shaking. Had she really driven this beautiful car? Although it felt more like *it* had driven *her* – she was just so relieved it had stopped when she had shouted at it. Is this what it was like to be a fairy? Able to make things happen – but not really being in control? Fun but incredibly scary?

Across the square, the shop was already open, a bread van parked outside. The sight of the huge loaf painted on the side of the van made Aoife realize that she was hungry again – she'd had eaten nothing since last night's dinner. While she was here... She felt in the pocket of her trackies. Plenty of money left from yesterday. She headed into the shop, grabbing a basket. Bananas, apples, a big bag of mixed nuts, a coffee cake, a litre of milk and some just-baked white rolls. At the counter, she held a twenty out to the man checking her purchases through the till. It was mad John McCarthy from the graveyard, the uncle of the man who owned the shop.

When he looked up to take the money, the old man did a double-take, as if the sight of her shocked him. 'Aoife O'Connor!'

She was suddenly very conscious that she had no shoes on, and that her clothes were in bits from crashing over hedges. She said as nonchalantly as possible, 'Yep, that's me.'

'Aoife O'Connor, who came in here yesterday with the hundred-euro note?'

'Yes why?'

John McCarthy eyed the money in her palm, but didn't take it. 'Would that be the change we gave you from that note or is it the same sort of money you came in with yesterday?'

Aoife began to feel uncomfortable, like she was being accused of something. Did he think she'd stolen the hundred? 'It's the change from yesterday. Sorry, is there a problem?'

'Not at all. That's grand, so.' He smiled with very few teeth, took the note and counted out the change into her palm. 'I'd say this twenty-euro note will stay as the good Lord made it, then, it not being fairy gold.'

She stared blankly at him. 'Sorry – what?'

He rolled his marble-blue eyes to heaven, and pointed to a large dead oak leaf lying on top of the till. 'And what do you think that yoke is that I found in the drawer only this morning?'

'A dead leaf. But what—?'

'See, your type of gold's not much use to us poor mortals. Sure, I had that Sinead Ferguson in here yesterday evening trying to buy sweets with another leaf the very brother of this one. Fair flittered, the poor girl was, when she couldn't find the fifty she says you gave her—'

'What's that about my daughter?' Thomas Ferguson had just come into the shop, his glasses askew on his bald head and his shirt buttoned wrong. 'Morning, Aoife.'

'Morning.' Aoife was stacking her purchases into a cardboard box as quickly as she could, in a hurry to get away.

John McCarthy said, 'I was just saying how the fifty Aoife here gave to poor Sinead turned out to be fairy gold and melted away.'

Thomas laughed, although rather sourly. 'Maybe that would explain what happened to the thousand my brother says was robbed out of his own till last night. He just got me out of bed to bring down a couple of coffees and a sandwich for the guard, because apparently they can't catch criminals on an empty stomach.'

'And would the drawer have been left stuffed with leaves like this one here?'

Thomas Ferguson looked startled at the oak leaf in John's hand. 'How did you—?'

'Fairy gold, Thomas – it turns to dead leaves in human hands. Doesn't it, Aoife O'Connor?'

Aoife fled out of the shop, across the square, slung the box of food into the BMW's passenger seat and jumped in behind the wheel. She was shaking. The garage till was full of leaves . . . So that was why there had been a dead oak leaf in her mother's purse . . . Oh God, she had cheated Dave Ferguson. She would have to bring the car back to him right away. Hopefully, the guards wouldn't arrest her. She touched the ignition, turned the wheel. Nothing. She leaned back in despair. Then, remembering she was starving, tore a chunk off the coffee cake and washed it down with the milk. Then, still hungry, crunched down an apple, and a handful of nuts. She had to talk to someone. Carla. No, not Carla – much as Aoife loved her, it had to be someone who wouldn't just be kind and gentle to her because they assumed she'd lost the plot. It couldn't be someone down to earth. It had to be someone who might believe the impossible . . .

Shay. He had talked to her about fairies. His own father, Eamonn Foley, had believed in them. She needed to talk to Shay.

The car started up again.

CHAPTER ELEVEN

Three kilometres beyond Kilduff, the Atlantic came to meet her and the cream BMW swung west along the coast road. Aoife clung anxiously to the wheel – the hundred-metre drop to the ocean was unfenced. But after a while she found herself gaining in confidence. The mistiness of early morning was fading, and the sun was getting hot. The land grew wilder, flushing from green to purple. The mountains rose higher with every bend in the road. To her right, the ocean was a vast blinding, rippling sheet, stretching to the horizon. The roof of the convertible slid open and the warm sea breeze fluttered her hair. Cautiously, she leaned her elbow on the door, fingers resting only lightly on the wheel; the car drove smoothly on.

After several kilometres of nothing but empty, rolling mountains, a turning appeared ahead – a farm track, hedged by wild rhododendrons and gorse, cutting into a greener valley between steep purple slopes. While Aoife was wondering where the boreen led, the car took the turn and drove bumpily along the track, stones spitting out from under its wheels. Stone-walled fields came into view, then a breeze-block shed and a long one-storey farmhouse with a blue tin roof. Two sheepdogs and a terrier came barking furiously down the boreen. The car swept through the pack into the farmyard and screeched to a halt, scattering chickens right and left.

By the time Aoife had opened the driver's door, the dogs had formed a growling semicircle around her. She ordered, 'Stay! Sit!' They bared their teeth, but didn't approach. Well-trained farm dogs. The chickens were settling already, like gold-brown leaves only briefly disturbed by a gust of wind.

No human came to meet her.

She'd never been here before, but it wasn't hard to work out where she was. John Joe Foley's old red Ford was sitting among the dismantled wrecks of several other cars in the corner of the yard. The car's bonnet was still crumpled up in an evil grin, and engine parts were lying all around. A blue tractor with no cab was parked on the other side of the yard. Washing hung on a line across the open-fronted turf shed: a set of blue overalls, two frayed white shirts and a Kilduff soccer strip.

Where was everyone? Where was Shay? Aoife checked her phone. Eight o'clock. Maybe he'd gone for the school bus already.

She glanced in through the open door of the barn, but there were only a few bales of hay, a half-built chicken coop, sacks of sheep nuts and three large containers of diesel.

She crossed the yard. The house was rundown but not badly kept. The walls had been whitewashed recently and the door was painted the same sky blue as the tin roof. The plastic guttering was broken but tied up neatly with nylon string. There was no knocker; she rapped on the door with her knuckles, and a few flies that had been warming themselves on the wood in the morning sunshine drifted upwards in an iridescent puff. Silence followed, apart from the breathy growling of the dogs. And then even they fell quiet. She tried to see in through the window.

'Stay right where you are!'

With a cry of shock, Aoife spun round. The man slapped his big hands flat against the door on either side of her, trapping her between his muscular arms.

He was in his twenties, well over six foot and very strongly built – huge muscled shoulders, and arms like iron. He was wearing dirty blue farm overalls, cousin of the clean ones on the line; he was handsome, black-haired and brown-skinned, but his hazel eyes were narrow with anger. He roared in her face, 'Where's ya thieving tinker friends – where are they hid? Nobody's stealing anything off me this time around. If I find them first, I'll burst them, so I will. This time I won't hold back.'

Aoife smiled as brightly as she could, to hide her alarm. 'I'm not a thief, I'm just lost.'

'Oh, you are, are you?' He looked her suspiciously up and down, from the goose grass tangled in her hair to her naked dirty feet. 'And where were you going when you got yourself so lost?'

'Do you know anyone around here called Shay Foley?'

His hard eyes flashed, then narrowed. 'And what would you be wanting with my little brother?'

So now there was no doubt – this was the violent, bullying John Joe. A shiver of fury ran through Aoife, followed by a fierce, wild determination. 'It's not Shay I've come to see. It's you.'

163

'What the . . . ?'

'I've come to tell you it wasn't his fault he crashed your car, it was mine.'

'*What?*'

'And I've bought you another, to replace it – see, there it is, it's really nice and it drives perfect—'

John Joe barely glanced at it; he brought his angry, handsome face even closer to hers. 'Let me get this right. Are you after saying to me that my thieving little brother not only stole my car but let a wee girleen like you drive it? Wait till I get my hands on him, the lying little—'

She cried in horror, 'No, that's not what happened! It wasn't his fault! I've bought you another one with my own money!'

'I don't deal with little girls too young to drive. It's my lying brother that will be paying for this—'

'*Just take it.*' And she dropped the car key into the front pocket of his overalls.

He fished it out instantly, with a growl like one of his dogs – but instead of throwing it back at her, he turned to look at the car. A long appreciative whistle escaped from between his teeth. 'Looks nice enough.' He strode long-legged towards it across the yard.

Aoife followed, heart still beating furiously, not sure if this was some sort of a cunning trap. She called encouragingly, trying to keep the tremble out of her voice, 'It's got red leather seats and everything.'

'I can see that.' John Joe was leaning in over the door, running his hand across the walnut dashboard. 'A vintage convertible – very nice.' Then puzzlement crept into his voice. 'Must have cost you a few bob.'

'It did, but . . .' She thought quickly. 'I claimed on my insurance.'

'Grand, so. Fair enough.' But he still didn't sound as if he completely believed her. A strange struggle was taking place in his face – his mouth twisting and eyelids flickering. It was as if some other inner self were fighting to get to the surface of his skin. He blurted out in a harsh, strangled voice, 'How old are you?'

'Eighteen!'

Instantly his face cleared; he smiled and said pleasantly, 'That's grand, then.'

Aoife took a deep breath; relaxed. Maybe this was the same as when she forced Dave Ferguson to sell her the car – maybe once she'd given John Joe the key, a deal had been done that couldn't be broken, despite the best efforts of his rational mind to fight back. 'So, is Shay still here?'

John Joe strolled cheerfully to the front of the car. 'Nope.'

'He went for the bus already?'

'Nope.'

'Then . . .'

He jerked his chin in the direction of the mountains bordering the sea. 'Back the bog, lambing. Working off what he owes me. Although now you've given me this, I suppose I can let him off.' He raised the bonnet. Then, after a moment's pause, walked round the car and looked in the boot. He stared at her. His mouth was making odd shapes again, eyelids fluttering. He said hoarsely, 'Where is it?'

Aoife wondered anxiously what could be missing out of the boot – the spare wheel? 'Maybe it's still in the garage. I could get it for you . . .'

A red flush was crawling up John Joe's neck, reddening his jaw line. He slammed the boot and thumped it with his fist, leaving a deep, frightening dent. 'I *said*, where is it?'

'I don't know what you're—'

'*The engine.*'

She glanced, startled, towards the open bonnet. The space where the engine should have been was empty.

The crimson had reached John Joe's strong cheekbones. He smashed his fist on the car again and again. Huge dents and cracks kept appearing – he had incredible strength. 'What are you doing trying to cheat me with this heap of junk! You wait here till that thieving brother of mine comes back and then I'll show him he can't make a fool of me!' He lunged for her. '*Come back here!*'

She fled past the barn, between the wrecks of cars, over the wall into the fields, the three dogs snarling and snapping after her. 'Home! Go home, dogs!' They obeyed her, dropping back. Less than a minute later, Aoife had reached the mountainside. Rather than zigzagging to and fro to ease the climb, she ran straight up the heathery slope. When she stopped at the top to look down, John Joe's small blue figure had come to a halt in the middle of his fields, the dogs clustered around him. She had outpaced him with ridiculous ease. She had just run half a kilometre up a nearly vertical slope, and she was not even out of breath. It was like having wings on her heels. It was as if she could fly . . .

Could she? *Could she?* If she was the fairy child . . . And she *had* to be – she had driven a car with no engine, and nothing rational could explain that away . . . If she was the fairy child, maybe she could fly. She had done so when she was little, on the day she arrived. According to her father's story, she had smashed the light bulb in the room.

Aoife raced across the heathery summit, holding out her arms like wings. Her green hoodie billowed out in the wind. She took a running jump. The blustering air caught her and carried her towards the edge of the cliff; she landed on all fours just before being swept right off, grabbing at grass, heart pumping with fright. The cliff face plunged hundreds of metres below her to the wild Atlantic. At its base, the ocean crashed on jagged rocks, sending up huge glittering clouds of spray. The skeletons of careless sheep were littered on thin green ledges all the way down.

Not the safest place to test her invisible wings.

Heart still pounding, she scrambled back to her feet and hurried west along the edge of the rolling land. The cliffs grew higher and steeper the further she ran. Far below her, the ocean roared and sucked. Gulls screamed and circled in grey flocks. The wind tore at her, threatening to push her to her death. She had to find Shay. She had to warn him that in trying to make things better with John Joe, she had ended up making things a thousand times worse. His brother thought they'd been trying to make a fool of him. God knows what he would do to Shay this time. She had to warn him not to go back to the farm.

Where was he, in all this wind-swept wilderness?

She would never find him.

Yet when she crested the next summit, he was right there, a few metres away from her, kneeling near the edge of the cliff in his faded jeans, a baby lamb in his arms.

Aoife collapsed beside him on the sheep-cropped grass. He didn't seem even to notice her – he was so utterly focused on what he was doing, stroking the soft curls of the new-born lamb. The lamb looked dead. The ewe, its mother, kept nudging it with her nose, bleating miserably. Once more he ran his hands over its curls, and this time it was as if a bolt of energy had shot through the tiny body. It raised its head and uttered a vigorous cry. Shay set it down and it sprang towards its mother and the pair of them walked away together. Then he sat back on his heels and smiled at her lying beside him.

She scrambled into a sitting position. 'I need to talk to you. I've done something really bad.'

A slow steady sweep of his green-brown eyes across her face. The bruise on his cheekbone had already vanished. The cut on his curved mouth was a thin dark line. He said lightly, 'Bad? You?'

'I drove to your farm.'

He was startled into seriousness. 'You did *what*?'

With a flicker of smugness, Aoife said, 'You're not the only one who can drive.'

'Did you run into John Joe?'

'Yes, and I told him I'd bought him a new car because it was my fault that his old one got wrecked.'

'Oh, for . . . What were you *thinking*? Aoife, you have to be careful around him. I told you, he doesn't know his own strength.'

'You're not kidding.'

He looked horrified. 'What, did he—?'

'No, no, he was fine with me. But he smashed up the car.'

'*What? Why?*'

'He got annoyed when there was no engine in it.'

Shay looked at her blankly, trying to work out what she was saying. 'You mean it got banjaxed when you drove—'

She said indignantly, 'I drove it perfectly well, thank you!'

'Then . . .'

'The engine wasn't *there*. Like, completely not there. And your brother got pure thick about it. So you have to keep away from him. He thinks we were trying to pull some stupid trick on him. But I wasn't, I swear. I thought it had an engine in it, I really did.'

He continued looking at her for a while, then turned to gaze out over the Atlantic, clasping his arms around his knees, the wind ruffling his hair and Mayo shirt.

After a while Aoife said quietly, 'I'm not lying, I swear.'

'I didn't say you were lying.'

'I know, but that's what you're thinking.'

Shay remained staring out over the sea that crashed against the cliffs so far below.

She moved closer, kneeling right beside him. If he wasn't going to believe her anyway . . . She said recklessly, 'Do you want to know what else? John McCarthy in the shop said the money I paid with in there yesterday turned to a dead leaf, and so did the fifty euros I gave Sinead, and he said it was fairy gold. Same with that money I used to buy the car – it turned into leaves and that's why Dave Ferguson called the police this morning. I gave a hundred to my mam, and there was nothing left in her purse but a dead oak leaf. I saw it myself.'

He glanced at her; his sun-browned skin had paled beneath.

'I found photographs of me as a little girl in a drawer which came unlocked when I touched it. Least, I thought the little girl was me. But my parents said she was their real daughter, and I was the changeling the fairies left in her place. That's why they moved to Kilduff permanently, so that no one would notice they had the wrong child.'

He shuddered. 'Don't listen to them. They're lying to you.'

'But why would they lie? And how else are all these things happening to me? I think they were telling me the truth.'

'No, they're mad.'

'Why do you think they're mad? It was you told me about the sheóg!'

'I told you what my father said. And he was mad himself, Aoife. He thought my own mother was a fairy.'

'Ah . . .' So old John McCarthy had been telling the truth. 'Tell me.'

Shay wrapped his arms around his knees, tightening his arms until the muscles showed, staring out to sea again.

'Shay? Tell me. Why did he say she was a fairy?'

He cast a wild, sad look at her. 'Aoife, who knows why he thought it? Because she was so beautiful, maybe.'

'He loved her.'

'Sure, he couldn't take his eyes off her. He was forever painting her. And then, at the same time, he said she was burning him up and killing him.'

'Ah . . .'

'She left him because of it, when John Joe was five.

She stayed away for seven years. But then she came back because she loved him still, and I was born, and my father went back to his painting, and telling her all the time that she was killing him, because she was from the otherworld. So in the end she said she was leaving again, and just walked away up the mountain. I was five and John Joe was seventeen. I wanted him to go after her, but he was so angry with them both and their craziness that he wouldn't go. So I went to fetch her back myself. She didn't seem to mind me coming after her, but she wouldn't come home. She held my hand. She brought me all the way up here to the cliffs. She spent a long time standing on the edge. Then she said she loved my father and was sorry for killing him. She said that she didn't belong in this life, that she didn't deserve to live in this world. Then she laughed and said that if she really *was* a fairy, maybe she could fly, and asked me did I want to see if I could fly too, because I was more like her than my father, and maybe I could. But I was only five and I got scared and pulled my hand out of hers. And she jumped without me.' Shay rubbed his hand across his face and groaned, from deep inside himself.

'Oh God, that's . . .' There were no possible words for it. Aoife got to her knees and put her arms around him.

He glanced past her towards the edge of the cliff, where the long grass bent double in the wind. 'I crept on all fours to the edge and I looked down. I hoped with all my heart that I would see her flying with the gulls. But there was nothing, only the sea breaking on the rocks. And I went home. And the coastguard were sent for and it took them a week to find her. And they did find her. So she never did fly, just fell. And my father died anyway, of the grief.'

'I'm so sorry.' She leaned her forehead against his shoulder.

He said softly, 'You're not a fairy, Aoife. Don't ever believe someone who tells you that you can fly.'

She could feel the pulse of his skin through the green and red material of his Mayo shirt; it seeped into the coolness of her blood and warmed her. She raised her head and looked at him. His green-brown eyes were dark with unshed tears. The cut on his lip was a faint line. She touched her finger to it. He opened his mouth very slightly, and closed it on her skin: the lightest of kisses.

The instant his mouth brushed against her, a bolt of gold shot through her heart, a vision of rapture, of flying – perfect, weightless, free . . . She leaped to her feet, exalted. 'It's all true!'

Shay caught her by the sleeve, his face turned up desperately to hers. 'It's not!'

Aoife's blood was fizzing, her skin on fire. 'I can fly!'

He cried in horror, holding her tighter as she tried to pull away. 'Stop!'

'I can fly!'

'No!'

'*Yes!*' She ripped her arm out of his grasp and fled along the grassy perimeter of the world, towards the west.

'*Aoife!*'

He was coming after her, his feet thudding on the springy turf, but she could outpace him easily even though she was running into the wind. She was so much faster than him now, even faster than when they had raced each other to the hawthorn hill. Beside her, to her right, the hundreds of metres of crumbling cliff fell sheer to the ocean. Gulls plunged from rocky outcrops into space.

'Aoife! Come back!'

I can fly. I can feel it.

'Aoife! Stop!'

She could. She could. She knew it in the very centre of her heart. From the moment Shay's lips had touched her skin, her blood had been flooded with a weird insistent clamorous joy:

I can fly! I can fly!

Although at the same time, in a softer whisper: *What if Shay's right – what if I'm not a changeling, and all this is a fantasy of my parents like the lenanshee was a fantasy of his father's? Then I'm going to die, like his poor mad mother died. I'm going to die, right . . .*

Now.

She turned and ran straight off the edge of the cliff.

CHAPTER TWELVE

At first it was all noise – the roar of wind in her ears, the screaming of the gulls, the shuddering crash of the ocean far below.

'*Aoife* . . .' His voice faded as she fell.

She screamed for him in terror – '*Shay!*' – but the speed of her headlong plunge stripped his name from her lips. The cliff face was rushing past her in a green-grey blur. The ocean was becoming brighter and clearer – huge inky white-streaked waves, bursting like snow against the base of the cliffs; rocks covered in red seaweed, rushing up to meet her, ready to splinter her bones to fragments and her flesh to pulp . . .

Fly! Let me fly!

Desperately Aoife spread her arms, and just in time she levelled out, slowing, gliding, the wind blowing through her clothes, the tips of the leaping waves spattering her feet, but not dragging her down . . . Rising upwards a little . . .

Flying!

A furious gust caught her and tossed her like a leaf, threatening to smash her apart against the cliff face; she scrambled in mid-air, flailing her arms, flipped over, lost her footing on the wind and fell again, headfirst.

Shay!

A grey mist spread suddenly beneath her, and she knew it was the end and closed her eyes. But instead of the freezing arms of instant death, a soft, warm, living blanket held her up.

It was the gulls.

They had swooped beneath and caught her on their backs, steadying her, their strong wings battering against her legs. Laughing, gasping with shock and relief and amazement, she rose again . . . Stretched out her own arms . . . Rolled in the air and was caught and steadied again . . . She was flying with the gulls, borne upwards on their wings, rising higher and higher . . . past mossy ledges . . . past a nest of gaping baby terns . . . the smiling woolly skeleton of a sheep . . . the bulging overhang of rock . . . the wind-blown fringe of green grass . . .

On the wings of the gulls, she rose slowly and smoothly over the edge of the cliff.

Shay had his back to her, weeping and struggling with his elder brother. 'Let go of me! She's jumped off the cliff!'

John Joe was red with rage, his eyes as wild as when he was mindlessly beating huge dents into the metal of the car. He was gripping Shay around the body, roaring in his face. 'What are you on about? That happened years ago! Stop trying to get out of what's coming to you!'

'I don't mean Mam! Let me go, I have to go after her!' With a huge effort, Shay freed his arms and tried to push his brother away. 'Let me go of me!' Sobbing, he punched John Joe furiously in the shoulder.

'Why, you lying—'

But before John Joe's huge unthinking iron fist had the chance to connect with his brother's jaw, Aoife seized Shay by his shirt and jerked him backwards off the edge of the cliff. The last thing she saw was the expression of terrified disbelief in John Joe's eyes.

They fell together through the sky.

She held him against her with one arm, and swept wildly at the wind with the other.

They fell.

His weight dragged them down, straight through the layer of gulls.

Aoife kicked and strained with every muscle to leap upwards.

They fell like stones. Straight down the vertical cliff towards their doom, while the gulls circled screaming overhead.

She had meant to rescue Shay from his brother, but she had murdered him instead. She couldn't fly for both of them . . .

He opened his dark hazel eyes and gazed at her. Then down at the jagged rocks rushing up to meet them, and then back at her, intently, as if just fixing his eyes on her face was somehow enough to save him.

She tightened her arms around him.

He rested his face against her neck, closed his eyes, ready for what was to come.

Straining every nerve, she braced herself against the wind . . . Think not of flying but of floating . . . Like falling paper, or a leaf through water, swinging from side to side, still downwards but slower . . .

Swinging . . .

Slowing . . .

A bone-shaking landing, skittering and rolling across sharp limpets and slippery seaweed into the water. The frenzied ocean swallowed her down, but Shay had his arms around her, swimming with her, pulling her back up onto the wave-lashed surface of the rock, pushing her up, climbing after her. Aoife lay flat, gasping like a beached fish. He was kneeling over her, water running off him. 'Are you all right? Are you hurt?'

She choked out, 'Grand.'

They had ended up on a low flat rock, a few metres square and about a metre out of the water, not far from the base of the cliffs. Dark blue waves were surging past them, boiling up white against the rocks. Shay stared around in wide-eyed disbelief, then up at the grey cliff face towering above them for three hundred metres, the summit hidden by the overhang. 'How in the name of Jesus did we make it all the way to the bottom without being killed . . . ?'

Getting her breath back, Aoife said, 'I'm so sorry – I didn't want him to hit you, he's so— *Crap!*'

A breaking wave had nearly washed her off the rock; Shay seized her and dragged her to her feet.

'The next will be higher. Stay with me till it's gone.' Even as he spoke, it boiled around their knees. Aoife's feet came off the ground, but he wrapped his arms around her waist and pinned her against him until the wave had sucked its way back into the ocean – then let go of her and dragged his mobile out of his soaked jeans. 'Tide's coming in fast. We've got to get the coastguard *now*.' He punched buttons, and groaned. 'Check yours.'

Her own phone was also waterlogged. 'Oh God . . . Won't your brother have already called them?'

'They won't come soon enough – he'll be sure we're dead. And he'll be right about that if we don't get somewhere higher in the next few minutes . . .' Between them and the smooth base of the cliff was a roaring cauldron of thick foam; the waves surged in and out of a low sea cave. To the right of the cave entrance was a narrow shelf, rising three metres out of the thrashing water. 'We'll have to try for that ledge. Here, hold me round the neck like I'm giving you a piggyback and I'll bring you across.'

Staring at the wildness of the waves, she said, 'It's all right. I can swim.'

'No, you're too light, the undertow is mad, you'll get swept out and then I'll have to come after you and we'll both drown. This way, at least we'll have a chance.' Shay sat himself on the edge of the rock, his legs dangling in the water. 'Come on, don't stop to think about it. Quick, before the waves get too big again.'

'Oh God . . .' Aoife knelt and passed her arms around his neck, and he slid with her into the water and swam for the cliff with strong, even strokes, his body twisting beneath her like she was riding a warm seal. They were only a metre away from the ledge when a huge wave took over and carried them past it through a thick curtain of spray, straight in under the low stone arch.

Being inside the cave was like being in a giant washing machine – thick white foam rushed up the walls and churning water rolled them over and over, tearing her from his back. She floundered, sank, then got her head out of the sea, choking. A rock shelf rose right in front of her and she grabbed for it, found handholds, scrambled up and turned to help him follow – just in time to see his black head being carried out of the cave in the white storm of water. '*Shay!*' She braced herself to dive back in, but already the waves were returning him. Dropping flat, she reached her hand down as far as she could. 'Over here!' Seeing her, Shay made a strong effort to reach her, but before he could get hold of her hand the waves pulled him out again, and it was nearly a minute this time before he was back, clearly exhausted now, beating the water feebly, not even really swimming any more – just desperately trying not to drown. When the sea had again pushed him to within a metre of the shelf, Aoife managed to grab a handful of his Mayo shirt. 'I've got you!' The swell was sinking again, sucking him with it. 'Shay!' His face was white, his eyes half closed. 'Shay, please!' Her right shoulder was coming out of its socket. His shirt was slipping from her grip . . .

'*Shay!*'

His eyes popped open. He glanced around as if surprised by where he was, then grabbed for the sharp edge of the shelf. Moments later he was kneeling on the rock, puking up water and shivering violently. Aoife crouched over him, rubbing his back. After a while he stopped coughing and sank down onto his stomach and lay limply, water running down his cheeks from his long black lashes.

'Don't go to sleep! Wake up!' She rubbed harder, frantic, trying to warm him, massaging his shoulders and arms and legs. 'Talk to me . . .' Shay remained flat and completely still. She lay down beside him, trying to press warmth into him with her whole body; she looked into his face – was he even breathing? 'Shay, don't do this to me . . .'

He opened one eye and winked at her. '*Wahu.*'

She sat up and slapped him sharply, between his shoulder blades. 'I thought you'd died on me!'

'Ow!' He sat up, laughing, then jumped to his feet as water flooded suddenly across the shelf. 'Tide's still coming in. Let's move back a way, see if we can find higher ground.' The shelf on which they had found refuge continued along the side of the cave, rising gently until it disappeared into blackness.

Alarmed, Aoife said, 'But the coastguard will never see us back there in the dark.'

'Doesn't matter either way – we won't be getting out of here until the next low tide.'

'Oh God . . . How long till then?'

'Ten hours?'

'*Ten hours?*'

'Hang on.' Shay was hunting through his jeans. 'Damn. Thought I had this little yokey-bob on me, sort of a key-ring torch thing, but I must have lost it back there.'

The sea poured over the shelf again.

After a short distance they had to get down on their hands and knees because a shelf of rock thrusting out over the ledge made it impossible to stand; then the way became so narrow they had to go in single file. Aoife went first. Gradually the blackness into which she was crawling grew so thick that she had no idea if they were still going up or down. She pulled out her phone – still dead: no chance of using it to light the way. The little locket came with it, the chain winding itself around her fingers. For safekeeping, she clipped it around her neck.

Down, down . . .

No. They had to go up.

A moment later Aoife scraped her head on the rock above and called back to Shay, 'Watch out – roof's getting low!' She got down on her elbows and crawled on. *Down* . . . Aloud, she said, 'Up. We have to go up.'

Shay's hand gripped her ankle. 'Aoife, wait – maybe we should turn round while we still can, see if we've missed a place where we can get higher.'

'No, this way.' She jerked her leg, shaking him off. 'It's this way. We have to go . . .' *Down.* 'Up. I'm sure this way is still rising.' But hardly had she said the words when the floor and ceiling met in a wedge. 'Ah, crap.'

'What?'

'I think it's a dead end.' *Down. Down.* Aoife felt around in the darkness, and there was the narrowest of gaps, just big enough to squeeze through, one at a time. 'No, it's all right. It carries on the other side.'

'Let me see.' Shay crawled in beside her, and then she could feel his warm hand next to hers, fumbling around in the cleft. 'No, it slopes down really sharply. If we climb in here and the sea tops this end of the ledge, we'll be drowned like rats in a hole. We have to go back and find another way.'

Down. Aoife thrust her head and arms into the crevice.

'Hey, what are you doing? Don't . . .'

Down. She pulled herself in.

CHAPTER THIRTEEN

She shouldn't have left him. Yet she couldn't go back, she had to go . . .

Down.

He would follow her. If she just kept going, he would have to follow. And if he didn't . . . He would. He *would*.

But what if he did, and he was right, and they were trapped and drowned?

Down, down, down . . .

It was the only way – Aoife could feel it in her heart. There was no going back. The roof was getting lower again and the blackness was as thick as oil, but she dropped flat and crawled blindly on, wriggling down the increasingly narrow tunnel, dragging and pushing herself forward with her fingers and toes, grazing her belly on the rock, scraping her elbows on the walls.

Moments later she felt as if her skull had been split in two by an axe. She lay gasping, hand clasped to her forehead. It was wet and sticky with blood. As the pain subsided, she took her hand away, and a faint light filled the tunnel. Her palm was smeared with light. As she stared at it, another iridescent glittering splash hit the sandy floor. Her own blood, shining like silver . . . *Shining?*

In her father's story, the changeling's hand had been injured and her blood had shone. The changeling was her. Maybe the magic was coming back to her, now that she was . . .

Now that she was what?

Down.

She had to go on, but she had a choice to make. The light of her own blood, slowly fading, was still bright enough to show her that the way had split into two tunnels, with a sharp dividing wall between them. One passageway was high enough for her to make her way on her hands and knees. The other was as low and narrow as the tunnel down which she had come.

Just as Aoife was making up her mind to take the easier path, she became aware of a distant hissing sound, rapidly growing in intensity. The next moment cold water spread out beneath her. Terror briefly gripped her, but the incoming ocean merely flowed on around her without getting any deeper, pouring down the narrower tunnel to her right. So that was the steepest way. That was *down*.

Before going on, she unclipped the locket and looped it over a spit of rock above the entrance to the narrower tunnel – then smeared a little of her own blood on the gold. If the light didn't fade too fast, Shay might see it there in the darkness – a small ghostly heart, showing him the way.

The new path descended much more steeply than the first. The rapidly running water, a couple of centimetres deep, made the rock slippery, and after a while Aoife was sliding as much as crawling on her elbows. And then, with a startled intake of breath, *only* sliding, like down the water chute at a fun park. But this wasn't fun, it was terrifying. She couldn't stop herself, couldn't see where she was going. Any moment now she was going to be tipped over the edge of an abyss, and fall and fall . . .

She fell.

And slammed so hard into solid rock that she thought she'd broken her shoulder. Waiting for the agony to die down, she lay there panting, then tried to move her arm, and couldn't. Maybe she really *had* broken her shoulder.

Her other arm wouldn't move either.

Nor her legs.

Was it her neck that she had broken? No, don't panic – she could move her fingers and toes. Somehow she must have got herself stuck in a cleft in the rock. Aoife struggled to free herself, but was unable to move. She struggled again. And again. It made no difference. She was completely wedged, lying on her front with her head twisted to one side. In the absolute dark it was impossible even to tell which way she was lying – staring into the crack in which she was trapped, or looking back the way she had fallen.

Nothing to do now but wait and trust that Shay would come. She strained her ears, listening hopefully to the silence. Water was still running somewhere nearby, gurgling faintly over stones, but there was no other sound.

Had he even tried to follow her at all? Aoife had been so certain that he would – but then, why would he? He had said they'd be drowned if they came this way, caught like rats in a trap, and she had ignored him. Maybe he had done the sensible thing, and let her go on alone.

After what seemed like hours, even the water stopped trickling, and then there was nothing.

Then there was something. A single bright pinpoint in the darkness. A random neuron firing in her brain? But the light stayed, until after a few minutes she was almost convinced it was getting closer. Even if it wasn't, at least it wasn't moving away – that would have been an unspeakable, horrible disaster. As she lay paralysed in the dark, this tiny pinprick, this eye of light, had already become the focus of all her hopes and dreams.

Come closer. Come closer.

She *wasn't* imagining it. It *was* getting closer. She loved the little light. It was her friend.

And suddenly – an unbelievable gift – there was sound. Not the sea water running again, but a low agitated whispering. And the whisperer was saying:

'Jesus and Mary, Holy Mother of God . . . JAYSUS!'

The light disappeared as Shay crashed violently into the rock beside her.

'Shay, are you all right?'

'Aoife, thank God . . .'

'Can you move?'

'Let me check. Yup, nothing broken. You?'

'I'm kind of stuck.'

'Hang on a minute. Where is it . . . ? You have to keep pressing this thing or— Ah!' The eye of light suddenly reappeared, probing towards her.

Aoife's heart swelled with joy. 'That's so beautiful, the light . . .'

'It's the torch I was telling you about – handy little key-ring yoke. Penknife on it too. Thought I'd lost it but I had it after all.' Shay was running the narrow beam over her face and body as he spoke. He said softly, '*Wahu*. Fancy meeting you here.' Aoife couldn't see his face behind the halo of the little torch, but she could hear the smile in his voice.

Smiling herself, she said, 'Yeah, well, you took long enough.'

'I know it. I got jammed in that tunnel a couple of times – thought I'd never make it through. Looks like you got a bit of a bump on the forehead yourself.'

'Can we cut the chat and get me out of here?'

He laughed. 'You're not really in a position to give orders, you know. Still, here goes . . .' He clenched the torch between his teeth and eased his hands in around her head. 'You really have got yourself stuck, haven't you?'

'*Aargh!*'

'I seriously wouldn't scream like that—'

'Of course I'm going to scream. You nearly ripped my ear off!'

'Sorry, I'm sorry, but don't scream. There's been no high-pitched girly screaming down here for billions of years. Supposing the vibrations set off some movement in the rock? It settles by a millimetre, your brains are toothpaste.'

'Thanks for the picture.' But Aoife tried to do no more than whimper softly as Shay eased first her head, then her shoulders from the crack, after which she got her own hands free and prised herself out with an effort that rucked her hoodie and T-shirt up over her stomach.

Shay switched the thin beam of light away from her, illuminating the narrow wet gutter in which they had ended up. There was a lot of wet sand, and small stones and shells, presumably washed down by the ocean. He cast the light upwards. The roof bellied tent-like just above them, an odd greenish colour, as if covered with moss. The long steep slope down which they had slithered had ended in a shallow drop of about two metres. The black rock was glittering wet but no longer running with water – the high tide must already have sunk below the narrow opening far above.

Shay said, 'We can probably climb back up. It's going to be difficult because it's so slippery, but it's the only way.' He turned the light towards her and cried in alarm, 'What are you doing? *Stop!*'

There were loose stones piled up at the back of the small crevice in which Aoife had been wedged and she was kneeling, pulling them out, jerking and tugging at the ones that wouldn't easily come free. They were egg-shaped and mottled green. 'Help me! There's a way through here!'

'No, stop! Do you want to kill us altogether? They might be holding something up . . . Aoife, *stop!*'

She stopped. But her heart was trembling with excitement. *Down* . . .

Shay groaned, 'Oh Jesus . . .'

Dust and tiny glittering rock particles had begun showering around them like dry rain. Startled, Aoife looked up. The greenish rock above their heads was rippling faintly, like water. A single stone fell from it, and rolled around in the gutter. Another stone hit her on the shoulder. She said anxiously, turning towards him, 'Shay?'

He was staring upwards with wide eyes as the dust sparkled down onto his face. A deafening bang jerked Aoife's gaze back to the roof. A zigzag crack like a bolt of black lightning had just ripped across it.

'Take my hand!' Shay fell on his knees, pulling her beside her. With his free hand, he crossed himself, gazing upwards. 'Hail Mary full of grace, the Lord is with thee . . .' The zigzag crack was spreading wider and wider, and now more stones were hailing down. 'Blessed are you among women and blessed is the fruit of thy womb, Jesus . . .'

A terrible roar, a peal of mighty thunder building, building . . .

He pushed her to the floor and crouched over her, trying to shelter her with his body. 'Pray, Aoife. This is it . . . Pray!'

She gazed up into his eyes. 'Hail Mary, Mother of God . . .'

He touched her cheek and murmured, 'Pray for us sinners . . .' For the first time Aoife noticed that he had her gold heart clipped around his wrist.

The stone shower was growing heavier. The rocks were hitting every part of her that he was unable to protect – hands, feet . . . His body kept jerking as the unbearable shower rained down on his back. 'Hail Mary, Mother of God, pray for us sinners Seamus Michael Foley and Aoife O'Connor now and at the hour of our death . . .'

The stones were rising faster around them, burying them. He sank down on top of her.

'I love you, Aoife O'Connor . . .'

The little key-ring light blinked out.

END OF BOOK ONE

BOOK TWO

BOOK TWO

CHAPTER ONE

Blackness. Silence.

Death.

Yet how could she be dead? She could feel his body, warm and heavy, lying over hers. The hard pressure of his jaw against her cheek. The softness of his lashes against her temple. His arms still tightly locked around her, protecting her from the falling rocks. The beat of his heart . . .

'Shay? Are you there?' Aoife's voice echoed loud in the enclosed space.

Blackness. Silence.

Or was it only her own heart, beating alone in the darkness?

She whispered, 'Shay?'

He did not stir. His body lay so heavily upon her.

He had to be alive – she could feel the warmth of him.

In the tiny amount of wriggle-room he had created for her by throwing himself across her, she twisted her head; her mouth slid across his cheek. Was his skin already turning cool? No, no, he couldn't be dead . . . She laid her lips to his velvety eyelashes. Deep beneath the earth, she breathed in the grassy farm-boy smell of him, overlaid by the saltiness of the sea water in which his hair was still coldly soaked. She tried to move her trapped arms, and finally, centimetre by centimetre, found a way to slide them up around him and hold him tight against her. 'Shay, wake up. Please, please wake up.'

Blackness. Silence.

Aoife tightened her arms around him. Her heart welled with grief and shame. 'I'm sorry, Shay. I'm so, so sorry.' He'd wanted them to crawl back along the ledge, to find another way; she'd insisted on squeezing through that tiny gap into the black bowels of the cliff. She hadn't *ordered* him to follow her . . . But she'd known full well that he would, and still she'd gone − driven downwards by that terrible compulsion, an emotional gravity impossible to resist, the same incomprehensible force that had driven her to leap from the cliff into empty air . . . Could a dropped stone resist falling to the earth? Yet she should have been stronger, fought against it, for his sake.

I love you, Aoife O'Connor.

If only she had answered him at that very split second: *I love you too.* But everything had been happening so fast, the deafening roar of the cliff sinking down on them. Then, by the time it had faded away into a last small trickle of stones, it was too late. Shay had taken the whole weight of the cliff upon his back, to save her.

At least she could say his own words back to him now. Now, she had all the time in the world. She whispered, her lips moving against his ear, 'I love you too.'

And listened as the echo of her whisper died away.

Infinitely soft: '*Wahu . . .*'

Aoife's heart bounded. '*Shay?*'

Blackness. Silence.

Her imagination.

Her muscles were stiffening, and her throat was sandpaper dry. How long would it take to die of thirst and starvation? A week? A month? Would it be very painful?

She shouldn't be hoping for him to be still alive, she should be praying for him to be dead. Wishing, for his sake, that he had gone first, without her, switched out for ever like the light of his tiny torch. That way he wouldn't have to wait with her in this dreadful dark for a long slow death.

It felt impossible to hope that he was dead.

'Shay? Shay? Can you hear me?'

No answer.

Blackness. Silence.

Deep, deep beneath the surface of the earth they lay together in their tomb of solid stone, locked in each other's arms, awaiting the end of time.

CHAPTER TWO

She came alert to a clatter of stones and braced herself, waiting for a second avalanche of rocks to finish the job, crushing the two of them to human paste.

Yet the weight on her was not increasing, but lessening . . .

A cool wisp of air drifted across her skin, and then, unbelievably, a young man's voice said in a Mayo accent: 'What the divil is this lad doing here?'

And a child's voice exclaimed: 'There's a girl with him!'

'Holy Mary, Mother of God . . .'

Had the coastguard found them? Had they actually managed to follow them down under the cliffs? Amazing! Unbelievable! Aoife tried to open her eyes, but they seemed glued together. Now someone was trying to ease Shay's body from her grasp, but her arms were too rigid to release him.

'She's as stiff as a board – is she dead?'

'Maybe. Careful, don't break her arms . . .'

Someone forced her hands apart, and Shay was gone. She tried to ask if he was alive, but her lips were so dry she couldn't peel them apart.

Now she was being lifted from her grave, in someone's arms, and then set down again on a flat surface. A hand was holding her wrist; she could feel a finger pressing against her vein. The deeper voice said, 'I think I can feel a pulse.'

The child's voice said, 'Will I give her some of my potion?'

The other laughed. 'Christ, no – you don't want to be poisoning her.'

'Just a dropeen. It's magic.'

'Donal, stop fooling yerself, ye've got no powers—'

'It's *magic*.' A thin metallic edge was being forced between Aoife's lips, clinking against her teeth; sticky liquid trickled across her tongue and down the back of her throat. An icy purple tide swept through her skull. Seconds later, she could open her eyes and her tongue came unstuck from the roof of her mouth.

She whispered hoarsely. 'Shay . . .'

'Hey, Ultan, she's after waking up!' The young boy kneeling over her was only about ten or eleven years old, snub-nosed and freckled with bright red hair, wearing a collarless shirt, a red necktie and short woollen trousers like something you might see in an old photograph from the fifties.

'What were you after doing trying to get through the tunnel, missus? That way is blocked.' The child not only looked old-fashioned, he talked like an old farmer from back the bog. 'Only for that we were out here looking for our cat and heard the crash . . . Where d'ye spring from anyway? I've been down here as long as anyone and I never seen you afore this. Here . . .' And from a leather pouch with a bronze ring at the neck he tipped a little more of the liquid into her mouth.

Another wave of ice swept across Aoife's brain and everything went bright purple, but then her vision cleared again and expanded. She could turn her head. She was still in the cave . . . No, a *different* cave; smaller with white, pink-veined walls and a moss-carpeted floor. Soft daylight was leaking in through the ferns and flowering brambles that curtained the arched entrance. Blue-and-green dragonflies darted in and out, and pencil-thin waterfalls bubbled down the walls. From the hidden world beyond came the sound of birds singing. *Please God let this not be a dream . . .*

The boy tipped yet another drop of liquid into her mouth. She sat up unsteadily.

The boy laughed, and tossed the pouch to someone behind her. 'See. Who says I'm too young to have got my powers?'

Aoife turned in time to see a plump youth of about seventeen catch the pouch; he too was wearing odd clothes – in his case an electric-blue eighties-style shell suit. Her first thought was that she'd seen this boy before, wearing those very clothes. But then she saw Shay, and forgot everything else.

He was lying on his back, white-faced and completely still, his eyes closed. She scrambled towards him on her hands and knees. 'Shay!' She stroked his black hair. His hands were folded on his chest, her gold locket still clasped around his wrist. 'Shay, wake up!'

The youth tipped a few drops from the flask

between Shay's slightly parted lips, saying, 'I guess it can't make him any the worse than he is now.' The juice ran out of the corner of Shay's mouth, as red as blood.

'He'll soon be back to himself,' said the younger boy, squatting down beside her. 'That stuff is powerful. Made it from berries of hawthorn. I do have special skills that way.'

'Shay, wake up! Shay, we've been rescued.' A terrible sob was pushing its way out of Aoife's chest into her throat. 'Wake up – oh please, wake up . . .' Why hadn't she said it while she had a chance? *I love you too.*

'Give him more, Ultan – a bird never flew on one wing.'

'I don't think it's going to do the trick, Donal.'

'It will, it's my *power*. You just haven't given him enough! Here . . .' The child grabbed the flask and tipped all the rest of it into Shay's mouth.

'Aah . . . Christ, what the . . .' Shay's eyes flew open and he rolled over onto his front, shuddering, coughing up foaming red liquid from the depths of his guts. His Mayo shirt was torn across the back, and his skin was violently bruised and scraped. 'Holy

Mother of . . .' He struggled to sit up and nearly fell backwards.

Aoife caught him, cradling him, supporting him. She was sobbing with happiness. 'Oh my God, you're alive . . .'

His head lolled against her shoulder. 'Is that you?'

'Can't you see me?'

'Everything's purple . . .'

'CAT! CAT!'

A tall, broad-shouldered, big-boned teenage girl with a bright red waist-length plait came leaping – flying, almost – over the high brambles and giant ferns that clustered around the entrance and landed, knees bent, in the centre of the cave. 'Come quick, I seen it asleep in the sun!' A year or two older than Aoife, she was wearing flared maroon cords with embroidered patches, a flowered blouse and strings of coloured beads swinging from her neck. She stared at Aoife – 'Where'd she come from?' – and then at Shay, slumped in Aoife's arms. 'What's the matter with your man?'

Donal boasted, 'I gave him my juice!'

'You did what? No wonder he's looks rough.

Come on, Ultan, we can creep up on the cat while it's sleeping.'

Ultan said to the child, 'You stay here.'

'Hey, no, I want to come! Caitlin?'

'Course you can. Don't humanize the kid, Ultan, he'll be grand. Hurry!' The girl leaped high over the brambles again, out of the cave.

'Donie, I'm telling you, stay here. Ye've got no powers.' But as the plump teenager forced his way through the thorns in Caitlin's wake, the small boy, with a wink at Aoife and a finger to his lips, sneaked after him.

Aoife cried hastily, 'Hey, no – come back, tell us where . . .' And then the child was gone.

Left alone in the cave, she bent her head over Shay. 'Can you see me yet?'

His green-gold gaze drifted up towards her, and seemed to find her face. He said dreamily, '*Wahu . . .*' and his eyes moved away again, slowly taking in the cave, the ferns, the trickling water, the dragonflies. He sat up suddenly. 'What the . . . ? I thought we were dead and a million miles underground!'

'I know! But then these two lads turned up

and dug us out and we were alive and here!'

'*How?*'

'I don't know! It's incredible! Maybe we made it all the way under the cliff and came out in the valley on the other side . . .'

Shay twisted to stare at her. 'That must be it. What an escape. I can't believe you're alive.'

'Me neither, about you.'

He said nothing for long moment, facing Aoife with his ankles crossed and his arms wrapped around his knees, his eyes moving slowly across her face, as if he were still uncertain she was real.

Maybe she should say it now. *I love you too.* But then, back in the cave with the roof crashing down on them, he had been sure they were about to die. And people might say a lot of things they don't really mean, in that sort of situation.

He broke eye contact, and glanced towards the cave mouth. 'Where did the lads go?'

'They ran off when this girl came in saying she'd found their cat.'

'They must live nearby. I wonder do I know them?'

'You might. I think I kind of knew the older

one myself, I just can't think where from . . .'

'Come on, we'll track them down and get a lend of one of their phones to call John Joe. Tell him there's been a miracle.' Shay stood up unsteadily. 'Ah Jesus, the state of me, I'm in bits . . .' Aoife offered her arm, but he waved it away. 'You're grand. Go on, I'll follow.'

The high brambles blocking the entrance were covered with blackberries as huge as grapes. Aoife grabbed a handful as she pushed her way through, cramming them into her mouth. They were so delicious, they brought tears to her eyes. 'Shay, you have to try some of these.' The birdsong became even louder as she pushed her way into the sunlit world – and caught her breath in disbelief.

She had been expecting to see the lilac bog land of north Mayo. Instead, she was standing on a white marble ledge gazing out over a vast pink and white blossoming forest of fruit trees, stretching for mile after mile unbroken to the horizon. Hundreds of rainbows arched above it across a turquoise sky, and around the horizon pure white mountains shone. A sparkling rose-quartz cliff sloped upwards behind her, its pointed summit disappearing into the blue; vines tumbled down its crystal walls, and from every crevice of the rock face thrust yet more blossoming fruit trees, haloed in pale blue clouds of butterflies.

Shay had pushed his way out of the brambles and had come to stand beside her. Aoife turned to him, wide-eyed, speechless. A strange joy was rising in her heart, like a warm tide. Was this the world of the Tuatha Dé Danann, the Land of the Young?

He, on the other hand, seemed a little sad. He said, a catch in his throat, 'So we did die, after all.'

'Oh . . .' The tide of her joy ebbed. 'Do you really think?'

'A cliff falls on our heads and we wake up in paradise. What else could explain it, apart from our being dead?'

'I don't know . . . I just feel so alive . . .' Really hungry, for instance, even after eating the blackberries. 'You think we're in heaven?'

Shay turned to her, studied her face, then slightly smiled. 'Well, I know I am, anyway. I'm not sure about you.'

'How do you mean?'

'Maybe you're not dead. Maybe in the real world, wherever it is, you're walking around, still alive.'

'But I'm here, with you!'

'Of course you are. My heaven wouldn't be perfect without you. And if this is *my* heaven . . .' Shay seemed suddenly very happy, though in a slightly wild way; the depths of his green eyes glinted gold, like the sunlit floor of streams. He took her hands, and his flesh was warm; he pulled her gently towards him, then transferred his grip so he was holding both her hands in one of his. He used his other hand to tilt up her chin. 'If this is my own perfect heaven, made especially for me . . .'

His mouth came close to hers.

Aoife held her breath. Vaguely she was aware that the birds had stopped singing, as though everything in Shay's heaven was waiting to see what was going to happen next—

A high-pitched, unearthly howling replaced the silence of the birds, and three voices were screaming and shouting at once.

'*CLOUD IT AGAIN!*'

'*I'm trying!*'

'*AGAIN!*'

'*It's getting away!*'

'*I CAN'T HOLD IT!*'

'*Move, move, move!!!*'

With a high scream, Donal came bolting out of the fringe of the woods, scrambled up to the ledge and shot straight past them into the cave – his cheek was badly slashed. Ultan and the big bright-haired girl came streaming after him, dragging a large net between them.

'Get in!' the girl yelled at Aoife and Shay. 'Cat's coming! Get in! Are ye fools or what? *Get in!*'

Once inside, Caitlin and Ultan hastily tied the net over the mouth of the cave, securing it to several thick tree roots that had forced their way in through cracks and crevices. Then they flattened themselves against the walls on either side of the entrance, watching the net like spiders watching their web. Shay pulled Aoife beside him against the damp marble wall; he said in her ear, 'Are these the guys that rescued us?'

'That boy there was one of them – I wonder what happened to the little one?' Donal seemed to have disappeared entirely – but then Aoife saw the top of his head bobbing about at floor level near the back of the cave; he had hidden himself in the hole left by the collapsed tunnel. 'And that cute little kid back there with the bright red hair.'

'What are they playing at, running from a cat?'

'I've no idea . . .'

Ultan reached out and tested the net with his hand. 'Caitlin, do you think maybe you should just blast it, soon as it appears?'

'Danu, no. Don't want to kill it. Just cloud it. Ye'll be able to give it a good dose when it's stuck in the net.'

'Just, it got a taste of Donal's blood—'

'Here it comes!'

A split second later, a huge white cat came leaping over the wall of brambles like a demon out of hell and crashed straight into the net.

Caitlin screamed: 'Cloud it! Cloud it!'

The creature was a domestic white cat – yet it was monstrous, nearly two metres long from nose to tail. It was struggling to free itself, rolling around in the net, screeching like a tortured soul, clawing at the strands, lashing with its tail. Aoife was sick with horror – she felt Shay pass his arm around her, holding her against him.

Caitlin shrieked, 'Ultan, it's getting free!'

'I've got it!' Thick black smoke was pouring from Ultan's hands and the beast was writhing, frothing at the mouth, eyes rolling, choking, clearly weakening, drowning in the fog . . . With a last furious effort, it tore the net apart with its teeth, broke free and headed straight for the back of the cave.

Ultan shrieked, '*Look out, Donal!*'

Donal's bright head popped up over the edge of the hole to see what was going on – and that was a terrible mistake. The cat seized his whole head like a ball of red wool, stuffing it into its mouth, wrapping its giant paws around his waist, sinking its teeth into his neck.

With an inarticulate but warlike yell, Shay launched himself from Aoife's side towards the monster, throwing himself full-length on the beast's back. The cat instantly bucked him off against the cave wall. At the same moment a hydrant of blue fire burst across the cave – it came from Caitlin's raised right hand and hit the cat square at the base of its spine, setting its tail on fire; the creature yowled and rose up on its hind legs, whipping Donal's body even harder from side to side – there was a sharp crack, and the child's muffled screams from inside the monster's mouth abruptly ceased.

Aoife still could not move. A terrible energy was rising through her and yet at the same time paralysing her, as if her body were being drained of blood and slowly refilled with freezing acid; with a great effort, she managed to raise one hand towards the dreadful sight of Donal, limp and broken-necked, being dragged around like a dead mouse . . .

The cat, now seriously on fire, dropped the boy and crashed over onto its back, writhing and mewing in agony. The others threw themselves upon it, Ultan wrapping the net around its paws and head, Shay jabbing with his key-ring penknife at the creature's ribcage – buttercup-yellow blood bursting from every hole he made. Caitlin was shouting at Shay, 'Stop, ya fool! We have to bring it back alive!'

At last the cat lay trussed too tight to struggle free, bleeding from its wounds, fur smouldering, hissing faintly in its throat.

Donal's small body was curled up in the corner of the cave.

Before Aoife could get to him, Shay had already

gathered him up, holding him against his chest like he had held the lamb on the cliff, touching the child's closed eyes, his wounded neck, his limp white hands. 'Come back . . . Come back . . .'

Ultan said, hanging over him, 'Donie, Donie, come on – you're in paradise, you can't die on us now, man!'

The leather flask was still lying among the stones, where Shay had knocked it from Donal's hands. Aoife pounced on it and shook it desperately into Donal's mouth. No red liquid dripped out.

Ultan groaned hoarsely, 'He used the last of it on you two, man. Generous to the last.'

Caitlin, standing further back with her arms by her sides, said grimly, 'Sure, it was only juice. He never had any real powers. Not old enough. Came home too soon.' Blue fire was still draining from her hands in fits and starts like they were gas rings on a cooker not completely turned off.

'He can't be dead!' Aoife was trying desperately not to cry. 'He can't be, he's too young—'

'Wait,' said Shay. 'Wait.' He pushed back Donal's bright red hair, lowered his head to drop a light kiss on the child's bared forehead.

The child stirred; eyelashes fluttered open; he smiled, his pale skin flushed, freckles darkened, his hair seemed to turn an even deeper red, eyes not pale blue but brilliant sapphire; he looked up at Shay and said in a voice as high and clear as a bell, 'Did you ever meet my mam and da? They're called Padraig and Mary McGoldrick.' And then his face slumped against Shay's shoulder, and he was gone.

CHAPTER THREE

They chose a final resting place for the child beneath a large spreading apple tree on the edge of the forest, and lined his grave with dandelions and kingcups, meadowsweet and wild violets. The warm breeze through the apple leaves shook down fruit and blossom into the freshly dug earth.

Aoife found it unbelievable, shocking, desperate, that her first act in heaven was to dig a grave, and for such a little boy. What manner of paradise was this?

And the guilt . . . Her heart was breaking with it. She was the only one who had done nothing to try to save him. Miserably, she pulled up armfuls of wild bluebells and threw them down into the hole. Ultan was sitting on the grass by Donal's body, his head buried in his arms. Shay was using his key-ring penknife to strip the bark from two willow wands. The girl was standing at the edge of the grave with her arms crossed over her flowery blouse and strings of wooden beads.

As she dropped in the last of the bluebells, Aoife asked through tears, 'Do we know where is his mam and dad?'

Caitlin slowly turned her head to stare at her. She was taller than Aoife, wide-shouldered and big-boned – her face strong and commanding, freckled pale, with stone-green eyes. 'How would we know?'

'We have their names – Padraig and Mary McGoldrick. Is there no way of finding them to tell them what's happened?'

The girl continued to stare at her. 'You do know he wasn't talking about his real parents, don't you?'

'But he said—'

'Those were the humans who brought him up, before he came home to this world. And what would they be doing here? We are fairies. This is *our* world.'

'Donal was a *fairy*?'

'Are you thick or what? Course he was fay, a changeling same as you and me. Only reason he had no powers, he came home too young. Did you imagine he was one of those stupid useless human children got themselves stolen by the banshees?'

The contempt with which the girl said 'human children' turned Aoife's skin cold – she glanced quickly at Shay, who was binding the willow sticks into a cross. 'Then shouldn't we tell his real parents, from this world?'

Caitlin shrugged, flicking back her bright red plait. 'Gone to the islands long ago. We're on our own here. Didn't you know? Danu's sake, will you stop crying.'

Aoife sobbed helplessly, 'Why should I? He was only a little boy and his parents don't even know he's dead.'

'He's not dead.'

'What do you mean he's not dead? We're burying him!'

'For Christ's . . . Danu's sake, this is *paradise* – don't you get it? We're fay! We don't die! Did the druid not teach you anything in Falias? Did you not pay attention to your instructions? If fairies get damaged in their original form, they just transform and come back in a different way. It's all in the book. It's not dying, it's being reborn. Ultan, pull yourself together – this is not a human funeral!'

'Sorry . . . Sorry . . .' The soft-faced lad was wiping his nose on his sleeve. 'It's just reminding me of when Trisha died.'

'*Transformed*.'

'When she got transformed. Reborn.'

'The daisies are coming up on her already, hey?'

'I know, I'm sorry.'

'So stop blubbing. The sooner Donal begins his transformation, the sooner he'll be after being reborn again, like Trish.'

'I'll get on with it, so . . .' Ultan raised Donal's body gently from the grassy bank where he had been lying, jumped down into the grave and placed him on the deep bed of flowers. He arranged the small legs stiffly straight in their short woollen trousers, and crossed the hands over the old-fashioned shirt, using the necktie to cover up the bite-marks to his tender throat. He laid a wild daffodil over the wound on Donal's cheek, and stood over the boy for a long moment before climbing back out onto the grass. Clearing his throat, he said, 'Caitlin, will you be wanting to say a few words?'

The girl rolled her eyes. 'I said, this isn't a human funeral.'

'I know, I just think it would be nice.'

'He's going to be transformed and come back to us. We're fay. We don't have to say goodbye.'

'Still, I'm thinking a few words . . .'

She turned away. 'You do it if you want. Just don't say anything thick and *sad*.'

Ultan took up position at the head of the grave, folded and unfolded his large soft hands. 'Donal . . . um . . .' He hesitated, large brown eyes rolling slightly up and to the left. Aoife assumed he was searching his head for the Catholic litany with which every person in Kilduff was buried, and knelt in the grass. Shay sank to his knees on the far side, his dark lashes lowered to his cheeks, the fresh-made cross lying on the grass by his side. The cat's buttery blood was still splashed across his shirt.

Ultan said: 'Donal . . . er . . . um . . .'

Shay crossed himself; the gold locket finely chained around his wrist caught the sun.

Caitlin was standing a short distance away with

her back to the tree, arms laced tight across her chest, as if – despite all her show of not caring – she was clutching a heavy weight to her heart. 'Get on with it.'

Ultan shot an anxious smile in her direction. 'OK, I have it now . . .' He brought his gaze back to the child lying in the hole at his feet. He rubbed his nose with the back of his hand, blackening it with a muddy streak. The feeling of his face being familiar came over Aoife again, though she still couldn't place him. Maybe from a photograph? He straightened his shoulders.

'Donie . . . Donal, you were – *are* – a very nice little boy and you deserve a bit of a rest after that terrible thing with the *cat-sidhe* – we're sorry about that – so lie here under this earth for as long as you want and then wake and grow upwards until you find the sun and wind and rain, and then you can be reborn as flowers and trees and fruit because you know things grow very fast down here, and then insects and mice and stuff like that, and eventually we know you will come back to yourself as a fay . . . And enjoy the journey, OK? We all love you and we're going to plant an apple right here on top of you, and we'll come back every so often and see how you're getting on with your rebirth, and when the tree is grown and has a few small apples on it, we'll pick one and eat it, and if it's very small but very sweet and not at all sour, then we'll know for sure it comes from you, Donie, so until then, you know, farewell.'

Licking salt tears from her lips, Aoife remembered the bee she had crushed in her hand, and how she had buried it in the school grounds outside the history room, and how she had known deep inside herself that through that process the bee would be transformed. That roots would sink into its flesh and draw up its energy and make a flower, and bees would drink from it, and make other bees. She tried now to feel the same certainty about Donal, but it was harder somehow. Maybe she didn't need to mourn the buried child. But still she felt heavy, like her heart was weighing her down. He had been so very small, and very sweet. And generous, as Ultan had said. He had poured all his hawthorn juice into Shay's mouth, and even though Caitlin and Ultan didn't believe it was actual magic, it had seemed to bring Shay back to life.

Ultan said, 'I'm thinking we should cover him now.'

Shay said, 'Wait a moment . . .' and stood up from where he'd been kneeling, and took a handful of earth and threw it into the grave so that it pattered across the boy's bare grubby knees, saying, 'All-powerful and merciful God, we commend to you Donal, your servant. In this world he has died: let him live with you for ever. We ask this through Christ our Lord.' Then he jammed the willow cross he had made into the grass.

Aoife murmured into her palms, instinctively, 'Amen,' but Ultan looked anxious and Caitlin shouted furiously, 'What are you – *human*?'

Aoife feared for a moment that Shay would tell the truth, and then the changeling girl would maybe start some sort of a horrible stupid angry argument before they'd even finished burying the fairy child. But he just stooped to pick up one of the split branches they had used to dig the grave and began to fill it in.

'Come on, Caitlin,' pleaded Ultan, following suit. 'Take it handy. He's new here. Come on, it's not easy to forget all the aul nonsense right away.'

The girl glared at Shay for a long, suspicious moment, before saying, 'Grand. Hurry up and fill that in, and let's get back to camp before the rabbit is overdone. I'm that sick of burned rabbit.'

The changelings' camp was a steep climb away, up a narrow rose-quartz path which zigzagged sharply up the mountain.

Caitlin ran ahead in long bounds – leaping high and gliding back down, brief bursts of something almost like flying. Ultan was only trudging slowly upwards. He had pulled off his shell-suit jacket and was carrying it over his shoulder. Underneath, he was wearing a Blondie T-shirt.

Aoife fell back to walk beside Shay, though the path was barely wide enough for the two of them. She said, 'Do you think it's going to happen – that that poor kid will be reborn?'

He said quietly, 'Daisies grow on every grave.'

'No, I don't mean like that – you know what I mean: I mean coming back to himself. That girl Caitlin said it was different for us—' She broke off; he wasn't one of 'us' – he was human. 'You know, perhaps you'd better not say anything about—'

She stopped, not wanting to offend him.

Shay said nothing to fill her awkward silence; he was looking closely into every cave mouth – one after the other crowded by blackberries and ferns. The wild, glinting happiness that had shone out of him when he'd thought he was in heaven had been replaced by a pale, serious expression. It was as if he were disappointed at not having died himself.

Aoife brushed her elbow against a bramble, and small blue butterflies flooded the air around her. Her heart lifted. 'I think that little boy will be reborn, you know. I think he'll come back to himself.' Ridiculous not to believe in magical rebirth, when they were in paradise.

Shay glanced at her. 'I hope so.'

'No, he will – I can feel it.'

The higher they climbed, the more of the world came into view – mile after mile of flowering wilderness, steaming in the sun, being watered now by a delicate rain-mist that lay across it like gold and silver dust. Silver rivers wound through it. Far in the distance were the smooth white mountains. A huge, solitary bird – an eagle? – was drifting under the arching rainbows on widespread wings.

Aoife pointed at it. 'What do you think that is?'

'*Careful!*' Shay's hand flashed out to seize her arm. The path had taken a sudden twist and she'd nearly stepped off into empty air. He kept hold of her arm for a moment, then slowly let it go. 'By the way, I think this isn't a mountain we're climbing. I think it's a ruin.'

'A ruin?' She looked around, puzzled, at the overgrown rock face riddled with cave entrances.

'I mean, a pyramid. A city.'

And instantly, Aoife could see that he was right. If it hadn't been for all the recent growth pouring in and out of every doorway and window, it would have been obvious. They had been passing not cave after cave, but dwellings thick with ferns, courtyards brimming with fruit trees, corridors choked with brambles. And many of the vines and ferns weren't even living, but were stone frescoes made green by moss. Not a mountain, but a pyramid of houses and overgrown gardens piled one on another. She stared up in wonder. A city . . . Or something that had been a city before nature had taken over: layer upon layer of grass-covered roofs, crisscrossed and linked by narrow streets and sets of steps heading in all directions, fading upwards into the rainbow-strapped sky. An abandoned city, but still beautiful and magnificent in its abandonment.

Caitlin said through a mouthful of the rabbit, 'Yeah, this here is Gorias, one of the four cities. It's overgrown because no one's lived here since the queen died. How come you didn't know about the Exodus?'

'We only just got here.'

'Still, didn't you get taught all about everything by the druid?'

Ultan, who was using a knife to poke around in a bubbling clay pot, said, 'Maybe after you stole his—'

Caitlin elbowed him.

'Aargh! Just saying!'

'Well, don't.' She turned to Aoife again, continuing in an airy changing-the-subject tone, 'I've been here a while myself. Nearly a year – hard to tell – time slips by 'cos there's no seasons. I teamed up with Ultan in Falias and we got sent out here to catch beasts.'

Ultan fished something like a pale purple potato out of the pot and offered it to Aoife on the point of his knife. 'Try this.'

It was violently peppery. 'Delicious.'

'Donal loved them.' He sighed and dug around for another piece.

The four of them were squatting on rough wooden stools around a small fire in the centre of a little courtyard, over which the clay pot was suspended on a wooden tripod. A bronze fountain gurgled nearby, and beds of grass were piled in three of the corners. There were narrow apertures in the outer wall through which Aoife could see the white mountains, and a net made of vines was strung across their heads from wall to wall – for protection against monsters like the cat, she guessed.

Caitlin took an old-fashioned bronze knife similar to Ultan's and speared herself a piece of the boiled root. 'So, where did you leave your kit?'

'Kit?'

'Your *kit*.' She jerked her thumb at the far corner, to a small heap of leather bags with drawstring tops. 'What you were given in Falias.'

'We haven't been to Falias yet. We've only just got here. The tunnel we came through collapsed on us, and Ultan and poor Donal pulled us out. We were so lucky they found us . . .' Aoife glanced at Shay. He was in the act of flicking his rabbit bone towards one of the window-slits; it flew through the narrow gap without touching the sides.

Ultan, watching him, blurted out through a purple mouthful of root, 'Good shot!'

Moments later, Aoife became aware that Caitlin was staring at her angrily, a piece of root suspended on the point of her knife halfway to her mouth. 'What? What did I say?'

'You're seriously claiming you came straight here from the surface world?'

'That's right.'

'You're lying.'

'I am not—'

'The only way from the surface leads directly to Falias. All the other ways are blocked. The people of Danu pulled every tunnel down behind them during the Exodus.'

'Well, this one *was* blocked, but we broke through it.'

The girl placed her elbows squarely on her knees, turning the wrist of her right hand upwards so that the knife was pointing directly at Aoife's face – still with the piece of steaming root jammed on the tip of it. 'Who *are* you, hey? What are you doing here?'

'I've been trying to tell you! We were in a sea-cave above and the tide came in, and we found this tunnel...' Aoife glanced at Shay again, but he was paying no attention to this discussion – he was watching a caterpillar crawl across his palm, and gently closing his fingers over it. 'And then I did something crazy and the roof fell in on us...' Shay was slowly opening his hand again – a blue bog butterfly spread its wings in the sun.

Looking at the butterfly and frowning, Caitlin said, 'So I'm wondering...'

Throwing the butterfly into the air, Shay said, 'And I'm wondering, how long are you going to keep poking that damn knife in my friend's face?'

Caitlin's eyes narrowed; she turned her shoulder to him and leaned even further forward on her stool so that it tilted under her, and held the blade even closer to Aoife's eyes. 'So I'm wondering...'

Aoife fought the instinct to pull back her head. Keeping her voice low and steady, she said, 'Wondering *what*?'

Ultan said warningly, 'Caitlin.'

'I'm wondering, are the pair of ye changelings at all, or just a couple of filthy, spying, dirty hu—'

Shay stood up and slapped the knife out of Caitlin's hand so hard that it flew across the courtyard and straight out of the same narrow aperture through which he'd flicked the bone.

CHAPTER FOUR

'*Humans!*' The girl was on her feet, pointing at both Aoife and Shay. '*Humans!*' Her hands were shimmering with violet flame, and Ultan was yelling at her, 'Don't do it!' and Shay was shouting, 'Not her, me – just me!'

Aoife's veins were flooding with cold acid – not slowly, like when the cat was savaging Donal, but very fast – and a moment later it discharged from her fingertips and rushed across the courtyard so that the space between her and the changeling girl became for a split second a dark watery blur.

Caitlin flew into the air so high that only the net prevented her from continuing over the wall and down the face of the pyramid. 'Aargh!' She crashed down again, striking her forehead on the bronze fountain, and lay slumped with her face in the bubbling water, hands still fluttering with blue flame.

Ultan yelped, 'Jesus . . . Danu . . .' He rushed to lift her out of the water. 'You all right, Cait?'

As soon as she got her breath, she shoved him fiercely aside – 'I'm *grand*. Don't be *mithering* me . . .' – and clambered to her feet, spitting out water like it was poison, furiously drying her hair with her fiery hands – the water steaming, as if she were using heated straighteners – before finally calming down and announcing to Aoife with impressive nonchalance, 'Grand so. Not too shabby. You're one of us for sure.' But then she snarled at Shay: 'But *you* . . .'

Aoife pushed in front of him; she was shaking from the explosive discharge of physical energy, exhilarated to have experienced such natural power. To find she could knock someone flying so hard, without even laying a finger on them . . . A dark joy filled her. 'Don't you touch him, or you'll have me to deal with!'

'I'll do my own fighting, thanks all the same.' Rolling up his sleeves, Shay moved out from behind her into view of the changeling girl. 'And I have some serious powers, psycho-girl, so if I was you, I'd back off now.'

'Yeah? Then why didn't you use them on me, hey?'

'Didn't seem right, two against one. Plus I wasn't

anxious to turn you into a wrinkled old crone if I didn't have to.'

Ultan flinched. 'Oh, by Jesus . . .'

'*Danu.*' The girl's already pale skin went slightly whiter, so that her coppery freckles darkened. She said quickly to Aoife, 'He can do that?'

Aoife lied as convincingly as she could: 'He surely can. You want him to show you?'

'No, God . . . Danu . . . I'll manage without that particular transformation, thanks.' Caitlin drew back and looked Shay up and down, with something between doubt and reluctant awe. Then she smiled – a black gap where her right canine tooth should have been. 'Grand so. Sorry I doubted ye. Let's start over. Fact, it's good we ran into ye. Me and Ultan, Donal and Trish, we were a team. Now it's just me and Ultan. You two can join up with us.'

She stuck out her hand to Aoife, who hesitated then shook it, but only for a split second – '*Ow!*' – because it was still shockingly hot from having been gloved in fire.

'Sorry – forgot about my power.' Laughing, Caitlin went to get three of the four leather bags from the corner. 'Now we've captured that cat-beast we can buy our way into Falias for a few days. Can't wait to be in a proper city again – the craic there is mighty.' She tossed one of the bags to Shay. 'Donal won't mind you borrowing his kit until he's reborn.' She plumped down on her stool and started pulling out the contents of one of the other bags to show to Aoife. There was a bronze knife, some silver wire, a long coil of rope with a hook tied to one end, a small purple blanket and a leather flask. 'You can have Trisha's kit. Everyone gets mostly the same stuff. Hey, what's this . . . ?' She gave the bag a last frowning shake upside down, and two old pre-decimal coins fell out – a sixpence and a halfpenny; also a lipstick and a black-and-white photo. 'Didn't know Trish was still carrying around her bits of human trash. No wonder she had bad luck.'

Aoife picked up the photo. It was of a girl of about eighteen in a flared skirt, and a boy of the same age in a parka jacket; they were standing under the eaves of a thatched cottage with their arms around each other. On the back of the photo was written in pencil, *David and me*, with a shaky heart drawn around the words. 'What happened to her?'

'Ran after a pooka – thought it was some human

boy she remembered from the surface world. I yelled at her to be careful but she flung her arms around it, and of course it shape-shifted and went for her throat.'

Ultan made a noise like he was going to be sick and went to stare out of one of the long narrow slits in the wall.

Caitlin was busy opening the third kitbag. She said cheerfully, 'My own kit came with this extra yoke in it – very useful if you want to know anything about anything.' She pulled out a book about thirty centimetres square and several thick. A pattern of gold hawthorn blossoms was pressed into the cover, and what looked like beads of red glass were stitched in bunches to the leather, clearly representing berries. She passed it over to Aoife. 'You can read it if you like.'

'Thanks.' But when Aoife opened it, the pages were covered in crude lines grouped in different patterns. 'Is this actual writing?'

'You can't read Ogham? It's the old druid language.'

'Can *you* read it?'

'Yeah, course, the druids showed me.'

Ultan snorted without turning round from the window.

Caitlin snapped, 'I *can* so read Ogham!'

'Sure you can – that's why we're always getting in such a mess. Like when you told Tricia all shape-shifters were female.'

'I still warned her to be careful, didn't I? Anyway, it's a really old book – of course it's going to be wrong some of the time.' She said brightly to Aoife, 'Want me to read some of it to you?'

'Please.'

'The recent stuff is the most interesting.' Caitlin opened the book near the end, cleared her throat importantly, and began in a sing-song story-telling voice, her eyes travelling back and forth across the page, 'One day this big fat ugly human priest saw the queen of the underworld riding a white horse across the bog and he fell in mad love with her even though he wasn't supposed to because he was a priest, and he followed her to Tír na nÓg and tried to kiss her. She told him to get lost because she was going to marry the Beloved the next day, and that pig of a priest got in a lunatic rage and stabbed her loads of times with an iron knife . . .' Aoife was beginning to suspect that Ultan was right – the girl couldn't read but was just repeating in her own plain-speaking way something she'd been told. 'And then the people of Danu brought the queen's body off to the islands, and they pulled the tunnels down behind them, so never again could a filthy human pig enter this land. And the beasts went wild, and things got a bit out of hand. So the queen's Beloved, who the people of Danu had left behind to look after the place, sent the queen's precious baby daughter away for safety. And then he called back the changelings from the surface world to help him sort everything out with their amazing powers.'

Leaning forward, very interested, Aoife said, 'I did feel like I was being pulled here. I felt so sure I had to go down.'

Caitlin closed the book and shoved it back into her bag. 'And now you can join us. We're using our powers to capture the beasts. And when we've caught enough of them and trained them to fight, there'll be a war against the humans.'

'What?'

Ultan sighed heavily. 'Don't worry, she's making that last part up entirely.'

'Am not! I heard the druid talking about it.' Caitlin flicked back her bright red plait, the beads around her neck rattling. 'And I'm not scared of going to war – I've killed a human already!'

Aoife stared at her. 'You've killed . . .'

'I set fire to a priest!' She was grinning boastfully.

'Oh, good God—'

'Good God nothing. It was absolutely brilliant. My mam . . . I mean, the woman who brought me up, Mary McGreevey, she used to tell me I was an evil, ugly child swapped out at birth for her real baby, but I never believed her. I thought she was just being pure mean because I was this big lump of a thing. But the day I turned sixteen I saw a tiny girl running past my house and I had this really strong urge to chase after her, and she ran into the priest's garden and his dog went for her, and I threw a stone at the dog and it burst into flames. Then I was really confused, and I went home and said nothing. But Father Hugh came to the house screaming that I was a devil child from hell, and my mam . . . Mary McGreevey, I mean . . . she screamed at me as well, and the stupid man got out his cross like we were in the Dracula film and started praying over me, so I pointed at him to see what would happen and he went up in flames.'

'Oh, good God.'

'I'm telling you, it was class. You should have seen his face. And there was my . . . Mary McGreevey . . . going hysterical and throwing her tea over him, but it was no use, he was melting into the lino like butter.'

'Oh, good God.'

'Stop saying that! And I ran out of the house and there was that little girl again, and I ran after her, and the next thing I'd fallen in the well at the bottom of our land and I was drowning. And I was sure that I really *was* a devil child and would wake up in hell. But when I woke up I was a fairy and in paradise, and one day I'm going to tell that to Mary McGreevey and see what she has to say to me then about me being ugly and stupid and evil and everything.'

'Are you from Ballinadeen?' Shay looked pale and shaken.

Caitlin stared at him. 'How do you know that? I don't remember seeing you around.'

'No, you wouldn't have—'

'Why not? Where are you from?'

He hesitated, then said, 'Further back.'

Ultan said, 'The Glen?' with an odd catch to his voice.

'Thereabouts.' Shay turned back to Caitlin. 'I've heard that story about the priest. I heard his robes caught on the McGreeveys' open fire and they couldn't save him, and the daughter ran off in a fright and drowned.'

Caitlin laughed harshly. 'Is that the aul lie they're telling everyone?'

Aoife was astonished. 'I didn't hear about that.'

'Because it was a long time ago.'

'Not *that* long,' Caitlin corrected him. And then she registered his expression, and her eyes narrowed. 'What are you looking at me like that for, like you feel sorry for me or something? Did my mam . . . Mary McGreevey . . . Did she die in the fire?'

He said quickly, 'You didn't kill her.'

She stuck out her strong, heavy chin. 'I don't care, you know, I don't worry about it – she's only human, not my real mam. I've cut my human ties.'

'All the same, you didn't kill her.'

Moving closer, his thumbs hooked in the elastic of his shell-suit bottoms, Ultan said, 'If you grew up near the Glen, did you ever hear tell about the McNeal boy who went up the mountain and never came down?'

Shay turned to him, frowning. 'I did, of course. He would have been the second cousin of our nearest neighbour.'

'Really? I don't remember ever meeting you.'

'But they remember you, if Ultan McNeal from the Glen is who you are.'

The plump youth looked pleased, but at the same time rolled his eyes. 'Well, I'd hope they would remember me. I haven't been gone very long.'

Aoife said, 'Oh . . .' She had just remembered where she knew Ultan from; where she'd seen his picture. On Carla's nan's mantelpiece. On a Mass card, the sort people send out to their friends and neighbours on significant anniversaries of a loved one's death. And he still looked exactly the same as in his picture. 'Oh . . .'

Shay shot a glance at her, then said to Ultan, 'How long did you say you'd been here?'

The youth shrugged. 'Time slips by here. A few months, maybe? If you really did come by that tunnel, I might see if I can dig through, get back to see them for a while.'

Caitlin snapped, 'You will not.'

'Ah, Cait, just for a week or so—'

'No. And stop dreaming about your so-called family and thinking they might miss you. You might have thought they were your real parents, but they knew all along they were only minding you because the fairies had their real child, and that you were an ugly, stupid devil child from hell.'

Ultan said nothing, kicking out the fire.

Caitlin stood up, swinging the kitbag over her shoulder. 'Come on, we have to get that filthy cat back to Falias, and it's a week's walk.'

On the way back down the ruined city, Aoife kept her distance behind everyone else. She needed space to think, to go over Caitlin's words. All her life she'd believed her parents loved her – hadn't even given it a moment's thought. Had they really only been pretending? Wishing all along that she was the real Eva, their own human child? She pressed her fingers to her eyes to hold back sudden, stupid tears. How could they have acted so kind when they didn't really want her?

Or maybe, just maybe, they had grown to love her. They *had* gone out looking for her when she ran away. She wished suddenly that she had some way of letting them know that she was all right. How long had she been gone? News travelled fast in a small town. They might have already heard about the red-headed girl who had jumped off the cliff with Shay Foley.

At the next twist in the path she bumped straight into him – he had been waiting for her. He took hold of her by her shoulders, as if he were afraid she might run off. He said urgently, 'I have to talk to you. We have to go home right now.'

'I know what you mean – I want to let my parents know I'm alive too. Maybe there's a way to send everyone a message—'

'No, that's not what I mean. I mean – *we have to go home*. Right now. And never come back.'

Aoife took a quick, disappointed step back, so that his hands fell from her shoulders. Below their feet the bird-filled forest flowered, and shining rivers coiled; above them, eagles circled under rainbows. This was the world where she'd been born and to which she had felt such a deep, powerful urge to return – and the farmer's boy just wanted to be safe above in the human world, where *he* belonged. 'I know this place is dangerous . . .'

He said sharply, 'I'm not *afraid*.'

'. . . but it's my world, Shay. It's where I come from. And there are other people here like me – other changelings. I feel like I belong.'

He glanced down the steep path to where Caitlin and Ultan were strolling on ahead of them, and said, 'Maybe digging out that tunnel won't be that big a job. I'd say we could do it.'

He hadn't even listened to her. All he could think about was leaving her. Aoife sighed, and said sadly, 'OK, but listen – you can't go that way, you'll be killed. We need to go to Falias. Caitlin said the only way back to the surface was from there.'

'But she also said it's a week's walk!'

'I know it's awful if John Joe thinks you're dead – I hate worrying people too – but what can we do? As soon as we get there, you can go home.'

Shay answered instantly, 'I'm not going anywhere without you.'

Aoife felt instantly much lighter – at least it wasn't her he was trying to get away from. 'No, seriously, it's a good idea you going first – you can tell everyone I'm safe as well.'

'I'm not going—'

'*Shay*. This is my world. I want to explore this famous city that Caitlin's on about. I want to discover stuff, like where I was born and what I can do. I want to meet other people like me. Just tell everyone I'm all right, and I'll be back soon.'

Shay cried, slightly wildly, 'How soon?'

'I don't know – a month?'

'*A month?*' He was staring at her as if she'd lost her mind.

'Why not? Once everyone knows I'm all right.'

'It's too long, much too long!' He had gone white, his eyes dark green and shining, like holly leaves.

'Shay, what's the matter? Tell me!'

He drew the palms down the sides of his face, hard. 'Aoife, do you realize how long Ultan McNeal's family have thought him dead?'

She had seen his anniversary Mass card on Carla's nan's mantelpiece. Ultan had said he'd been away a few months, but it must have been longer, for him to have had at least one anniversary. 'A year? Two?'

'Thirty.'

'*Thirty?*'

'And his father is still mourning him. And his mother is dead.'

'Oh God, poor Ultan, he's lost all track of time—'

'And Caitlin McGreevey's mother is in the graveyard above in Ballinadeen.'

Aoife groaned. 'So she *did* die in the fire.'

'No. She passed away when I was a little kid, of old age. The fire that killed the priest happened nearly half a century ago.'

Aoife stared at him. 'But—'

Shay said in an anguished voice, 'Aoife, it's like the legend of Oisín.'

'Oisín . . .'

'The Fianna hero who followed the fairy Niamh to the Land of the Young. He thought he had only been away for three years, because he never grew older and nothing ever changed, but when he returned, three hundred years had passed in his own world and all his family and friends were dead. Suppose it's like that for us, Aoife – suppose time is flying by above, while we are trapped down here? What if by the time we get home, everyone is old or dead?'

CHAPTER FIVE

Ultan insisted on helping – he jumped into the hole left by the collapsed tunnel and began hurling rocks aside. He was a strong farmer's lad himself, under his soft layer of flesh.

Caitlin stood screaming at him: 'Ultan, stop it – you're not allowed! You want the dullahans after you, hey?'

'Banshees and lenanshees go to the surface all the time, don't they?'

'They're different, they're *ancient* types. We're the children of Danu and we have to stay here!'

Ultan was struggling to lift a small boulder. 'What about those guys in Falias who sneak back for the human food? I'm after hearing *they* don't wait for anyone's permission.'

'Don't go quoting those lunatics at me. If they want to risk getting sucked dry by a dullahan for the sake of a packet of cheese-and-onion Taytos, that's their business.'

'Sucked dry?' He laughed loudly and deliberately. 'Ha, ha, ha! You're making that up.'

'It's in the book!'

'Sure it is. You're forgetting you told me before, them things have no heads.'

'Oh, for . . . Isn't it obvious? They carry their heads around with them, under their arms. How else do you think they call your name?'

Ultan looked startled and nearly dropped the boulder on his foot. 'I did wonder about that . . .'

'First they call your name and then they suck you dry.'

'Stop *saying* that. You're full of crap.' But he climbed out of the hole and stood on the edge of it, with his thumbs hooked in his elastic waistband. 'Anyway, there's no point trying to dig our way out with our bare hands – we won't be getting through there without a proper machine to help us. Or super-strength as a power.'

Aoife stopped digging as well. Ultan was right – the rocks were getting so big, they were impossible to lift. Shay was still frantically clearing away what he could, but it was obvious that it was an impossible task. She climbed out of the hole and said to Caitlin, who was trussing up the unconscious cat even tighter, 'Is it really a week's walk to Falias?'

'More like two weeks. Lugging this thing with us is really going to slow us up.'

Aoife did a quick mental sum, with a wide-eyed glance at Shay. Two weeks – two hundred weeks – four years. Carla would be at university. She felt dizzy and panicky at the thought. 'Do we really have to bring that monster with us?'

Caitlin knotted another strand of net. 'Won't get into Falias without it – we have to bring a live beast with us if we're going to be allowed in.'

'Is there no quicker way?'

'Nope. I can fly pretty well, but Ultan here . . .'

'You lepping about the place like a giant rabbit,' said Ultan sharply, 'doesn't count as flying.'

'. . . but *Fat Boy* here is way too heavy to get off the ground.'

'*Hey!* It's just not my power, all right? Anyway, what about the boat we saw at the lake?'

Caitlin said fiercely, 'I'm not getting in that flimsy little—'

Aoife cried, 'There's a boat?'

'No!'

Ultan rolled his eyes. 'Don't mind her, she's only lying 'cos she's scared of water.'

'I'm not scared of anything! I just don't like it!'

Shay had already vaulted out of the hole. 'Come on, let's go and find this boat.' He seized one corner of the net and started dragging the unconscious cat towards the entrance.

Caitlin sprang to her feet. 'Danu's sake, be careful. What's the rush?'

'We're in a hurry to get to Falias, aren't we?' He scraped the cat's body over a pile of stones – it groaned and extended claws like shark's teeth.

'Take it handy, ya fool, don't bash it around! The zookeeper won't accept it if it's dead – we'll get no payment, no city passes, nothing!'

'Then the quicker we get it there, the better. Look at the state of it: it's burned to a crisp – it's half dead already.'

'Wasn't me jabbed it full of holes! I told you not to hurt it!'

Ultan said anxiously, 'Cait, he's right, we should take the boat. Supposing it does die on us, and we get stuck out here in the wilderness for six more months?'

'Oh for— Ugh. Grand so, but stop *dragging* it. Lift, *lift*!'

The four of them bundled the cat through the brambles and down towards the forest. At the edge of the trees the changeling boy came to a determined halt. 'I want to see how Donie is getting on.'

Caitlin scoffed, 'Come on, ya soft fool, there'll be nothing to see yet – stuff doesn't grow *that* fast.'

And Shay said grimly, 'We're in a hurry, aren't we?'

But Ultan's round face grew stubborn and he dropped his corner of their burden. The cat's jaw smacked off a stone; its teeth went through its tongue, and drops of yellow blood rolled from its lip.

'*Careful, ya fool.*'

'I'm not going anywhere without saying goodbye. It'll only take ten minutes.'

Aoife did the sum, and shivered. Ten minutes. Sixteen hours in the human world. Yet not to visit the child's grave . . . 'Look, let's do it. It's only a short distance away.'

They couldn't find the grassy glade with its soft pile of earth – it was as if it had been swallowed by the forest. Ultan didn't want to give up looking, and was only persuaded to do so when Caitlin threatened to abandon him. But as they headed back towards where they'd left the cat – the plump changeling lad in tears – Aoife spotted a slim flicker of white beneath the trees. She looked closer. It was the willow cross. 'It's there! Oh, it's beautiful! Ultan, cheer up, it's a miracle!'

The air around the grave was heavy with the drug of perfume; vibrant with the beat of wings. Every flower and fruit they had planted had forced its way towards the sun – around the rough white willow cross spread a deep carpet of dandelions, kingcups, fluffy meadowsweet, violets, wild bluebells; the intertwined grove of slim young apple trees blossomed and fattened with red fruit. Pale blue, deep red and large white butterflies quivered on every flower; bees were buried headfirst in every blossom; caterpillars dangled on thin threads, swaying in the warm flower-sweetened breeze; birds scrambled and hopped from branch to branch, snatching beakfuls of apple.

Caitlin stared in astonishment. 'No, you're wrong, this *can't* be where we buried him.'

Aoife cried, 'It is – you can see the cross. And

why can't it be? Didn't you say he'd be transformed?'

'But not this quick. It wasn't like this with Trish. We stayed with her for two days at least, and she only got as far as grass and daisies.'

Ultan said hopefully, 'Maybe it's because Donie was so young.' He plucked one of the small apples and bit into it. Juice spurted. He grinned broadly through a mouthful of rosy white flesh – 'God, that's sweet!' – and offered it to Aoife.

She nearly refused, remembering what he had said over the grave about how if a future apple were small and sweet, they would know it was Donal coming back to life. Eating something that was part of Donal seemed like an act of cannibalism. But a thought came to her of Father Leahy proffering the communion wafer while intoning in his bored, flat voice: *Take, eat: this is my body, which is broken for you: do this in remembrance of me.* She bit down. The fruit tasted nothing like communion bread – the explosion of sweetness startled her into laughing; she tossed it to Shay, who took a bite, raised his eyebrows, passed it on to Caitlin. The changeling girl consumed the rest in two crunching mouthfuls, and wiped her hand across her mouth.

'All right, maybe it is him, but I'm still not getting this. It's too weird. Something different has happened here.' She was frowning at Shay as she spoke, a deep freckled furrow between her ginger eyebrows. 'I just can't work it out.'

Shay shrugged. 'Nothing to work out, far as I can see. Come on – you want to get to Falias before the cat dies, don't you?'

'Wait a moment . . .' Ultan was filling his kitbag with the small sweet apples.

Impatiently, Shay took the knife out of his kit and hacked down two straight branches of ash. 'We can thread these through the net and shoulder one end each – it'll make the going easier.'

Aoife was alarmed to find out from Ultan that the lake was at least ten kilometres away – yet the going wasn't as slow as she feared. Stringing the net on the poles made it easier to carry, and the changelings didn't walk but ran steadily. Now she was worried that Shay would show himself up as human, by not being able to keep pace. Yet he loped easily along in front of her, his long legs covering the ground. She found herself thinking that it was just as well he played Gaelic football and was so fit – it was as if he had fairy blood himself.

Ultan was munching his way through fruit after fruit as he trotted alongside Aoife. 'Just spreading Donie around,' he explained breathlessly as he fired yet another core into the undergrowth.

'But how will he come back as himself if he's spread around?'

He shot her a startled look. 'Hadn't thought of that. I wonder how that rebirth thing works . . .'

'You don't *know*?'

'Not been here long enough to figure it out. But I've been reliably informed it does.'

'By . . . ?' She jerked her chin towards Caitlin, running next to Shay with her head held high.

'I know what you mean. But that druid fellow was pretty strong on the subject, and he seemed, you know, wise. Beardy, anyway.'

The grass path dived deeper and deeper into the forest, through a tunnel of blossom – cherry, plum, pear, apple, quince. The yellow-green foliage shimmered with birds, and the undergrowth was alive with creatures. Rabbits fled across their path, one of them pursued by a long red streak of fox.

Hedgehogs watched them pass with button eyes.

The cat was lying with its head towards Aoife, its yellowish tongue flopping out through jagged teeth; every so often it took a breath, and each time it exhaled, its red nostrils flared and hairy lips quivered. The rancid stench of its breath turned Aoife's stomach every time – that, and the odour of scorched hair. Parts of the monster's dirty white coat had burned down almost to the skin; its tail was more raw flesh then fur. Occasionally its fiery eyes flickered open, and fixed on hers. At those moments it was hard for her to resist holding its gaze – its eyes held a malicious depth which she found both compelling and revolting. Once, after they'd stared each other out for a full minute, the beast closed its foul mouth and made a deep rumbling sound in its throat, alarming Ultan into nearly dropping his end of ash pole.

'It's growling at you!' He raised his palm and fired a black cloud of smoke into the cat's face; it passed out again, clearly in a weaker state to start with than when he'd tried to gas it before, in Gorias.

Aoife said, impressed, 'What *is* that thing you do?'

'Don't know really. Keep away from me when it's happening, though, 'cos if you catch a dose you'll wake up puking three days later. I know all about it – first person I ever gassed was my own self, by accident.'

'Ouch. When did that happen?'

'My sixteenth birthday – changeling powers usually kick in at about sixteen. Well, whichever power we're going to have.'

'You only get one?'

'Yep. Caitlin's convinced she can fly as well as do fire, but it's only a bit of lepping about. Her fire's good, though. Me, I got poisonous smoke. Weird, huh? Course, I had no idea I was a changeling. Got over-excited 'cos it was my birthday, gassed myself, and my dad did his absolute nut 'cos he thought I'd been at the poteen.'

'Bad luck.'

'Second person I gassed was my arsehole of a maths teacher. That's why I headed off up the mountain in such a hurry. And then this tiny boy beckoned me from far off across the bog, and when I ran after him, I fell in a hole and that was me gone.'

'You saw a sheóg?'

'Course I did. That's how we get called – out across the bog, into a bog hole, done.'

Aoife cried, 'I saw a little girl!'

'There you are then.'

'I thought I'd imagined her.'

'No, that's the way we all get called back. They send the human child up for us.'

She stared at Ultan in horror. 'Sheógs are *human* children?'

'The very ones we got swapped out for in the first place.'

'The babies which we . . . ? Our parents' own . . . ?' She felt like she was going to be sick with the shock. The tiny girl in the bog had been the real Eva, and Aoife had left her there – had cruelly abandoned a lonely, frightened child. 'What happens to the sheógs? *Oh God, this is horrible!*'

'Stop, don't be panicking. I'm sure they just make their way back down. There's enough of them around – the supply doesn't seem to dry up at all. And the banshees really love them. There's times when you see them pass by with a whole cartload of the little tinkers, off on some jaunt.'

Aoife still felt shaken to her core. 'Are you

definitely sure? Did you ever find the little boy you were swapped for?'

'No, but that doesn't mean he isn't here. All toddlers look the same, don't they? I don't have any picture to go off, and I didn't get a good look at him in the mist out on the bog.' Ultan added with a rather forced brightness, 'If I do ever find him, I might bring him home – then my parents would surely be glad I'd run away.'

'Ah, they wouldn't . . .'

'They would if they had their real son back again. I was an impostor, wasn't I? It wasn't like they intended to adopt me.'

Aoife would have liked to tell him about the Mass card; the thirty anniversaries over which he had never been forgotten. But that would mean telling him that his father was very old and his mother was dead. And although there might come a point where he found out the truth, it seemed too cruel to blurt it out – especially as she had no actual proof to show him. 'I'm sure your parents loved you a lot.'

Ultan pulled a face. 'Truth, they were always so good to me I wonder did they realize I wasn't their own, and that they'd lost their real son to the fairies.

Then if I did find him and leave him home on their doorstep, secretly like, would they know him for who he was? Would they understand it was the child they'd lost as a baby? Would they understand that no one gets any older in Tír na nÓg? Maybe he'd end up in care or something.'

'I'd know my sheóg if I saw her. My parents had a whole drawer of photographs of her, hidden away.'

'So they knew all along that you were a changeling?'

'Yeah. My dad . . .' Aoife paused. Not her dad – the human man who had brought her up. She tried again: 'James . . .' But that sounded ridiculous and wrong. She could picture him so clearly, his silver-grey hair, brown eyes blinking owl-like behind his glasses, reading aloud to her beside the fire. 'My dad had a ton of books about this place. I thought he was just into old stories.' While all the time, he was doing serious research – trying to build a picture of where his human child was now. Convincing himself there were no dark things in paradise. He was so wrong about that.

The murderous cat slept on, swinging from side to side as the four of them ran steadily down the woodland path. The noise it had made earlier *could* have been a growl. But – and Aoife found this idea much more disturbing – she suspected it had been a purr. Would they ever reach the lake and be able to set the beast down? They must have been running like this for over half an hour now . . . Automatically she pulled out her mobile from her hoodie pocket. Still destroyed, of course.

'What's that you've got there?' Ultan was looking at the mobile phone.

'Crappy old Nokia. I wanted to check the time, but it's not working.'

'Funny-looking clock.'

'What? Oh . . .' Of course, Ultan was from the eighties – which explained the shell suit. He would never have seen a mobile phone. She pushed it back into her pocket.

Just in front of her, Shay was showing no sign of tiredness. Just as well, as Caitlin kept giving him odd lingering looks like she still had her doubts about him. Yet fit as he was, surely no human could keep up this changeling speed for much longer. Even Ultan was breathing hard; he was feeling his stomach with a cautious faraway expression. And suddenly the trees opened out onto a sandy beach, and there it was – a shining lake, with flocks of white water birds drifting on its silk-blue breast like snowy islands.

'Got to go!' announced Ultan abruptly; he dropped his end of the pole and disappeared among the trees.

'Serves him right for eating all those apples,' said Caitlin as they lowered the cat onto the beach. She scanned around her and said, clearly relieved, 'Ah, boat's gone. Probably some pooka took it. Or it floated off and sank.'

'Is that it?' Shay pointed to a black currach drifting a long way out on the water – almost half a kilometre away in the middle of the lake: tarred animal hide stretched over wood, the sort of home-made boat sometimes still in use out on the islands.

'Ah, we'll never get to that!' Caitlin was mightily delighted. 'Oh well, that's life, so it is – we'll have to just carry on as we are, on foot . . .'

But before she'd finished speaking, Shay had already dived into the water and was striking out across the lake with clean sideways sweeps of his arms.

'Swimming?' Now Caitlin was disgusted. 'Are

you sure that boy's a real changeling? There's something not right about him. I can't put my finger on it . . .'

'Of course he's a changeling. I can swim – can't you?'

'Ugh, no, can't abide the water. I always thought that was a general fairy thing. And that boat is an absolute eggshell.'

'If you can't swim, I could teach you—'

Caitlin snapped: 'I can swim. I'm not *scared* of the water, I just don't *like* it.'

The sun was roasting, and the sight of Shay swimming so casually and easily gave Aoife a strong desire to jump in the lake herself. She trotted along the bank and dipped her bare toes in the water. It was deliciously warm. She stripped off her hoodie down to her Nirvana T-shirt, jumped in and did a fast breast-stroke towards the boat; the water was so clear, she could see the flickering gold-silver-blue mosaic of stones far below. It felt like flying. Brown-spotted trout passed beneath her in arrow-shaped squadrons.

She was gaining on Shay. When she was still a few metres distant, she dived down deep and swam beneath him and rose out of his sight on the far side of the narrow boat. Aoife grabbed the starboard bow, and pulled herself half out of the water at the exact same time as he grasped the other side. Their eyes met across the currach, and he laughed. '*Wahu*. Fancy meeting you here.'

'Oh, I often swim this way.' Aoife rolled over the side, and sat panting on the floor, between two seats, with her back against the curved lathes.

Shay climbed in himself, and sat beside her. 'Nice boat. Must be five, six metres long.' He hunted around. 'Damn. No oars. We'll have to make some – or maybe they got left on the bank. Help me swim this to the beach.'

'Hang on, give me a minute. Just half a minute.' Aoife tilted her head back against the side of the boat, lifting her face to the sun. It was so nice just to lie here for a moment. The sun was warm on her skin, and she felt very tired.

'Aoife?'

'Mm?'

She opened her eyes and he was kneeling beside her, gazing urgently at her. He said, 'You know, back in the real world—'

'Hey, this world is real! It's where I come from!'

'Sorry, I didn't mean . . . I mean, back home, when you found me on the cliffs, you were so sure you could fly. What happened when you jumped?'

Aoife sat up, folding her arms around her knees. 'Well, I sort of flew.'

'Are you sure?'

'Yes . . . Not, like, amazingly well or anything. The wind was so strong, and I would have got smashed into the cliff, only for the gulls helped me steady myself. And when I tried with you, you were too heavy. All I could do was float a bit, just enough that we didn't get killed.'

'Then why not try again, now? There's only a light breeze here, and flying would get you to Falias a lot faster.'

Aoife shook her head. 'I don't think it would work. Ultan said we only get one power, so maybe just a bit of gliding is all I can manage. We all seem to have a bit of fairy speed and lightness. Besides, even if I could fly, what's the point? Like I said, you're too heavy for me to carry.'

'But that doesn't matter. You could go on by yourself, let everyone know we're all right, then I'll come after you as soon as I get to Falias and find the road back.'

She said crossly, 'I'm not leaving you here in this place by yourself – anything might happen.'

Shay shrugged. 'Ara, I'll be grand.'

'Double standards! When I suggested you went without me, you practically lost the head!'

At first he hesitated like he wanted to deny it, then gave in and laughed. 'All right, but truth to tell, it's wasn't so much I was thinking about whether you'd be safe without me.'

'Oh? Then what was it?'

'It was when you said you were planning on staying for a whole month. What I was thinking was, I'd be a lot older than you by the time you came back – eight years would have passed, and I'd be going on twenty-four. And I was thinking you wouldn't be much interested in me then.'

'Oh my God, Shay Foley, the cheek of you – who says I'm interested in you now?'

His eyes widened, and he flushed. 'Ah, I didn't say that . . . I'm sorry, I wasn't meaning . . .'

Aoife couldn't stop laughing at how mortified he looked. Reserved, cautious Shay Foley, who would always rather listen than talk, had been utterly caught out speaking his thoughts aloud.

Her laughter was lightening her blood, making her fizzy. She jumped up and the currach swayed delicately beneath her feet. It had been drifting towards shore while they weren't looking, as if caught by a current, and the bank was much closer now. 'Let's see can I make it to land without falling in . . .'

She stretched out her arms and ran forward and sprang up, and the spring did take her high into the air, and the warm breeze cushioned her slow descent – but it was only what Ultan called lepping about like a giant rabbit, even if Caitlin had referred to it as flying. She splashed down into the lake halfway between the currach and the shore and swam back, hauling herself over the side again, rolling her eyes.

'Annoyingly crap.'

'Still, pretty impressive.' Shay was smiling, though still slightly flushed across his cheekbones from her teasing; not looking straight at her, he glanced up at her sideways from under his dark lashes. And suddenly Aoife remembered. Out on the cliff, when she'd touched his lips with her finger, and he'd kissed it, and the bolt of sweet lightness had poured through her blood . . .

'I flew when you kissed me,' she blurted without thinking.

Shay's smile widened, flattened the curve in his lip. 'Kissed you?'

And then it was Aoife reduced to blushing awkwardness. After all, what she was calling a kiss had been a mere nothing, the lightest closing of his mouth on her skin. 'I don't mean a proper kiss. I mean . . .'

'Aoife, I know what you mean. And like you said, it wasn't a proper kiss.'

'I know, I know.' She scrambled to her feet – she needed an excuse to go 'lepping' out of the currach again. 'We're nearly there now – I might just get back in the water and swim the boat to the bank.'

Shay stood too, and pulled her to face him. 'Or maybe you should fly.' His eyes were on her face, but he was no longer smiling. 'Aoife . . .'

'What . . . ?'

'Maybe if I kissed you properly.' He put his hands on either side of her jaw, and stroked her lips very lightly with his thumbs. 'Aoife . . .' His curved mouth drew close to hers.

'*NO! STOP!*' Caitlin was leaping up and down on the bank in huge ridiculous bounds, waving her arms.

He murmured, 'Ignore her—'

'*NO! DON'T! STOP! DON'T!*'

Aoife pulled back. 'What if something's wrong?'

'I'm sure everything's fine—'

'*NO! DON'T! STOP! DON'T KISS HIM! I KNOW WHAT HE IS! DON'T KISS HIM! YOU'LL GROW OLD AND DIE!*'

CHAPTER SIX

Caitlin flung the rope with the grappling hook, using it to drag the currach the last bit of the way to land while all the time screaming at Aoife: 'Get out of the boat! Don't let him kiss you!' and even more dementedly at Shay: '*Don't even touch her!*' She gave one last mighty jerk to the rope; the stern smacked into the beach.

Aoife made a grab for Shay's arm, to keep her balance. To her shock, he raised his hands and stepped away from her, saying flatly, like all the joy had been knocked out of him, 'Best do what she says.'

'Oh my God . . . *What* are you on about?' She stared in confusion from him to Caitlin. 'What's going on?'

'Move further back! I know what you are!'

Still with his hands raised, Shay stepped back over the plank seats in the centre of the currach. 'Calm the form – see, I'm not even touching her.'

'But you were going to, weren't you? You couldn't

help yourself, could you? You have a *grá* for her! Just as well I realized in time, before you turned her into a wrinkled old crone!'

Aoife flipped from being mystified to badly wanting to collapse in hysterics. She didn't dare catch Shay's eye – he clearly felt the same way, because he had sunk down on the small seat in the bow, his face buried in his hands. She said to Caitlin, trying her best not to laugh, 'Chillax, it's grand – give us a hand with the cat into the boat.'

'I'm not getting in a boat with that one!'

'It's grand, he has his power under control.'

'No, no, he can't help himself!'

'Really, it's all right, he's—'

'*Pooka! Pooka!*' Ultan came hurtling down the sandy shore, dragging up his shell-suit trousers as he ran, black smoke streaming behind him like he was a small plane. 'We've got to get out of here!' He flung himself full-length into the currach, and the fragile vessel lurched and water churned over the low sides as he floundered around on his knees, coughing, still in a mist of his own now-greying smoke, searching around under the seats. 'Quick, row! Where're the oars?'

But even without the oars, the boat was already moving away from the land as if whatever current had floated them in had suddenly reversed itself. The grappling hook trailed its long rope in the water. Caitlin, trapped on the beach, ran first to her left then to her right, eyeing the widening gap with horror, crying, 'Come back!'

Aoife shouted, 'We've no oars! Just grab the rope and we'll pull you in!'

'Oh, sweet Mary and Jesus . . .' The changeling girl took a running jump and launched herself furiously into the air. Her distaste for the water gave her height – not only did she clear the gap – already a good eight metres; she was only saved from over-shooting the boat altogether by Shay jumping up to steady her. The narrow boat rocked fiercely as the girl landed, and for a moment she clung to him. Then she pulled back with a shriek – *'Don't kiss me!'* – hitting him in the chest with her fists.

Still holding her by the upper arms as the currach slowly stabilized, he said in a low voice, 'Keep the head, I'm not about to kiss you.'

She threw off his hands. 'Just you don't even think about it!'

'Yeah, try and control the passion, man,' said Ultan, highly amused. He looked a lot less scared now that there was a good stretch of lake opening up between the boat and the land. 'I know it's hard to resist her charms but be strong like me.'

'Get lost, McNeal.' Caitlin hopped back over the centre seats and joined Aoife in the stern, staring in disgust at the shore. 'Oh for— Are we caught in a current or something?' The beach was receding rapidly into the distance, the cat still lying trussed on the sand. Aoife's hoodie, with the dud phone in its pocket, was in a small green heap beside it; everyone's kitbag apart from Caitlin's lay carelessly around. Caitlin reached over the side, paddling furiously with her hands. 'Hey – help me get this turned round! We have to row back for the cat!'

Ultan said, arms stubbornly folded, 'No way, I'm not going back to land with that thing around.'

'We have to, or the zookeeper won't let us in! How do you even know it was a pooka you saw? I bet you were after seeing an ordinary horse or something!'

'It wasn't in horse form, it was— *There it is now!*' The beach was by now small in the distance, but the vast creature shuffling out of the forest was still terrifying to behold – horned, stooping, covered in black hair and with claws for hands. It went straight for the cat, picked it up in both hands and bit off the creature's head. Yellow blood spurted up in a narrow fountain.

'Aargh!' Caitlin slapped her forehead with her palm. 'This is a total disaster of a day. Weeks of tracking and nothing to show for it.'

Aoife knelt frozen in the stern, transfixed by the grotesque scene. The goblin was munching its way down the cat's body, pausing occasionally to spit out shards of bone. In the depths of Aoife's mind flashed up the dark intelligence of the cat's eyes as it had gazed on her and purred; she experienced a brief, uncomfortable sorrow, as if there were something she should have done to save it from such a terrible fate.

Moments later, the beach had disappeared as the lake narrowed into a river, passing between hills covered in oak trees, heading straight towards the brilliant white mountains. Bulrushes and reeds lined the shallows, rustling with moorhens, and an otter sprawled on its back on the grassy bank – it had a fish in its paws, which it was eating up one side and down the other like a corn on the cob, much more dainty in its manners than the goblin devouring the cat.

Caitlin had retrieved her rope and grappling hook, rolling them up and stuffing them into her kitbag, and was now studying an ancient map drawn on the centre pages of her book. 'I don't believe it – this stupid river is taking us towards Falias.'

'Sound stuff.' Ultan was basking in the same posture as the otter, head back, eyes closed against the sun.

'It's not sound! We don't have a beast – we have to get back to Gorias where the cat-beasts are!'

'Ah, come on, Caitlin – relax for once and enjoy.'

Aoife got carefully to her feet, arms out to balance herself; she stepped over Ultan's legs and moved up the boat towards Shay. He was sitting in the bow, staring intently ahead.

'Where you going, hey?' Caitlin glanced up from her map-reading. 'I'm warning you, that one is getting a *grá* for ye! I can't keep saving your arse if he gets it in his head to kiss you again.'

Ultan murmured, 'Ah now, let her off – you had your chance. He was fair desperate to shift you and you turned him down—'

'Course I did – he's a lenanshee, ya fool. One of them fairy lovers who suck the life out of you if they get a fancy for you.'

Aoife, with one foot on the central seat, froze in the act of stepping over it.

Shay did not turn round. His shoulders visibly tensed, as if he knew she was there watching him, but he did not turn.

Behind her, Ultan was saying, 'A lenanshee? Him? Aren't they supposed to be mad good-looking?'

Caitlin's voice said, 'Are you blind? Look at him!'

There was a long pause, then Ultan muttered uncomfortably, 'All right, sound – I suppose if I were a lass . . .'

'Right. He's a lenanshee right enough. Remember how he threatened to turn me into an old woman? You see how Donal came alive when your man kissed him, but then went out like a candle? You see how fast everything started growing on the child's grave?'

'Even so . . .'

'You see that thing your man did with the caterpillar?'

'Huh?'

'Transformed into a butterfly, just like that.'

'Jesus . . . I guess you're right. That's a strange fellow to have along for the ride.'

'He comes anywhere near me, you get between us, OK?'

'He seems quiet enough for now.'

'That's what they're like, ya fool. They *lull* you. It's all here in the book, I'll read it to you.' There was a pause, and the sound of riffling pages. Caitlin put on her story-telling voice: 'Avoid the kiss of the lenanshee, unless you wish to write a load of crap poetry or go mad playing the fiddle and end up looking like a wrinkled old prune and die young.'

Aoife still felt unable to move. She gazed at Shay; he was holding the side of the boat with his sun-brown hand. The gold locket wound around her wrist glittered in the sun. In her mind's eye, she could see and hear old John McCarthy in the graveyard, elbows sharp in his worn black jacket: *Beware of the leannán sídhe, Aoife O'Connor. Stay away from the lover from the otherworld.*

Caitlin was calling to her: 'Danu's sake, ya fool, come back here and sit down.'

Aoife unfroze, and stepped over the seat. She said, 'Shay?'

The changeling girl tutted disgustedly to Ultan, 'Some people just won't listen. Serve her right if he can't control his *grá*.'

'Shay, are you all right?'

He said, without looking at her, 'Do you think you could make this thing go faster? I need to get back to John Joe and the farm before the summer's out. He'll never manage to bring in the turf without me.'

Aoife stared at the back of his dark cropped head. 'I don't know what you want me to do about it. It's up to the current how fast we're going.'

'You're wrong – it's you powering this boat.'

'*Me?*'

He said impatiently, 'Aoife, come on. Didn't you drive a car with no engine?'

'Oh . . . I guess I did . . . Maybe it *is* me.' She felt suddenly rather proud of herself.

'So would you mind speeding it up?'

Shay had repeated his request so coldly that tears pricked her throat. 'Sorry, but I don't know how, OK? I would if I could, I'm in just as much of a hurry as you are, but I don't even know how I'm making it move in the first place.'

'I'd say it's just by thinking about where you want to be going.' Still he didn't turn his head to meet her eye.

Aoife crouched down just behind him, against the side of the boat, and fixed her eyes on his profile, willing him to look at her. His mouth was set firmly, upper lip deeply curved, no smile at all. The smooth sweep of his neck was tight with tension. 'You're right. When the car brought me to your farm, it was because I wanted to see you.' She touched her fingers to his arm.

He flinched. 'Best not come near to me. Best keep away.'

The tears rose in her throat again. 'Why should I keep away?'

'You heard Caitlin. You *have* to keep away.'

'That's crazy!' Aoife lowered her voice. 'You know she makes stuff up. Why would you believe anything she says? She's just got that into her head because of what you said about turning her into a crone. If you were a lenanshee, you'd know.'

'Like you knew you were a fairy?'

286

'When my power came, I knew—'

'But not right away. You thought you were imagining things.'

'No, I did know, deep down. I just couldn't believe it at first.'

Shay turned his face a small way towards her, but kept his lashes lowered. 'And that's how I've always known – deep down. Knowing but not believing, because it was so impossible to believe.'

'But what made you think—?'

'My mother showed me how to hold a caterpillar and turn it into a butterfly, just by feeling a love for it.'

Aoife sighed. 'That's amazing!'

'No, it isn't. The butterflies would only live for a few minutes – half an hour, at most. I never lost a newborn lamb, but the ones I saved always got sick and died within the year. I told myself it was a coincidence, or I'd got the sheep mixed up, but deep down I knew there was something wrong about me. I kept away from other people. I tried not to talk to anyone, because I was afraid I might bring the same harm to them.' Shay groaned, pressing his fingers to his eyes. 'God help me. Why didn't I keep away from you?'

'You've never done me any harm!'

'Not yet. But what if I do get a *grá* for you? I'm a beast. Like the pooka.'

'No!'

'Aoife, if you'd seen my father die – an old, old man at thirty with all the life and energy sucked out of him. My mother burned him up.'

'Your father loved her – she didn't mean to hurt him.'

'But she destroyed him, Aoife. And she knew it. That's why she killed herself, jumping from the cliff. She wanted to take me with her. She said I was like her. Maybe I should have kept hold of her hand.'

'And die as well? That's a terrible thing to say!' Aoife went to stroke his shoulder, to comfort him, but he shrank from her again.

'Please, Aoife, don't . . .'

She dropped her hand. 'Listen to me. The only thing that happened when you kissed me was I knew I could fly.'

'And what if flying for you is like painting was for my father? It was beautiful, what he did, and he was lost in himself when he was doing it. He said he felt more alive when painting her than at any other time.'

'She was his muse—'

'She was the drug that killed him.'

'It was love.'

'No, it was her burning him up. Don't look at me like that. I mustn't go getting a *grá* for you. I can't risk doing the same thing to you.'

'But what if—?' Aoife stopped. She wanted to say: *What if it's too late? What if you already have, and I for you?*

Shay was holding his head in both hands, like it ached. From his sun-browned wrist, the gold chain dangled.

I love you, Aoife O'Connor.

He'd been wearing the locket since he'd followed her under the ground, and had never once offered to give it back.

He followed her gaze, ran one finger over the gold heart, then, with a swift movement, unclipped the catch, shook the chain from his wrist and handed it to her. 'You'll be wanting this back.'

'No, really . . .' Aoife felt tears well up in her eyes, and couldn't trust herself to say anything more.

'It's yours. I kept meaning to give it back to you. But I got used to wearing it and forgot I had it.' Shay kept on holding it out, the locket trembling from his fingers like a delicate pendulum, catching sparks of sunshine.

In the end there was nothing else she could do but take it. The heart was warm, from his flesh or from the sun shining on it. As soon as she took it, she experienced a fierce tug, like someone had tied a string to her heart and pulled. As if something about the locket was physically dragging her onwards. The boat suddenly, massively, increased its speed.

CHAPTER SEVEN

The woods flashed past; in seconds they were powering through the mountain pass – the white marble sides of the gorge soared far above them, capped with emerald trees.

Kneeling in the prow of the boat, Aoife felt her sadness lift as the boat rushed on. The speed was exhilarating, almost like flying. Her red-gold hair streamed behind her and the material of her T-shirt thrummed against her skin, drying in the wind and sun. This must be what a motorbike rider felt, burning up the outside lane, blood pounding with speed and power. She clutched the locket tight in her pocket. Somehow it was pulling her on – and it was getting stronger, the feeling of it, as if she were getting closer to her destination. And that destination must be Falias, because that was where she wanted to go.

Shay's hair and shirt were drenched with spray; he shouted at her over the noise, 'You're amazing! I wonder how many powers do you have?'

She shouted back, 'Ultan said we get one each.'

'But you have so many—'

'Then he must be wrong: we do get more.'

'Or you are special.' He said 'special' with a very warm, wide smile at her, his eyes running over her face. But then he turned his head away, saying, 'I mean, especially good at this magic thing.'

At the back of the boat Caitlin was screaming in outrage, '*Slow down! Slow down, you stupid boat, you're going to kill us!*' and hammering her fists on the black, tarred sides of currach as if this could get its attention, and Ultan was howling, '*I'm going to be sick!*'

Shay looked at Aoife, eyes dancing now, laughing.

And then he was gone.

The currach had up-ended over a waterfall. Aoife clung desperately to the side of the boat as Ultan, with a high-pitched scream, nose-dived past her down the roaring face of the cataract. Caitlin came tumbling after him, but managed to get a grip on Aoife's leg and hang on. A microsecond later the currach toppled even further forward and plunged down the deafening drop. Below, Shay was disappearing into a wide blue pool, in a clean dive. Ultan vanished after him, with a mighty splash. Caitlin and Aoife rode straight down the waterfall in the boat, both yelling, Aoife clinging to the side and Caitlin clinging to her, until it crashed prow-first into the boiling foam and sank, taking both of them with it.

Thrown out of the currach, Aoife drifted underwater, half stunned, waiting for her downward momentum to slow before heading upwards. The deep pool swirled warmly around her, sunny, creamy blue with bubbles and – this far beneath the surface – blissfully quiet. The currach, now levelled out but upside down, was settling on the floor of the pool beneath her. A couple of metres above was a wriggling cluster of legs – long ones in jeans surrounding short, plump ones in electric-blue trousers: Shay dragging Ultan to the bank. Caitlin's book and kitbag came floating past her towards the surface.

Caitlin?

On the point of swimming up for air, Aoife realized that the girl was nowhere in the water. She must be under the boat.

Lungs straining, Aoife dived downwards and seized hold of the rim of the currach, exerting all her strength to roll it onto its side. As it tilted, the changeling girl came floundering out – eyes bulging, mouth bubbling.

Instantly Aoife kicked towards the light, but it was like trying to swim up through mud – Caitlin had seized her around her neck from behind, and every time she tried to prise her loose, the big, strong girl gripped her tighter. Aoife struggled on until the open air was only a metre above her, thin yellow sunbeams striking through the water. She *had* to breathe in the next few seconds or her head would explode . . . She seized in desperation at the intangible straws of light . . . They slipped through her fingers, and the surface got further away.

Bright pictures began flashing through her head. Autumn in the field behind the small stone house. The ash tree outside her window, leaves bursting off in gusts of wind. Her Facebook page, full of messages regretting her death. Her guitar, plastered with stickers, a ribbon tied around it. In the kitchen, her mother, dark blonde hair scrunched up into a ponytail, sitting at the table poring over photographs. In the back room, James reading, looking up to find her there . . . Smiling at her with tear-filled eyes that reflected an empty room.

Carla, darling Carla, in bed, face pressed into the pillow, pale, sick and forlorn . . .

Oh, she would never get home. She would never see any of them again.

No, she had to try – she had to get home. *Keep trying. Keep swimming. Think of Shay.* Shay, his mouth so curved, his eyes so green . . . Shay, floating like an angel towards her through the blue sky, reaching for her . . .

Aoife held out her own arms and opened her mouth to welcome him, and cool water poured into her lungs, putting out the fire.

He was kissing her, which was strange when, before, he had flinched from her touch. His lips withdrew. She could feel the solid warmth of his hands pressing on her heart. His mouth back again, on hers. She didn't have any urge to kiss him back – his mouth felt different from how she had imagined.

Now she could hear his voice nearby, raised over a constant noise of thunder. 'Breathe into her, then push. Get the water out. Harder. Breathe—'

'I'm *doing* it.' Ultan, on the verge of hysteria.

'He's making a pig's ear of it, hey?'

Ultan snarling, 'Hey, who nearly drowned her in the first place, hey, hey, hey?'

Stomach spinning, Aoife jerked into a sitting position and vomited a belly-load of water in one, two, three body-clenching waves. It was several minutes before her body had finally finished convulsing; then she sat shivering weakly with her forehead on her knees. And finally opened her eyes. Her first thought was that she really *was* in heaven now, floating in the middle of a rainbow. But a moment later she realized that she was sitting on a marble ledge beside a massive waterfall, which was pouring into the deep pool from which she had been rescued, then out again over the far edge. The air was thickly misted with rainbow-coloured spray and Ultan's round brown stare was hovering centimetres from her own. He shouted above the roar of the water, 'Are you right now? Just as well yon lenanshee's after swimming like a fish, even if he doesn't dare kiss girls. That was me giving you the aul kiss of life by the way – don't be worrying that you're going to start changing into a wrinkled old crone or anything.'

'That's great.' Aoife rubbed her mouth with the back of her hand. 'Thanks a mil.' Shay was crouched behind Ultan, smiling rather madly at her like he didn't know how to stop. She smiled at him. 'Thanks for pulling me out.'

He grinned even wider. 'Not a bother.'

Ultan said, 'Hardest job was persuading Caitlin to let go of you, she's that scared of the water . . .'

Sitting with her knees pulled up and head down, the changeling girl snarled, 'I'm not scared, I just don't *like* it, so stop going on at me about it. It's all right for you. You never drowned thinking you was a devil child going to hell.'

Ultan fell silent, pulling a guilty face.

Shay stood up and went to get the purple blanket out of Caitlin's kit; he dropped it around her shoulders. She shrugged angrily – 'Don't touch me, lenanshee boy!' – and he moved away, walking through the blinding spray to look down over the edge of the ledge.

Aoife followed him; standing beside him, she felt her heart clench with shock at how high they still were. The waterfall down which they had fallen was only the first of many. After this first pool there was a second waterfall, which fell into another pool, and then a third, a fourth . . . Five in all, before the river became horizontal again, winding calmly away through a dark green hilly forest. A thin white line – a road? – ran alongside the river, and the forest was dotted with clearings in which there were tiny earth-coloured structures – maybe houses and farms.

And only a few kilometres away, a massive rose-quartz pyramid rose straight out of the forest, shining white and crimson like blood-streaked snow, and glinting in the sun as if every door and window were made of gold. It was so brilliant to look at, it hurt her eyes.

She turned to Shay in wild excitement, shouting over the thunder of the falls: 'Falias! We're nearly there!'

He shouted back, with a look of desperation, 'Yes, but how are we going to get down?'

'There has to be a way!' But the face of the marble cliff down which the cataracts thundered was utterly smooth – apart from the ledges of marble that framed each pool. 'We've got the rope in Caitlin's kit – maybe we could lower ourselves down the side of the waterfalls, from pool to pool. Even if it's not quite long enough, we could sort of swing and drop into the water.'

'Not a bad idea . . .'

But when Aoife really looked, she saw that it was a terrible idea. The second waterfall was much bigger than the first, maybe fifty metres, and the rest were easily as much again. 'No, I'm an eejit, it's too dangerous – and even if it worked, it would only do it for the first drop, because we couldn't bring the rope with us.'

'It's all right – I'd lower each of ye, and then dive with it.'

She turned to Shay in horror. 'Are you *crazy*? You'd be killed!'

'Sure, didn't I do it already?'

'But the first waterfall wasn't so high, and the pool was really deep! You can't dive fifty metres into a pool that might be much shallower than this one – it's like suicide!'

'What's the alternative? We have to get to Falias. I say let's do it.'

'*No!*'

'If you have a better idea—'

Aoife shouted, over the roar of water, 'Kiss me!'

Shay flinched back, eyes wide. 'No—'

'Yes, kiss me! Kiss me like you were going to kiss

me in the boat – properly, so I can really fly! I want to be strong enough to fly with you! Kiss me properly!'

'I can't do that to you.'

'You can! One time won't hurt me, I'm sure of it!'

He stared at her. Then smiled very oddly and said, 'No, it won't work.'

'*Why not?*'

'I would have to have a *grá* for you, like my mother for my father.'

'Then . . .' Her voice faltered. 'But you . . .'

'Aoife. There's no point. I have no *grá* for you at all.'

Aoife closed her eyes and opened them again. He was still looking at her. His eyes were the dark green of the forest so far below. She said coldly, 'Kiss me.'

He said, 'No.'

She darted forward, brushed her lips across his mouth, turned and jumped.

She wasn't flying properly, but she was gliding – arms extended for balance, skiing on her stomach down a long transparent slope of air, over the powder-blue waterfalls towards the dark green woods below. It was so exciting that she found herself screaming mindlessly, like she was on a roller coaster at the fair; her wet clothes were rippling against her body, quickly drying out in the rushing mixture of wind and sun. Minutes later, the dark forest came rising to meet her. She dropped her left hand, tilted, rolled in the air and managed to right herself just before she tipped into an out-of-control spiral which would have sent her headfirst in among the trees. Instead, she glided in low over the dark red-berried branches, and landed gently on her feet on the road she had seen from above.

CHAPTER EIGHT

She had landed just in time – she could feel the last drop of power from that brief stolen kiss draining away as her bare feet touched the earth. At once, Aoife knew that she had done a terrible thing. She had abandoned Shay, with no way of getting back to him. And now he would try that crazy stunt with the rope, and get himself killed . . . As she raced back down the road towards the falls, she threw herself repeatedly into the air, desperate to fly. Each time she remained afloat only for a few hopeful seconds before drifting leaf-like down again.

At the foot of the mighty torrent, the last waterfall pounded deafeningly into the final pool – pale milky blue streaked with white, heaving in smooth swells like molten marble before funnelling through a gap in the rocks and becoming a wide, fast-running river. Nearly two hundred metres above her Aoife saw the tiny white lip of the highest pool. It was impossible to see what was happening there, so far above.

Aoife screamed, pointlessly, at the top of her lungs, *'Shay!'* The woods to her left shook in a gust of wind, and black crows went screeching up in their hundreds – thousands – blanketing the sky like sudden night.

Why had she jumped? *Why?*

Not just the need to be home – it was anger.

Standing there like a fool, asking him to kiss her. And he: *There's no point. I have no grá for you at all.*

Anger that she had assumed that he really *did* have a *grá* for her, and was only hiding it from her, restraining himself . . . Anger at herself, for being so stupid. When he had offered to kiss her properly, in the boat, it had only been so that she could fly home ahead of him. He was being kind, and she had misunderstood. Stupid. *Stupid.*

The vast black flock of crows drifted down again, and the sun poured like honey through the stilled, bright air.

Behind her, the dusty white road looped round a bend.

A road meant people. From far above she had seen clearings dotted through the forest, with round structures that were surely houses. Whoever lived in them could help. Aoife turned and raced back up the road. Round the bend was another corner, far ahead. She hurried on. The road was stony and rutted as if used by vehicles; the river alongside her babbled wide and shallow over stones. The crows crowded along the dark green branches above her, gazing down with gold-rimmed eyes – all the trees were yews, dark-needled, red with poisonous berries.

Corner after corner, and nothing in sight . . . Maybe she would have to run as far as Falias itself. But which way? She couldn't see the pyramid city from the ground. She slipped her hand into her pocket and took hold of the locket. At once the invisible string jerked at her, this time so unexpectedly hard it made her gasp, as if it might nearly wrench her living heart out of her chest . . . Not onwards, but to her right, into the woods. At the same instant, dogs startled her by barking somewhere nearby, a cacophony of deep-throated baying. Dogs meant a farm. And a farm meant people.

Following the sound, Aoife turned through an opening between the trees, and ran along a grassy avenue rich with the sappy scent of the yews. Crimson yew berries and dry brown needles carpeted the ground. Every branch rustled with the sleek black bodies of the crows. After a short distance the track brought her out into a clearing, in the centre of which stood a circular house of clay and logs. To her disappointment it was clear that no one lived here – the thatched roof broken down and green with moss; thick brambles choking the door and every window. Just as she was turning to go, to seek help elsewhere, the dogs she had heard suddenly came bursting round the side of the empty building, a dozen of them, barking and howling in excitement.

They were as big as ponies, black with bone-white eyes.

Aoife fled straight for the nearest tree and scrambled up it as fast as she could, sending a cloud of crows screeching away. Only when she was at least five metres above the ground did she dare stop and look down. Her heart was pounding, her hands wet with sweat. But the enormous dogs didn't even seem to have noticed her – they were racing around the ruined house, still barking and yelping, throwing themselves at the walls, darting their long pointed snouts through the windows, trying to leap up onto the rotting thatch. The windows were too small for them to squeeze through, but as she watched, the largest of the dogs discovered the door and started forcing its way through the mass of brambles. The others crowded in behind their leader, long tails extended tensely, narrow jaws dripping.

In the sudden silence, from inside the abandoned house came the high thin sound of a child weeping in terror.

For a very, very brief moment Aoife almost convinced herself it wasn't a child at all, just a frightened animal. The huge dog pushed on into the house. Still Aoife stayed hidden in the foliage.

And then the scream.

'Mam! Help me!'

Horror swept over her; ice poured into her blood.

'Mam! Help me!'

She had to do something, quickly. Her veins were filling with power – but slowly, much too slowly. She leaned out of the tree, clinging tight to its swinging branches. 'Oi, dog! Over here!' Her throat was so dry, the cry came out as a squeak. She tried again. *'Dog!'*

The massive beast paused, its head still deep in the doorway, then shook itself and pressed on. The other dogs, pricking up their ears, turned to look up at her across the glade, baring needle-fine teeth in silent snarls, creamy foam dripping from their jaws. But then they closed in again around their leader, which had now disappeared up to its ribcage in the brambles.

A shriek from within. '*Mam! Mam!*'

Aoife was ready. She raised her hand, and a long dark blur cut straight through the air, across the clearing, engulfing the beast. But the monstrous dog did not go crashing to the ground. It barely reacted at all. It merely paused in the doorway, and its long tail flicked once, at the extreme end. The other eleven dogs seemed confused – trembling, twisting in circles, long black snouts swinging, bone-white eyes turning from the house to Aoife.

After a long, terrible pause filled only by the child's screams, the lead dog seemed to come to a decision: it backed out of the brambles, swung round and paced across the clearing towards her. Its hind legs were longer than its front legs, giving it an odd crouching gait. Reaching her tree, it gazed up at her with gleaming white eyes and pulled its lips back into a crazed smile – its gums were bright red, thickly crowded with thin yellow teeth. Up close, Aoife could see that the beast's long rough coat was not black but a very dark green. Even though she was already five metres above the ground, she hastily fled up another couple of branches. The dog placed its huge paws on the trunk of the tree and rose to a standing position, as tall as a bear. Its breath blasted up to her, stinking of rotten meat. It sprang, snapping for her bare feet, only just failing to catch them.

The child was screaming again. *'Mam! Help me!'*

The massive dog leaped up at Aoife one more time, jaws drooling, then dropped to the ground and strolled back towards the house.

'Mam!'

Sweat broke out of Aoife's every pore. She raised her hand but there was not yet enough power in her veins to fire again – even if it could have made any difference.

'Mam!'

Her heart squeezed like a fist. She screamed – pathetically, even to her own ears, *'Down! Stay!'*

The dog paused, then sloped round in a tight circle, lay down and rested its nose on its paws, still gazing up at her with that crazed rabid smile. As if saying, *I'm in no hurry. I'm going to have my cake and eat it. First you. Then that little cupcake inside. Or maybe the other way round.*

If she leaped as far as she could, and hit the ground running, maybe she could make it as far as the doorway, and if she could get inside, there might be some way for her to defend the child. Once she had made up her mind, the decision felt natural and surprisingly easy. No other child was going to die while she was around, like poor little Donal. Aoife crouched on the branch, feet together, knees bent.

The massive dog started to rise.

'*Stay.*'

It lay down again, still with that dark, sardonic grin. The other dogs gathered around their leader, whimpering with uncertainty, many lying down themselves. A strange, calm, extraordinary thought floated through her head: *Farm dogs.* '*Stay!*' she screamed one more time, then clenched her fists and exploded out of the tree, right across the clearing, over the heads of the pack, and burst through the overgrown doorway into the house.

'Hello? Hello?'

Aoife stood panting, listening. Silence. No dogs barking or trying to follow. She was breast-deep in a sea of blackberries, ferns, bindweed and nettles. The high windows in the cob walls were dense with briars, and only a few threads of dusty sunlight leaked through the rotted thatch, in which mice and small birds pattered.

'Hello? Hello?'

Impossible to see where the child was hiding, in all the undergrowth and shadows. She stumbled a few steps further into the overgrown room, and in the darkness nearly stood on the child, crouched in a shaking ball among the briars, thin arms wrapped over its head – a little, soft, prickle-less hedgehog.

Aoife hunkered down, not sure whether to touch the little thing, or if that might terrify the poor creature further. What to say? She decided this changeling was probably a girl: she was dressed in a pink dressing gown with a Disney motif on the pocket from *One Hundred and One Dalmatians*. The dressing gown was very dirty. *Everything* about the child was dirty – hands, bedroom slippers, tangled short blonde hair. 'Hello, sweetie.'

The child squeezed into an even tighter ball.

'Don't cry. I'm called Aoife and I'm not going to hurt you . . .'

Muffled against her knees, the child sobbed something inaudible.

'What did you say, sweetie?'

The little girl said more distinctly in a shrill, trembling north Dublin accent, 'Go away. I hate you. I'm not your sweetie, I'm my mam's sweetie. I want my mam.'

'All right, swee— honey. I'll help you find her.'

'They told me this way was home but the dogs came after me. I want to go home.'

'Of course you do. Tell me where you live.'

'In Dublin. In the house with the blue door . . .' The child suddenly looked up at her with tearful eyes so icy blue they were near transparent. *And I want my mam.*

A deep emotion swept through Aoife's body, like something essential had clicked home – but painfully, like a dislocated joint. Nearly crying herself, she held out her arms. 'Come here to me, honey. I'll take care of you.'

'No, you're a stranger – I don't know you . . .'

'But I know your mam, very well.'

'I don't believe you.'

'I do, and she gave me something to give you, so you would know I was telling the truth. You want to see it?'

The little girl wavered between hope and disbelief. 'No . . . Is it Smarties? No.'

'It's not Smarties, it's better.'

'Ice cream?'

'Wait . . .' Aoife dipped her hand into her trackies pocket, and for a bad moment thought she'd lost it, but it had only been pushed deep into the corner. She fished it out and extended her palm.

The child peeped at it from behind her knees; then her blue eyes widened and she unravelled herself just enough to snatch at the locket. She flicked the gold heart open to see the old photos of Aoife's parents looking so young, and her tears started falling again, like small strokes of chalk down her dirty freckled face. 'I want my ma. I want my da.'

Aoife gathered the child into her arms, and this time the little girl didn't resist but clung to her. Even for a four-year-old, she was extraordinarily light – mere bones; Aoife could hardly feel the weight of her at all. Standing up, she pressed her lips into the short scruffy hair. She said, 'You're safe with me, Eva.'

And her parents' real daughter, the girl from the photos hidden in the drawer, the child who had been taken by the fairies eleven years ago and yet was the same age as she had ever been, said, 'I want to go home.'

CHAPTER NINE

Still the dogs were silent. When Aoife peered out, the shadowy glade was empty of everything but drifting butterflies. Maybe the pack was hiding, ready to tear them apart. Yet she couldn't stay here – she had to get back to the mountain falls. The little girl passed her thin arms around Aoife's neck, and laid her small head on her shoulder – Aoife was reminded of how Carla's little sister Zoe would sometimes insist on being carried home by Carla at the end of a long, tiring day. It felt both strange and heart-warming, having Eva hug her in the same way – like having a little sister of her own. Stroking the child's skinny back, she said, 'Let's go for a walk, honey.'

Instantly the little girl struggled to get down. 'I don't want to! The dogs will eat me!'

Aoife kept hold of her. 'They're gone, honey. Anyway, they're just stupid dogs. We're not scared of stupid dogs.'

The child kicked her in the hip. *'Yes we are!'*

'Don't you want to see your mammy and daddy?'

Eva sobbed. 'Yes . . .'

'Then we can't stay here. Be quiet and brave, and I promise I'll bring you home safe.'

The child sobbed again, but quietly, her lips pressed tight together.

'Good girlie.' Holding the child high up out of the way of the thorns, Aoife pushed her way through the chest-high brambles, hastily scanned the empty glade, then sprinted as fast as she could for the avenue. Reaching the dusty road, she turned towards the falls. She had failed to bring help, but maybe there was something else she could do – maybe there was a route to climb that she hadn't noticed before.

Eva had her head up now, braver, looking around as the world flashed by. 'You can run very fast. Are we going home?'

'We just have to see some friends of mine first.'

The ice-blue eyes narrowed. 'You said we could go home! You promised!'

'I do promise.'

A small fist struck her shoulder. '*When?*'

'As soon as I can, honey. I swear to God.'

The sun was lower in the sky, and the many

waterfalls crashing down the giant marble cliff were no longer pale blue but pastel pink. The pool at the base of the cliffs boiled and bubbled. No sign of the others on the tiny marble rim above. Had they already tried to get down? Had Shay dived? A bird of prey was circling in the air, just above the second pool. Was his body floating there, food for predators?

And now the bird was plummeting . . . descending in a tight rapid spiral down the smooth face of the cliff beside the falls. Not a bird of prey, but a falling body.

Aoife let the child slither to the ground and rushed forward in terror, her hands raised to the sky, trying to summon power. Maybe she could somehow catch him, hold him up . . .

The sound of terrified screaming was becoming audible over the crash of the falls beside her. '*AaaaaaaaEEEEEE!*'

Her mind was black with panic, swirling . . . There was nothing in her hands, no power, nothing in her blood, nothing . . .

'. . . *AAAAAAAAAAAEEEEE!*'

Not Shay but Ultan, exploding through the clouds of spray, about to land on her like a sack of rocks.

'. . . *EEEEEEaaaaaaaaaaa* . . .'

Miraculously, he had sprung back up into the air – ten, twenty metres. Now he was falling again, shrieking – '*AaaaaaaaEEEEEE* . . .' – face contorted with the speed of his descent. Rising again . . . His screams swelling and diminishing and finally dwindling to gasps of distress as he bounced more and more gently to a halt and ended up spinning slowly two metres above her head, making hoarse strangled squeaking noises. A thin rope was knotted around his chest and stomach.

Aoife was laughing hysterically with relief. 'What the—? You bungee-jumped?'

He squealed in an unnaturally high voice like he could hardly breathe: 'Bungee-*what*? Get me down!'

'Hang on—'

'I am hanging on! Does it look like I'm doing anything else?'

She wrenched a long branch from a yew, hooked him by the front of his shell suit and dragged him down towards her until she could get hold of his legs and pull him the rest of the way. She hugged him tight. 'Oh, Ultan . . .'

He pushed her away, fumbling with the rope tied

around his middle. 'Don't squeeze me – this yoke has me cut in two as it is!'

'Here . . .' As soon as Aoife touched the knot, it came undone and jerked out of her hand, shrinking up into the misty air like elastic contracting. 'I can't believe that rope was long enough to get you down.'

Ultan was sucking in lungfuls of relief, visibly expanding around the waist. 'I know! Me too! I'm telling you, that's the last time I ever let myself be seduced by a lenanshee.'

'*What?*'

'Talked me into it! Said he could lower me to the next pool, then he'd dive after us and lower me to the next, but soon as my feet were dangling in the air, down I went like a stone and I was that sure the damn yoke had snapped on me – all I could see was the ground coming up to meet me and— *Mother of God, here they come!*'

A wild shrieking signalled the rapid descent of Shay and Caitlin on the rope, Shay with his arms firmly around Caitlin's waist. As they nearly hit the road and bounced back up again, Aoife could hear the changeling girl screaming: 'Quit hugging me, ya sick lenanshee! I told you I can fly!' And the next moment she sprang free of Shay's arms, double-somersaulted through the air and crashed face-first into the water beside them, fire spurting from her hands like she was a malfunctioning Catherine wheel. The heaving flood extinguished her in a cloud of steam, spun her round, then swept her down the river where, just before disappearing round the far bend, she managed a desperate doggy-paddle to the bank. Climbing out, she pulled off the kitbag, and stood with her back to them, grimly emptying it of water.

Ultan jogged off towards her, calling, 'Great lepping, ya mad rabbit!'

Shay untied himself and dropped – he tried to catch the end of the rope, but it sprang back up into the watery air; he watched with a frown as it shrank from sight. Then he stuck his hands in his pockets and turned his gaze to Aoife, saying, with an uncertain smile, '*Wahu . . . ?*' like he wasn't certain whether she might do something utterly crazy if he spoke to her – like kissing him then flinging herself off a cliff. Before she could think of what to say or even what manner of neutral expression to adopt (cool? friendly?), he had transferred the same warm smile to Eva. 'Hello there. What's your name?'

Eva had crossed onto the bank from the road and was regarding him from a cautious distance, hands in the pockets of her dirty pink dressing gown. She said in her shrill north Dublin voice, not coming any nearer, 'I'm Eva O'Connor and I'm from Dublin.'

'Well, it's nice to meet you, Eva O'Connor. Have you been here long?'

The little girl drifted closer to Shay. Her distrust of strangers seemed to have melted in his presence. 'Ages and ages. But *she*' – she jerked her chin at Aoife – 'she says she's going to take me home.'

'Is she now.'

'Yes, she *promised*.'

'Then I'm sure she will. She's pretty reliable.' He squatted down in front of Eva and brushed his right forefinger across the locket that was now clasped around her neck. 'I see she lent you her special necklace.'

'It's not hers, it's mine.'

'Of course it is.'

Aoife said, 'Seriously, it *is* hers. Her parents gave it to her.'

'Ages and ages ago,' said the little girl. 'For my last birthday. When I was four. So as I don't forget them ever.' And as if practised in so doing, she flicked open the heart-shaped locket with her finger and thumb and kissed the faces of Maeve and James O'Connor.

Shay's hazel eyes caught Aoife's, astonished. 'Is she . . . ?'

'Yes.'

'Aoife knows my mam. Do you know my mam?'

He said, still looking at Aoife, 'Not as well as Aoife does.'

'Aoife's bringing me home. Are you coming home too?'

'I am, of course . . .'

'To Dublin?'

'No, Kilduff.'

'I don't know Kilduff.'

Shay's eyes switched towards the yew forest, and darkened with shock. He sprang to his feet, snatching up the child while grabbing Aoife's wrist and yanking her hard against him. He hissed, '*Don't run. Keep still.*'

'What the . . . ?' She craned to look over her shoulder. 'Oh . . .'

The dogs had followed her; they were stealing out from under the shadows of the yews, taking up position in a line on the dusty road, twelve of them, heavy-shouldered and thick-necked as bulls, and all of them smiling their grim, spit-dribbling smiles. Thirty metres away, down the bank, Caitlin and Ultan had their backs turned, oblivious. Eva pressed her face into Shay's smooth brown neck. She said in her high voice, 'They're just stupid dogs. We're not scared of stupid dogs.'

He set his cheek briefly to the child's light blonde hair. 'Good girl. Now, we're going for a swim, so hold tight . . .'

Aoife said, 'I can sort this.'

'This is *not* the time for doing something crazy.'

'I'm not crazy.'

'*Aoife* . . .'

With one quick twist, she wrenched her wrist out of his grip and ran forward, screaming at the lead dog: 'Sit! *Sit!*'

The beast cocked its elongated, bony head and lowered its haunches to the ground, settling them carefully. Once sitting, it raised its snout and fixed its pale eyes on hers – their whiteness had a rainbow shimmer, like monstrous opals. A high, rustling whimper rose from the dog's throat – a sickly whine.

She said, '*Stay*, dog.'

The dog wrinkled back its dark lips to reveal its clusters of thin yellow teeth, edged in thick white spittle.

She said, 'Lie down.'

He lay down. Another dog, younger and smaller than the rest, flesh puppy-soft, his head only as high as Aoife's waist, followed suit. She snapped at those still standing: '*Lie down!*' Each one, as it met her eyes, drew in its tail between its legs and pressed its belly to the ground, laying its drooling head on the dusty road between its mighty paws; massive ribcage rising and falling with its foul panting.

'You're not scared of dogs, are you?' the little girl was saying to Shay behind her. 'Dogs are just stupid.'

'Twelve cooshees, Ultan. Twelve! We're marching home to Falias with twelve demon dogs! This is way impressive. Who knew it could be so easy? All that time chasing after the cats, and we could've just whistled for these thick eejits. You'd think it'd have been in the book! Useless piece of druid crap.'

'Maybe cooshees don't act so easy around everyone. It's Aoife they seem to like.'

'That's just 'cos they met her first. Dogs are all the same. If you show no fear, they know well who's boss.'

Clearly unconvinced, Ultan said, 'Right.'

The dogs had formed a tight guard around Aoife – heads tossing, tongues lolling, tails in the air like flags. Night was falling, and the low hills of yews rose dark green against the sunset to the west, and the sky above was a deepening turquoise pricked by stars. Shay was striding along on her left, his old silent self. Eva was riding on his back, her skinny arms locked around his neck, legs dangling down to his waist, little feet jogging up and down. Her bedroom slippers were decorated with Sleeping Beauty motifs.

Caitlin and Ultan were half running, half walking along in front – keen to get to the city, now that they were so close. The changeling girl was still expounding cheerfully on their good luck: 'We'll make the zookeeper give us money as well as passes. Sure, twelve cooshees must be worth a fortune.'

'Yay – then on to Falias and spend, spend, spend!'

Aoife called to them, 'What sort of things do you do there?'

Ultan turned to jog backwards for a moment. 'Music! Craic! Magic competitions! Ah, we can have great fun all together. What d'you want to do first – eat or go dancing?'

'Eat! I'm starving!'

'Good stuff. The food is mighty – pork, roast potatoes, cheese. No more burned rabbit!'

Aoife glanced at Shay. 'I really *am* starving – maybe we can grab a quick bite to eat while we're passing through?'

He glanced at her and shrugged. 'Sure, while we find out where is this road home.'

Caitlin jeered over her shoulder, 'Falias *is* her home, hey! No one's going to be giving a changeling permission to leave paradise; not until the war. Link up with your own kind, lenanshee boy – they'll show you the way to the surface. I know you lot have a famous *grá* for humans.'

Shay paused in mid-stride, stared at the changeling girl, then at Aoife.

Aoife was trembling – shocked, but at the same

time pleased for him. 'That's so brilliant for you – you can get home whenever you like!'

He said coolly, falling back into his stride, 'I told you, I'm not going anywhere without you.'

'But if it turns out I can't and you can, at least you can tell my parents I'm safe.'

'Could you take a message to mine as well as hers?' asked Ultan quickly.

Caitlin scoffed, 'Give over, the two of ye – cut your human ties. Your aul parents don't care a damn about you, they're just delighted to be rid of ye.'

Eva, who had been nodding off, raised her head suddenly. 'Are we home yet?'

Aoife said to Shay, 'And that's another reason for you to go. You can take Eva with you.'

'I told you, I'm not—'

Caitlin shouted, 'Hey! He's not taking that kid anywhere: sheógs belong to the banshees, not the lenanshees! Soon as we get to Falias, you've to give her back!'

Aoife snapped back angrily: 'I'm not giving her to anyone!' and the guard of dogs suddenly rushed at the changeling girl, bristling and growling. Aoife ordered hastily, 'Down. Quiet.'

Caitlin, who had instantly sprinted for the trees, came back snarling, 'Just get your stupid beasts under control, all right?'

'Shay's taking Eva home.'

'Grand so. Whatever you want.'

Ultan said, 'That's the way, Caitlin. Show no fear.'

The road had turned away from the edge of the river and they were climbing rapidly uphill through the trees. The fallen needles made a soft carpet beneath Aoife's bare feet. The sun was gone, and the sloping woods were heavy with shadow. In the distance, above the pitch-black trees, the rose-gold sunset seemed to increase in strength as the night behind them darkened.

The child sat resting her chin on Shay's black hair, watching the darkening world with her ice-blue eyes. Seeing Aoife gazing at her, she smiled and stretched out her small hand.

Taking it, Aoife cupped it in her own. And had a weird, chilling moment of recognition. A straight, pink, diagonal line across the palm. She looked at her own hand. A single faint silver line: the scar from that forgotten accident on her first bike. She peered again at the much fresher mark on Eva's hand. 'How did you get this, honey?'

'The nurse said if I kept still, she could make me better. The other little girl cried, and her blood came out shiny. The nurse pressed our hands together. It made me better.'

Aoife placed her palm on Eva's. The scars would have been the same length, except that her hand was much larger now.

The child said sadly, 'The nurse took me away and kept me for ages. Then she said I had to go home and get back the other little girl.'

'I know, honey. I saw you.'

'No, she sent me to the wrong place. It wasn't Dublin, it was an empty, lonely place, and I couldn't find the fairy child.'

Remembering – re-experiencing – that first violent tug on her heart, Aoife said, 'You did find her, honey.'

'I didn't – a big girl came running after me instead. And I was scared and ran away up the hill and I lost Hector.' She started to cry.

'Hush, hush – that was me, and I found Hector for you.'

'You did?' The tears dried instantly.

'He'll be waiting for you, honey, just as soon as we get you home.'

The child jogged along on Shay's back for a long minute, then said, 'After I came back, they said to go this way instead. But then the dogs chased after me and I got lost and I never did find her. Do you think they'll be cross? Maybe I should go back and look for her.'

'Honey, you found her – she's me.'

The little girl looked at Aoife dubiously, then gave her short-cropped head a violent shake. 'No. You're a big girl, and she was only little, like me. I think they'll be cross and take me away in the cart.'

'No one's going to be cross with you. My friend here is going to take you home.' Aoife looked at Shay, who said nothing; his eyes were more black than green in the dusk, like the rough coats of the dogs.

The track had narrowed to a path, barely wide enough for two to walk abreast. The yew trunks twisted, thick strokes of charcoal in the dark emerald light. Up ahead, through the branches, the sky was the same rich fiery crimson.

Caitlin stopped and said quietly, 'Ultan, look at that.'

'What?'

'Ssh . . . Keep your voice down. Lights on the river.'

The water, now far below them, had been a ribbon of blackness, but suddenly there were lights – dull, flickering lights that drifted fast beneath the overhang of trees, alternately hidden and revealed. A unpleasant, nauseous perfume drifted on the breeze.

Ultan said, 'Good stuff – it's people on boats, with lanterns. We must be nearly at Falias.'

'Ssh, I don't think it's people, I think it's *them*.'

'What . . . ?'

'*Them*.'

'How do you know?'

'Book says they travel in groups and smell like day-old puke . . .'

'Ah Jesus!' He made to run for it, but Caitlin grabbed him by the arm. 'Stay quiet, don't move – they're not stopping, we don't want to attract their attention.'

The procession was passing directly below them now and Aoife could hear the faint splash of oars. She whispered, 'Who's *them*?'

'Headless dullahans. It's all right, they'll go on by.' But even as Caitlin said this, the first of the boats slowed and drew in to the shore.

Ultan took a sharp breath. 'What are they stopping here for?'

'I don't know.' Caitlin's voice was panicky. 'They can't want anything with us. We didn't do nothing wrong – not me anyway. I'm not trying to steal the sheóg.'

'Let's run—'

'*No, they'll think we're trying to escape! Just stay still and keep quiet!*'

The rest of the boats were clustering in behind the first, the lights disappearing now, hidden by the trees. The splash of oars had also ceased. The four of them stood silent on the path above, holding their breath, listening and watching.

One by one, the lights began to reappear – this time not on the river but coming up through the steep woods. Three points of orange light . . . four . . . The smell grew worse. The pack of dogs whimpered and scuffed at the path with their heavy claws, snuffling loudly.

Aoife hissed, '*Quiet!*' gripping the nearest two by the scruffs of their necks.

Ultan whispered shakily, 'They're getting closer.'

'If they call the sheóg's name, I say we dump her and run.'

'*I want my mam!*'

Aoife snapped, 'Stop scaring her, Caitlin! Hush, honey, no one's going to hurt you . . .' Eva, weeping, was struggling to get down from Shay's shoulders. Aoife let go of the dogs to comfort the child – and in an instant, the pack was gone, howling and snarling, hurtling downhill through the ancient yews.

For a moment they stood shocked into frozen silence, staring after the rampaging dogs as they disappeared into the trees. The deep, fierce barking echoed back and forth in the dark woods, ranging from side to side and down towards the river. Yet there were no other answering sounds – no fighting, no shouts, no running of feet; even the orange lights had suddenly gone out. It was as if it were only the beasts themselves running wild in the forest – frightened farm dogs on a windy night chasing imaginary ghosts around the yard.

Ultan said, relaxing, 'Nice one. I think they've

frightened them off – fair play to— *Mother of God!*'

The cries of the cooshees had abruptly changed – several of the dogs were not barking now, but screaming. Then yet another changed its tone, then another, from courageous challenge to hideous howls of pain. Eva shrieked shrilly and covered her ears with her hands.

'Quick, let's go!' Caitlin took off at full speed up the path, followed by Ultan. 'Quick, now, while they're busy ripping them cooshees to bits!'

Aoife groaned, 'The poor dogs—'

'*Leave them!*'

Shay touched Aoife's arm. 'Come on, she's right – nothing we can do.'

'The poor brave dogs.' Swallowing her grief, Aoife ran after the others.

The path climbed and twisted, narrower and rockier. Roots caught her feet. Behind in the woods, the beasts were screaming. Ultan cursed and fell. Aoife sprang over him, and turned to help him up. Shay waited for them, Eva in his arms, her frightened little face buried in his shoulder. 'Are ye all right?'

Ultan gasped, hands on knees, 'Grand. Are they following us?'

The three of them stood listening for a second – the sounds of ghostly battle were still ebbing and flowing through the woods, but more sporadically and further back. Aoife thought she saw a lantern flare briefly, but only as the faintest orange spark. At the same time, a deep, ferocious barking started up down near the river, before mutating into a high-pitched, almost ethereal scream – a blood-chilling, gut-wrenching death-cry.

Shay shuddered. 'Come on.'

As they ran, Aoife dropped a little behind the others, listening. The canine screams had ceased now; all she could hear was the breathing of Shay and Ultan and the scuffing of their feet as they mounted the hill ahead of her, up through the dark woods towards the crimson sky.

About a quarter of an hour later, the trees thinned and they came out on the crest of a steep hillside. Caitlin was standing with her back to them, her hands on her hips, silhouetted against the brilliant sunset.

Yet it wasn't sunset, because the sun had long set. It was the pyramid city, its rose-coloured walls lit by a thousand golden fires that burned on every balcony and in every courtyard.

*

Falias up close was vast – much vaster than it had appeared from the top of the waterfall, because from there the lower two thirds of the pyramid had been hidden, and only the tip visible. The city that was now before them rose up out of a deep, circular valley; most of it burned gold, but its upper levels were pale blue, and the very point seemed to float above the rest, a delicate minaret of silvery white. The hill at their feet formed one side of the valley. On the far side, half circling the pyramid like a vast protective hand, was a hemisphere of marble cliffs, reflecting the city's lights as a solid sparkling wall of rose-gold. Above was a warm green sky, with a round yellow moon. The river emerged below to their left and swept round the city's foot, so bright with mirrored fire that Falias appeared to rise from a sea of crimson lava.

'Nearly there . . .' Shay started immediately down the hill. But Caitlin ran after him, grabbing him by his torn shirt.

'Stop. We can't just turn up.'

'Why not?'

'Because we can't get in without a pass and we

need money, and we can't get either without handing over a beast to the zookeeper.' She plumped herself miserably down on the dark grass. 'Danu, I so want to get back in. What d'ya let them cooshees go for?'

Aoife said sharply, 'They saved us from the dullahans!'

'They didn't need to, stupid dogs – we could have sneaked off and got away. It's your fault for not keeping them under control. This is a complete disaster. Even that burned-up cat would have been worth something to us. If stinko-boy there hadn't taken a dump near a pooka—'

'I didn't know it was there!'

'I bet it was the awful smell that attracted it, like blood to a shark.'

Shay hefted Eva higher in his arms. 'We have to chance it anyway – there's got to be a way.'

Caitlin said fiercely, 'Don't you listen? We can't get passes off the zookeeper without bringing him a beast!'

Ultan said, 'Well, let's go see him anyway, and explain we did have loads but we lost them.'

'Oh, for— Why bother?'

'I'm starving, Cait. He feeds the animals, doesn't

he? If he can feed them, he can feed us. And maybe he can get us some new kitbags before we go back out.'

'I'm not begging animal food off Seán Burke! I'd rather starve!' Caitlin's eyes were flashing, yet at the same time she sounded very young and hopeless. She sat cradling her kitbag in her arms like she was using it for comfort; like it was a doll. 'I'm telling you, we have to go back to Gorias – we have to get ourselves another beast.'

Aoife stepped away under the trees and waited a while until her eyes got used again to the dark green dusk. The fallen needles were spongy under her feet; the bitter smell of them sharp to her nose. There was an utter stillness in the woods – the sounds of the desperate dogs had long faded to absolute nothing. She felt a deep sadness at having abandoned the dogs to their fate. What were dullahans – creatures or men? They were *headless*? With what had they ripped the dogs apart? Claws? Weapons? Bare hands?

She listened, and the wind moved in the wood and branches bent. The needles on the floor shifted. The hairs rose delicately on her neck . . . So hard to see more than a few metres into this tree-cluttered darkness. She took another step forward. A darkness slunk through the trees . . . And another.

'Here, boy?'

She was only whispering, but her voice cracked with strain. Supposing it was the dullahans. The sweat rolled down the hollows of her neck and under her arms.

Five, six shadows, closing in around her. Aoife stayed where she was, her arms extended. They pushed their long bony heads against her back and chest; their thick fur was wet with stickiness. She stroked one after the other, running her hands up the ruffs of their huge necks. She counted only seven of them. The younger, smaller dog was present, but the biggest, the king of them all, was among the missing.

CHAPTER TEN

'Seven cooshees? Sure you have. Lovely creatures. I seen one once. A dead one, mind.'

'We had twelve—'

'Course you did.'

'But they got in a fight—'

'You'll get that. So, where's this famous seven— *Mary, Mother of God, ye were serious! Get them away from me! Them's dangerous beasts!* Oh, my heart . . . Don't you be after coming one step nearer, girleen – you get them straight over there into that cage – there, the one that's open . . . Holy Mary, Mother of Christ, and all her saints . . . Close the door on them! *Close it now!*'

'I have to get out again first, don't I?'

Aoife jumped out of the high wooden cage, then slammed it shut against the dogs, which were whining and jostling to follow. 'Sorry, lads . . .' She slipped her hand through the bars, stroking the bony nose of the youngest cooshee – badly slashed around the head and missing an ear, but otherwise one of the survivors.

Caitlin said, 'Now. Seven beasts. We want passes and money.'

'Tie the rope, tight . . . *Tighter*.'

'All right, all right.' Caitlin wound the thick sugán rope repeatedly around the doorframe, knotting and re-knotting. 'Safe enough for you now? Scared of cooshees? I'm not, they're safe as houses. Thought you were a zookeeper.'

'Can't help the job I was given by the Beloved. Lovely man, lovely man, not saying a word against him. Said I was perfect for this job even though I never minded nothing before but two cows and three chickens— *Tight*.'

Caitlin snapped, 'It *is* tight! Give us the passes and lots of money.'

'Don't be in such a hurry, girleen. I have to answer for every penny that goes through these hands.'

'There's seven there, Seán Burke – count them for yerself!'

The zookeeper drew nearer to the filthy cage; he had a head like an outsize conker, dusted with a cobweb of grey hair as fine and fluffy as a cat's. Every

340

item of his clothing was heavily patched – shirt, trousers, even the heavy boots on his feet. 'One, two . . . God save us. *Ye* might say seven, but if ye stirred these up together in the one pot ye'd be lucky to have enough to make one—'

Caitlin snarled, 'There's no rule we have to bring them in absolutely perfect. They're still in good working order. 'Tis only a few ears.'

'And three with stumps for tails – d'ye think I'm blind? And look at these horrible gashes across their backs – what did ye do to them? They've been whipped to pieces with something right powerful. I'm going to have to get the vet to them – it'll cost me a fortune, so it will.'

Shay's voice came from the darkness. 'We haven't got time to stand around chatting with you – we're in a hurry, so we are.'

The old man's eyes shifted, searching. Barely half a kilometre away across the valley, the city of Falias shed its brilliant light, but here between the high wooden cages all was shadowy. 'Who said that?'

Shay stepped forward. 'I did.'

'No time to chat, is it? That's very sad, very modern.' Then the zookeeper's gaze fell on Eva, who was now asleep with her cheek pressed to Shay's shoulder, mouth distorted. His face lighting up with interest, he hobbled over to peer more closely at her. 'Well, well, well. Is that your own sheóg, if you don't object to my asking?'

'She's mine,' said Aoife quickly.

'Yours?' He turned and looked her up and down, and his expression changed from blustering meanness to something deeper – cleverer. Like the ancient farmers at the mart judging the worth of cattle, hands in their shabby black coats and caps pulled down low. 'So you're the . . . A new arrival, are ye? That's very, very interesting, so it is.' He leaned closer to her, attempting a friendly smile, his face as creased as the patched leather boots on his feet and his teeth sticking out at curious angles. 'Why don't you come up to the house, girleen, and I'll find you a special pass?'

Aoife winced at the foulness of his breath. 'Four passes and some money.'

He cast up his faded, watery eyes. 'All right, all right – daylight robbery, but come on, the lot of you. I have the water on and I'll make ye all a nice hot cup of tea.'

Ultan's plump face lit up with sudden longing. *'Tea?'*

'Not *real* tea, laddie, not unless ye've brought a handful of Barry's with you.'

'Oh . . . ' Ultan's face fell again. 'No. I haven't.'

The zookeeper said sympathetically, 'I know, 'tis desperate, the food and drink ye get here in paradise, isn't it? No decent tea, no Kimberley biscuits. Unless ye know the right people, that is. But I'll do me best.' And he shuffled off between the ramshackle cages, beckoning to them, grinning and bobbing – servile yet powerfully insistent.

Aoife said to Ultan, 'We'll just have to get the passes and go; we haven't the time for tea.'

'I don't mind – if it's not Barry's original, I'm not interested.'

'Shut up about stupid Barry's,' grumbled Caitlin, hitching the kitbag up onto her shoulder again.

Seán Burke plodded along the muddy track in front of them, a stick in his hand which he occasionally poked into a cage to disturb whatever misshapen creature was curled up on foul straw trying to get some rest. If any hissed or snapped at him, he leaped back very nimbly for his age – which must have been well over eighty. It hadn't struck Aoife that there might be changelings here who hadn't been called home to paradise until they had grown old. How had this man spent his life, before he found out who he really was? He reminded her of two or three ageing bachelors in Kilduff: fanciful types, full of extraordinary stories about aliens and monsters – or 'pure shite', whichever the listener chose to call it. 'Away with the fairies', people said of them – and maybe they should have all gone away with the fairies years before, but they had stayed behind instead, trapped in the pub with only themselves and the barman for company. Had Seán Burke been walking back along the bog road late at night, full of brandy, when the sheóg finally called him home – and had he run after her like he was young again?

'Jaysus, will you look at the state of these craiturs,' said Ultan.

In one cage, a strange beast with toad-like skin and one leg was asleep on heaps of dirty straw. In another that looked empty, a small child-sized being suddenly materialized out of thin air, leaping and clinging to the bars with human hands – for a second Aoife thought it *was* a child, then saw its wizened face and claw-like nails. The little creature was naked, its body covered with a thick reddish coat of hair, matted with sticks and leaves.

'Grogoch.' Ultan grimaced. 'Disgusting thing.'

'Dangerous?'

'Only to priests.'

'*Priests?*'

'Can't stand 'em . . .'

'But why?'

'Ask Caitlin – apparently everything about everything is in that fancy book of hers.'

'I don't have no *book*,' hissed Caitlin over her shoulder, jerking the strap of her kitbag tighter so that it rode higher over her shoulder blade.

'But—'

'But *nothing*.'

Ultan dropped his voice to a whisper. 'Oh. Right. Sorry.'

'You thick or what?'

'Sorry.' He leaned in close to Aoife's ear. 'She stole it off the druids, and fat lot of good did it do her – she can't even read the useless yoke.'

The old man was peering at them over his shoulder. 'What's all the whispering about back there?'

'Nothing!' Caitlin glared threateningly at Ultan.

The building that the zookeeper had grandly called the 'lodge' was set apart in a clearing of muddy ground. It was circular like the cob house, but built of rough dry stone. A thatch of reeds jutted out all around it, extending almost two metres from the walls like the wide brim of a hat. Smoke, tinted orange-pink by the torchlight, rose from the high apex of the thatch. Inside, the floor was flagged with grey stone and the furniture was an odd mixture of roughly made sugán stools and heavy oak chairs, carved with fruit and flowers, that must have been salvaged from a grander residence. A small bed was covered in fluffy rust-red blankets. Stacked against the far wall were several rows of drawers with bronze handles, like something from an old-fashioned chemist's. There were keys in some of the drawers; a few stood half open. A copper pot with bronze claws for feet was boiling over an open fire, and bunches of dried herbs dangled from the rafters.

'Come in, sit down, the lot of ye – ye must be longing for some tea . . .' Seán Burke had climbed onto one of the stools, and was pulling down handfuls of the brittle, shrivelled leaves, picking and choosing, clicking his tongue against his loose yellow teeth. 'Dandelion, nettle . . . Basil, where's me basil?'

Aoife sighed, 'We don't have time for tea. Can you just give us the passes?'

Caitlin said, 'Yeah, and the money, you aul slobberer, and then we can get ourselves a proper decent drink in Falias.'

'Hold on there, now – where's yer rush? Ye must be tired to yer bones, all of ye. Sit down by the fire, warm yerselves while ye wait.'

'Wait for *what*?'

'Mm . . . I have to find another three passes, they're behind in the shed.' As he spoke, the old man stepped up onto the hearth beside Caitlin and threw his handful of herbs into the boiling water.

'Look, we don't want your disgusting tea.' But Caitlin said this in a softer, less urgent tone, as sweet steam rose from the pot and swirled thickly around the room.

'Lovely smell, ain't it?' Seán Burke set four clay cups on a tray, ladled in the boiling herb-water, and hobbled around handing them out. 'Drink up, all of ye. Let a poor lonely old man show ye a small bit of hospitality.'

It was hard to refuse – with a grimace at Shay, Aoife took the steaming cup; she was thirsty, and the scent reminded her of home, somehow. The sweetness of the garden, coming through her window on a soft summer night.

The zookeeper was saying to Shay, 'Lay the little sheóg down on the bed there – it's not much but it's grogoch fur; strange little beggars moult like nothing else. I'll be back nearly afore I'm gone.' And the door of the house opened and shut as he went off into the night.

Aoife inhaled more steam from her cup, and an intense wave of sleepiness washed over her. She sank down on one of the stools. Shay was also sitting down, on the fur-covered bed beside the sleeping child, head on hand, his cup resting on his knee. Ultan, who had taken one of the sturdier chairs beside the fire, tried a careful sip. 'Ouch – too hot.' He took another. 'Ouch . . . ' Then he started snoring incredibly loudly.

Caitlin, yawning, picked up the poker and

prodded him. 'Oi, Fat Boy, you're after frightening the animals.'

Aoife inhaled deeply again. Her mother's face drifted into view . . . She opened her eyes with difficulty. Shay was raising his cooling cup to his lips. She mumbled, 'Don' . . .' then tried to stand up and crashed sideways off the stool, her drink spilling across the floor. Shay set down his cup and came over to help her up.

'Are you all right?'

'Don' . . .' She made a desperate effort to control her tongue. 'Don't drink . . .'

Caitlin's face appeared at the blurred edge of her vision. 'She's right. I been having a good dig at Ultan with the poker and he still won't wake up. That cheating sneak of a zookeeper is up to something. I bet he has plenty of passes right here. Let's find them.' Still yawning, she marched over to the rows of little drawers, pulling out the ones that were already half open. 'Nails . . . string . . .' She turned the keys in the drawers that had them – 'Ugh, more herbs' – then tried the ones that had no keys. 'Locked. Bet they're in one of these.'

'Hang on.' Aoife got shakily to her feet and went

over to join her. 'Sometimes you just have to . . .' One after another, the locks clicked open beneath her fingers, as she'd known they would – like the drawer in her parents' bedroom, and the locker at school, when she'd forgotten her key.

The changeling girl threw her a puzzled glance. 'How many powers do you have, hey?'

'It's just a knack.'

'No, no – opening locks, that's a real power; it's on the list.'

'Oh. OK.' Aoife felt pleased with herself.

'And you can fly too, nearly as good as me. Ultan calls it lepping about, but we know it's flying, don't we?'

'Mm.'

Shay had joined them, and was checking through the drawers which Aoife had unlocked. 'What do these passes look like? These?' He held out a handful of small green and blue enamelled pebbles, like tiny worlds.

'No, that's paradise money – good find. Take as much as you can. And look for some thin red stones – that's what the passes look like.' Caitlin turned back to Aoife. 'You should meet this old fart of a chief druid, Morfesa. He was always on to me about how no one could have more than one power, always said I couldn't fly even though I showed him I could.'

'I wouldn't mind meeting a real druid.'

'Yeah? I'm not going near that beardy freak again.' Caitlin, head down, began rifling through the newly opened drawers herself. 'Ha! I knew it – here they are, loads of them. I'm taking four – no, what the hell, thirteen. That's the number of beasts we had today; not our fault the pooka and them dullahans picked off a few. We can use the other passes another time.' She glanced towards the door. 'Where's that aul slobberer got to, anyway?' She shoved a lot more than thirteen of the red stone wafers plus several drawer-fuls of enamelled pebbles into her kitbag and slung it over her shoulder. Then she suddenly launched a fierce assault on the unconscious Ultan, punching his head and kicking him in the legs. 'Wake up, you thick lump of a fool! What d'ya want to drink that tea for?'

As she gathered up Eva from the bed, Aoife cried, 'Stop! You're going to hurt him!'

'He can't feel it. Ugh, I've half a mind to leave him here, the big eejit.' But she wrestled the changeling youth out of his chair, dropped him – 'The fat fool!' – then started dragging him towards the door by his legs, his head thumping painfully across the stone flags.

'Jesus, wait!' Shay hastily stooped and grabbed Ultan under the arms. 'You'll give him brain damage!'

'Won't make no difference. Come on, let's get out of here, afore Seán Burke finds out we've been going through his drawers.'

CHAPTER ELEVEN

The bridge over the river was empty; small lavender fires burned in braziers along its length. Its parapets were made of white stone ornamented with vines and leaves and fruit, and at the far end it led to massive gates of solid bronze, which reflected the lilac light of the fires and the crimson glow of the river. Down the carved walls on either side of the gates tinkled rivulets of water, spilling from the open mouths of carved animals and from the cupped hands of tiny figures. A mighty scene was depicted on the doors – a mountain top, with figures descending from a fiery cloud, carrying spears and riding horses, and surrounded by hooded creatures.

Aoife murmured to herself:

'They landed with horror, with lofty deed,
in their cloud of mighty combat of spectres,
upon a mountain of Conmaicne of Connacht . . .'

353

'What's that, hey?'

'Something I heard somewhere.'

'Can't stand poetry.'

There was a smaller door, a postern, in the gate, and two red-headed changelings in parka jackets were sitting on either side of it, playing cards. They looked up as the others approached. Aoife was carrying the sleeping child, and Ultan – now half awake – was staggering drunkenly along with his arm around Shay's shoulders. Caitlin fished around in her clinking bag and pulled out four passes.

'Five,' said one of the pair, a youth who looked about seventeen.

'The little one's a sheóg.'

The other changeling, a girl of Aoife's age wearing a very short mini-dress under her parka, stood up abruptly. 'Whose sheóg?'

Aoife said, 'Mine.'

The girl said anxiously, 'I think we're supposed to call someone if—'

The youth was already opening the gate; he was smiling at Eva, who was still asleep in Aoife's arms. 'Take care of the kid. I had a little sister her age, back at— I mean, you know, up above.'

'Ugh, Eoin,' said the girl, disgusted. 'You're so full of sentimental humanized crap.' She sat down again and threw a card onto the ground. 'Your go.'

'That's the *tenth* ace you've used in this game.'

'Bet you wish you could do that.'

'Yeah, being able to cheat at cards is such an amazing power.'

'Better than farting music.'

'In the surface world, among my friends, that was considered pretty cool.'

'Well then, why don't you go back to . . .'

Aoife stepped in through the small postern doorway.

Inside, all was noise, bustle, music. She was in a large square lit by flaming torches; the place crowded with teenagers, eating, drinking, singing and shouting. On a plinth in the centre of the square stood a huge bronze statue of an elk; two girls were balancing on its antlers, and as Aoife entered, they leaped simultaneously into the air and glided away across the cobbled square, then had an argument about who had got furthest. Sitting on the side of a marble fountain was a boy playing a fiddle at great speed, smoke rising from his strings. A younger boy was juggling blue flames – as Aoife watched, he accidentally set his hair ablaze, yelped and dived headfirst into the fountain.

Shay appeared at her side, still supporting Ultan – who threw his other arm around Aoife's shoulders and slurred, 'Than' Chri' we here at las' – I love this ci'y . . .'

'It's amazing.'

'Le's go fin' something to ea'.'

'Me and Aoife have to—'

Aoife interrupted Shay. 'No, Ultan's right, let's eat first, just quickly. If I don't get some food into me, I'm going to pass out and then I won't be going anywhere even if I do get permission.'

Caitlin came striding past, wooden beads swinging. 'Come on, you lot – what are you hanging about here for? Temple quarter has the best street food.'

They followed her up a narrow street of glittering houses carved from the solid rose-quartz pyramid. They passed bronze arches that led into courtyards full of fruit trees. Chaffinches and blackbirds hopped in and out of open doorways. Three young changelings with hair of varying shades of red – from orange-gold to crimson-black – were sitting on a step; they were busy knocking down a set of small wooden dolls, shooting blue blasts of power from outstretched fingers. Eva, now awake and clinging around Aoife's neck, laughed delightedly.

Caitlin turned aside into another wider thoroughfare, this one lined with food stalls – wooden trestles heaped with toffee apples and dried plums, roast birds, pale golden cheese. Plenty of the blue-green money was changing hands. Down the street towards them, pushing through the crowd, came a group of older men and women in white robes, holding leather books, branches of mistletoe and small harps. Aoife stopped at a cheese stall, then looked around for the changeling girl; she was hurrying away from them along a darker, less crowded laneway. 'Hey, where's she going? She's got all the money . . . Caitlin! . . .'

The girl did not turn. When they finally caught up with her, she said coolly, 'Took your time.'

Ultan protested, 'You ran off on us without saying!'

'Did not. Just, I know a better place further on.'

'Ah, Caitlin, the best eats are all back there.'

'Didn't you see the mistletoe-and-harp brigade? I'm not staying here while a bunch of druids is on the prowl looking for sacrificial eejits. Come on, follow me.' Caitlin dived into an even narrower side street, and then another and another, until there was no light of fires or passers-by, but only moonlight. Several turns later, they were in a narrow alley lined with plum trees, the fruit rolling and slippery beneath their feet. A high wall blocked their way, unexpected in the dark.

Ultan, just ahead of Aoife, peered around. 'Where's she gone now—?'

'*Over here!*' Caitlin's pale green eyes were on a level with the pavement, glinting like the eyes of a rat. 'Come on down!'

'Ah Jaysus, where are you taking us?'

'Didn't you say you wanted Barry's tea?'

'You mean . . . *What?* Caitlin, these are serious guys!'

'Which is why this is a good place to keep our heads down. No druids in here.' Her eyes disappeared below pavement level.

The bronze basement staircase led down to a wooden door, through which Caitlin disappeared as they followed her down. It led into a vaulted cellar, poorly lit by four or five candles.

Once her eyes got used to the dimness, Aoife could make out a number of changelings much older than the norm – in their thirties, even forties – standing arms folded at a stone-built bar, drinking out of wooden cups in absolute silence. Very young changelings of Donal's age were moving between them, carrying clay bowls.

Caitlin seemed to know the place well – she stopped a little girl in a flounced white communion dress. 'Anything interesting on the menu today, Katie?'

The child consulted the piece of slate in her hand, written on with chalk. 'Tinned frankfurters, Laughing Cow cheese, Tayto crisps.'

'Cheese and onion?'

'Course. A packet of Kimberleys but they're a bit stale. Wedding cake. Fanta. Barry's tea.'

Ultan breathed, 'Excellent.'

'We'll have the wedding cake, Laughing Cow cheese, a few cans of Fanta and some Taytos. And a pot of Barry's for Fat Boy there. And bring us some light into that corner.' Caitlin marched off towards the back of the bar, where there was a collection of sturdy sugán stools.

As they followed her, Ultan murmured to Aoife, 'These guys are dangerous, but the food here is great.'

'What on earth is this place all about?'

'Some of the older changelings like to get their hands on human food. I don't know how they manage it, but they source some really nice stuff. They claim they get it off new changelings who happen to have it on them when they're called down. But everyone knows one or two of them are sneaking it in from above.'

'They know a way to the surface world?'

Shay looked round sharply. 'Is that true?'

Ultan whispered, 'Ssh, keep your voice down – you'll get us thrown out.'

As she took her seat, Aoife turned to study the drinkers at the bar. They were soberly dressed, most wearing suits and ties, and all keeping themselves to themselves. One of them had a small plastic bottle of Coca-Cola in front of him, from which he was sipping very slowly.

Caitlin slapped her arm. 'Don't be staring at them! They don't like it!'

'But if they know the way—' Aoife met Shay's eyes.

'Danu's sake, let's at least get some food into us before the two of ye start asking stupid questions and we all get our throats cut.'

'*What?*'

'I'm telling you, these are serious hard guys. You got to be a lunatic to risk getting your name called by a dullahan just for a bag of Taytos – even if you can get good money for it.'

The child came over with a lighted candle, which she jammed into a crevice in the wall beside them, and then with two tin bowls which she set on a fifth stool. The Laughing Cow cheese came in individually wrapped triangles; the wedding cake was roughly cut, and one of the figures that had topped it – the bride – was still stuck into the icing of one slice, though her head was missing. Caitlin unwrapped a cheese triangle with ill-concealed relish. 'God knows why anyone would still want to eat this human crap.'

'I'm in heaven – cheese-and-onion Taytos!' Ultan ripped open a packet with his teeth and began cramming them into his mouth. 'Where's my tea?'

'Coming.' The child ran off again.

Eva sat on Aoife's knee looking around. 'Is this home?'

'No, honey – later. Do you want some cake?'

'Crisps and Coke.'

'Is it possible to get her some Coke?'

'No, it'd cost every coin we have, and I wish you'd stop lugging that stupid kid around with us,' Caitlin said irritably. 'You're like a banshee with her. People are looking.'

'No one's looking.' It was true – every single patron of the bar had their backs firmly turned.

Except for one small man, who had just come down the stairs and was staring straight at them across the shadowy room. Aoife became horribly aware of the wealth of stolen enamelled money and red passes at the bottom of Caitlin's kitbag. 'Crap.'

Shay, a slice of wedding cake in his hand, followed her eyes. 'What's the—? Oh, I see.'

The zookeeper was coming towards them, almost bowing – his usual peculiar mixture of servility and authority. 'Come along now, lads and lassies.' The drinkers and eaters at the bar didn't look behind them or move a muscle.

Caitlin stood up, face flushed. 'You owed us them

passes and money, Seán Burke – those cooshees are worth a fortune and you know it.'

'Quite right, quite right. Come on now, yer carriage awaits. The Beloved wants a word.'

Ultan nearly choked on his crisps. '*The Beloved?*'

'Lovely man, lovely man . . . Gave me my first job here, insisted I was the man for it, even though I warned him about my heart . . .'

Caitlin said in a trembling voice, 'Is it this stupid sheóg here that's got us in trouble? You can take her and good luck.'

Also standing up, Aoife snapped, 'No, you can't!'

'Leave her or bring her, whichever ye decide, girlies. 'Tisn't the sheóg the Beloved is after. And no one's in any trouble. All he wants is to get a good look at ye all, 'cos ye're all so lovely. Come along, stand up there, lads.'

'Oh God . . .' Ultan was cramming the rest of the crisps into his mouth as fast as he could, cheeks bulging. 'At least let me eat another bag . . .'

'Take it easy, lad, there'll be plenty more meals for all of ye. 'Tis just an invitation to a pleasant chat, not a walk down death row.'

Taking a slow, unhurried bite of his cake,

Shay said, 'Supposing we don't want to be going anywhere?'

'Ain't no one here going to help you, my lad, if force turns out to be necessary. But why would it be? Sure, there's nothing wrong here at all. Now get up and follow me.'

And still the men at the bar sat with their backs turned.

The coach blocking the narrow lane at the top of the steps reminded Aoife of the horse-drawn vehicles travellers used for funerals in Clonbarra – high-wheeled, polished black. It sat in silence, the door open. The coachman was hunched on the box, the hood of his cloak pulled up, a long white whip in his hand. A lantern hung from a hook beside him, burning with a rotten scent. Four small black horses were harnessed to the vehicle; they stamped and tossed their heads.

'Climb up, take a seat!' The zookeeper gleefully ushered them up the steps of the coach. The interior was empty. Two hard benches faced each other across a narrow aisle. There were no windows apart from a small rectangular shutter behind the rear seat, which was bolted. A whip cracked up front, the carriage jerked, jangled; the high wheels creaked and began to roll away. Seán Burke ran alongside them for a few paces, holding open the door. 'Say hello to the Beloved from me, and if he has any other kind of a job going – something in an office, say . . .' He slammed the door on them, plunging them into darkness. Aoife kneeled up on the back seat, fumbling for the shutter and jerking it open; the coach was already thundering along very fast, careering wildly round torch-lit corners.

Caitlin threw herself down on the opposite bench, a furious expression on her freckled face. 'I don't know what this is about but it's definitely nothing to do with me. I didn't steal anything.'

Ultan crouched down holding his hand out to Eva, who was sitting cross-legged on the floor with her back to the bench, eating Taytos. 'Come on, just one.'

'No.'

'Poor Ultan's tiny tum is hollow with the hunger—'

'*No!*'

Shay joined Aoife on the back seat, also kneeling to look out, his head close beside hers. He said under his breath, 'I'd say if all this buck wants with us is a chat, we should sit quiet and let him do all the talking.'

She smiled – it was so like Shay Foley to advise silence as a strategy. 'But if we want to find the way home, maybe he's the best one to ask.'

'I'm serious, Aoife. I don't think we should let him know what's in our minds. I don't like being dragged off to see him like this, whether we want to or not.'

'Me neither, but I suppose it's not as if he's the devil. The people of Danu left him in charge of the queen's daughter, so he can't be a monster. He was the queen's Beloved.'

'Then what does he want with us? We're nothing to him.'

'Maybe he likes to welcome new arrivals. Or maybe he wants to know how we captured all those cooshees. The zookeeper said he'd only ever seen a dead one before.'

Shay fell silent, staring out of the small window, his cheek so close to Aoife's that she could feel the heat of his skin. They were rattling along more crowded streets now, the driver making very little attempt to avoid what was in his path. Changelings who had just leaped out of their way remained frozen in position as the coach crashed by – mouths open, arms wide. A stall shuddered and nearly keeled over, ripe plums smashing on the cobbles. Clouds of pink chaffinches rose twittering.

Caitlin suddenly unfolded her arms and slapped Ultan across the head. 'This is *your* fault, ya thick eejit!'

'Ow! No it's not! How is it?'

'You went mouthing off about my book!'

'*Your* book?'

'And that aul slobberer of a zookeeper must have heard you and told the Beloved!'

'Ow! Give over hitting me! You shouldn't have stolen it in the first place!'

'How else would we have managed out there? It saved our lives a ton of times!'

'Caitlin, you can't even read it—'

'*I can so!* You're just jealous. And now I'm going to have to dump it before they search my kit.' She stood up and pushed in between Aoife and Shay, the leather volume in her hand, readying herself to toss it from the moving coach; then sank back onto her seat again, mournfully turning pages. 'But it's been so *useful*.'

The coach thundered on between thick marble columns. Heavy bronze gates swung shut, and a long dark tunnel began to unfurl behind them, echoing violently with the sound of their passing. The walls curved away into dimness as the coach travelled upwards in increasingly steep circles, leaning more and more to the left. As it swung round the tightest curve yet, Shay slid heavily against Aoife. 'Ah – sorry.'

She laughed. 'It's OK.'

But he grabbed the back of the seat and jerked himself away from her, looking pale, as if what had happened were far from OK – as if the very feel of her against him was a violation of his space. Not looking at Aoife, he said loudly to Caitlin, 'So, this Beloved guy – what's he like?'

The girl said grumpily, 'How would I know?'

'Doesn't he run this show?'

'Yeah, but I never, like, *met* him.'

Ultan asked pointedly, 'Then why don't you read us all about him out of your precious book?'

Scarlet-faced, Caitlin stood up again, and this time didn't hesitate but hurled the book out of the back window. It bounced several times along the stone road, pages flying open, and ended up face down. 'There! Happy now?'

Ultan said, 'Oh, absolutely. No one coming this way will notice that lying there in full view.'

'Who cares if they do? We'll be miles away by—'

The carriage screeched to a halt, horses whinnying loudly; they all went flying.

After a long moment, all four of them got back to their feet and peered out of the narrow window. The stolen book was still guiltily visible under the archway through which they had just passed. Speechless, they turned and stared at the windowless door. No one opened it. Then came the sound of leather and metal tack being unhitched; horses' hooves clopped evenly away, fading into the distance.

Looking up from her crisps, Eva said calmly, 'Are we home yet?'

'Not yet, honey.'

'I want my—'

'Oh, for . . . I'm sick of all this messing!' Caitlin rattled the door handle furiously. 'Locked! Will I just burn our way out?'

Ultan said sourly, 'Sure, set this tiny enclosed space on fire with us in it.'

'Will I?'

'*No!*'

'Hang on.' Aoife pressed her palm to the bronze latch. The door opened wide, and the sweet scent of fresh hay flooded in. (Caitlin complained loudly behind her, 'Why didn't she do that before, the fool?') She jumped down to the stone straw-covered floor. The shafts of the coach were empty, the points resting on the ground. A single torch, set in a conical bronze bracket, showed red leather reins hanging from a hook and a heap of hay in one corner. They were in a stable – a long one, with a low arched ceiling. Tens of wooden stalls stretched away into the dark; the tall figure of the coachman was leading the four horses into the darkness, his hood pulled up over his head, the orange lantern dangling from his hand. 'Hey!' Aoife called after him, running forward a few paces. 'Wait! Where are we? Stop!'

The coachman stopped and turned. Under his black hood, where his head should have been, a cloud of flies hummed busily around the raw stump of his neck. The lantern in his hand was not a lantern after all, but his own decomposing head.

For a long shocked moment Aoife could not move.

The dullahan took a single pace towards her, and the rotting orange head opened its mouth – a long pale tongue protruded, and a mouthful of maggots spilled onto the stable floor.

Aoife slowly lifted her hand. Her arm was shaking. No power in her fingers.

A low voice very close to her said quietly, 'Go.'

The headless coachman turned on his heel and continued on into the darkness, the four horses clopping softly after him.

It took her a moment to find the speaker in the dim light – but then she realized that he was only a few metres away, leaning casually against the side of the nearest stall. He was wearing a long black coat over a loose dark shirt; his face was in shadow, but a shuttered lantern was sitting in the straw at his feet and by its faint light she could see that he was wearing heavy leather boots.

She said shakily, 'Thank you.'

'I'm glad to be of service to you.' He reached down for the lantern, opened the shutter and held it towards her at arm's length, studying her face. His eyes widened, and he caught his breath as if what he saw were very surprising, or very gratifying, or both. He said softly, 'You're welcome home.'

'Thanks – we only just got here today . . .' Aoife glanced behind her, expecting to see the others climbing down from the carriage. They were, but she could hardly make them out because the carriage was so far off – a black silhouette against the light of the single torch. It was as if, instead of taking a few paces after the coachman, she had run a hundred metres deeper into the stables. She turned back to the man. 'Where is this place?'

'You don't know?'

'No . . . How would I?'

He brought the lantern up to his own face, illuminating it in light and shadow. He said, 'Maybe you remember me?' There was amusement as well as warmth in his lamp-lit gaze.

'No, sorry . . . Who are you? Do you look after the horses? Are you the groom?'

He laughed. 'You might say that. Come. Look closer.'

Aoife looked, and for a passing moment something about his face reminded her of Killian – although this man was dark, not blond, and his eyes not pale grey but black. More than that, he was taller and older than Killian – in his early twenties, at least.

She said, 'I'm really sorry, I definitely haven't met you before.'

He looked a little sad now, his head on one side. 'But you've hardly been away from me at all.'

'Away from . . . ? Did you use to know me when I was a child, here in paradise?'

'You truly don't remember me?'

'Look, who *are* you?'

He came a step nearer, still holding the lantern up beside his face. Up close, his eyes were not black after all, but an intense deep inky blue under long, slightly upturned, dark copper lashes. He said, 'I am Dorocha. I am the Beloved.'

CHAPTER TWELVE

The uppermost tip of Falias, a minaret suspended above the city, had been hollowed out of a single white crystal, and its walls were so delicate that the moon shone through, flooding the chamber with a ghostly light. Arches opened onto the balcony that circled the entire minaret; blue silk drapes fluttered in the night breeze.

A round oak table was set in the centre of the room, laden with platters of half-eaten roast chickens, torn-apart lumps of pork, joints of beef. Tall wax candles burned brightly between the plates. Half-empty silver jugs of rose-coloured drink leaned drunkenly in bowls of melting ice. The centrepiece of the spread was a life-sized swan constructed of spun sugar – it had looked real until Ultan greedily snapped off its head. Now he was happily sucking its beak and breaking off sugar feathers to feed to Eva.

Aoife pushed her wooden plate away – she

had reached bursting point. Shay, to her left, was still eating as if he had plenty of room left, using a bronze knife to hack his way through a plate of pork and obscure knobbly vegetables. Caitlin was wolfing down her fourth chicken leg; she had her kitbag in her lap, one arm tight around it. Dorocha, the Beloved, was sitting on the stool next to Aoife, his elbows resting on the table. Leaning forward, he asked Caitlin, 'Is that good?'

She nodded vigorously, holding the bag tighter, wiping her greasy mouth with the cuff of her flowered blouse. 'Reminds me of Christmas dinner at my aunt's. My mam – I mean Mary McGreevey – never gave me nothing but boiled potatoes and hardly any ham, she was that mean . . .'

The man turned to Aoife. He had shed his long black coat once he had escorted them to his dinner table; his thick linen shirt was loosely laced down the front with a thin strip of red leather. In the mixture of moon- and candlelight, he was very pale-skinned with high, shadowed cheekbones; his hair was not black but a deep volcanic red, like iron ore; his eyes were a starry midnight blue. 'Did *you* have chicken, ever?'

'Oh yes. Every Sunday.' An image came pouring into Aoife's mind: after Mass, herself and her parents at the kitchen table; roast potatoes. Her heart ached suddenly at the memory.

Dorocha was gazing even more closely at her. The flickering candles burnished his copper lashes with sparks of gold. 'You look sad. Were you not content in the surface world?'

She cleared her throat. 'It's not that – I was just thinking I need to let my parents know I'm still alive.'

'That can be arranged. Tell me about yourself, Aoibheal.'

A touch on her bare foot – Shay's own foot, under the table. Urging her to silence. But she was too delighted by Dorocha's offer to care. This man had been so helpful since she had met him in the stable – entirely different from the Beloved she had imagined. Not powerful and old, but young and easygoing – at the most only ten years older than her. He had insisted they eat and drink before they discussed anything of importance. He had brought them to his own apartments, high in the ethereal minaret. She said, 'Aoife, not Aoibheal. Could I really send them a message?'

He nodded. 'Of course.'

'Could I take the message myself?'

He raised his eyebrows. 'Is paradise so dull?'

'No, not a bit, it's just . . . Could I, though?'

Dorocha was smiling into her face with puzzlement. 'First, tell me – what was so much better about your life among humans that you are so eager to return?'

'I wasn't saying it was better . . .'

'How did you pass your time in the surface world?'

'How did I . . . ? Oh God, I wouldn't know where to start.'

'Try. I would like to know.'

'I don't know . . .' Such simple things, too ordinary to talk about, yet hard to describe. School and home. Writing songs with her guitar. Facebook and television. Trying to beat her own time on her bike. Texting Carla – what was Carla doing now? Three days ago they had been choosing dresses to wear, taking a bus, going to the cinema. 'It's not exactly exciting stuff.' She felt a stab of guilt for talking as if her best friend were ordinary.

Dorocha smiled and poured her out a cupful of the rose-coloured drink. 'At least I trust you were happy while you were gone. Your foster parents promised to be kind to you, in return for the banshee minding *that* little thing.' He tipped his head towards Eva, who was leaning on Ultan's knee, still eating sugar. 'Remind me, what were your human parents' names?'

Another touch on her foot from Shay. 'Maeve and James O'Connor.'

'And did they take good care of you, as they promised?'

Aoife took a slow sip from the cup – it was sweet, slightly fizzy, and tasted of the rosehip syrup her mother had insisted on giving her every time she'd had a cold. The memory was both comforting and sad. 'They did take good care of me, yes.'

'You sound unsure.'

'No, it's just . . .' It was a difficult, strange thing to come to terms with – that their kindness to her had all been for the sake of another child: their real daughter; the one over there, her head resting sleepily on Ultan's knee.

Dorocha said softly, leaning towards her, '*Did* they take care of you, Aoibheal?'

'Aoife . . .'

'Because if they treated you badly, tell me, and I will destroy them.'

'What? No! *What?*'

She stared at him in horror, but he was smiling, his hands raised – slightly mockingly – as if to ward off her anger. 'You were fond of them?'

'Yes! Very! They were fine! Good! Perfect!'

He lowered his hands. 'Then nothing will hurt them.'

'All right. OK.' But she was shaken by the casual easiness of his offer. She took another sip of the rosehip drink, for the homeliness of the taste.

Dorocha pulled a ring out of his pocket – a small, rainbow-coloured thing – and spun it idly on the table top. 'I alarmed you. I apologize. You still have a liking for those who raised you. But I have good reason to despise all humans.' He caught up the ring and pocketed it again. 'You must have heard that a priest – in the name of his God – chose to murder my queen. That he stabbed her to death in her bed, with an iron blade so she could never be transformed. If ever I close my eyes . . .' He lowered his copper lashes until they touched his high cheekbones, then shuddered deeply and raised them again, looking straight at her.

Gazing into their deep blue darkness, Aoife said, 'I'm so sorry for your trouble.'

'I never sleep, Aoibheal. Never.'

'I'm so sorry.'

'Humans are murderers.'

'Not all of them—'

'They cause us *pain*.' Dorocha slapped his hand on the table. 'And any child of Danu who has suffered at their hands, they can come to me and I will avenge their pain.' He glared at each of them, then barked at Caitlin, whose pale green eyes were bulging with sudden anxiety: 'Will I avenge *you*?'

The changeling girl blinked. 'You mean . . .'

'Will I destroy this . . . this . . . What was your mother's name? Mary McGreevey?'

'No! God no. Don't go troubling yourself about her. I loved her boiled potatoes, and there was plenty of them.'

Dorocha studied Caitlin's face for several seconds; she flushed, and he laughed. 'The things we do to protect those who have wounded us.' He switched his gaze to Ultan. 'You?'

Ultan flinched. 'No, no, you're good, not a problem, everyone fine. Lovely childhood. Happy out.'

'Happier than in paradise?'

'Yes. What? No! You mean . . . ? Christ . . . Much better here, in paradise.'

But the man had become calmer; smiling now. 'It takes a while for any changeling to cut their human ties. And yet they must.'

'I've cut *my* ties,' Caitlin blurted loudly. 'I killed a priest.'

'You did? A priest, by the Fear Dubh! With what power?'

'Fire! You should have seen his face when—'

'Brave girl. When you return the book to the druid Morfesa, you may tell him I gave you permission to take it.'

Caitlin turned a yellowish white. Her mouth was still wide open to tell her boastful story but the words were now trapped in her throat.

Dorocha leaned slightly towards her, his forearm on the table. 'Did you really think that no one would notice you pick it up, down there in the stable? I can see better and further in the dark than I can in daylight, and I can see better in daylight than any other being.'

Not waiting for her to recover her speech, he

turned his head to look past Aoife to Shay. 'And you, with the black hair . . . How did you find the human world? Are you also finding it hard to break your human ties?'

But Shay was – or appeared to be – entirely absorbed in selecting an apple from the deep clay bowl of fruit.

The man shifted position, rested his other elbow on the table, and his chin on his hand. The firelight shone off his hair, bringing out the depth of the red, like the last coals smouldering in a dying fire. Once more, something about his face – the angle of his high cheekbones, the length of his eyelashes – reminded Aoife of Killian. He shot her a light smile, the shadow of a wink; then jerked his chin slightly towards the farmer's son. She turned; the apple had fallen from Shay's hand and was rolling in a wide complicated pattern among the clay bowls and silver cups before it came back to Shay and stopped. He looked at it for a moment, then picked it up again. Again it slipped from his fingers, and this time trundled slowly past Aoife's plate and into Dorocha's open palm.

Shay followed the apple with his eyes until the

man's long fingers closed around it, then withdrew his gaze and sat doing nothing for a moment. Then reached into the bowl for a pear, and started eating it.

The man laughed.

Shay looked sideways at him; took another bite of the pear.

The man said, 'So, did *your* foster parents treat you well?'

Shay said nothing.

Aoife said, 'They did, of course.'

'Wait, let him tell me himself.' Dorocha sat up and tossed the apple back into the bowl. 'Did they reject you?'

Shay glanced at him, his cheekbones darkly flushed, and remained silent.

'You don't like to talk about it . . . Your father beat you? Your mother didn't care for you?'

Aoife said, 'Look, please stop asking him these questions. His brother raised him after they died.'

In the quiet of the room Dorocha sat with his gaze fixed thoughtfully on Shay. The silk drapes fluttered in the night breeze and a barn owl drifted past the window on white outstretched wings. Somewhere there was music, too faint to make out the tune.

Eventually he said, 'There is something unspoken here. You are very dark-haired to be a child of Danu. You have a human look about you.'

'He's not human!'

'He's definitely not human,' said Ultan, almost at the same time. 'Is he, Caitlin?'

'No he's not,' said Caitlin, but she sounded slightly wild – clearly still frightened by being caught out about the book. 'But he's not one of us neither. It's not our fault, I swear – we found him in Gorias, he tagged along, he's a lenanshee—'

'A lenanshee?' The man's eyes widened – something between surprise and caution. 'A *lenanshee*? Are you certain of this? Let me look at you.'

He stood up and moved round the table. Shay also got to his feet, and turned to face him, his lips set, eyes steady. The two were of a similar height. Dorocha studied him very closely, with a half-smile. His mouth was narrower than Shay's, without the curve, the bones of his face more delicate; skin paler. He said, 'I suppose you do have the look of a lenanshee. Especially around the mouth – and the shape of your eyes. But not the *colour* of your eyes. The child of lenanshee, perhaps, by a human . . . But what colour is your blood?' He ran his forefinger quickly down Shay's wrist, and a fine thread of bright red spilled out. 'Human.'

Aoife stood up very fast; ice spilled into her veins and her fingertips stung.

Without lowering his eyes from the man's gaze, Shay placed the palm of his other hand over the wound for a few seconds, then took it away. The cut had healed to a faint pink line.

Dorocha raised his eyebrows at the scratch. 'Lenanshee skill. Interesting. Half and half.' He looked up at Shay's face again. 'Was it your mother who was the lenanshee? A foolish choice for your father to make.'

'It wasn't his choice.'

The man nodded, as if in genuine sympathy. 'No. But nor was it hers. There is no *grá* like that experienced by a lenanshee. They cannot help the hunger of their love. They cannot release the soul they are consuming alive. Soon you will experience that *grá*, and when you do, you will understand your mother better.' He paused, then tilted his head very slightly. 'Or maybe you have discovered it for yourself already . . .'

Shay lifted his head and his shoulders stiffened; he kept his eyes firmly fixed on the man's face. 'No, never.'

After studying him closely, Dorocha nodded. 'I see. Too young, perhaps. When you are older, you will feel it.' He turned his eyes suddenly towards the nearest archway, one finger raised, head on one side, listening intently. 'I think . . . Why not? They live very close to the summit of Falias, close to the ceiling of this world. I think . . . Yes, I hear them. They are coming. It is your human blood that calls to them.'

Shay's eyes widened with shock, and Aoife cried in fear, 'What are you talking about?'

Caitlin and Ultan leaped to their feet, scattering chicken and sugar pieces, yelping, 'Pooka?'

Dorocha laughed at them. 'Not a pooka – lenan-shees! And there's no need to be afraid. It is only human blood that is of interest to them. Whenever the queen had company . . .' His voice broke slightly. 'Whenever a human man . . .' He paused, recovered himself, then murmured to Shay, 'They will try to steal your heart. Resist them,' and walked out through the sea-blue curtains onto the balcony.

The air was filling with young girlish voices, and for a moment Aoife thought they must be coming up the stairs from the stables, but then it was as if the song they were singing was drifting in from the night beyond the balcony. She drew close to Shay, who had remained motionless where he was; she touched his arm but he quivered as if every sinew in his body were too tight, and shook her off. His hazel eyes were wet with tears.

'Shay? Are you all right?'

He glanced at her briefly, but not as if he really saw her, then called to Dorocha: 'What is that song?'

The man was leaning on the stone parapet, gazing down. Without turning his head, he said, 'You don't recognize it?'

'No.' Yet at the same time Shay touched his chest, as if unconsciously, as if his heart were saying something different – that it knew the song, and was stirred. 'Unless . . .' His eyes, fixed on the balcony, flashed wide in amazement. 'Ah!'

Aoife spun to look – 'What is it?' – and a moment later saw what had so astonished him: two slim white clusters of fingers grasping the base of the stone columns of the parapet. Then a pale figure came swarming hand over hand up the outside of the balustrade; a beautiful face with turquoise eyes rising into view over the railing, like a mermaid peering over the side of a drifting boat.

Shay took a step forward, saying, 'Who is she? *Who is she?*' Again Aoife put her hand on his arm, and again he shook her off – not as if he were annoyed with her but as if she were utterly unimportant to him. He added, in a kind of desperate agony, 'She's so *beautiful!*'

The girl clinging to the balcony glanced down behind her, then threw her leg over the railing. As she climbed in, another pair of hands grasped the balustrade. Two pairs . . . three . . . five or six slender girls in dresses of rich ivory lace, climbing quickly over the railing out of the night, as agile as squirrels.

'Ah God . . .' Shay was staring from one to the other, intensely, but ever his eyes returned to the first one he had seen. 'She's like a picture come to life . . .'

The lenanshees gathered in the curtained archway, peering with great interest into the candlelit room. Their gorgeous dresses clung to their bodies, falling a little below the knee. Then the first of them sauntered further in, with a sway of the hips and toss of her long black curls. The others followed, looking around, all with the same intense turquoise eyes; they seemed fascinated by their surroundings, running their fingers down the blue silk drapes; touching the crystal walls, licking their fingers to taste crumbs of sugar from the table. One paused by Ultan to run her hand over his round cheek – he flushed a dark, rusty red, and she laughed and prodded his plump flesh with her forefinger, as if to mock him for even thinking of her. A second took hold of Caitlin's heavy jaw and studied her plain face and missing tooth with a shudder. Another tugged lightly at Aoife's tangled hair and glanced at her torn, muddy clothes with amused disgust. But the first of them went up to Shay and took his arm.

When Aoife had done the same thing only moments before, he had twice pulled away. This time he did not, but stared down into the lenanshee's pale, heart-shaped face as if transfixed by the very look of her. He said in a low, trembling voice, 'Do you know me?'

'Come with me, Shay Foley,' the lenanshee

murmured, and touched her finger briefly to his curved mouth.

'How do you know me?'

'Not here. Come with me and I will tell you everything.'

He said on a deep breath: 'Ah . . . I must be dreaming.'

Aoife's heart filled with fear. She said, 'Shay . . .'

But he didn't seem to hear her. Instead, he spoke to the lenanshee, his tone a terrible haunting fusion of sadness and longing: 'As soon as I saw your face . . .'

'Yes . . .' breathed the lenanshee.

'I think every night of my life I have dreamed of you.'

Aoife's heart sickened and turned cold.

The others were crowding around Shay now, taking hold of his torn shirt, his brown strong hands. His hazel eyes met Aoife's over the girl's head, anxious but happy. 'I have to go with her. Will you be all right?' As if he were pleading with her to release him from some promise that she had never asked him to make.

With every nerve in her body she wanted to cling

to him; to drag him from the lenanshee's clutches. She kept her hands by her sides and, trying hard not to cry and aware that she sounded utterly childish, said, 'Just do whatever you want.'

'I have to talk with her, Aoife. There's a reason—'

'You don't need to explain.'

'I'll come back, I promise. I'll just be a short while . . . Don't go anywhere till I get back. A few minutes. Ten minutes – half an hour at the most.'

They were urging him now towards the narrow crystal staircase that spiralled down into the stables. The first of them had her arm around his waist. He moved with them, unresisting, his eyes again on the girl's face.

His father's love for a lenanshee had killed him. '*Shay, no, wait!*' But Dorocha's hand caught Aoife's arm, holding her back.

He said in her ear: 'Let him go. He has chosen her. He has human blood, but he is also a lenanshee. He will be as safe as anyone can ever be who has fallen in love. This is not your fight.'

Shay called over his shoulder as he moved on towards the archway, 'Wait for me, Aoife.'

'Please be careful . . .'

'Wait for me.'

And he was gone with them down the twisting stairs.

After a long moment Caitlin said, 'Ultan, shut your mouth.'

CHAPTER THIRTEEN

She had curled up on the bench to wait, and she must have fallen asleep, because the night had passed – the faint breath of dawn drifted in from the balcony, and the crystal walls pulsed with a pale pink light. Ultan had crashed out senseless on the floor, the front of his shell suit sparkly with crumbs of sugar. Caitlin was slumped with her head sideways on the table, using her kitbag for a pillow. Eva sprawled across Ultan's chest, also asleep. And Shay . . .

There was no Shay. He had not come back. After all his determination to go home – for both of them to go home – he had chosen to spend the whole night in paradise. Even though a day here meant three months had slipped by above. Summer, gone. The turf for his brother's farm brought in already, without his help.

Out on the balcony was Dorocha, a tall dark figure against the pinkish dawn, gazing down over the city like a soldier on watch. Aoife joined him, shivering, folding her arms on the stone balustrade. 'Have you been standing here all night?'

He shot her a smile. 'I told you, I never sleep.'

'You must do some time.' The morning air was soft on her face, and there was a strong sweet scent of spring flowers. On every side, the yew forests crept to the summits of the circling cliffs. Eagles circled far above, golden wings blazing in the sun which had not yet risen over the side of the valley. Small birds sang from every stone carving; the minaret, like all the city walls, was decorated in vines and gargoyle faces – Aoife could see now how easy it must have been for the nimble, light-footed lenanshees to climb up to the balcony. She leaned out further over the stone rail. Far below, at the foot of the city, the lights still burned a strong ruddy colour – fires in change-ling homes and courtyards. But under the minaret were tiers of dwellings where the light pouring from the windows and doors was a soft bluish colour. Over the dawn chorus of the birds she could hear the distant cool clear notes of a single flute.

Stepping closer to her, Dorocha said, 'The lenan-shee quarter is a shrine to the beautiful. See the colour of the light? They burn oil of bluebell. Beautiful.'

The stone of the parapet chilled Aoife's arms through her hoodie. 'Very.'

'And the lenanshees themselves – also very beautiful, don't you think?'

'Very.'

'Their eyes, their hair . . . No wonder men adore them. Are you cold?'

She pressed herself against the railing, to stop herself shivering. 'No.'

'Maybe it's because the floor is wet?'

'Oh . . . I see what you mean . . .' Lost in her misery, Aoife hadn't noticed that she was standing in a shallow skim of water that was running across the tiles of balcony and out through the balustrade – she glanced up to see where it was coming from. Everywhere down the pale pink walls of the minaret, golden droplets fell. Three floors above, the peak of the minaret was a circle of white blossoming hawthorns, spread out above them like lace parasols; dew fell from the branches, and trickled down from between the roots. For some reason, the sight of the hawthorns seeming to weep brought tears to Aoife's own eyes. She scrubbed the dampness away with the back of her hand.

With a look of surprised concern, Dorocha said, 'Are you sad again?'

'I'm fine . . .'

'Is it because you wanted that boy to stay here with you?'

'No! No, of course not. It's not like that. We're just friends, that's all.'

'The love of a lenanshee is a very dangerous thing.'

'That's why I'm so worried about him.'

'I didn't mean dangerous for your friend. He is a lenanshee, despite his human blood. He will enjoy their company.'

'Oh . . . That's good, then.'

'Yet you're still sad?'

Tears rising again, she burst out: 'I can't help it. I miss everyone so much.' And it was true, so true. She had never felt more lonely, more deserted, now that Shay had abandoned her and no longer cared about going home. She needed Carla, desperately. 'I miss my friend. I could so do with talking to her right now.'

'What is this girl's name?'

'Carla. Carla Heffernan. She's been my best friend for ever.' And suddenly the tears spilled out and ran down her face. 'Oh God – sorry, this is stupid . . . But Carla's just like a sister to me. I so want to see her. I *need* to see her. Can I go home now?'

Dorocha said coolly, 'No.'

Aoife sobbed. She had known it would be his answer. 'But *why*?'

'Every changeling must break their human ties.'

'I can't just stop loving the people who I've known all my life—'

'Aoife? There's someone here you might want to see.' A sleepy-looking Ultan was beckoning to her through the archway.

'Oh, thank God.'

But it wasn't Shay.

It was a woman with long black hair, who was sitting at the table with Eva perched rather awkwardly on her lap. As soon as Aoife entered, the little girl slipped down and ran to meet her, throwing her arms around her knees.

The woman rose gracefully to her feet; her tall body was enfolded in a scarlet cloak which fluttered in the warm breeze from the balcony. She was tall – much taller than the lenanshees; just as beautiful, although in a different, ageless fashion: skin white as milk, and eyes so black they were like the space between the stars. An early memory stirred in the centre of Aoife's mind – the sound of lambs in a field; a garden path. Being afraid, and lonely, and not wanting to be abandoned. Another girl's mother, asleep in the chair by the fire wearing a new green cardigan. Another girl, her own age, lying in the bed, in a clean pink dressing gown. A child in the grip of her own mortality. The banshee had taken out a bronze knife. Fay blood would cure the human child of death.

The banshee held out her arms, and Aoife flinched back, clenching her hand, remembering the exquisite pain of the knife slicing across her palm. But it was Eva who the woman was gazing at, with ravenous love in her black eyes. In a low, intense voice, the woman said, 'Come here to me, little girl.'

Eva clung harder to Aoife's legs and whimpered.

Aoife said firmly, 'She's with me.'

'The child is mine.'

'Not any more. She's my sheóg – I found her, and I'll do what I want with her.'

The woman turned her beautiful face very slowly to Dorocha. 'Who is this?'

Dorocha shrugged, and threw himself down in his high-backed chair. 'A changeling newly returned.'

'Did you call me here to be insulted by her?'

'No, it was because I have an errand for you.'

The banshee said in a deep, cold voice: 'I do not run *errands*.'

'Then think of it as a deal.' The man nodded at Caitlin's leather kitbag, from which the changeling girl had just raised her head, with a sleepy but startled look. 'There is a book in that thing which Morfesa will pay you for.'

Again, the banshee slowly turned her head, this time to study the bag. 'The book that was stolen?'

'Not stolen – borrowed. That girl has returned it.' Dorocha jerked his chin at Caitlin, who hunched low on her stool in a failed attempt to look small and inconspicuous.

'Why does she not bring it to Morfesa herself?'

'She is afraid of the druid.'

'*Hey! I just don't like—*'

'She is afraid he will make a sacrifice of her.'

Caitlin made a slightly strangled noise in her throat, but said no more.

'Very well. I will take this.' The banshee snatched

up the kitbag from the table in one hand, then walked straight across to Aoife and seized Eva by her arm. 'You come with me, sheóg.'

Grabbing hold of Eva's other hand, Aoife cried, 'Leave her alone! She's with me!'

'I don't take my orders from you. You have no powers.' And she dragged at Eva with such inhuman strength that Aoife was forced to release the screaming child or see her ripped apart. In a single motion, the banshee gathered up the little girl and strode away towards the stable steps, but Dorocha was on his feet again, barring her way.

'Set the sheóg down. The changeling is fond of her. The druid will give you others from the temple when you return the book.'

The banshee hesitated – reluctant to comply, but interested. 'How many?'

'Three.'

'Morfesa has agreed to this?'

'Tell him, it is a proposal from the Beloved. If he refuses you, come back to me. But until then . . .' He lifted Eva out of the banshee's arms and set her down on her feet so that she could run back to Aoife, then walked with the woman to the crystal stairs, where he stood talking to her in a low voice. The banshee glanced across at Aoife occasionally, pulling her red cloak tighter around her; eventually she turned and left.

Caitlin muttered, instantly bolder, 'Danu's sake, what a bitch.'

Still hugging Eva, who clung to her, Aoife crossed the room to stand before Dorocha. 'Thank you.'

He smiled at her, and said, as when he had dismissed the dullahan, 'I am glad to be of service to you.'

'No, it was kind of you to let me keep her.'

'I only want to make you happy here.'

She drew herself up tall, shoulders back, meeting his eyes. 'Then let me take my parents' daughter home. She'll never find the way by herself. She thinks she still lives in Dublin.'

His smile didn't falter. 'No.'

Frustration and anger made her face hot. Her voice came out louder. 'Why not, if you want me to be happy? If my parents have their own daughter back, they'll be happy themselves, and then I can be happy here. It's only fair – if you have me, why can't Eva go back to them?'

Dorocha dropped his head slightly to one side, appearing to consider her question, then shrugged. 'Why don't you ask your lenanshee friend? The road is open to his kind. He could bring your little sheóg, if he liked.'

Two different emotions swept through her: gratitude, that he would let the child go home; loneliness, at the thought of Shay going back without her. 'Thank you. Can you show me where to find him?'

'But it will be hard for you to persuade him to abandon his new love.'

Aoife half closed her eyes as misery swept over her; then opened then again. 'He's my friend, he won't say no.'

'Yet she is so beautiful.' And Dorocha's dark eyes lingered on every part of her, eyebrows raised, mouth twitching in amusement.

At once she became acutely, painfully aware of how ridiculous she must look — every part of her filthy and scratched by brambles, her hair in knots, her clothes encrusted with dirt and stinking horribly of cooshee, her trackies torn almost all the way down the right seam to her ankle, her toenails wedged with dirt. She repeated loudly, determined not to let this man undermine her trust in Shay's friendship for her, 'He will do it for me, if I ask him. Can you show me the way to the lenanshee quarter?'

'Of course.' Still his eyes travelled laughingly over her, from tangled hair to naked feet. 'But if you feel a need to wash yourself before you walk among them . . .'

Under his cynical gaze, Aoife felt herself weaken. She remembered the lenanshee who had looked her up and down with such disgust. And the one who had prodded Ultan's plump cheek mockingly, and the other who had shuddered at Caitlin's missing tooth. If she were to walk into their perfect world, looking like this . . . She could imagine the horror and the laughter. And she felt suddenly that she wouldn't be able to bear it if she saw the slightest sign in Shay's face that he was in any way ashamed of her. 'Maybe if you've got somewhere I could clean up a bit . . . ?'

'Of course. And when you are clean, I have dresses that will fit you, far more beautiful than any lenanshee has ever worn.'

For a brief moment her heart lifted. If she could look as beautiful as they . . . But then, why fool herself? 'You don't have to go lending me a dress; just a wash will do.'

'Aoibheal—'

'*Aoife.*'

'He is with the most beautiful girl he has ever seen. He promised to return to you last night, and he did not. He has no desire to return to the surface world. If you want to win even the slightest part of his attention, I strongly advise you to accept my offer.'

The fragile crystal staircase that rose through the wall of the minaret was narrow and twisting; they climbed in single file.

Caitlin had insisted on coming too, despite repeatedly declaring that she had no interest in dressing up. 'I'm a changeling soldier, I don't want to look like the bloody Rose of Tralee.'

Bringing up the rear, Ultan said, 'Don't worry – it'd take more than a dress to do that to you, state of you.'

She snarled, 'Shut your mouth, Fat Boy.'

When they reached the next floor of the minaret, double doors of bronze appeared before them. Dorocha thrust them open, and stood aside with a mockingly dramatic sweep of his arm. 'The treasures of the queen of the Tuatha Dé Danann! Take anything you wish, all of you.'

Moving past him into the chamber, Aoife stared around in amazement. Dresses of all colours spilled from copper-bound wooden chests; were heaped in corners; hung from silver poles. They were soft rose pinks and poppy reds; brilliant dandelion; sage green; the rich lilac of bluebells in evening light.

Sliding to the floor from Aoife's arms and running in among them, Eva cried, 'So pretty!'

Caitlin said nothing – but she let out a breath that trembled with desire. Ultan, who had perked up at the word 'treasure', was clearly disappointed. 'Just girls' clothes?'

Dorocha laughed. 'You, Ultan McNeal, follow me. I have other treasures that might amuse you.'

'Gold and jewels?'

'You have lived too long among humans. Try not to think of every wealth as mineral.'

'Then what—?'

'Come with me and see.'

The doors swung closed, leaving Aoife, Caitlin and Eva alone in the vaulted chamber. The windows high in the wall were curtained in deep blue, but fat wax candles burned brightly in brackets, supplementing the sunlight that glowed pinkly through the crystal walls.

'Pretty,' said Eva again, in an awed voice.

'They are.' Aoife walked along one of the rows of dresses, stroking them with her hand. They seemed to have been woven from actual living flowers – still soft and sweet-smelling and beautiful. She thought of the heart-stoppingly beautiful lenanshee girls in their floating lace dresses. Dorocha was right – these dresses were even more wonderful.

Leaning against a central pillar was a huge sheet of copper, burnished so brightly it served as a mirror. She paused as she passed it; she did look awful. Her face was splodged with mud and her hair was like a bramble bush. A large wooden comb lay on a marble block beside the mirror, along with a basin of water and a linen cloth. A small wooden stool stood beside the block. Taking the cloth, she dipped it in the water – it was warm and scented – and washed her face and arms. With a glance towards Caitlin, who was wandering around looking stunned, she stripped off her trackies, sat on the stool and washed her long legs and narrow feet. It felt good, getting off all the mud. She dragged the comb through her long, tangled hair, and studied herself in the mirror. Better. At least her hair wasn't greasy – in the last twenty-four hours it had been soaked in the sea, a lake and a waterfall, and bleached by hot sun. Gold threads glittered in the rich dark red. Her pale, oval face had caught the sun, bringing out the strong colour of her blue-green eyes.

'Oh my God – I mean, Danu – Aoife, look at this . . .' The tall, muscular changeling girl appeared from between the rows, holding out an item of silvery lace, very similar to the beautiful lenanshee dresses but thickly embroidered with pearls. She seemed to have completely forgotten her earlier contempt for dressing up. Her freckled face was alight with joy. 'I've never, ever, ever seen anything like this. I never even had a dress, 'cos my mam said I was way too ugly, not like her stupid human baby would have been. It's gorgeous, don't you think? Do you think it would it fit me?'

It *was* heart-stoppingly gorgeous, and it was obvious that it wouldn't fit. 'I don't like it, Caitlin. See, there's so many pearls sewn onto it – the bodice looks way too uncomfortable and the skirts must be much too heavy. Let me find you a different one.'

'No, I want *this* one.' And she glared at Aoife, like she suspected her of wanting it for herself. But when Caitlin tried it on, it wouldn't even fit over her shoulders. Her stone-green eyes dampened, like pebbles washed by a wave; she stuck out her chin, and held the dress out to Aoife. 'Go on then, you have it. It's bound to fit you perfectly.'

'No, I'm serious, I don't like it at all. How about this one on you?' The dress Aoife had pulled off the silver pole was as light as air: created of feathers, the sleeves had the fluorescent beauty of a kingfisher, and the full high-waisted skirts spread out in the glowing greens and blues of a peacock's tail. When she held it up against Caitlin, it swept the floor – another gown not made for action. But the changeling girl's eyes were starry at the beauty of it.

'Oh . . . Do you think I could . . . ?'

'Sure you could, it's perfect for you. Let me comb your hair and help you on with it.'

She re-braided Caitlin's bright red hair, and helped her on with the floating dress. Although it was designed as a full, loose gown, it was a struggle getting it on over her broad, strong body and Aoife had to stretch it across her muscular back, and realign the feathers to cover the gap between the silver wire fasteners, which she had to unfold and re-bend to get them to meet. But Caitlin couldn't see behind her – all she could see was herself in the mirror, and her face was no longer the face of an angry murderer of priests, but that of a little girl wearing a new dress to her own birthday party. Her pale green eyes softened, and without the scowl she was suddenly almost as pretty as Sinead – and far less cat-like. 'I never . . . If my mam— I mean, if Mary McGreevey could see me now . . .'

'She would say how beautiful you were.'

'Yes,' breathed Caitlin. She picked up the wet cloth and rubbed her cheeks. 'I am.' And when Eva plucked at the feathers and said, 'Caitlin looks like Big Bird!' she smiled fondly at her, wide enough to show her missing tooth.

Caitlin's enthusiasm was infectious. There were hundreds of dresses, so beautiful . . . But Aoife had her pride. She didn't want to look like she was deliberately dressing up to impress Shay; she just wanted not to look laughable. She took down the simplest dress she could find, and pulled it over her head. It hung straight to her knees. The hem had been dipped in dark blue dye, and from this rays of gold shot up to the paler rose-pink of the shoulders – the sun rising from the sea. There was a pair of red leather shoes under the rail, no more than slippers with no heel. She tried them on and they fitted perfectly, as soft as butter to her feet.

She went to stand beside Caitlin at the mirror. Good enough – no point in pretending she could be as gorgeous as a lenanshee. At least now she could go to find Shay without feeling like a complete fool.

The bronze doors creaked and she turned eagerly, thinking it was Dorocha come to bring her to the lenanshee quarter. But it was two changelings of maybe twelve and thirteen, one with an auburn bob and the other with such pale gold-red hair it was like liquid sunshine. They were wearing purple dresses and had bare feet.

Aoife said, 'Can I help you? Did Dorocha send you to bring us to him?'

'Oh no, not yet,' said the taller girl with the darker bob. 'Not until everything's ready.'

'Ready for what?'

Instead of answering, the girl went to take down a small gold casket from a niche in the wall. And then stood and whispered to the other girl, both of them staring at Caitlin, who was still wafting around in front of the mirror admiring herself in the splendid feathered gown. After a few seconds the big changeling spun round to face them, arms folded and feet squarely planted apart.

'All right, what are ye two staring at? I was told I could take any dress I wanted and I did. Have ye got a problem with that?'

'No, no, sorry—'

'Are ye taking the mick?'

'No, no! We were just wondering—'

'*What* were ye wondering, hey?'

'Please, does the little sheóg belong to you?'

'Not me.' Caitlin jerked her head at Aoife. 'That one keeps dragging the kid around with us everywhere. We had the dullahans after us because of it. Banshee wants her back, hey? Fine by me.'

But the two girls were no longer paying any attention to her or to Eva; instead they were staring at Aoife, and going pink and pale by turns. Then the one with the pure gold hair nudged the older, who came to herself and advanced slowly towards Aoife, opening and holding out the small casket.

In it lay a single pearl, threaded on a fine copper wire. 'The Beloved says you might like to put this on.'

Aoife caught her breath. The iridescence of the pearl reminded her of the rainbows that spanned the wilderness around Gorias. 'No, really – I can't wear that. Sorry, what's your name?'

'Niamh.'

'I need to find Dorocha. He said he'd take me to find my friend.'

'I'll wear it,' said Caitlin, taking off her hippy beads.

'Is there something else you would prefer?' Niamh asked Aoife. She said over her shoulder to the younger, 'Fetch the ruby flowers, Saoirse. And the ruby circlet for her hair. And a more suitable dress than this. The bodice of rubies, with the train of poppy petals to match. And take the pearl away—'

Caitlin made a strangled noise.

Aoife said with a sigh, 'My friend here would like to try this on.'

The two girls glanced at each other in surprise,

and Niamh said, 'You want to make your friend a gift of this pearl?'

'Not that it's mine to give away . . .'

But Niamh had already turned and slipped the thin wire over Caitlin's neck and settled the pearl in the hollow of her strong throat. Caitlin turned back to the mirror and sighed in pleasure. 'Have you got any more of these?'

'Oh no, that is very rare. It was stolen from the largest living oyster, by a selkie.'

'Selkie?'

'A seal wife. They take human husbands and coax them down beneath the waves.'

Caitlin laughed loudly. 'I'd say the lads don't last long.'

'No.'

'Well, if you haven't any more of these yokes, how about those rubies?'

Again the two girls looked at Aoife anxiously. Aoife gave a slightly despairing wave of her hand. 'Sure, go ahead.' Who was she to stand between Caitlin and her long-thwarted desire to adorn herself? Besides, she had had a thought. Eva looked very shabby herself in her grubby pink dressing gown and slippers. It would be nice to send her home looking as if she'd been well-cared for.

The queen's dresses were too big, but in one large wooden chest lying against the back wall she found some soft jackets of rabbit fur. She called the little girl over to try them on, but they kept slipping off her shoulders. A smaller darker casket, banded by copper, stood directly under one of the blue-curtained windows. She lifted the lid and found heaps of children's dresses.

'Oh, Eva, look at these!' She pulled out armfuls. Like the flower dresses, they were extremely soft and scented, but tougher, as if the flowers had been dried before being woven into flax. 'Which one would you like to wear?'

'Pink.'

'OK, hang on . . .' Near the very bottom of the chest, Aoife finally unearthed a short dress made of old-fashioned cottage roses. She pressed it to her face; it still carried that summery scent. She helped Eva off with her dressing gown. Underneath was the Sleeping Beauty nightie she had been wearing in one of the photographs. She took it off, then fetched the wet cloth and wiped all the mud from the child's pale skin, and combed her hair, then pulled the rose dress over her head. Eva gazed back at her with her round ice-blue eyes, her blonde hair curling down almost to her shoulders. Aoife said, 'Ah, you look so pretty, sweetie.'

The child's mouth tightened; quivered. 'Only my mam calls me sweetie.'

'Sorry, honey. Now, come and show the others how lovely you look.' She took Eva by the hand and led her back through the racks of dresses. 'Look at our little sheóg now! Isn't she lovely?'

'Very nice,' said Caitlin, still focused entirely on her own image in the copper mirror.

But the other girls, Niamh and Saoirse, turned to look and their eyes filled with tears, as if the sight of the little girl in the pink dress were very moving.

Aoife asked, 'Is everything all right?'

'It's just strange . . .'

'Strange?'

Saoirse said, 'To see a different child in that rose-petal dress.'

'Was it not all right to borrow it?'

Niamh said hastily, 'Oh, no, you can do what-ever you want with it! It's just, it seems so strange

– I mean, how much you've grown in such a short time . . .'

Aoife stared blankly at her. And then at Saoirse. 'I'm sorry. Did I know you two when I was here before?'

'Oh, Aoibheal—'

'My name's *Aoife*.'

'That's your human name.'

'But it's what I'm used to being called.'

'Ah, darling, you've changed so much in every way – and even more beautiful than before you left! But I'm still Niamh and this is Saoirse, and we haven't changed at all – don't you remember us even a little bit?'

It was the same as when she'd met Dorocha in the stables, when he seemed hurt that she had no idea who he was. 'I'm sorry, no.'

'But it's such a short time since you were sent away! We loved playing with you. I remember when we used to dress you in that very dress, the one the sheóg is wearing now.'

'That was *mine*?'

'Of course. All these dresses, all these jewels – they're all yours. Everything here belongs to you now.'

'What? *How?*'

'The Beloved said we have to dress you for the temple. Please let us help you to choose something more suitable, Aoibheal.'

'*Aoife.*'

'But don't you remember your mother calling you Aoibheal?'

An image of Maeve rushed into her mind, sitting at her computer in the same old green cardigan she always wore. 'My mother called me Aoife.'

'No, she called you Aoibheal. Do you really not remember the queen?'

'Why would I remember the queen?'

'Ah, Aoibheal, how could you forget your own mother? She loved you so much.'

'My . . . mother?' Aoife's legs felt like water. She moved towards the mirror, and sank down on the low wooden stool. Caitlin stood staring at her with her mouth open. The two girls in purple dresses hovered over her anxiously, as if not sure what to do to help.

'We're so sorry.'

'We thought you knew your mother was the queen. Now can we dress you?'

She closed her eyes and pressed her hands hard to her face. This was crazy – impossible. This was a dream. A nightmare. The daughter of a murdered queen . . .

'Aoife?'

'It's OK, Caitlin, just give me a moment.'

'Aoife?'

'*What?*'

'If all this stuff is yours, can I keep the dress?'

'What? Oh . . . Yes.'

'I mean, it fits me perfectly, so it's got to be way too big for you.'

'Keep it.'

'And the pearl?'

'Yes.'

'I don't suppose the rubies—'

'Yes! *Yes!*'

'OK. Thanks.'

Aoife took her hands from her face, opening her eyes. 'No, wait!'

'Oh, for . . . It doesn't take long, does it, before people who come into money get all selfish and greedy?'

'I'm not talking to you . . . Niamh! Saoirse!'

The two changelings in purple dresses came back towards her, holding up the dress of white lace and pearls that Caitlin had been unable to wear. 'How about this beautiful dress, Aoibheal? And you could wear the white diamonds and the crown of white-gold hawthorn with rubies for berries, and a train of swan feathers—'

'If I'm her daughter, why didn't he tell me right away? Where is he?'

'Waiting for you to dress yourself, Aoibheal.'

She jumped to her feet. 'If you won't tell me, I'll find him myself.'

The two girls cried despairingly after her as she ran, 'No, no, you can't go to him yet, not until you're ready . . .'

CHAPTER FOURTEEN

She raced up the twisting crystal staircase.

A door made of amber was set in the turn of the
stairs; it glowed a deep orange-gold from a low light
behind it, and in the amber were the shadows of
hundreds of bees, perfectly preserved as if drowned
in solid honey. A memory flickered – she placed her
right hand over the silver lock; it clicked open and
the door swung back, revealing another circular
room where the walls were draped in black velvet.
The only light came from a fat yellow wax taper,
over a metre tall, burning in a stone candlestick set
between the door and a small four-poster bed. The
bed had its black curtains closed. Aoife darted across
the room to drag them aside. Inside, the black drapes
and covers were splashed across with streaks of silver.

Back out and on up the stairs, and another door,
of gold. She could hear voices within – Ultan crying
out in alarm, and Dorocha shouting: *'Back! Back!'*
She threw the door open. Bronze-bound caskets

brimmed with treasure: gold rings, silver chains studded with amber, gold cups set with lapis lazuli, amber collars large enough to slip over a man's head. Fur cloaks were stacked up against the sunlit walls. In the centre of the chamber was a huge copper cauldron, upturned, and Dorocha was standing on top of it, laughing and stabbing down at Ultan with a three-metre spear – a flint head lashed to a wooden shaft. Breathing hard, the changeling youth was blocking the man's blows with a wide-bladed bronze sword almost as long as he was tall.

Aoife forgot her rage in horror. '*Stop!*'

Dorocha cast aside the spear, leaped down to the floor and came striding across the room towards her with his hands held out. Behind him the spear remained suspended in the air, darting back and forward like a shark, twisting and turning, still parrying the blows of Ultan's sword with ease. Half delighted, half panicking, Ultan cried, 'Help, they won't stop fighting each other! They just keep going!'

Dorocha clicked his fingers in the air, without even looking back; both weapons clattered to the floor. He barked over his shoulder, 'The game is over, Ultan McNeal. Leave us.'

'Oh, is it? Right . . . Us? Oh, it's Aoife. Hey, Aoife, what's the matter? Is everything all right?'

Dorocha had come to a halt before her, his hands still extended. She looked into his pale, fine-boned face; his midnight-blue eyes.

'Aoife, is everything—?'

She said hoarsely, '*Ultan, go.*'

As the boy left the room, closing the door behind him, Dorocha raised his eyebrows and said, 'It seems you can command the changelings of this world. Now, command *me*. Ask me anything you wish.'

But Aoife found herself unable to speak. It felt suddenly absurd to ask if she was the daughter of a queen. Dorocha's gaze slipped over her from head to foot – from the rough, sweet lavender tie in her red-gold hair to the sunrise dress, to the soft red slippers. Clearly disappointed, he murmured, 'You have chosen very plainly. Did my girls not come to you? You need a dress more suitable for this moment.'

She found her voice. 'The girls did come, and they said something strange.'

'And you want to know if it is true?'

She sighed. 'Yes.'

'It is.'

'That I am—'

'The queen's daughter.'

'Oh God. This is such crap.' She needed to sit down again, but there was nowhere except the floor. She turned and walked to the sunlit, glowing wall; leaned her hands against it; bowed her head and closed her eyes. Dorocha touched her shoulder. Without looking at him, Aoife said in a trembling voice, 'If it's true, why didn't you *tell* me?'

'I couldn't believe you'd forgotten, after such a short time.'

'A short—?' She slapped the wall with both hands, hurting them. 'My whole life!'

'Still the same impatient Aoibheal—'

'Aoife! I'm Aoife! This isn't me being impatient, this is about everything being crazy!'

'Aoibheal—'

'Aoife. *Aoife.* I can't change names overnight, not after being called that name all my life.'

'All your life?'

'I've been away since I was four – that's eleven years!'

'Only forty days.'

'*Forty days?*' She jammed the heels of her palms

against her temples, strode away from him across the room, and leaned her elbows on a chest of scented cedar, gazing down into a sea of misshapen golden coins.

Dorocha came to stand beside her. 'Aoibheal.'

'Aoife.'

'Aoife. There, see, I am following your wishes. Aoife, listen to me. You are not what you think you are. You were away in the human world for only a short time – only enough for you to grow older and come back to me.'

'Come back to you?' She straightened up to face him. 'Are you my father?' Her ribs were uncomfortably tight around her heart. She was certain he would say *Yes*.

Instead, he looked amazed. 'Why would you think I was your father?'

'But you said, to come back to you—'

'I am the Beloved, Aoibheal.'

Aoife's heart, released, gave a single heavy thump. 'Then who is my father?'

'Was.'

'Ah . . . Is he dead as well?'

Dorocha took the small ring from his pocket, and

spun it into the air, watching it. 'Of course he is dead. He was a man.'

'But who . . . ?'

'Who can tell?' The ring glimmered above their heads, rainbow coloured. Then fell into his hand. 'Even after the Tuatha Dé Danann were driven from the surface of reality, your mother retained a passion for its heroes. The blue-painted Firbolgs. The dark Milesians. The tall, broad-shouldered Fianna . . . There was a young warrior of their company once, whom she met by a pool beneath the hawthorns. Then there were the golden kings of Tara. Which of them was your father? Even the greatest of heroes is at the mercy of death. Every one of them slipped through her fingers like dry sand, until she had outlived them all.'

Aoife sighed. 'And that was when you became her Beloved?'

Dorocha pulled a cynical face – amused, self-deprecating – and tossed up the ring again, higher, his eyes fixed on it. An unbidden thought came to her – how beautiful this man was, with his dark red hair and blue-black eyes, and high, tilted cheekbones. Agelessly beautiful, like the banshee. 'I was always your mother's Beloved, Aoibheal. When she found me in paradise, I was a wild dangerous beast, but she tamed me. She pampered me and trained me to bring her any human man of her desire, fetching him down beneath the earth to be reborn in her arms. I watched and waited for her to forget these passing fancies, and turn to me. She was the queen of rebirth, as I was the king of death. Together, we could be all-powerful. But she did not want to ally herself with me. I was too forcible for her liking. Your mother had a love of weak and fragile creatures.' He shot Aoife a slight smile from under his lashes. 'Maybe that's why she kept her fondness for you, when so many fairy mothers neglect their children. She brought you everywhere with her, even when she went to walk in the surface world to wash her hair in the soft water of the bog pools – and there you would age a little every time. In the end she stopped bringing you to the surface. She was right. She was immortal. Why would paradise need a second queen? It would only make trouble. But all children need to grow up, even the daughters of queens. So I brought you to the surface myself, after your mother's death.'

Another memory: a breath of night air – so damp

and grassy. The elderflowers of the lane. 'It was you in the carriage at my parents' gate.'

'It was. I found it hard to part with you. I had kept you by me for a while, watching you play, dressing you in flower dresses. I missed your mother. I can still see her heart beating, spraying its silver fountain across the bed.'

Aoife shuddered, remembering and understanding the glittering patterns splashed across the black drapes of the bed in the room below. Her mother's blood. 'She was still alive when you found her?'

Dorocha said pleasantly, 'And I took that iron arrowhead and I slit that priest screaming from throat to groin, and before he died I dragged him up to the very summit of this city and threw him tumbling down its walls until he was lost in the river below. And now the queen's pool overflows for ever through the hawthorns, and washes away his blood. The rose in the white quartz is human blood. The river that circles Falias is red.'

'Ah God . . .' Aoife took a step back, staring at him in horror.

He laughed, as if her reaction amused him. 'And

when he was gone, I came back to find her. And I was all alone with her, but she was dead. And then her people took her away, and I was left again with banshees and lenanshees and all the strange beasts of this world. It was hard to be without your mother in the beginning. I had played the tame beast to my queen for so long. But then I realized I was no longer a servant. I was free at last. The travelling magicians of Danu had left for the islands, moving west as they always do. The tables were turned. I began to call their children home, and give the little conjurers *my* orders. But some returned too soon, without their powers. I sent all the little darlings out to catch the beasts, knowing only the strongest would survive.'

Aoife's heart sickened. 'But that's murder . . .'

'How? I touched none of them with my own hand.'

'I saw a little boy get killed.'

'Not killed – *transformed*. Aren't you a believer in rebirth, like your mother? She had no fear of death – except by iron.'

'*He was a little boy!*'

Dorocha laughed. 'And too young for power, just like yourself.'

'I'm not too—'

'You're not yet sixteen! And you will never grow any older!' His eyes were bright with humorous excitement. 'When your sheóg came back without you, I could have strangled the silly little thing! Life burns up so fast on the surface – I thought you would be sixteen before I had my hands on you again . . . Too late to keep the tables turned on the magicians! But in less than an hour I knew you were here, making your way through the wilderness towards me. The sheóg drew you to me. She was my hook of flesh and blood. You could not stop yourself, whatever the danger of the journey. You were helpless.'

'Not helpless—'

'You were helpless. And *afraid*.' Dorocha said it like it truly delighted him. 'You were and will remain powerless, my queen.'

'*I'm not your queen.*'

'But I have all the power we need. The children of the people of Danu will serve you, because you are their queen. And you will serve *me*, because I will be—'

'Serve *you*?'

Still laughing, he flicked up the ring again, caught

it and tossed it to her. A terrible heat seared through her skin of her palm. The ring was made not of rainbows but of fire. Aoife threw it from her with a cry of agony. He snatched it out of the air and held it poised before her between thumb and forefinger, grinning and twisting it like he could tempt her with it, like a sweet to a child.

'Take it, my queen. It is your wedding ring.'

With a cry of revulsion, she turned and fled for the door.

'I *said*, take it.' Dorocha's hand was on her shoulder, and his fingers dug deep. Weakness spread down her arm, as if his nails were the teeth of a spider piercing her skin, sucking the energy from her.

Aoife struggled wildly. '*Let go of me.*'

'You'll not run away?'

'No.'

'Promise?'

'Yes.'

He let her go. Instantly she ran for the door, but he was easily there before her, smilingly indignant. 'Now, Aoibheal, that wasn't very honourable.'

She swerved and stumbled away between the chests of treasure. He came after her, grinning, dancing to cut her off; she doubled back and broke for the door again, and again he was right before it, his arms open to catch her. The bronze sword was in her path, lying where it had fallen. She stooped to lift it – it was shockingly heavy.

His face bright with amusement, Dorocha held his arms wide, boastfully exposing his heart to her.

Straining every muscle, sweat stinging her face, she tried to swing the mighty sword at him, but couldn't hold it up – the point fell forward and rang loudly off the floor.

He sprang from foot to foot, a mocking dance. 'Ah, Aoibheal, don't imagine you can use a weapon of death against me. Only I can make Nuada's sword sing. I am the Fear Dorocha. I am the Fear Dubh. I am the Beloved. I am the king. I am the last act.'

Aoife struggled again to lift the sword. The power in her blood was rising now – she could hear the steady pulse of it in her ears; feel the tingle of it in her skin.

'Put it down, Aoibheal. Only I can wake it. You are a child. A powerless child.'

It was still too heavy to lift above the horizontal,

but the hilt was stirring in her hands; she would sweep it at his waist, then spring past him.

Shaking his head, he said sadly, 'Now behave or I will murder you here and now, as I murdered your mother in her bed before I cast her human lover down the walls.'

The sword flung itself at Dorocha's heart.

He lurched back several paces until he was half sitting on the edge of one of the open caskets; he gazed down in astonishment at the centre of his chest, where the tip of the blade had sunk deep between his ribs. For a moment Aoife could not move either – as if the blood in her veins were liquid stone. As they both watched, the heavy hilt of the sword sank very gradually towards the floor, causing the point of the blade to turn upwards, deepening and widening the cut. A river of ink poured through the rent in his shirt. Dorocha raised his head and stared at her with eyes the same blue-black colour as his blood. Hurt. Surprised.

Then, with one smooth circular motion of his arms, he wrenched the sword free with both hands and hurled it at her. It streaked past her ear like a blast of freezing wind, and clattered away harmlessly between the treasure chests.

He leaped for the spear where it lay against the wall.

Aoife ran for the door, slamming it behind her and slapping her hand over the lock – it clicked into place, just as the bronze point of the spear came plunging through the gold surface, missing her cheek by centimetres. She raced down the stairs, but Eva was running up them towards her, crying tearfully, 'You said you were going to take me home!'

'Here . . .' But Eva dodged past her open arms and ran on upwards. '*No, come back!*' She turned and ran after the child. As she passed the door of the treasure chamber, the thick slab of gold was shuddering and creaking in its frame, bending outwards, splitting . . .

After the next sweeping turn in the staircase, the walls changed from crystal into living wood, first pale twisting roots and then branches of blossom, the powerful scent dizzying her almost as much as the constant turning of the stairs. She burst into the open, and she was in another space, brilliant with sunlight. Crimson water lay across the floor, covered in floating blossoms. Aoife ran splashing through the water to the far side of the circle. They were caught in a living cage of thorns, at the very summit of the city. On the stairs behind her, the footfall of leather boots. So Dorocha had heard her, knew that she had run up, not down . . . She picked up the child. She could squeeze through the thorns and jump. But there was no Shay from whom to steal the slightest kiss, and she might fall like a stone and die, with Eva in her arms. The lenanshees had scaled the walls using the carvings of vines for handholds . . .

'Eva, we have to climb down.'

The child struggled in her arms. 'No!'

'I'll hold you tight.'

'I want to go home!'

'Soon, honey . . .'

'Now! You said the empty place where I saw the bus was home!' The child slipped from her arms, ran across the blood-red floor – and disappeared. The shallow surface of the water did not even ripple.

'Eva? *Eva!*' Aoife scrabbled to and fro on her hands and knees. It was like searching for the child in the pool above, only this time the water was a centimetre deep and the floor not mud but red stone tiles. 'Where have you gone?'

'Back to the bog where every sheóg belongs.' Dorocha was leaning with one hand against a hawthorn bough; he had laced his shirt over his wound, though the material was stained as if with ink. 'Stand up, Aoibheal. I have locked this gate. Only the lenanshees and banshees can freely take this road. You haven't the power to open it without me.'

'You have to let me go after her! I have to help her! She's only a little kid – she'll die out there by herself!' Aoife made a desperate effort to claw up one of the stone tiles; she tore a nail, and a silver thread leaked out into the crimson water. 'Please let me go after her!'

'Marry me first.'

'You murdered my mother!'

'Marry me and I will bring you to the surface world myself. We will travel together, in my coach.'

'That's crazy. There's no time. Let me go now. I'll come back to you, I promise.'

'Like you promised me you would not run? I'm not a fool. I'm not your tame beast. Marry me.'

'No!'

'Very well. Then let us sit here, hour on hour. And for every hour in paradise, a hundred hours will pass out on the cold bog above. It is autumn there now. And your precious little sheóg will wander the bog, and the sun will rise and the sun go down, and the night will be cold and the day hungry; at last she will tire and lie down for ever in the heather, and the ants will eat her down to the bone.'

CHAPTER FIFTEEN

He was angrily insulted when she refused to waste time by changing into a more beautiful dress, or cover herself in her mother's jewels. But if he wanted her to go along with this farce, then this was the way it was going to have to be – good enough for him that she had already changed out of her hoodie and trackies. All she wanted was to get this ridiculous wedding over and done with. Why should she care what she was wearing?

It wasn't like she was the only one underdressed. Most of the changelings who had been called into the temple for this hasty coronation and fake wedding were in their everyday clothes – faded trouser suits and beads from the sixties; tartan flares from the seventies; punk Mohicans that had gone limp without hair gel. There in the bedraggled crowd before the altar, gazing up at Aoife where she stood exposed to everyone's view, was Ultan in his fluorescent shell suit. Caitlin, moulting feathers, was waving enthusiastically and giving her the thumbs-up – then nudging her neighbours, flashing her selkie pearl and ruby chains, clearly boasting that the new queen was her best friend for ever.

Along the walls of the temple stood ranks of dullahans, black-cloaked, the rotting stench from their heads tainting the air, the hum of the insects beneath their hoods filling the air with the sound of a summer's day. Lenanshees clustered together, a sea of lace dresses, singing songs that Aoife had never heard yet which seemed familiar. She couldn't see Shay among them, nor the one who had spirited him away. Banshees in red cloaks moved through the crowd, cooing over the human babies in their arms. Women in caps of dappled sealskin left wet footprints as they walked. Just within the high doors, wide open to the bright sun, Seán Burke stood clutching the reins of a tabby kitten-beast. Beside Aoife, at the altar, another very small old man stood burning a pile of oak leaves. Caitlin's book lay open at the druid's elbow; he paused to consult it, slowly turning the pages.

Aoife was sick with impatience. A little girl was lost on the empty bog above. Every minute here, a hundred minutes there. *Please God let her not fall in a bog hole and drown* . . . Surely she would make her way to the road. A passing car would stop. And then . . . The guards would be called. The real Eva O'Connor had literally disappeared from the face of the earth eleven years ago, and yet she was still only four years old. The little girl would tell everyone that her parents lived in Dublin, and then social services would take her away, just as the banshee had before. She would spend her childhood in care, never to be found.

Seven druids were circling, chanting. Children, also in white robes, squatted with their backs to the rough-cut block of marble that served as the altar. The smallest of them was yawning. A tall female druid touched Aoife's cheek with a twig of mistletoe. She flinched, turning her face away . . . And he was there. He had come after all. Striding long-legged through the open doors, with his beautiful lenanshee by the hand. He stopped at the back of the crowd, scanning the hundreds of faces around him. The young woman rested her cheek against his upper arm, gazing up at him with turquoise eyes; her delicate dress drifted around her like sun-struck mist and her hair tumbled in black ringlets. Aoife stared at the two of them – such a picture – then tried to turn her gaze away. Too late – Shay had caught her looking and stood gazing directly at her across the heads of the crowd.

Aoife took a deep, slow breath – then smiled. Important to show him that she was all right, in case he tried to stop what was going on, and slowed the ceremony down even more. He nodded back. Hot tears inched up her throat. She kept smiling even wider – now it felt like an inane clownish grin, making her cheeks ache. His hazel eyes left her face, and swept down over her clothes. She was covered in the wet blossom from the pool above. Without thinking, she brushed her hands down the front of the dress. Stupid reaction – what was she doing? Trying to prettify herself for him again? The elegant beauty at his side reached up to touch his face, calling his attention back to her again. While not taking his eyes off Aoife, he took the girl's hand and lowered it gently to his side, lacing his fingers firmly through hers. She raised his hand to her lips, and kissed it. The tears reached Aoife's eyes; she blinked and looked away.

Dorocha, his elbows on the altar and his chin in his hands, was watching the druid burn his leaves. Catching Aoife's eye, he winked. She marched furiously to his side. 'What are we waiting for? This is taking for ever. If you want to get married, it has to be *now*.'

'Patience, my queen.' He took her hand and pressed it. Even though he held it only gently, thin trickles of pain sparked up her nerves, and her knees threatened to give way, forcing her to lean against the altar for support. He raised her hand and pressed it to his chest. She closed her fingers into a fist. Beneath his shirt, where his heart should have been, she could feel with her knuckles the smooth outlines of the hole. Gazing at her, Dorocha murmured, '*My heart . . .*' and shoved her fist into the cavity. Instantly she was drained, sucked dry – every drop of her pouring into him. When Shay had even touched his lips to her finger, she had been filled with his energy – had flung herself from the cliff, certain she could fly. With Dorocha, it was as if all her power were pouring into the empty space behind his ribs. He slipped his other arm around her, keeping her on her feet, bringing his lips close to her ear. 'We are one. This is how it will feel, for all eternity.' He spun her slowly to face the crowd and raised his voice. 'Morfesa, the queen is ready to be crowned.'

The old druid grumbled, glancing at them, 'The ceremony is not complete.'

'The queen is bored and tired by druid nonsense.'

'The ancient text insists on a full—'

Dorocha released Aoife's fist, reached behind her for the ancient leather book and hurled it straight into the middle of the changeling throng, sending Caitlin scrabbling for it among everyone's legs. The old man screeched furiously: 'That is a treasure of the Tuatha Dé Danann!'

'Ah, those pretty magicians,' said Dorocha softly, seizing Aoife's hand again, pressing it back against his chest. 'Dabblers and wanderers, no better than druids.'

'*Heroes, every one of them!*'

'What nonsense . . . You, the abandoned children of heroes!' cried Dorocha suddenly, pulling Aoife with him to the edge of the dais. 'Here is your new queen, to be crowned this minute by the great, the all-powerful druid Morfesa!'

The old man glared, but the female druid

hurried forward with a small circlet of mistletoe and hawthorn and set it on Aoife's hair. There was a loud 'Hooray' from Caitlin, who was on her feet again, with a suspicious bulge under her feathers; her cheer was echoed enthusiastically by Ultan and, rather more cynically, from the back of the crowd, by Seán Burke. The bedraggled cluster of changelings clapped and chattered to each other excitedly. Shay, pushing forward into the crowd, raised his hands over his head, also clapping – very slowly and deliberately, and holding Aoife's eyes as he did so – not smiling at her, but expressionless. The young lenanshee followed him, still gazing up at him.

Dorocha pulled Aoife against him, and she tried to move away, but he tightened his arm around her waist. A dry sob forced its way up out of her chest. She hated being forced to lean against him, in the way the lenanshee was now again leaning lovingly against Shay. She tried at least to stand straight, but her bones were water. From the high gold roof, hawthorn had begun falling in a white mist, blurring the world like snow and sweetening the air, masking the stench of the dullahans. Dorocha was forcing her fingers apart. An intense heat scorched her – he was holding the fire-ring to her fingertip. She tried to find Shay, but she could no longer see him through the haze of pink and perfumed snow. 'Marry me,' Dorocha murmured, and pushed on the ring.

It would not slip over her finger.

He tried again, frowning, saying in a low voice, 'Do not resist me, Aoibheal.'

'I'm not resisting you.' Her voice was shaking.

'Don't be afraid.'

'I'm not afraid.'

'It will only burn for a moment, as it sinks into your flesh.' Yet however hard he tried, he could not seem to force it over her finger. His grip on her was growing so intense, she feared the bones in her hand would break. The druids were drawing closer around them, a white-robed circle, arms folded, gazing with more curiosity than concern at the strange little struggle.

Pale and sweating, Dorocha glared at them. 'What is this ridiculous spell, Morfesa?'

'Push it on . . .' But Aoife's voice was an inaudible whisper. His grip had tightened beyond the endurable, and her vision was darkening. Her legs could no longer support her; she was a rag doll slumped against him.

The old man was saying rather smugly, 'As I said, the ancient text insists on a full ceremony—'

'Then perform it!'

'If you hadn't thrown away the book . . .'

She needed to scream at them all not to waste any more time, just to force on the ring, but her throat wouldn't work and no words rose.

'Aoife!' Shay's voice came loud over the sudden silence of the crowd.

Instantly Dorocha's grip loosened; he patted the back of her crushed hand, and said in a much calmer tone: 'Morfesa, that girl in the feathers has your book – the one heading for the door. Send one of the children after her.'

'*Aoife!*'

'And here comes another of my wife's not-so-faithful retinue. Make sure to send your farmer boy away, Aoibheal, before I refer his name to the dulla-hans. It would be a shame to spoil our day.'

Again, Aoife tried and failed to speak. Her sight was still blurred by the receding pain, but she could hear the rustle of the parting of the crowd, and the whispers, and the sound of his bare feet striding over the stone. Running up the steps of the dais. His voice, close to her: 'Aoife, are you all right?' Even this near, his face seemed ghostly and unreal. She felt his hand on her arm. Hard strong fingers; his energy flowing into her veins. Giving her strength. He came suddenly into bright focus, as if a lens had been adjusted – his forest-green eyes with depths of golden brown, his strong flushed cheekbones, his rich black hair. Faded jeans, the torn red and green Mayo shirt. 'Aoife, what's the matter . . . ?'

'*Tell the lenanshee boy to leave us alone.*'

Aoife stepped out of Dorocha's embrace, and stood by herself: shaky, but at least on her own feet. She said clearly, 'Leave us alone.'

Shay's head jerked back like she'd slapped him. 'Aoife, I'm just here to ask what's happening with you, and are you all right, and what's this buck doing to you?'

'Nothing. Go away.'

'Is this really some sort of coronation? That's so—'

She said coldly, 'Shay, go away.'

'Because that joker is telling you to make me go

away? If you're really the queen around here, you should be telling *him* what to do.'

Dorocha interrupted sharply, 'Enough of this, lenanshee boy. I am marrying her. Now, leave us alone.'

'*Marrying her?*'

Aoife took a step closer to him. 'Shay, this is none of your business. Now, go—'

'None of my business? Are you serious? You can't go getting married!'

'Why not?' A spurt of warmth in her heart.

'You're only fifteen!'

Her heart cooled again, and at the same time, a stupid, irrelevant memory surfaced: him pulling up in the battered red Ford, and her saying, so shocked – *You're only fifteen!* and him, faintly offended – *Nearly sixteen.* 'If you can drive a car—'

'For Christ's sake, that's hardly the same thing!'

Aoife lowered her voice. 'Shay. Go away. I don't have time to talk about this. Go back to your girl. That's where you belong.'

'Ah now, Aoife . . .' A faint smile was rising in his green-gold eyes. 'Ah, now, she's not really my—'

'*Go!* I don't want you here!'

His eyes stopped smiling. He said, calm and cool, 'Grand, so.' And turned on his heel.

'Now . . .' said Dorocha, with a sigh. 'Where is Miss McGreevey? Let us rescue the book, and we will perform the whole ceremony if it takes all night.'

'Wait.' It was the tall druid who had interrupted them – the woman who had crowned Aoife with the hawthorn. 'There may be another matter. I wonder if the queen is desired by this lenanshee? I've heard no other love can overcome such desire. She would not be able to marry another until the lenanshee renounced her.'

'Ah . . .' Dorocha's dark eyes lit up. 'Of course. How simple. I forgot the *grá*.'

Aoife cried quickly, 'No, that's wrong – he has no *grá* for me. He's told me that before. He has no *grá* for me *at all*.' Shay had turned back at the top of the steps. Running over to him, pushing him roughly, she cried, 'Go on, go away—'

Dorocha was at her side, his hand on her arm. 'No, lenanshee, stay. Tell me, is this true?'

Aoife whipped her arm away before her energy could begin to drain. 'No it's not! He doesn't love me!'

'Let him say it himself. Is this true – *Shay Foley*?' As he uttered Shay's name, he raised his voice as if to project it out across the whole temple, so that 'Shay Foley' rang off the marble arches and gold panels and thin columns of rose quartz. All along the walls of the temple, the black-hooded dullahans took a single pace forward, sending a ripple of alarm through the changelings gathered under the altar.

'Shay! Tell him you have no *grá* for me!'

He gazed at her despairingly. 'Aoife—'

'*Tell him!*'

Dorocha raised his arm, snapping his fingers. The dullahans raised their heads in their hands, and the lenanshees stopped their singing and stood poised, glancing around fearfully with turquoise eyes. The banshees were drifting towards the temple doors, pulling the flaps of their red cloaks over the human babies in their arms.

'He doesn't! He doesn't feel anything for me! Give me the ring!' Aoife seized it from Dorocha's hand, and tried to force it onto her finger herself. It was like holding a hot coal. 'Why won't it . . . ? Oh God, oh God . . .' The pain was too great; she was weeping, deep gut-wrenching sobs of agony.

Shay was trying to take it from her. 'Aoife, what are you doing . . . ?'

She glared wildly at him, sweat and tears pouring from every inch of her. 'Is it true? Do you have a stupid *grá* for me?'

'Aoife, I'm so sorry . . .'

The dullahans were raising their heads in their hands; the rotted mouths were opening, orange light gushing out through decomposing eyes. A deep, still wordless roar was filling the temple. The lenanshees were gone, only for the girl who had arrived with Shay. The changelings themselves were hurrying away, amid sparks of fire and wisps of smoke. A few were flying, slowly, a couple of metres off the floor; a couple vanished as they ran. Caitlin was trying to get out of the door, but a white-robed little boy was hanging onto the back of her dress. Ultan was shouting at her: *'Just give it to him!'*

'Oh God . . .' The ring fell from Aoife's hand and rolled away, a circlet of fire bouncing softly down the steps into the empty space where nobody was left – only the lenanshee girl standing there watching.

Dorocha screamed across the emptying temple, *'Shay Foley! Shay Foley!'*

And the black ranks of the dullahans took it up, marching in swinging lines towards them, the melting lips of their lanterns forming his name, a sonorous terrible shout arising: 'Sha—'

She caught Shay's face in her hands, covering his ears. 'Don't listen!'

He placed his own hands over hers, staring into her eyes.

The lenanshee in her white lace dress was still standing her ground, gazing at the altar. The black-hooded army was pushing past her. '*Shay . . . Foley . . .*' The lenanshee grabbed the black sleeves of those nearest, and they paused mid-stride, before marching grimly on.

Aoife could hear Dorocha shouting at her as well – not in the deep, graveyard voices of the dullahans, but high and demented, screaming at her to let the boy go, dragging at her, cursing her for being like her mother, a lover of the weak – but he had no strength compared to hers. Standing pressed against Shay, she could drink the pure simple energy of him, feel the pulse in his veins, his heart thudding hard against her chest. And she knew, as she had known before, when she'd asked him to kiss her so that she could fly, that all his energy belonged to her.

'*Shay . . . Foley . . .*'

She mouthed: 'Kiss me.'

He hesitated. She laughed and dragged his mouth down to hers, and pressed her lips to his. And after the briefest moment of resistance, he sighed and softened and kissed her back.

She exploded into flight. The dullahans instantly lifted their heads towards her, rotten mouths snapping at her ankles; their hoods fell back and clouds of flies rose up – but she was gone through the high doors, Shay in her arms, skimming over the changelings fleeing down the street outside, Caitlin and Ultan staring, waving . . . Up, up, past layer on layer of city streets, green flowering gardens, cobbled alleyways, buildings of gold and lapis lazuli and bronze, rose quartz sparkling with the tears of the hawthorns that dripped, dripped, dripped down the city walls, then up past the lenanshee quarters – white archways from which blue light streamed, then circling the delicate crystal minaret, an upward spiral, all paradise spread out on every side, its marble mountains and abandoned pyramids, powder-blue waterfalls, silver rivers, flowering woodlands . . . The sun hot on her back, and Shay in her arms . . . Her eyes were on fire, heart pounded, skin sweated; she was possessed with a furious joy. Up, up, up, further into the rainbow sky . . . Eagles swung away from her, startled . . . Rainbows so close she could touch them . . . Solid light . . . She flipped over onto her back to glide beneath them, so that Shay was lying on top of her.

'Hey!' He tightened his arms around her.

'Ow! Can't breathe!'

'Sorry.' He relaxed his grip, though only slightly. He glanced over her shoulder towards the ground, and tightened his hold again, and clamped his legs around hers. 'Aoife, I don't know if you've noticed this, but we're very high up.'

'I know! If you'd only kissed me before . . .' Aoife let go of him and stretched out her arms to the sides, feeling the force of the wind against the backs of her hands, giving herself entirely to the moment.

'Jesus Christ, Aoife . . .'

She teased him: 'You want to fly by yourself? It's fun. You can do it.' She tilted sideways.

'Aoife!'

'Go on. You have lenanshee blood.' She swept with him out in a wide circle, under the arching rainbows. For a while he kept his arms locked tight around her, his heart thudding hard against her, and the heat of his body burned through her clothes. But gradually she felt him relax. He loosened his grip, and laid his cheek next to hers. His eyelashes stirred stiffly against her skin. He murmured in her ear, 'Where are we going to go now?'

'Where do you want to go?' As far as Aoife was concerned, she was already doing the one thing she was born to do – fly. What else was there to worry about, ever, in this world or any other?

'Home.'

The burning joy drained from her blood. *Eva*. This was what everything was about – this was the meaning of this journey, even though she hadn't understood for a long time. She had to find the little girl who was lost. She had been searching for her parents' child since that first day when she had seen her running in her pink dressing gown down the hawthorn hill. Now she had to bring her home. She banked in a sweeping circle and surged back towards the minaret. The hawthorn circle was the size of a silver coin, rapidly growing larger, the trees parting beneath her like a flower to the light, like an opening, welcoming hand. She plunging headfirst through the sweet cushion of blossom – no thorns, no thorns – straight for the stone floor . . . The lenanshee boy in her arms closing his eyes . . . Not stopping, not slowing . . .

The water blood-red, then black.

CHAPTER SIXTEEN

Empty bog. Empty road.

It was just as it had been when she stood here with him on this hill before; when she had forced him to drive her out here to look. Except there were no blossoms on the hawthorns now, only a few shrivelled red berries. They had been gone for little more than a day, but this was a world of autumn skies and browning heather. No bog cotton. No flowers. A scatter of miserable grey sheep.

Empty bog. Empty road.

No child.

How many days had passed since Eva had tried to go home? She would have been found, a car would have stopped – someone would have seen her, as Aoife had spotted her before. Maybe this time the little girl wouldn't have got scared and run away . . . Maybe there would be something about it on the news, and she could track her down that way . . . But how to get her back? No one would ever believe . . .

With a slight choke in his voice, Shay said, 'Oh.'
'What?'

Before Aoife had even turned to him, he was gone, running down the green hill and out across the bog, faster than she had ever seen him run. In the direction he was running, a rose-pink dot in the rusty heather – a patch of flowers, surely. She started to run herself. The flowers were gone with summer . . . It must be a lamb, a pink brand on its wool. She ran faster. But the lambs were gone too.

When she reached him, he was kneeling on the wet ground, cradling the child against him, sobbing. 'Pray for us sinners . . .' Her little face was pale blue, her eyes half closed – a rim of white visible through her blonde lashes. Her short hair plastered flat to her skull by the rain. Stains of blackberries around her mouth. Her rose-petal dress ragged and torn. Days out on the bog, nights of cold and dark, and only blackberries to eat. 'Pray for Eva O'Connor, Hail Mary, Mother of God, pray for her . . .'

Aoife could hear her own voice howling wordlessly. She clenched her fists, pressed her lips hard together. Stop making that noise. She breathed in deep through her nose. Stop. Think. 'Wake her. Kiss her. You're a lenanshee. Bring her back to life.'

Shay pressed his lips to the child's forehead. Her lashes fluttered, a little colour came into her cheeks, and then her head fell back, as Donal's had done before.

'Again!'

This time, only the tips of her lashes quivered before they again fell still.

He sobbed. 'Aoife, it's too late.'

'*She's not dead.*'

'She's growing cold—'

'*Then rub her hands!*' Aoife seized the child's small hand, translucent as fallen petals. There was the scar that matched her own, a thin pale blue line across the white. Blood sisters. 'Give me your penknife!'

'What—?'

'*Give it to me!*'

Tears running down his face, Shay fumbled in the pocket of his faded jeans and pulled it out – the key-ring with the torch that once, in the blackness of the cave, had seemed like all the magic she'd ever needed. She prised open the penknife with her teeth and stabbed the point into her hand, slicing along the line of the old scar and through the throbbing burn left by the ring.

Shay groaned, 'Oh God, Aoife . . .'

She cradled Eva's fragile hand, took a quick breath, then slashed the knife across it and pressed her palm to the child's. Her hand so much larger, dwarfing the little child's, engulfing it. The human blood running into her, and her blood running into the child – fairy blood to cure the human child of death, fanning awake the smallest flame of life. 'Kiss her again – bring her back for me!'

Again he bent his head, touched his lips to the child's white forehead. Again her lashes fluttered . . . This time a little more . . .

'Again!'

The blood still flowing. Eva's eyes opening, icy blue with a hint of silver. Her mouth opening now – a weak, trembling cry, as if her lungs were new born. Aoife herself weeping and covering the child's face in kisses, while still pressing their palms together.

'Eva – Eva, how long have you been—? Ah, you wouldn't know . . . I'm so sorry we took so long . . . Did no cars pass? Did no one stop?'

The child's sobs were getting stronger; she was

taking deep shuddering breaths. 'I tried to find Hector – then it was dark, and I wanted Hector, and no one came and I'm hungry and *I want to go home.*'

'We're taking you home, sweetie . . . honey. We're taking you home.'

A tractor with a trailer-load of turf was rattling along the bog road. Shay ran to wave it down. It creaked to a halt, and the eighty-year-old farmer eating a sandwich pushed open the door of the cab, looked down at Eva in Aoife's arms with teasing good humour. 'Is it a fairy you are, little girl, running out of the bog in that pretty dress?'

'I'm a sheóg and Aoife is a fairy.'

'Well, that's grand, so.' He took a bite out of his sandwich. 'I could do with a few wishes.'

Shay said, 'Would you mind giving us a seat as far as the road?'

'For an aul pot of fairy gold now . . .'

Aoife had no pockets – she pushed her hand into Shay's back pocket instead, pulled out a wad of euros and slammed it down on the step of the tractor. 'There. And my sister is hungry – is there another half to that sandwich?'

The old man's mouth dropped in shock. 'Oh merciful Jesus, put that away, will ya, I was only joking—'

'Take it. There's plenty more where that came from.'

'I will *not* – have ye robbed a bank? Here, I have a whole tin of the sandwiches – the old woman makes me enough for an army – ham and cheese do ye? It'll have to; they're all of them ham and cheese and always have been.'

The tractor took them as far as the Clonbarra road, and left them there – the old farmer still indignantly refusing money. With Eva now clinging around Shay's neck, they trudged on towards Kilduff. Rain was falling now – not the light, misty dew of paradise, but proper, heavy, sodden rain, making them three times as wet as they had been after climbing out of the pool. The leaves on the trees poured rivers and the ditches gleamed with rain-polished sloes and blackberries. The little girl, although no longer hungry, was shivering; she started to cry a little. A white Toyota was coming in the opposite direction. As it passed them, Sinead's face was at the side window, her mouth making strange distorted shapes at them through the rainy glass. Aoife cried, 'Oh, it's the Fergusons!' and waved frantically. The Toyota actually increased its speed, disappearing round the bend with a screech of wheels. Exasperated, she said, 'You'd think they'd stop for us in this weather, even if they are going the wrong way. It wouldn't kill them to run us back as far as Kilduff from here.'

'Maybe she didn't recognize us.'

'No, I'm sure she did. Maybe they'll come back.'

But the Toyota did not return. They walked on. The rain was running off Shay's short black hair and pouring down his face; dripping in silver drops from his long lashes. He had placed one square hand flat over Eva's head like it could act as an umbrella. The rain ran in a thin silver line down the brown sweep of his neck, down under the torn collar of his Mayo shirt. For the first time in a long while, a song lyric came into Aoife's head:

I dream of this:
Under the hawthorns he raises me with a kiss.

Shay was smiling at her. 'You know, I like that dress on you, even if you do look like a drowned rat.'

462

'Great. Thanks a million.'

'You still have that thing on your head.'

'What the . . . ?' She felt the top of her head – the circlet of hawthorn and mistletoe was still there, caught in her hair, and she pulled it off and threw it into the hedge. Then had an epiphany: 'Look, what are we doing – what are we walking for? I know we're back in the real world, but that doesn't mean we have to pretend to be human. How about you . . . you know, and we fly to Kilduff?'

For a moment Shay's face lit up, his smile widening, entirely flattening the deep curve in his upper lip. And then faded again. 'Aoife, I really don't think that's a good idea.'

'Oh, for . . .' She walked faster, leaving him behind – would have run off on him entirely, only for not wanting to leave Eva.

He caught her up, splashing through the puddles. 'Aoife, believe me, it's not about not wanting to kiss you.'

'I know, I know, I get it. It's not me, it's you. Grand. Wonderful. I appreciate your concern for my well-being. Thanks.'

'Aoife, I need to tell you—'

'Really, it's all right.'

'The lenanshee that came to find me—'

'I *said*, it's all right! You don't need to tell me anything.'

'But I want to explain—'

'Shay, there is absolutely no need for you to explain to me about every girl you decide to go off with. I'm not some kind of mad stalker type.'

He blurted his next sentence out in one long breath before she could interrupt him again. 'She told me that if I had feelings for you, I should stay away from you.'

Now she just wanted to laugh – and did, bitterly. 'And you believed her.'

'Yes.'

'Well, there you go then.'

'Aoife, stop walking away from me – look at me – you're getting this all wrong.'

She turned on him angrily, stopping dead in the middle of the road. 'OK. So tell me, how am I supposed to get it *right*?'

Under the strong umbrella of his hand, Eva was only half awake, eyelids swollen, cheeks as pink as the rose-petal dress. Gazing steadily at her, Shay said, 'My mother killed the one she loved and she has to live with that for ever.'

She felt the urge to protest – *But your mother is dead* – and stopped herself. 'I know that's what you believe—'

'It's not her body in the graveyard, Aoife.'

She stared at him, the cold rain trickling down her neck. John McCarthy's old-man voice was playing in her head, shaky and crackly: *That's not Moira Foley in there. 'Tis a log of driftwood. They fairies do love to play tricks.*

'The girl who came to find me? That was my mother, Aoife.'

Still she stared speechless. Shay gazed down at her over the child's sleeping head, his green eyes shining as if the rain had filled them up – his face soft with emotion: happiness, grief, longing, loss.

Aoife found her voice. 'Oh, Shay.' In the drenching rain, she stepped forward and put her arms around him. 'Shay.' And Eva, in the warm space between them, stirred and smiled in her sleep.

A car beeped. As Aoife pulled away from him, conscious that they were standing out in the middle of the road, a woman in her seventies with blue-rimmed glasses wound down the window of a rusty VW. 'I guess ye'll be after a seat. I have all this shopping in the front, but if you push over my bag on the back seat there'll be room for the three of ye.'

'Thanks a million.'

'No trouble, pet. Can't be letting you young lovers walk in this weather, specially with a little child. That's it, move it over – don't forget your seatbelts.' The woman kept glancing in the rear-view mirror as she drove towards Kilduff at thirty kilometres an hour, clearly wanting to hear the full story. 'You're all three of ye very wet – ye look pure drownded like ye came straight out of the ocean.'

Leaning her head against the window, staring out at the wet green world of home, Aoife smiled. 'Yes, it's raining pretty hard out there.'

'And you in your pretty flowery dress! And he in his bare feet! Are ye hippies on your travels? I was a hippy once, beads and all. Where are ye headed? A festival? I love a good music festival.'

'Just Kilduff.'

'Ah, Kilduff. 'Tis a very tragic town since those two poor teenagers died in May. Did ye know them?'

Aoife glanced at Shay, a shiver going through her. 'Sort of . . .'

'Sure, as wet as ye were I thought for a moment ye were the pair of them returned from the sea.'

Still holding her gaze, Shay's eyes widened. He must also have just figured out the full story with the Fergusons – they had seen ghosts: the drowned dead come to life, drenched with sea water. No wonder the car had speeded up. Clearly, just walking in on everyone was going to be a difficult business. In the bag beside Aoife, among crumpled handkerchiefs and packets of medication, was a mobile phone. She leaned forward between the seats. 'Would you mind very much if I use your phone, just to text some people? I've been away, I've got to find out what's happening. I can give you some money for it.'

'You're welcome, pet, I have free calls and texts, but it won't be any good to you – 'tis one of those new ones, my daughter insisted on getting it for me – it's impossible to . . .'

Aoife was already texting.

Hi Carla ☺

Almost immediately, a text came back:

Who this?
A friend ☺
I don't have this number
Cos not my phone ☺
Who IS this?

Aoife showed Shay the screen. He shook his head. She hesitated, then texted:

Carla I need to tell u something very weird

After a few seconds Carla replied:

About what
About Aoife

A bare second later:

i don't know who this is but if u say one wrong word about my best friend who died i will find out who u r and u will be very really really incredibly sorry u exist on the same planet as me

Warmth flooded Aoife's heart, and tears her eyes.

Carla I love u
Is this Killian ☺☺☺☺

Aoife laughed, and wiped away the tears:

No sorry someone else who loves you
WHO IS THIS TELL ME NOW OR I WILL STOP
ANSWERING YOU

There didn't seem to be any easy way to do it.
Biting her lip, she texted:

This is Aoife ☺☺☺☺☺☺☺☺☺☺☺☺

A long, long pause. Then the phone rang.

The woman driving chirruped: 'Do you mind
answering that, pet – that will be my daughter, she'll
be delighted it's not me answering, I always touch the
wrong thing and cut her off, tell her I'm two minutes
from Kilduff, I'll be at hers in thirty minutes . . .'

But it was Carla's number. Aoife tapped the green
phone icon and put it to her ear, closing her eyes.

In a low, fierce, tearful voice, Carla said, 'Sinead, you bitch, I know this is you, and isn't it bad enough you pretend to see a ghost walking down the road and now you're pretending to be her, this is a new low, you are lower than the snake's belly, wait till I tell Killian this and I am going to tell everyone and put it all over Facebook and—'

'Carla, it's not Sinead. It's me.'

Silence.

'Carla, it's me.'

Silence.

'Carla, it's OK, it's Aoife.'

Carla said in a very small voice: 'Aoife?'

'Yes.'

Hesitantly: *'Aoife?'*

'Yes.'

'AOIFE?'

'See, Sinead wasn't lying about seeing me—'

'Oh my God, you ARE a ghost!'

'No!'

'I don't care! I don't care if you're a ghost! Just don't hang up on me!'

'I'm not a ghost, Carl, I swear, it's really me, just me. Carl, I'm sorry, I have to go—'

'No, don't go again! Are you kidnapped? Tell me where you are – just describe it to me – tell me what you can see! I'll find you—'

'I don't mean *going*, I'm not going anywhere – I mean I'm here at the top of our lane, I'm not going anywhere, only home.'

'Oh my God . . .'

'And I have to go home now, but I'll come and see you later today, I swear. I haven't seen Mam and Dad yet—'

'But where have you *been*? Why didn't you ever call me? Are you with Shay? And is Shay alive too?'

'Yes, Shay's here. Carla, I'm sorry, I'm on someone else's phone and they're giving me a lift home, and we're nearly there now. I have to go – I really love you—'

'*Don't go!*'

'I have to. This is our turn off.' She tapped the woman on her shoulder. 'I'm sorry, it's here, do you mind?'

'Aoife, listen, listen . . .'

But instead of stopping, the woman turned into Aoife's lane and thundered along slowly over the potholes. 'I'll take you all the way, pet – ye don't want to be getting any wetter.'

'Thank you, that's really good of you—'

'Aoife, who are you talking to? Listen, listen to me, don't go yet!'

'Carla, it's OK, I have another minute now – I'm listening.'

'I love you and I'm so glad—'

'Love you too, Carl.'

'No, listen.'

'OK. Go on.'

Carla took a deep, shuddering, tearful, happy breath. 'I just want you to know: whatever happens, if this is a dream, I'm so glad you were in my dream.'

CHAPTER SEVENTEEN

There were four cars parked in off the road next to the house, on the track up to the turf shed – the Volvo and the Citroën, and two others she didn't recognize.

The woman dropped them off in the lane, did an elaborate fifteen-point turn, then rolled down the passenger window and leaned across. 'I just have to ask because I couldn't help hearing you on the phone. Are ye two really Aoife O'Connor and Shay Foley, the star-crossed lovers?'

Shay glanced at Aoife from under his long lashes – a green-gold flash of amusement. She felt herself flush. 'Well, we're Aoife and Shay, anyway.'

The old woman beamed, and her faintly wrinkled cheeks became as red as apples. 'Goodness me. Nothing this wonderful has happened to me since my hippy days. We were all mad into other realities then. I'll be telling my daughter about this but she will never believe me. My daughter is very modern, you know. She doesn't believe in visitors from the other realms.' And she drove off slowly and bumpily, leaving them by the blackberry hedge at the side of the house.

The rain had eased off to nothing, and the sweet smell of wet blackberries was all around them. Eva had woken up when they climbed out of the car. Now she stretched out her arms, yawning, and Aoife took her from Shay. The little girl blinked around her crossly. 'What are we doing here? You said we were going home.'

'You are home, sweetie.'

'No, I live in Dublin.'

'This is where your mammy and daddy live now, sweetheart.'

'They live in *Dublin*.'

'Well, then, yes, but now they're on holiday.'

Eva looked surprised, then hurt. 'On holiday? Without me? I want ice cream. Did they forget me?'

'They never forgot you, honey . . . Ssh now, a moment.'

The door of the house was opening, and two men came out onto the porch, pulling on their coats. One was Martin Flynn, of the coastguard. The other was

John Tiernan, one of Aoife's old school teachers from the Kilduff national school, a very quiet man and a member of the deep sea diving club. His voice ringing clear as a bell through the shadowy late afternoon air, Martin said, 'God help us, John, that's a very sad house.'

'It is.'

'There's nothing worse than losing a child that way, and worse again to have no body to bury. I hate always telling them the latest search turned up nothing.'

'Desperate.'

After a short pause Martin said, 'Did he encourage her to jump, do you think? It seems to run in the family.'

Shay was standing so close behind her, Aoife could feel him tense. She glanced back at him and mouthed: *Will we tell them now?* but he shook his head, and pulled her further back behind the blackberry hedge, out of sight.

The school teacher said, with sudden volubility, 'Martin, we'll never know what was in a pair of teenagers' heads, and maybe that's a good thing. It's no good to anyone trying to figure it out. It'll only make matters worse, going over and over it again. Things are bad enough as it is.'

Coats buttoned, they walked in silence to their separate cars, and one after the other backed out into the lane, turning to their right, not seeing the returned ghosts standing in the gap of the wet hedge.

When they were gone, Aoife said, 'Do you think I should just go right on in?'

'It's hard to know how else to do it.'

'I don't want to give the poor things a heart attack . . . Maybe I'll go round the back.'

'Like that will be less of a shock.'

She laughed awkwardly.

Shay said with sudden determination, like he'd been considering it for a while, 'Look, I'm thinking will I walk back on up to the road, get a lift onwards.'

'Oh . . . What? Now?'

'I need to let John Joe know I'm alive.'

'You could call him from my house?'

'I'm like you. I don't want to be giving him a heart attack either. Actual fact, I'm hoping I'll find him in the pub in Kilduff, and at first he'll just think he's seeing things. Let him in gently, like.'

'Right.' Aoife managed a weak laugh. 'Yeah, I guess.'

Shay stood hesitating. 'Look, I'll see you very soon.'

And then the thought of him just walking off, into the damp autumn dusk, became unbearable. 'No, wait. My dad will give you a lift.'

He laughed genuinely. 'I don't think your dad will be interested in driving me around the countryside when he's just got you back from the dead.'

'Eva as well, don't forget. Especially Eva. I'm not sure they'll be that interested in me. After all, Eva's their real daughter.'

'Ah no, you're as much their daughter as she is.'

Aoife shrugged. 'I guess.' But she wanted to say: *The people we love don't always love us back.* 'I don't know if they feel that way. They never asked to look after me. It was all only for her sake.'

Eva was struggling and sliding down out of her arms. 'Put me down! I want to see my mam.'

'You're wrong. Of course they love you for yourself.'

'I want to see my mam!' Eva was dragging at her hand, tugging her towards the house.

Shay reached out for her other hand, then didn't take it, letting his own fall to his side once more. *The people we love aren't always able to love us back.* 'Look, I'll call you later, all right?'

'I haven't got my mobile.'

'Have you a house phone?'

'You haven't got your mobile either.'

'I'll call from my brother's phone. What's your number?'

She told him. 'But you won't remember it.'

'I will, I'm good with numbers.'

'Repeat it back to me?'

'Really, I have it. Aoife, listen, you're going to be fine. Everything will be more than fine. Just get in there.'

'*I want to see my mam!*'

'Aoife, go on.'

But then, as she turned to go, Shay called her back – 'Wait a minute!' – and lifted his hand and very lightly touched her nose with the tip of his forefinger. '*Wahu*, Aoife,' he said softly. And then, 'Take care.'

Lifting Eva, she moved carefully across the lawn to peep in through the kitchen window from the growing shadows. Her father was standing with his back to the window, one hand on the electric kettle, the way he always stood waiting for it to boil. His head was lowered.

Eva asked, 'Who's that?'

'That's your daddy, honey.'

'My daddy has black hair.'

Suddenly James turned and stared straight at them, or rather, straight in their direction into the darkening garden – as if he had heard something. He was pale and his eyes were puffed up with weeping.

'Daddy?' said Eva doubtfully, touching her fore-finger to the golden locket.

'Yes, sweetie. Just his hair went grey.'

'OK. Will we knock on the window?'

'No – ssh – let's go round the back—'

'Are we going to give them a surprise?'

'That's right, honey.'

With Eva on her hip, Aoife climbed the ash tree easily, using only one hand. Her bedroom window was unlocked, and she leaned out of the tree to pull it open, then lifted Eva across the gap and followed herself, nearly knocking a lighted candle to the floor.

Her bedroom was like a shrine. It *was* a shrine. There was a ridiculously large picture of herself on the chest of drawers; a jar of wild roses, five candles and two plaster angels were grouped around it. The bed neatly made and the covers turned down and everywhere unnaturally tidy – all clothes put away; her guitar leaning in the corner; the computer desk a paper-free zone. The torn edges of the music posters were neatened with Sellotape. There was even a set of her own song lyrics hanging on the wall, mounted on blue cardboard and laminated. *Under the hawthorns, he raises me with a kiss . . .*

'Is this house *your* house?'

'Ssh, honey, just whisper.'

'That's you! And you! And you!' Eva pointed to the walls with enthusiasm. There were many more photographs than before. The sort that she wouldn't have bothered with herself, because they didn't have Carla in them. Aoife moved softly around, gazing at them. She'd never realized how many pictures her parents had taken of her, year after year. Grinning in a centimetre of snow. Knee deep in a river, holding up a fish. Lopsided on a donkey. A holiday in Cork. They must have had a full drawer of photographs somewhere – photographs of her, their fairy daughter.

'Can I see my mam now?'

'Ssh, honey.'

'Is it still a surprise?'

'That's right. Don't make any noise until I tell you.'

Holding Eva's hand, Aoife eased her bedroom door open a crack.

Across the landing, her parents' bedroom door was nearly closed. Before she could open the door any wider, her father came into view up the stairs, a mug of tea in each hand. He glanced sadly towards Aoife's bedroom, then used his foot to push open the door of his own. 'Thought you might want a cup of tea, love.' He went in, turning on the light, leaving the door ajar behind him.

Eva tried to pull her hot little hand out of Aoife's; Aoife looked down with a frown and a slight sideways shake of the head, putting her forefinger to her lips. Then led the child out onto the landing.

Through the half-open door of her parents' room, they could see Maeve sitting cross-legged on the bed, dark blonde hair grown longer and tied aside in a plait, her back resting against the oak headboard, staring blankly in front of her. James stooped over her, pressing one of the mugs into her hand. She smiled up at him weakly, tears running down her face. In a choked voice, she said, 'I almost wanted them to find her, James. Do you believe that? It just hurts so much, not knowing. Then, at the same time, of course I don't want them to find her. I want to carry on believing she went back to her own world. That she's there with Eva, somehow. And they're happy together, in paradise.'

'That's what I hope for, sweetheart.'

'But does paradise even exist?'

'I think it does.'

'But we don't know for sure, do we? And we told her she could fly. And then she jumped . . . with that poor boy.' James sat down on the bed next to her, passed his arm around her. She pressed her wet face to his shoulder. '*Oh God, Aoife.*'

In this room too there were photographs everywhere, covering the walls. And, framed, on the oak chest of drawers. Aoife's face, but also Eva's – all the hundreds of photos from the drawer. No longer locked away.

'If only I knew where they were!'

'We have them here, Maeve. Both of them. Here.' And James pressed his hand to his heart. 'That's what matters in the end. Wherever they are.'

There was no easy way, but it had to be done now. Aoife crouched down beside Eva, and whispered very, very softly in the little girl's ear. 'Keep quiet a bit longer, honey. We're going to go stand where they can see us. All right?'

Eva nodded solemnly. Aoife straightened up. Hand in hand, they moved a few paces forward, to where the bedroom light could fall through the door onto the two of them. The slender changeling in the sun-rise dress with her red-gold hair, and the sheóg in a dress of dried rose petals, with her short blonde curls.

Maeve had lifted her head from James's shoulder and was frowning towards the dark, rainy window. 'What was that?'

'What, sweetheart?'

'I thought I heard something.'

He glanced upwards. 'Birds on the roof?'

'No, maybe the wind . . .' She turned her head towards the door. And after a long moment said, in the strangest voice, 'James?'

'What are you looking at?' He turned to look as well.

For several shimmering, silent seconds, Maeve and James O'Connor stared at the vision on the landing. Their eyes enormous in white faces. Each with a steaming mug of tea in one hand.

And a moment after that, Eva tore her hand out of Aoife's and went rushing into the room, leaping onto her parents' bed, knocking the tea flying and screaming: '*Surprise!*'

Maeve was kneeling up in the bed, screaming too, crying, howling, her arms around the tiny child. 'Oh, it's not possible, oh, it's not possible, James, do you see her too, have I gone mad, have I died, she's here, oh my God, my love, where have you been – *She's still four, James!* – are you well? *She's not dying!* Oh my love, my love, my love, my love, my love . . .'

And James as well had his arms around the grinning four-year-old, who kept on and on shouting at the top of her healthy little lungs, 'Surprise! Surprise! Surprise!' And occasionally, 'I want ice cream!'

Aoife, out on the landing beyond the door, stood watching the broken family instantly remake itself – the tight circle that had been on display in those pictures hidden in the drawer. It reminded her of the studio shot – her parents posing on the photographer's couch, with their arms around their only child, in her blue velvet dress and beret. The picture she had thought for a short while was of herself.

Eva was shouting now, 'She found me! Mam's friend found me!' and Maeve was trying to stand up now, with the little girl clinging like a monkey around her neck. *'Friend?'* And James was striding towards Aoife, weeping, with his arms held wide.

'You said you were our *friend?*' He pulled her into a bear hug, his wet cheek pressed to hers, holding her so tight she feared her ribs would crack.

Maeve was sobbing to Eva, 'She's not my friend, sweetie.'

And the little girl said doubtfully, 'But she's very nice and this is her house.'

'Of course it's her house! She's our daughter, Eva! She's your sister!'

'But I don't have a sister—'

'Yes you do, sweetie. You really absolutely do.'

'OK. Was she away at school?'

'That's right, sweetie. But now she's home.'

'And is this her house?'

'Yes, and yours too, sweetie. And mine. And your dad's.'

And Aoife's father, still with his face pressed to hers, kept on and on repeating, 'Never leave us again. Oh God, never, ever, *ever* leave us again.'

There was so much noise, between the constant joyful shrieking, and James furiously cooking spaghetti bolognese because his girls must be starving, and Maeve unable to stop crying, and going from Eva to Aoife, and from Aoife to Eva, and Eva being more delighted with Hector than anything else, that by the time James said, 'Maeve, phone . . .' it had rung off.

The telephone sat silent by the coats in the hall. No caller ID.

Standing behind her, Maeve said, 'I don't suppose it would have been for you, sweetheart.'

'I guess not.' Aoife kept on staring at it.

Maeve said, gently caressing her hair, 'I know this is going to take a bit of getting used to, but you see, everyone thinks—'

'I know. You don't need to tell me. Sinead spotted us walking down the road and had an absolute panic attack.'

'Oh, the poor child.'

'Mm.'

'We better start making some calls about you soon. Just as soon as I can believe it isn't a dream myself. Darling, come and eat.'

They had barely made the kitchen doorway when the phone rang again. Maeve reached it first. 'Hello? Hello? Sorry, speak up, it's very loud where you are . . .' She was frowning, smiling, shaking her head, turning to Aoife with the receiver in her hand. 'It *is* for you.'

It was very, *very* loud where he was. Music blaring, people shouting and screaming, glasses chinking. Shay said something into the receiver, but too low to make out.

'I can't hear you! Are you in the pub? How's John Joe doing?'

He said more loudly, 'Grand.'

(Someone was shouting, 'Good on ya!' and another, 'Here's a pint of the black stuff, John Joe! Drink up, there's more on its way!')

'Not too much of a shock?'

'Not too bad. Blamed it on the drink, but I think he has it straight now. Aoife, listen, there's something I forgot to say to you before . . .' And his voice dropped again.

'I still can't hear you! Move somewhere quieter!'

'I can't – this is the pay phone stuck to the wall. And everyone here is very excited. Just listen . . .' Again his voice tailed off.

'I still can't hear you!'

'Oh, come on . . .'

'It's not my fault, you keeping not saying it loud enough.'

'All right. Grand. Fine. *I love you, Aoife O'Connor!*' And to the background noise of absurdly drunken cheering, he shouted: 'Now, did you hear *that*?'

ACKNOWLEDGEMENTS

For their invaluable advice and constant support: My son Jack and daughter Molly.

For being my target readership: My daughter Imogen and son Seán.

For first draft feedback: Aideen Kane, Sabine Lacey, Sinead Leonard, Una Morris, Derek O'Flaherty, Morag Prunty, Denis Quinn, Aideen Ryan, Cathy Whelan; Zoe Costello, Ming Flannelly, Dearbhla Forkan, Gemma Lacey, Katie McHale, Derry Quinn, Meabh Walsh; the girls from St Mary's.

For their professionalism: Marianne Gunn O'Connor, Vicki Satlow, Kelly Hurst, Sophie Nelson.

For being herself: Rachel Falconer.

For being himself: Tim Lacey.

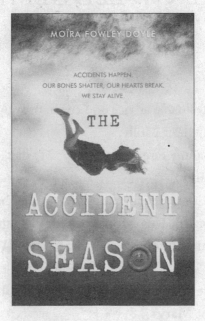